CITY OF LOST GIRLS

CITY OF
LOST
GIRLS

DECLAN HUGHES

WILLIAM MORROW

An Imprint of HarperCollins*Publishers*

HarperCollins books may be purchased for educational, business, or sales promotional use. For information please write: Special Markets Department, HarperCollins Publishers, 10 East 53rd Street, New York, NY 10022.

FIRST EDITION

Library of Congress Cataloging-in-Publication Data
Hughes, Declan, 1963-
City of lost girls / Declan Hughes. — 1st ed.
p. cm.
ISBN: 978-0-06-168990-1
1. Loy, Ed (Fictitious character)—Fiction. 2. Private Investigators—Ireland—Fiction. 3. Murder—Investigation—Fiction. 4. Los Angeles (Calif.)—Fiction. I. Title.
PR6058.U343C57 2010
823'.914—dc22   2009041251

10 11 12 13 14 OV/RRD 10 9 8 7 6 5 4 3 2 1

To Diarmuid O'Hegarty

He hadn't even wanted to kill the third girl.

No, that wasn't right, God forbid he should sound like some kind of seething maniac, he hadn't even wanted to kill the first girl. It had just happened. He knows this is a notoriously inadequate, worse, a barely articulate explanation, but there it is. Not that it hadn't come unprompted. Oh no, there had been a perfectly good reason for killing the first one. Or at least, he thought so at the time. And no, he hadn't always wondered what it would feel like, or whether he'd be capable of killing if it ever came to it; he hadn't felt an overwhelming sense of triumph either, or freedom or euphoria or whatever it was a genuine psychopath supposedly craved by his actions; at the time, he hadn't felt anything much beyond panic, then sadness and guilt, tinged with relief that he had overcome the practical obstacle that had suddenly confronted him. It was only later . . .

He tried to explain it to the second of the Point Dume girls, who he thought exhibited an intelligence and an empathy the others had lacked.

He had been mistaken in that, but he still feels it was a good analogy, even if it was unlikely in the extreme that he'd ever set it out for anyone again. Imagine, he told her as they grazed on buffalo wings and drank the semisparkling Prosecco he liked, Prosecco dei Colli Trevigiani, the one in the blue bottle, imagine you awoke to the the sound of an invading army on the streets of your city. By lunchtime, they are in control. By nightfall, the knocking on the doors has begun. Suddenly the world has changed. Resistance would amount to suicide. What do you do? Because through sheer good fortune (still the primary, perhaps the sole determinant of success in life) they don't want you, they want the blacks, or the Jews, or the bankers. (He hadn't said bankers *back then, but he'd say it now, of course, and he'd get a laugh. Or at least, he imagines he would. He certainly would be entitled to a laugh. But he'd rarely had much success in making girls laugh. In a way, that is part of the problem.) So why not tell the soldiers what they want to know? The Jews are hiding in the attic or in the cellar, they have two dogs you'll need to poison or shoot, the children are in the shed at the bottom of the garden, thank you and good night, Officer.*

Because, for all our talk of merit and distinction and hard work rewarded, life is measured out in split-second moments when it could go either way—did anyone see you push the other kid off the swing? Did your wife smell your girlfriend's perfume on you? Did your boss see you out for lunch on the day you called in sick? And of course, it's not that these moments won't arise, it's how you conduct yourself when they do that counts. Because we call it good fortune, or luck, or grace—he calls it grace, God's grace, if truth be told, yes, the grace of God, old God Himself, either you believe or you don't and not a lot you can do about it either way—but you have a role to play in that luck, that grace, how it impacts, how it intervenes in your day-to-day, how it makes your fortune, your future, your fate. So in that moment, you have to lie, to prevail, to persuade—the other kid pushed you, too, the perfume was your sister's, the lunch was with your oncologist, anything that works. The Jews are in the attic, and here I am, finishing my dinner, free.

And each time you do it, you're telescoped back through all the other times you've done something like it, right back to the first one, the first desperate scrape, the first time you mouthed the prayer: O God, please God, help me, if You only get me out of this, I promise I'll never, never, never again . . .

He has lost track of how many times he has said that prayer. He said it the very first time, of course, just as he said it when the second Point Dume girl was dying. He found it decreased his anxiety levels and helped to leaven the extent of his rage. The first time was the most un-expected, not because it was without precedent—he had had difficulties with girls before—but because of the way he chose to react. It was simple and, he conceded, sordid, in its way. The girl—he called them girls but they were always well into their twenties, he had no interest of any kind in children, never had, even when he had been a child himself—the girl had been blond, greasy cheeks and brow shining through streaky makeup, denim cutoffs, low-cut top, eyes bloodshot, pink nail varnish chipped, red mouth wide and slack and glistening, she'd heard he worked in the industry and that was it, her yeasty breath in his face, her damp hands tugging at him. Later on, he'd come to realize that she was one of a type. A grip had told him that she—or rather, girls who resembled her, and once he started looking around Los Angeles it sometimes seemed as if they all did—was a classic fraying-at-the-edges Hollywood skank. But this was the first time he'd worked in L.A., and girls like this were new to him. Besides, he had thought there was something else around her eyes, he didn't know what . . . a certain sadness that he understood, and might like to share, to commingle with a certain sadness of his own.

Back at his place, he'd poured the cold Prosecco from the blue bottle, even then it had been a favorite of his, he'd tried to get her to sit and talk, he'd asked her questions, told her a little about himself, but she didn't want any of that, she didn't want to behave like a person, like a human being. She couldn't sit still. She'd asked him to play some music, and when he couldn't find what she needed, she tuned the radio station her-self, classic rock, appalling stuff, plastic riffs and shrieking vocals, and she danced for him, like a stripper, and he sat and watched because that was what she wanted, and then she came closer to him, she was in her un-

derwear now, black panties and a red bra, not only did they not match, they weren't even the same line or brand, he felt ashamed for her as she came closer and knelt before him and unbuckled his belt and unbuttoned his jeans. He wasn't close to hard, wasn't going to get hard, not this way, not with her, not now, he had felt a tremor in the bar, but nothing since, not as she tugged and yanked on his cock and then took it all into her mouth, not such a great feat really as it was shrinking by the minute and the harder she worked, the more it shrank, until it felt as if it had vanished altogether, as if she had swallowed him down to the root. She looked up at him through bleary, glazed eyes that were suddenly glaring, and he thought perhaps she was angry because of his inability to get an erection, but then she spat him out and said:

"Let go of my arms!"

and he realized, in his anxiety, in his inability, he had been squeezing her forearms, squeezing them tighter and tighter,

"Let go of my arms, you asshole!"

and now his palms were all slick with something greasy, what was it? He released one hand and saw it was beige brown and shiny. Fake tan? And blood, there was blood, too, and he saw that he had opened wounds on her arms, track marks, he realized later, from intravenous drug abuse, the makeup had been there to conceal the needle marks,

"I'll call the cops if you don't let me go, you dickless Irish fuck,"

and maybe if she hadn't said that, in such an abrasive, shrill caw of a voice, and if she hadn't wrenched her body back and shook her frizzy dried blond head about, and if she hadn't said it again,

"I'm calling the cops, you crazy motherfucker!"

and if she hadn't started screaming, yes, it was the screaming that pushed him over, combined with the fear of the LAPD, of going to jail in Los Angeles, the idea was terrifying, unthinkable, and it was a big break for him, this movie, America, everything, he couldn't let it be jeopardized by this filthy little. . .

(He knows he only learned the term later, but he feels ever since that he had thought it at that moment . . .)

Filthy little skank . . .

His hands were on her neck so quickly, his thumbs pressing hard against the cartilage of her larynx, his fingers gripping the back of her neck, that by the time she started to pummel him with her weakened hands, she was already drifting away, the light in her bugged-out eyeballs guttering as she died.

He hadn't felt much at the time beyond panic, then sadness and guilt, then relief. It was only later, looking back, he felt more. It was the look of it he remembered, the look of the girl as she expired, as the light in her eyes flickered and dimmed. The dying of the light. That's not why he killed the first girl, of course—because he hadn't known then what would happen when he played it back in his mind, reran it, unspooled it like a movie. It had been raining outside, he remembered, and as he was strangling her, he thought of lines he had always liked in Macbeth: "There will be rain tonight/ Let it come down." *He didn't kill the third girl because of some lines in Macbeth, though. He did it because he knew that later, he would hold it in his mind's eye, the exquisite framing of it, the flash of red, the fade to black. He would hold the grace of her light within him.*

CHAPTER 1

Jack Donovan, *the* Jack Donovan, in a darkened Dublin bar, great handsome bull's head tipped back, plume of still-dark hair coiled over broad black-shirted back, full pint of stout held aloft to the east, shot of whiskey to the west, and the feet all pounding in a ring around him as he sinks the dark pint to rising hoots and cries, and then a roar as he knocks the shot back and lifts the empty glasses up through the flickering light: to east, to west, to north and south, a bacchanalian benediction, and bows until his hair sweeps the floor. Josh Tyler steps forward in jeans and Mastodon rock-band T-shirt, slight, unshaven, pint of Guinness in hand, wrists braided and bangled, just another skinny student on the lash if you didn't know about the Oscar nomination or the thing with Mischa Barton. He embraces Donovan, kisses him on the lips, lifts the pint and tips it slowly over their joined heads. Donovan lifts his face into the falling beer, and Tyler steps aside and drains the glass over his director with a flourish.

"Ladies and gentlemen, a Jack Donovan picture," he says, and Donovan bows to whoops and cheers, elevated, as is everyone watching, by the Hollywood anointing: showman Jack, braggart Jack, broth of a Paddy Irish boy Jack, back shooting moving pictures on the streets of his hometown.

There's a voice in my ear: dry, amused, ironic.

"Only trouble is, it's always the *same* Jack Donovan picture."

Mark Cassidy, Donovan's director of photography, elegant, Anglo, almost camp, with him since the no-budget movie they made in Dublin nearly twenty years ago, the one that started them all off. If it was always the same picture, Mark Cassidy should know. So should producer Maurice Faye, Jack's representative on earth, diplomat, scammer, fixer extraordinaire, elfin, tweed waistcoat, hoop earrings, raven thatch now silvering at the edges, phone at his ear as he slides out of the pub to take another call from the West Coast. So should Conor Rowan, First AD, chubby, ruddy, strawberry blond crop, permanently furrowed brow, implacable sergeant major, charged with waging total war for the good of the group. The home team, the gang of four, Jack Donovan's men since they were hungry guttersnipes dreaming of celluloid glory over the gantry of this very pub with barely the price of a pint between them.

I smile at the crack, always the eye-rolling same from Mark, only happy when he's cringing. I assume Mark means that wherever they go, and for as long as they've been going, and no matter what kind of film they end up making, it will all come down at some stage to Jack Donovan, carouser extraordinaire, professional Irishman, the life and soul of the all-night party, Jack Donovan howling at the moon, raging once more against the dying of the light, surrounded by the fans and the fakes and the flakes, the casts and the crews and the camp followers, Jack Donovan, lightning rod, channeling the savage energies, tapping the occult information, transmuting the base energies of a Dublin pub through his own alchemical powers into something altogether *other,* something exalted, into some strange kind of . . . magic, yes, no less than the intangible quality that pervades all of his movies, even the misfires (perhaps especially the misfires), a roiling, kinetic sense that the veil between this world and the next is gossamer thin, in places a mere shadow, that the concrete, the ordered, the rational, *that* is the illusion: magic is immanent in the world, and Jack summons it up, like some ancient fire starter, some witch doctor, some shaman. Or so it seems to us, to all of us, even Mark Cassidy, all of a hush now as Jack holds his hand aloft, the vibrations in the room at a precarious pitch, nothing to hear but the clink of glasses and the breath of a hundred souls, and just as I realize what he's going to do, Mark turns to me and shakes his head, aiming maybe for jaded incredulity but stalling at wonder, and Jack opens his mouth and the first line sails out in that extraordinary voice, pure tenor, not as fine as it was, wood-smoked and whiskey-basted by one careless owner but still mighty, and the expressions on the faces of those who'd heard rumors of this but never dared dream it might be true, let alone that they would witness it, as *E lucevan le stelle* from *Tosca* fills them, fills us all with sad joy and desperate longing for a love we didn't know we'd lost, for a home we'd forgotten we missed.

Afterward, as people are first too stunned to applaud, and then as they do, the noise they make like thunder, and as reality descends in murmurs and in muted shouts, the evening running down, Mark turns to me.

"Typical bloody Donovan," he says, his voice an acrid buzz. "If he'd sung *Nessun dorma,* the room would have erupted. But Jack always wants to leave the audience yearning."

As he says this, it seems to me that there are tears in his eyes. But I can't be sure, because there are certainly tears in mine.

It may still be the same Jack Donovan picture, but Maurice

and Conor are on their feet as well, still crazy, still in his thrall. Even Josh Tyler, whose last day of shooting was today, whose party this was, is happy to let Jack take center stage.

What's the matter with these people?

It's simple, really.

Jack Donovan is the matter with them.

I should know. A long time ago, he was the matter with me.

I make a brief appearance in a Jack Donovan picture (don't reach for your popcorn or you'll miss me). In his adaptation of *The Dain Curse* (1997), the Dashiell Hammett novel, I am "Irish man in bar." I even have a line. I was working as a private detective in Los Angeles back then, and Jack and I had become friends. We were in Hal's Bar on Abbot Kinney Boulevard in Venice one night while he was casting.

"Hey Ed, say 'whiskey.'"

"Whiskey."

"There you go. You could be Irish man in bar, right?"

"I could. I often have."

The movie starred Nick Nolte and Drew Barrymore and Lisa Eichorn and Michael Madsen, and if it didn't really work, everyone agreed the book didn't entirely work either. Besides, Hammett's mix of Californian religious cults, sexual deviance and violent gunplay was hospitable enough to the elements people loved in Jack's films: sharp dialogue, quirky humor, a strange, poetic sense of yearning, a fraught exchange of status and power between a beautiful older and a beautiful younger woman and an uneasy sexual relationship between a young man and woman who may or may not be related. A couple of the performances won Golden Globes, and there was an Oscar nomination for best adapted screenplay. (Jack's movies without exception got best screenplay nominations. According to Jack, it was because he always buried a quotation from Yeats or Joyce or Heaney in there, to act as a watermark denoting Quality Irish Literature: This Is The Real Deal. That may sound cynical on his part, but I believe it was actually self-deprecating: those quotations were never out of context, or at least, they never seemed so to me. And the screenplays were better written than anyone else's, although that didn't always make them better movies. But what would I know? When it comes to Jack Donovan, I am far from being a reliable witness.)

So there I am, waiting for Jack Donovan, and because I'm not drinking, I don't feel much like extending him the usual indulgence. Apart from on a film set, where he is always on time and available, Waiting For Jack is what everyone who knows him gets used to doing. Maybe it started out because of a romantic life that to be kind you might describe as "complicated." Maybe it goes back to his childhood (more of both of those later). Maybe he reserves any sense of order, discipline or basic forward planning for his work, allowing himself to be completely unruly and chaotic in his life. Chaos. That's something else we'll come back to. Whatever the reason, I'm not interested. Madeline King, Jack's PA, is coming toward me, late twenties, dressed in black, legs to here, all dark curls and twinkling smiles and professionally casual Galway charm.

"I know you're waiting, Ed—"

"I'm not waiting. I'm leaving."

"Stop. It's the usual fecking nightmare with Jack—"

"It's one from which I awoke a long time ago. Jack called me. And I didn't mind the concert, or watching Josh Tyler play John the Baptist, but I'm not hanging around like a supplicant here. It's late."

Madeline does a slight, smiling double take at this, and checks the time on her phone.

"It's nine o'clock. That's not late sure. From what Jack told me, it's certainly not late in Ed Loy's world."

I say nothing. It's true, a few months ago, nine o'clock wouldn't have been late, would barely have been early. But that was before I'd met a woman who puts her kids to bed around nine, and who has to be caught within the following hour or so, otherwise she's asleep. A woman who doesn't drink on a school night. A woman who wouldn't have fitted into Ed Loy's world at all and in almost every respect still doesn't, apart from the minor detail of my having fallen in love with her.

Madeline rolls her eyes at a text message and says: "The thing of it is, Jack has gone on. He wants you to follow. There's a car waiting outside."

I don't know if I roll my eyes, but I feel like I should. *Jack has gone on.* How many times have I heard those words? I don't think I ever once arrived at the appointed meeting place without Jack having left word behind the bar or with the waitress that he had *gone on,* and that I should follow. He would always have a car waiting for me, but frequently he would have departed the second spot by the time I'd show up. Usually it was just a schlep across town: from the Formosa to Bar Marmont, or Musso's to the Ivy. Once, though, during the private plane years, or was it months, however long the big deal with Warner's that didn't work out lasted, Jack had *gone on* to LAX, and was waiting for me on the runway. We flew to New York "for dinner at Patsy's on Fifty-sixth Street, because Frank says it's the best," Jack said, suddenly, improbably on first-name terms with Frank Sinatra. And I think there was a trip to Mexico "to find the real mezcal," but the details are very hazy. They didn't last long, but those were the days. But those were also the days when I didn't much mind who I woke up beside, or where. Those days are gone.

"Tell him he has my number, we were were due to meet an hour ago, I have somewhere else to be."

Madeline clutches my arm.

"Please," she says. "I can't tell you what this is about, but he won't go to the Guards. He said you were the best. He needs you."

I look at her, at her pale cream skin, at her deep blue eyes, stricken with anguished concern and evident adoration for Jack.

Poor Madeline. I can recall an Emma, a Susie, an Amanda, two Aprils and a Cindy. It ended in tears every time. I haven't seen Jack in a while, but from what I'd been told, it looks like it always will.

Before I can reply, Conor Rowan is there, red brow furrowed, mouth in a mirthless smile, beaded with sweat, perma-hassled and reveling in it.

"Excuse me folks, Ed. Maddy, I know it's not your area, it's not mine either, but Geoff had to go and I said I'd catch you, one of the extras, she's a friend of yours, Nora Mannion . . ."

"She's a friend's sister, I put her in touch with the casting agent, I don't really know her. If she's not working out—"

"No, she's great, Jack's really happy with her, herself and two other girls have a look he really loves, black hair, blue eyes, that whole Connemara thing you have yourself."

"Grand so. Glad it worked out."

Madeline's pale skin reddens as the compliment hits home. She nods to Conor, then inclines toward me to exclude and dismiss him and fixes me with a peremptory look, waiting for me to consent; when Conor speaks again, she flinches visibly.

"Except, Nora, could be she's done a runner."

"What do you mean, a runner? You know what—"

"She wandered off late this afternoon. One of the trainee ADs lost track of her. Jack wants to cut away to her first thing tomorrow—"

"You know what these young ones are like," Madeline snaps, impatient, side of the mouth, an improbable oul' one all of a sudden. "She's probably on the tear."

"Geoff followed it up. Her mobile goes straight to message. The girls she was staying with, they said she doesn't drink, this is not like her—"

"She's twenty-one, she's not old enough to be like anything yet. This is her, finding out what she's like. Now, I have a thing here, Conor, for Jack, I need to do."

Conor gives her his blank smile, as if he understands, and is personally disappointed by his own behavior, but he isn't going to go away until he gets what he wants. Madeline responds with a young one's petulant sigh.

"*What?*"

"Ring the sister. Ask if there's anything, you know. Anything we should know, why she—"

"She's just an extra . . ."

Conor's smile intensifies and his face gets redder, and Madeline stops short without him having to interrupt her. When he speaks, it's as if to a stubborn child.

"Jack wants to cut away to her tomorrow, do you understand what I'm saying to you? He's using the three of them like fates, or furies, you know, the way he does. He's already shot on her, made her focal. So if we can't get hold of her, it'll be a fucking disaster. We'd have to reshoot with a replacement, and we can't afford to do that. Or we'd have to tell Jack to cut the three of them altogether, and that would still entail major reshooting, which would be worse, because not only can we not afford the reshooting but Jack will be pissed off because he can't do what he wants to do. That will be, if you know anything about this business, and I don't know if you do since this is your first job, or about Jack Donovan, an apocalyptic fucking crisis. So he'll want to know everything is being done."

Madeline has been torn a new one, and it seems she has to take it. Her tone is as even as she can make it.

"If it's so major, why didn't he tell me about it?"

"Because he relies on us to do these things without being asked so that he can devote himself entirely to being Jack Donovan, which is his job. And enabling that to take place is ours. You got me?"

"All right. I'll find out what I can, I'll call you with whatever I have. Five minutes. All right, Conor?"

"Always a pleasure," Conor says, and wheels away, his mouth set in his trademark grim smile.

Madeline mutters "asshole," bites her lip, pushes air through her nose like a thwarted pony, then tosses her hair and turns to me. But I'm not looking at her, I'm reading a text on my phone:

Girls to bed too late, me too sleepy and too sorry, rain check, will you still xxxx me tomorrow?

So now I have all the time in the world.

"Where's the car?" I say, feeling not a little thwarted myself.

Madeline asks me if I need her to come with me. I tell her that since I don't work in the film business, I can probably survive traveling by car without an assistant with my ego unbruised, and that in any case, she evidently has better things to be doing than minding me. Like keeping her job, I think. As I leave, the slight figure of Josh Tyler is surrounded by a ring of adoring women, their faces aglow with the light of his celebrity. All the stars in heaven.

CHAPTER 2

In the nightclub, which is overfurnished and -carpeted and -decorated and has always felt to me a bit like being in your granny's good room, except with a bunch of drunken idiots looking over their shoulders to see if anyone famous is in, Jack Donovan is ensconced behind the velvet rope with a lively group that includes an Oscar-winning film director and two former supermodels (you'd know their names), neither of whom looks like she's getting any older, and a couple of world-famous Irish rock stars (you'd know their names, too). Jack beckons me to the table, but I shake my head and hang by the bar. Everyone looks happy enough to see me, and I wave and smile to assure them I love them all dearly, but I've had enough glamour for one night. Maybe if I was drinking it would be another matter. Even if all my sobriety has been in vain, it's too late to start now. Isn't it?

Jack joins me at the bar and claps a beefy arm around my shoulder.

"All work and no play, Ed," Jack Donovan says.

"This is work, Jack."

Jack takes a step back and looks at me, his expressive face and flashing eyes crinkling into a thousand questions and insinuations.

"Man alive, you look well, Ed. The eyes, the skin. More than just off the booze. There's a rare bounce of light coming off you, a fine old glow. "

That's how Jack Donovan talks sometimes. Like the opera he sang, it's corny, and then beyond corny, and then suddenly more real than anyone else's speech, until you wish everyone could talk like that all the time.

"Am I permitted to inquire after the lady's name?" Jack says.

"Anne. Anne Fogarty."

"And she has kids, does she?"

"Two daughters. How did you know that?"

Jack shrugs, an elaborate affair that involves his entire frame, his outstretched hands turning like the arms of a crane shifting in the wind.

"You're not the type to go running after young ones, Ed. And with women our age, if they're not married, it's usually because they don't want to be, or they used to be. And if they used to be, they often have children."

"That's neat reasoning, Jack. Seems to me you don't need a detective. Whatever this problem you have is, you can solve it on your own."

"Besides, Tommy Owens gave me the lowdown."

"Tommy Owens?" I say. "I didn't know you knew Tommy."

"We met that time he was out in L.A. with you. Remember? He gave me his number. Still the same. Thought I'd talk to him first. Get the lay of the land when it came to Ed Loy, this year's model."

I nod. A lot had happened between Jack and me. We had been friends, and I had worked for him, and then we stopped being friends and I didn't want to work for him anymore, hadn't wanted anything to do with him, until now. Now, in the flesh, I'm more than pleased to see him. It has been too long.

"I never got the chance to say I was sorry, Ed—"

I shake my head, put an arm on his shoulder.

"It wasn't me that needed an apology. But I know you tried to make things right. Another lifetime, Jack."

"Never since, Ed, I assure you—"

I cut him off again with an upheld palm. I don't want to talk about it, don't want to think about it. Sooner or later, we would get to it anyway. The past is always out there, a land mine buried and forgotten about, ready to blow the present apart at any moment. I know that. But I don't want to let it in tonight. However bad it seems, and God knows it got pretty bad back in L.A., it was a long time ago, and in another country, and tonight, it's good just to see an old friend. And if that isn't worth breaking a few weeks off the booze, I don't know what is. Which is probably why I end the night with a dawn swim in the Forty Foot, drunk as a lord.

I join Jack's table for an hour or so, and am handed a champagne flute full of a dark pink liquid I recognize as a Bellini: Prosecco and peach puree. One of the famous Irish rock stars is as famous for talking as he is for being a famous rock star, and the other film director had been an actor not known for his diffidence, but neither can get a hearing tonight. Jack is in full flow, talking up his movie as if he was pitching it to investors, rather than in the middle of shooting it.

"It's the fulcrum of our emotional, our sexual, our psychic history: Monto, the largest red-light district in the whole of Europe for over a hundred years, Nighttown, Joyce calls it in *Ulysses,* where most of the girls have been trafficked, as we'd say now, lured, bewitched by the brothel-keeping madam, the enchantress, the Greek goddess Circe, and then kept virtually as slaves, and it lasts right through the war of independence and the civil war until the mid-twenties, when the Legion of Mary puts an end to it—and what replaces the brothels? The Magdalene laundries, the reform schools, and the industrial schools run by the Church, where women and children were trapped and abused for decades. All the lost girls: stretching back, children of empire, stretching forward, children of the Republic, and at the center, the two wars, the first between the IRA and the British army, and then between factions of an IRA torn asunder by a disputed treaty. And amid the warren of brothels, there are safe houses for both sides, hiding holes for spies and informers, whispering johns and whores telling tales, all manner of intrigue and betrayal and hypocrisy, of passion and heartbreak and death: the unwanted babies drowned, the diseased whores smothered. And that's the bloody heart of the movie, the violent, delirious, debauched birth pangs of a nation in the filthy side streets of the red-light night town, dirty old town, Dublin town . . ."

There is a pause after this, everyone punch-drunk on the rhetoric, Jack Donovan stealing the air out of the room once again. Jack drains his glass and grips it like a trophy. Then the rock star who likes to talk picks up the jug of Prosecco and peach juice and says:

"Federico Fellini . . . will you have a Bellini?"

At which, the entire table explodes in mirth, a blessed release from the intensity. Jack laughs, too, but within minutes, he starts to look ill at ease, agitated, unhappy in his own skin. It's a contrast I remember well in him, the soaring leap of imaginative fancy, as if he was singing an aria, followed by the descent to cold hard earth, the well-worn flight path from elation to despair. After a few minutes, during which he affects a show of attention to the rock star, who is saddling up his own winged horse of speculation and reminiscence, and then, with apologies and embraces, indicating to all that he has an early start and business still to do, Jack and I retire to a small room equipped with an antique desk, leather armchairs, a wall planner and a couple of wooden filing cabinets. A trim lady in her fifties in a low-cut ivory dress with luminous blond hair and skin that glows burnt orange, like glazed pottery, appears. Jack looks at our drinks and makes a face. I drain mine and do the same.

"Two Irish Manhattans, Glenda, Jameson whiskey, of course, with the vermouth half and half sweet and dry."

"Will you be wanting cherries, boys?" Glenda says, laying it on thick, a Northside Circe tempting us with dubious potions.

"Always, Glenda, always," Jack says, licking his lips and laughing a big barroom laugh. When Glenda departs, Jack frowns, as if he is preparing with difficulty to unburden the contents of his troubled mind. What he says, however, is:

"A Manhattan made with scotch is called a Rob Roy. There should be a proper title for one made with Irish whiskey. Ed?"

"Are you sure they can make a mixed drink at all here? Dublin has not gotten any better at that, Jack," I say. "There are still a lot of places where you ask for a Martini, they give you a tumbler of vermouth and ice."

"Which is why I've been in here tutoring them in the occult ways of the bartender. Now they can manufacture a perfectly respectable Sidecar, Old-Fashioned and Negroni, and a superior Martini. The point being, the Irish Manhattan. A Robert Emmett?"

"Too many syllables. An Oscar Wilde?"

"Too hackneyed. And we'd risk appealing only to a niche market."

"A niche market who buy cocktails."

"A Padraig Pearse. A De Valera. A Michael Collins."

"A Manhattan is not a Collins drink. A Great O'Neill."

"Red Hugh O'Donnell. A Red Hugh. *H-U-E.*"

"Red Hue is good."

So when Glenda brings the drinks, Jack tells her about the

christening with great excitement, and Glenda gives us a smile pitched judiciously between flirtatious and maternal and brushes the side of Jack's face, a gesture that is part stroke of the cheek, part pat of the head.

The Red Hues are very good, so good, in fact, that my reason for being there at all almost deserts my mind until Jack pulls an envelope from his breast pocket and takes a few sheets of notepaper from it.

"*The Mystery of the Spiteful Letters*. Wasn't that an Enid Blyton, Ed?"

"I think so."

"The Famous Five, or the Secret Seven?"

"The Five Find-Outers, I think."

"That's right! Who's this they were again, Julian, Dick—"

"That was the Famous Five. Are they the problem, Jack? Is this why you needed to see me? Those letters?"

Jack Donovan nods his head, suddenly unwilling to meet my eyes. He is shielding the letters with his meaty hands, an embarrassed expression on his face, as if, after all this time, he's made it to the doctor's waiting room and his cough has mysteriously disappeared. He makes fluttering movements with his fingers and twists a grimace of a smile onto his face, as if he is about to dismiss the likelihood of the letters amounting to anything serious. But no sound comes out of his mouth.

"Probably best to let me see them so," I say.

Jack passes the letters across the table, drinks the remainder of his Red Hue and leaves the room.

There are three letters, and they have been assembled in the traditional fashion by cutting out words from magazines and newspapers and pasting them together so that they make a sentence. They read as follows:

1. *All praise to God the Father, all praise to God the Son,*
   and God the Holy Spirit, eternal Three-in-One.

2. *Flanked by thieves, Jesus remained Lord. But all three died the same death.*
3. *Once, twice, three times a dead man. He will know neither the day nor the hour.*

Jack comes back into the room with two drinks. I am still halfway through my first, and feeling every sip, unlike, apparently, Jack, who takes a long hit on his fresh drink before he sits down.

"Stupid stuff really, not sure why they have me so rattled," he says, making his eyes twinkle and his brows rise as he asks me to reassure him that everything is all right and there is no need to worry. With every client (for that is what Jack had just become), there is a moment like this. Just as you hope your doctor will tell you that all you need is to go home and have a cup of hot tea and two paracetamol and your cough will magically vanish. Anonymous letters often fulfill their purpose simply by being sent; the idea that the threats they make would ever be acted upon never enters the sender's head. Often, but not always.

"So why *do* they have you rattled, Jack? Do you have a notion of who they could be from? Do you think it's someone who might be threatening you, who actually wants to turn you into a dead man?"

Jack shakes his head.

"I didn't think I knew anyone who would send something like this. But that said . . . I meet a lot of people, you know what I mean?"

This last comes with a lubricious gleam, I guess in the unlikely event that I'll have difficulty understanding what he means.

"We're assuming it's a woman, then."

"Well, it's a woman's thing, isn't it? Anonymous notes. Ringing you up and not saying anything."

"You've had calls also?"

"Not from this one."

"From which one?"

"Ah, that's not relevant. A mad one, she was . . . sitting up with a bottle of brandy and a telephone, I sorted it out. You know the kind of thing I've always had to put up with, Ed."

Of course I know, Jack. That's why I stopped wanting to have anything to do with you. Don't go back there, Loy. You go back there, you'll remember why you should have nothing to do with Jack. But you want to take this case. Why? Because . . . it's time. Because you're ready, at last. Because no matter what, Jack Donovan is a friend of yours, and a man sticks by his friends, even if—especially when—they do things you don't agree with. And because the little voice in your head says you should, and the day you stop listening to the little voice in your head, you're finished.

"How did the letters arrive? Through the post?"

"By hand. They just appear, in my coat. In the pocket of a notebook."

"Okay. Well, we could set up surveillance on the set, get a fix on who is delivering them."

"Okay, good."

"But you probably know already, don't you? You know, but you don't want to deal directly with it."

Jack grimaces again.

"Do you want me to give you a list?" he says.

"What do you want me to do, Jack? Either you're worried or you're not. If you are, tell me why and help me narrow it down. The biblical stuff, the Trinity, does that ring any bells?"

Jack twists in his chair again, heaving his great bulk about like a figure trapped in a landscape that hasn't been drawn to scale.

"My sister. My older sister, Marie. She's . . . we're not close. She resents . . . has always resented me my career, my success."

"Did she have similar ambitions?"

"She worked in the theater. As an actress, then when that didn't work out, as a director. She wrote plays, had her own company, first they did kind of socially committed stuff, going around community centers and so on, and then they changed to a kind of theater-in-education outfit touring schools. None of it ever quite caught fire. She tried writing plays, got a couple produced, again, didn't really lead anywhere. All the time she's broke. And I'm, not to make myself out to be a great fellow, I'm paying her bills, so on. I bought her a house, in the mid-nineties, just before the boom, a little cottage in Ringsend, that's where she wanted it. For cash. So she doesn't have a mortgage. Worth a lot now, less than before, but a lot more than she didn't pay for it. And she's got a job, she's a script editor for that RTE TV soap, whatever it's called.

"So you know, she's doing all right, she's not exactly a tragic case. But it's not what she hoped for. She wanted to be, I don't know, in the National Theater in London. Or at the BBC. Or in Hollywood. And she's just . . . she's got this idea that I stole her life, I had all the luck . . . because it wasn't even my intention to do this, I was training as a singer and then sidestepped into film, that somehow I deprived her . . . like there was only room for one talent in the family. It's not rational. But it's what she thinks."

"And the religious stuff?"

"In the past few years, she's joined a Catholic group, Communion and Liberation. I don't know that there's anything wrong with them. There isn't the sinister vibe you get with Opus Dei. But the last couple of times I've met her, she talks of nothing else: Jesus this, the incarnation that. Gone into it very deep. The Holy Father. And there's a crowd of Latin-mass folk she's got in with as well, the Tridentine mass, very traditionalist Catholic. The Society of Saint Pius the Tenth—SSPX. Now, they are a creepy shower, proper back-to-the-fifties merchants."

"I still don't get it. She's your sister, she doesn't like you, she's very religious. Even if she did send you these letters, mightn't they be more in the way of a spiritual wake-up call? Man must die to be reborn, Jesus was greater than you, and He died among thieves, don't be getting above yourself, type of thing. I mean, she's not threatening you, is she?"

Jack nods as if he's agreeing with me, then produces an envelope, out of which he gingerly prises a folded sheet of thick art paper. Rust-colored fragments shed from the page as he flattens it out on the table and pushes it toward me. There are two images daubed there. One is an upside-down crucifix; the other is the finely etched rendering of a fetus in the womb. The drawings are dark red in color, and if I'd been asked to guess, I'd say they were painted in blood, or at least painted to look that way.

"A few years ago, Marie got pregnant. Wasn't with the father, didn't want to be with the father, called me and asked me what she should do."

"She's your older sister?"

"I know. It's always been this way. Because our parents died when we were so young, or not *because* of that, but . . . that's what I've always put it down to, Marie missing our father, wanting me to stand in and then resenting me for it, never able to sustain relationships with other men. Anyway. She calls me, and I say, do what you want, if you really want to keep the child, I'll help support it. If you want a termination, we can arrange that also. And she says, in this tight voice, very emotional, very clenched, 'if I *really* want to keep *it*,' and then she says, '*termination*.' Which is to say, I am weighting my advice, I am using mimsy words for brutal procedures, I am biased toward encouraging her to have an abortion. Am I? Maybe I am. Maybe I don't think it's entirely reasonable of my sister to depend on me to support a child she wants to have without a father in the picture. I offer to, sure, but maybe I don't toast her to the rafters and strew the bunting around the village. She hangs up on me. Calls me again the next day and says she wants to have an abortion, in L.A., and can I arrange it. So I do, and a week in Shutters on the Beach afterward to rest and recuperate."

"And she's never forgiven you."

"Something like that. Another debit entry in the ledger."

"And . . . what? This is your sister. I assume you're not saying she's a danger to you."

"I don't even know that she's the one sending the letters."

"But if she was. What exactly do you want me to do?"

"Get her to stop."

"It's family, Jack. You don't feel up to dealing with it yourself?"

"She makes me feel guilty. And she wears me out. I'm exhausted with her. And I know I've done everything I could for her, and her problems are not my problems, but . . . what I suppose I'd like you to do is, ask her to leave me alone. I've . . . I don't want to deal with her anymore. See her anymore."

"Tell her you love her and kiss her good-bye."

"I know. I know you've done that for me before. I . . . it's not the same."

"They were never your sister before. Otherwise . . . okay, forget about it. Anyone else?"

"You're laughing at me."

"I'm not laughing, I'm . . . smiling through the pain. Just tell me who else you think might have written the letters."

"There's my ex-wife."

"Your ex-wife. When did that happen?"

"When you and me were on the outs. She was a runner on *Twenty Grand,* the film I made after *The Dain Curse.*"

"I saw it."

"You were the one, then."

"That bad?"

"A metaphysical road movie set in the Sierra Mountains, starring a cast of unknowns and Harry Dean Stanton. Lord God Almighty, Ed, was I on drugs?"

"I don't know. Were you?"

"Of course I was, but that's no excuse. The business it did, let me tell you, it made *Kundun* look like *Star Wars.*"

"And you met your wife on the set?"

"That's right. Teri. I mean, Geri. Fuck."

At this moment, Jack at least has the grace to blush.

"Geri. Geraldine," he says.

"As opposed to Teri. Teraldine."

"Fuck off."

"How do you forget the name of your ex-wife?"

"It's late. And these drinks are strong. Anyway, I didn't forget her name. I *misspoke* her name."

"I'm sure she'd appreciate the distinction."

"Of course she wouldn't appreciate the distinction, that's why she's my ex-wife."

"Forgetfulness—excuse me, 'misspeaking' like that is apt to turn wives into ex-wives."

"Do you want me to tell you about her or do you just want to sit jeering at me?"

"Sitting and jeering is working well at the moment, actually. And for the record, I liked *Twenty Grand*."

"Well, that makes the entire painful, humiliating and very nearly career-ending experience worthwhile."

"I'm glad."

"You didn't happen to see *The Late Late Show* last week, did you?"

"I didn't," I lie.

"Speaking of career-ending experiences."

"Never mind *The Late Late Show,* Jack. Geraldine."

"Geraldine was and is Irish, from Dublin, South County Dublin, Foxrock to be precise. She was in the costume department, the design assistant, so she was their eyes and ears on set, keeping the actors sweet while making sure they didn't roll up their sleeves or unbutton their collars between takes, you'd be surprised how dumb actors can be about all that stuff. Anyway, she was a dab hand at keeping everyone sweet, being bubbly and flirty and easy on the eye, but she was completely useless at the

main part of her job, so the thing very quickly became a con-
tinuity nightmare. And as if that wasn't bad enough, she wasn't
endearing herself to her department in a variety of other ways
either, vanishing when she should have been on set and coming
in late and generally behaving as if for some obscure reason she
could do exactly as she pleased."

"Apart from screwing the director, I wonder why that was."

"So the costume designer fired her. Quite correctly."

"And what, to cheer her up, you married her?"

A comedy twinge of shame flashes across Jack's increasingly
bleary features.

"Something like that. She was so upset. And . . . I don't know,
I didn't even like her very much, she was a spoiled little prin-
cess with a deluded sense of entitlement, she didn't have much a
sense of humor, wasn't even that keen on sex, or as I was later to
find out, wasn't that keen on sex with me. I don't think she even
liked me very much either. It was just, I felt I was the reason she
had lost her job, although the costume people told me later that
that wasn't true, she was rubbish at her job long before she began
to think she could get away with being rubbish at her job because she was screwing the director. And there she was, hanging
around, crying, waiting for me to make it right."

"So you proposed to her. Out of embarrassment and inap-
propriate guilt, with a dose of white-knight-to-the-rescue for
good measure."

"Like I said, you and me were on the outs, Ed. I had no one
around to tell her I loved her and kiss her good-bye. God forgive
me, I didn't even like her."

You didn't like any of them, Jack. That's been the problem all
along.

"And how long did it last?"

"Long enough for me to buy a big house around the corner
from Mummy in Foxrock. I was still in post on the movie, Geri
found the place. I never actually set foot in it. We agreed to di-

vorce before *Twenty Grand* was finished. Mostly because, when she paid an unannounced visit to L.A., she caught me in bed with someone else. And that was the end of it."

I shake my head.

"Until? There isn't enough there for upside-down crucifixes and fetuses daubed in blood. What happened next?"

"What happened next was, I bumped into her one night about five years later, about five years ago, in this very spot, and drink had been taken and bygones had become bygones and I finally got to see the house I'd bought, indeed, to spend a night or two or five, to be precise, there. And very nice it was, too, although I'm not sure we liked each other anymore by the end of it. And then I went back to L.A., only to hear a while later that Geraldine was seven months pregnant and I was the father and maybe this would be the making of us, destiny once more, true love will find a way. And while I'm an anything-for-a-quiet-life-at-heart type of guy, as you know, and often to be found on the passive-to-pussy-whipped scale where the ladies are concerned, I sort of hoped if and when I had kids, it might be with someone I actually liked, or failing that, who at least liked me. And I wondered about it all. I specifically wondered about the fact that Geraldine, who had always been built like a boy, had grown hips and a belly by the time we got together again. Not that I didn't like any of it, I did very much, but I just wondered. And I wondered about the drink as well: it had been very much taken by me the night we met, and continued to be throughout the week, but not by her, half a glass and then she'd stop. And what I wonder was if she was pregnant already."

"I say it again, Jack, you can do your own detective work. Save yourself some money."

"So I congratulated her, said I'd be happy to do what I could, and asked for a paternity test. And she freaked out, and wept, and said I was a shit, and that she'd never lie about such a thing, and how dare I not trust her, and so on. But she wouldn't agree to the test. So I didn't acknowledge the child. Children. Twin girls. Called them Jacqueline and Joan, you know? Fuck."

Jack is telling the story as if it plays in his favor, but when he reaches the child's new names, his mouth sets firmly and his eyes darken.

"Jacqueline, Jack, Joan, John, you know? Fuck. And this . . . it had just happened a couple of times in L.A., women I could barely remember, and I was all ready to pay out, but my lawyer said, you've got to protect yourself, this is not an uncommon scam, and with both of those ladies it was, so it was in my head, the possibility she had set me up? And I felt anyway, I was paying her so much maintenance she wouldn't be short of a buck."

"But you still have doubts, that you may actually be the father?"

Jack Donovan drains his drink.

"My head says, no question: if she wouldn't agree to the test, it meant the girls weren't mine. But . . . I don't know, I guess for a man to doubt a woman's word like that, over something so . . . sacred. It's still pretty bad, I feel guilty about it. I feel like I've betrayed her trust and denied my own—even if she was lying and somebody else was the father."

"Okay, Jack. I'll go and talk to them both. Anyone else?"

Jack sighs, as if the notion is absurd, then shoots a cagey glance toward the door and leans in to me.

"You know Madeline. My assistant, and current . . . you know. Beautiful Galway girl, very smart, apart of course from her unaccountable lapses in judgment when it comes to men. And I suppose you'd call getting involved with a coworker a textbook definition of insanity on my part: repeating behavior that has had nothing but disastrous consequences in the past, expecting it to work out this time. If I do expect that."

This is a plot too thick for me.

"You think *Madeline* is sending you anonymous letters and

freaky drawings? She was the one pleading with me to help you. She's crazy about you, Jack."

"Which is what I'm saying to you. What's up with that? She's too smart to fall for me. What's her angle?"

"It would be nice if I thought you were taking this seriously."

"I am, Ed, I just . . . look, I don't want to talk about it anymore. Go see Madeline as well. I don't think she's sending them herself, but she might be helping whoever is. Please?"

"You're asking me to spy on your girlfriend?"

"I'm asking for your help, Ed. And maybe I can't explain why this has got under my skin the way it has. Maybe I can't, maybe I don't want to. Maybe the women will fill in the gaps. I'm just asking for your help. Please?"

Jack all plaintive now, pleading Jack, innocent Jack, what-have-I-done-to-deserve-this Jack, and the winsome smile then, at his own bewilderment. Does he think I'm going to refuse him? Does he not understand I still feel guilty about abandoning him back in L.A., even if I do have right on my side? Sometimes you can do the right thing and regret it nonetheless. Somebody once said if it came down to a choice between betraying his country and betraying a friend, he hoped he'd have the guts to betray his country. I don't think that would be the right thing to do, but I know what he meant, and I hope I'd have the same kind of guts. I was tried and found wanting before. Not this time. But there's no need to burden Jack with that level of friendship. It'd only embarrass him. It would certainly embarrass me.

"I charge a thousand a day, plus expenses. I'll need three up front. In cash."

Jack narrows his eyes and a cagey grin snakes across his mouth, as if, much to his relief, I have forfeited the high moral ground to him at last. Like every client, he has had to tell me things about himself he would have preferred to keep secret; in return, he gets to remind me that I'm a hired hand. That isn't the whole story, of course, and Jack has aways been a generous man, but sometimes I wondered if his generosity was a way of keeping me at a distance, of reminding me of my place, and therefore, of his. He takes a silver money clip out of his jeans and thumbs green hundred-euro bills onto the desk, his grin widening as they pile up. Jack loves to spend money, but then he loves everything about it: the deals, the budgets, the stakes; the way it makes you feel, the things it lets you do. It doesn't make you happy, he used to say, but it completely changes your life, and sure isn't that as good as happiness? Better, in fact!

There were five other directors like him in Dublin in the early nineties when he had made the break, five who'd made little independent films around the same time, and at least two, maybe three, were better than Jack was, or at least, their movies were: Jack would say so himself, and indeed, as the years wore on, he liked to remind people of the fact, his way of saying that he had come through on a lot more than sheer talent. And the fact was, none of the five, each of whom has continued to work in the industry, had wanted full-blown Hollywood success as badly as Jack; each had been content with a kind of independent, art-house, succès d'estime level of operation; none wanted to engage with what they loftily referred to as "suits." Jack was under no illusions: filmmaking was an art and a business, and you could no more ignore one than the other. When he met Maurice Faye, a film buff who'd been running a chain of pubs in Galway by the time he was twenty-four and was keen to get into the movie business, he'd found his ideal partner.

Jack passes the thirty bills across to me, his grin broad, his eyes twinkling. At least as many bills again remain in the clip, and I have a slight twinge, as if I've been hard done by: it's never easy being around someone quite so flush, and so damn casual with it. Jack whips up the clip and winks and claps his hands, as if to say: *now the deal is done, now the money is down, the world is remade once more: let's sit up and watch what happens. Make it happen, Ed.* And I wonder what the artificer wants to happen, what the manipulator hasn't told me, what secrets the old rogue holds that he wants me to expose.

Glenda arrives with fresh drinks: under the new, sober dispensation I have arranged for myself, this should be my cue to leave. I have already had more than enough, especially since I started from the position that I wasn't going to have any. But I can't leave now, nor do I want to. Money and booze have changed things, but that isn't all. I finish the Red Hue I had, and sink the one I am given, and another couple besides, and we talk about this and that, everything and nothing, or so it seems, like it wasn't ten years since we'd met but ten days, talk like we know one another's mind inside out, which is not and never has been and never will be true. Sometimes it seems that way, though, and tonight is one of those times. So when Jack suggests, or rather, announces, at four in the morning, a swim, it seems like the most natural thing in the world, as I guess it would to a man who has forgotten what it's like to be drunk.

Jack's car takes us out in stately splendor along Strand Road in Sandymount and the coast road by Monkstown and Dun Laoghaire Harbor and deposits us in Sandycove beside the Forty Foot, in sight of the Martello Tower James Joyce once lived in and fled from and used as the setting for the opening scene of *Ulysses*. The Forty Foot used to be called the Men's Bathing Place but it's now open to swimmers of both sexes and ultimately, if the water is cold enough, which it generally is, of none. After the brief interval of indigo that passes for night as Dublin heads toward the summer solstice, a musky summer predawn is softening every hard surface as we walk down the steps of the Forty Foot and strip and fling ourselves off the rocks. Before we get in, Jack warns me gravely not to piss in the sea. It doesn't seem to me that where or when I piss is any of his business, but when it looks like I'm going to say something to this effect, he stops me and says he has his reasons.

We swim in silence, Jack getting out regularly to dive back in again. I stay in the water, looking up at the white Art Deco–style house that flanks the Joyce Tower, a little glimpse of California on the south Dublin coast, and recall that the last time we swam together, it was in the ocean at Zuma Beach, north of Malibu, and that my mother had been with us, indeed, that the trip had been Jack's idea. Jack had worked hard to charm my mother for no other reason than that she was my mother, taking her to tea at the Biltmore, and to see Tony Bennett at the Hollywood Bowl, and my mother was very taken with Jack; you could say he was the highlight of her trip. And she always asked after him, and continued to do so with more than a note of reproach in her voice after she learned we had fallen out, as if, in any such rift, the fault would obviously be mine. Now she is no longer able to ask anyone anything, but I think of her often, of course, and I think of her now, as we swim at dawn in Sandycove.

When it is too cold to stay in the water any longer, and when Jack breaks the unreal spell an early summer morning casts by announcing that he is due on set in an hour, we get out and get dressed, and Jack declares that we will now take a piss at what he calls the urinal with the greatest view in the known world. I'm not an expert on urinals with views in either the known or the unknown world, and I imagine it's a fairly small field on which to post odds, but I'm prepared to bet the urinal at the Forty Foot is among the favorites: a half wall with a gutter beneath, washed by the water but rank with piss and seaweed; above the wall you can see whatever there is to see right out across Dublin Bay to Howth promontory on the Northside; this morning, we can see the sun rising slowly above the sea. Jack says we could have pissed in the sea, but then we would have missed out on the perspective, the perspective *gained*, he says, emphasizing the last word. And we wouldn't want to miss out, would we? No, Jack, we wouldn't. As I had forgotten, as I am reminded again this morning, every hour spent with Jack Donovan is a lesson in not missing out.

CHAPTER 3

Anne Fogarty sometimes wonders if her daughters disrupt the morning routine deliberately, with malice, or at least, mischief, aforethought. She has it all worked out: shower at 7:10, dressed by 7:25, wake the girls and leave their clothes ready for them and straight downstairs to set out breakfast cereals and prepare lunches. They used to have porridge when they were little, and Anne has fought the good fight against cereals with added sugar for a long time, but when the kitchen table began to play host to scenes of female aggression and hysteria worthy of a women's prison, she gave in, drawing the line at honey in the title or anything that colored the milk brown. First they both wanted Cheerios, which was easy, too easy as it turned out; Aoife quickly decided she preferred Rice Krispies Multi-Grain Shapes, and then Ciara, ever anxious that her elder sister might be gaining even greater advantage, decided she preferred them as well; within a couple of days, exhibiting her customary restlessness and discontent, divine or otherwise, Aoife moved on to Frosties.

Now upon the kitchen counter sits a veritable library of breakfast cereals; they remind Anne of the slogan for the Armada books she used to read as a child: "Imagine how colourful they will look upon your bookshelf! Four for ten shillings, eight for a pound!" She bagged a cache of original Armada Books at a church fete a few years back for half nothing, Enid Blyton mostly, but also some gymkhana books by Christine and Diana Pullein-Thompson and a dozen Chalet School titles by Elinor M. Brent-Dyer. However, she has failed in her attempts to persuade Aoife to share in her childhood enthusiasm: Aoife, even at seven, favored books in which young American girls dreamed of boyfriends, clothes, and makeup, and refused to contemplate anything published in what she sniffily referred to as "the olden days" ("Mum, what was it like growing up in the olden days?"). Anne has been meaning, once she summons up the moral force, to try the Armada Books on Ciara, who, while no less stubborn than her sister, is at least not as argumentative.

Anne sets the bowls of cereal on the table, pours milk into a jug and goes out into the hall to yell up the stairs. This would be an excellent opportunity for one or other girl to register her objections to the choice of outfit her mother had laid out for her. (Anne and several other parents have tried on more than one occasion to get the PTA to introduce school uniforms, but they have been defeated by what Anne thinks of as generic "school project" parents who object to anything even faintly redolent of discipline or authority; one of the mothers among this rather sanctimonious, hippyish group whose marriage has recently broken up and who has taken, in what looks very much to Anne like her late forties, to wearing denim miniskirts and very tight low-cut tops, would benefit greatly from some kind of uniform herself, Anne has forborne from observing, as would the parents who wear pajamas and Crocs when they drop their children to school.)

But the outfits are approved, or at least consented to, this morning, and the cereal choice also passes without demur, and as her two tousle-headed daughters tuck into their breakfast in relative silence, Aoife reading a Meg Cabot and Ciara lost in a Teen Titans comic, Anne thinks this just might be the morning it all goes smoothly, the morning *Hello!* magazine could be admitted into her lovely home to see how idyllic it all is. Maybe they could take a photograph of Ed Loy's text, which she looked for first thing she awoke, and is looking at again now, sitting at the breakfast table with a hot mug of tea and a slice of brown bread with the last of Kevin's mother's marmalade. (The etiquette of divorce is uncertain and improvisatory, and lapses of dignity are inevitable: Anne feels one coming on in the next couple of days, as she doesn't see how she can survive without more of Kevin's mother's marmalade, and yet fully understands not only that she is no longer entitled to it, but that if she contacts Iris directly to ask for it, she will lose face in some not entirely definable but nonetheless certain way. She and Iris are still in contact anyway, of course, Iris being the girls' grandmother. Maybe it wouldn't be such a big deal. Maybe she could say Aoife liked it? Could it ever be ethical to use your child in order to get marmalade? She might ask Ed Loy that, it would make him laugh, at the very least. Most things she says seem to make him laugh. In any case, if she told Iris Aoife wanted marmalade, Iris would ask Aoife if that were so, and Aoife would say "Ewww!" and "No Way!" and Anne would be Found Out.)

Ed's text reads . . . no, she's not going to repeat it, she finds they work best if she glances at them quickly and then turns away. When he first started texting her, he'd send things like *Yes.* and *See you later.* and *After nine.* and while it's always nice to know a man is more direct and practical than you are, there's a limit to how much of that a girl can take. So she told him he was only to send her dirty texts, and when he refused (he blushed, in fact, which took her aback: she didn't think he was the blushing type, knew for a fact he wasn't, except, it appeared, in print), she sent him some samples he could use as templates, and eventually, when she had been away on holidays with the kids for a week and he was home alone and drunk, he used up all the templates and got into the swing of things himself, and the one he sent her last night was very good indeed, so much so that Aoife had asked her what she was smirking at and she said she certainly wasn't smirking at anything, she had just remembered something, which was one way of putting it. Just as well Aoife had got her own phone for her tenth birthday, so she leaves Anne's alone now.

Anyway, there was no point in mentioning the text to Ed, as he would shake his head blankly and affect not to know what she was talking about. She couldn't remember fancying anyone the way she fancied him, not even Kevin, or at least, not for ages, she could feel it in her teeth, for Christ's sake. Even if she and Kevin still occasionally . . . out of habit more than anything else, sometimes he stayed over if there was a birthday and they'd all had too much to drink, and even though he'd stay in the spare room, she found herself needing to . . . check up on him . . . obviously it wasn't a good idea, but as she said, divorce etiquette is uncertain, and she is only human . . . and she knows fine well Ed Loy was carrying on with that Donna Nugent one when they met, not that he had promised anything but she couldn't bear the idea of anyone else getting her hands on oh for God's sake Anne get a grip, it's eight o'clock in the morning you horny old cow.

True to form, with hair brushed and shoes on and lunches in schoolbags and all looking set to be A Banner Morning in the Fogarty household, Ciara suddenly gets all teary at the possibility that she might have had a project to do for the last four weeks (the first Anne has heard of it) involving family trees and photographs of grandparents and a *scale model of the family home* set in location with neighboring houses, said project being due this morning, and once Anne has tamped down a perfectly human reaction to scream *Four Weeks And You Tell Me Now?* she says she will come into the class and talk to Miss Redmond herself and explain . . . what? That she is on heroin, and can't be expected to help with homework? That she never looks in Ciara's homework journal because she is too busy gallivanting with a fancy man? (There is no mention of this project in the homework journal.) That sure Ciara is allowed do as she pleases because she is a little dote, isn't she? Anne doesn't know. Mum will make it right, in some undisclosed fashion. At eight o'clock, she had felt on top of the word, efficient, desired, loved, a capable, sexy woman more than ready for the day; ten minutes later, with Ciara's tears dried and the girls in the back of the car (the plan had been to walk because it was so fine, but at this stage, to be honest, fuck that), she wonders whether, once she's dropped them at school, she can just cancel her appointments and crawl back into bed.

She can't, of course, and doesn't need to, Miss Redmond having explained that the project is only *beginning* and will run for four weeks, she is handing out fact sheets about it today and parents can consult with their children and help to plan the work together. Mrs. Mini Skirt casts a superior look in Anne's direction, another salvo in the ongoing low-level attrition between the Mums Who Work and the Mums Who Don't; fair enough, Anne supposes, she has been a bit untogether, but if she were wearing kitten heels and *shorts* like Mrs. Miniskirt is this morning, she'd at least take care to try to not look superior to, well, anyone, really.

Anne swings back to the house to grab a cup of coffee and fill a tote bag with her pile of samples and magazine references. In the long wait for the lights at Donnybrook Church, she glances at the bag and wonders whether she'll even get to remove its contents. A few years back, it had been so different: no sooner would she get through the door than the client would be pouncing on the samples and squealing over the color schemes, credit card vibrating like a tuning fork in anticipation. One woman could stand for many: Merilla (possibly not her given name), the Lancastrian wife of an Irish boy-band singer living in a 3,500-square-feet new-build mansion in Portmarnock, immaculate if a little portly at nine in the morning in brilliant white Juicy Couture tracksuit, snow-blond porn hair framing hard features made even harder by a full face mask of orange makeup, brilliant white acrylic nails, rings on every finger and, for all Anne knew, bells on every Ugg-encased toe, twin babies safe in the care of a silent Brazilian nanny. Anne had to explain patiently that the references she had prepared for French Rustic, English Country House and Swedish Gustavian designs for the house were *alternatives*, and that it would be difficult to combine them, especially if, as it seemed, Merilla wanted bathrooms, kitchens and reception rooms in all three styles. Difficult, but not, as it turned out, impossible, especially given the extent to which Merilla was prepared to pay for the privilege. The result, which looked like the interiors of three houses in one, certainly pleased Merilla, who exclaimed, "It's absolutely gorgeous, just like a hotel so it is." Anne was less keen, and when Merilla was desperate for the house to be featured in an interiors magazine, Anne, fearing career-ending humiliation, went out of her way, using every contact she had made in the business and reeling in several favors, some dating back to school days, to ensure that it would appear nowhere. Eventually, Merilla concluded that the problem had been an excess of subtlety and commissioned a new designer to incorporate Arts and Crafts, Tuscan and Classical/Etruscan themes into the house, which by then had swollen to five thousand feet with the addition of a glass-and-steel extension.

In its new incarnation (with sole credit going to the second designer, Anne having successfully written herself out of its dynamic history), the house was featured in every magazine and property supplement in the land, serving as a cautionary tale of high Celtic Tiger vulgarity and the ever-present danger of having more money than taste, or indeed, sense. Not long afterward, amid the storm of humiliation this and her husband's public affair with the judge of a reality-TV talent contest provoked, the marriage broke up amid a welter of slur and counterslur and Merilla retreated to Burnley, where, from what Anne can make out, she lives a busy life gaining and losing weight, taking and not taking drugs, finding and losing unsuitable boyfriends and giving exclusive interviews on these and every other aspect of her life to the tabloid newspapers and glossy magazines that must have reporters assigned to her around the clock.

The house in Portmarnock went on the market five years ago for four and a half million. You could pick it up for 1.2 now, but nobody wants to, figuring, perhaps correctly, that even that is too much to pay for such a folly. There is still a lot of money around, but there aren't many Merillas left these days, and even the people ready and able to spend are either too cautious, not knowing what economic rupture might come down the line next, or simply too embarrassed to risk looking like middle-class Marie Antoinettes.

In fact, Anne has begun to wish she could charge a consultancy fee for the first meeting, because for the last six months or so, the first meeting generally turns out to be the only meeting. It is also a very long meeting, and it tends to revolve not so much around interior design as interior psychology: how to fill the days now the money supply has tightened. Anne feels a little like a district mental health care nurse, driving door-to-door providing psychotherapy for recovering spendthrifts. *But don't you understand?* she wants to scream as another anguished housewife explains bravely that rediscovering how to make do and mend is so much more fulfilling *spiritually* than all that dreadful materialistic self-indulgence, *my living depends on your preposterous vanity and greed, you spoilt rich brat!*

As she parks on the tree-lined street outside Geri Foster's thirties detached Foxrock house, Anne's hopes are not high, even though this meeting is at least a follow-up. Much of the initial meeting had been taken up with Geri sighing and tossing her curls around and talking wistfully of her acting career and how she needs to get it back on track again after a long time spent behind the scenes. Anne had never heard of her, although that is saying nothing much; she doesn't go regularly to the theater, and so only catches up with new Irish actors when they are so famous you can't avoid them. She looked her up on the Internet Movie Database and drew a blank, but maybe she had another professional name. She appeared to own this house, so maybe she had been incredibly successful back when the girls were babies and Anne's brain had taken a five-year vacation. Anything was possible. Somehow her instinct told her it was unlikely, though. At their first meeting, Geri Foster had struck Anne above all as being lost.

Not that she is unfamiliar with lost girls. After all, she had very nearly been one herself. And she still has her moments. Applying her makeup in the rearview mirror now, she wonders if that was the attraction for Ed Loy, if he sensed that once upon a time, all had not been well. Of course, they met when she hired him to investigate her father's unsolved murder, so it wasn't as if he'd been trawling the farmers' markets and cafés in search of a bored suburban mum. The idea makes her grin; Ed, in black suit and white shirt and Church's shoes, invariably looks incongruous in the park or on the beach among the baseball caps and shorts and chinos, and positively outlandish in a domestic setting, even if he is giving it his best shot.

But he speaks to the girls like he is interested in what they have to say, a facility their parents don't always have the time or energy to maintain, and he remembers to distinguish between them:

that Aoife hates to be teased, for example, whereas Ciara adores it; or that Aoife loves to run and swim, whereas Ciara prefers to sit for hours on end, drawing and listening to music and dreaming. And he never says how was school or are you looking forward to your holidays; instead he comes armed with things to tell them, funny or scary stories or news about comic books and new movies, as if they are people in their own right and he feels he should be interesting to them. As a result, they genuinely like him in a way that has taken them all by surprise, particularly as Aoife was in the throes of a full-fledged love affair with her dad and had initially felt her loyalty to Kevin was incompatible with anything other than hostility toward Ed. This faltered because Aoife doesn't have a talent for hostility, because Kevin was very laid-back about the whole thing, and seemed to like Ed (most men did, Anne had noticed, apart, she supposed, from the ones who were trying to kill him) and because Ed knows how to pay people—women and little women—attention in a way that doesn't seem—hell, that probably isn't—self-serving. And it's very difficult not to respond to that.

Now when he visits and the girls are still up, or if they're around at weekends, they run to him before she can get anywhere near, and scream and hug him, and she finds herself having to turn away. It's hard not to feel excited by that; equally, it's impossible not to feel anxious. She knows Ed's daughter died when she was almost two years old; she would be Ciara's age now, he had told her. She doesn't know what to make of that, doesn't want to talk about it (nor does he), but she thinks about it a lot, and sometimes she sees something in his face when he's with the girls, an expression of such intense, aching sadness that it's impossible not to feel for him.

And yet at a certain level, she doesn't give a damn about how he gets on with anyone but her. Yes, she feels convulsed by occasional surges of the Where Are We Going With This pheromone, but that is as if to say, even if she has no interest whatever in watching *Desperate Housewives,* she feels on some level that she is obligated; in other words, she's a woman, and occasionally she feels a compulsion to corner a man and emotionally blackmail him into making promises neither truly believes will bring them happiness. She succumbed to that urge once; never again. Now she is a divorced woman who doesn't want any more children and who has a reliable father for those she has. And what she missed, more than anything, was what she has now: a man she is powerfully attracted to but doesn't know, perhaps can never know completely. A man, if she is being honest with herself, with more than a hint of danger about him. Not violence, not roughness, just the sense that he cannot let himself be contained. Her twenties had been spent in thrall to any number of men, boys in truth, who were far too dangerous: too much adrenaline got to be as enervating as too little. One ended up in jail, and one was dead; eventually, they'd all been dangerous, but fools with it, and none had been kind or tender enough. She supposes it had something to do with her father dying when she was in her teens: instead of looking for security, she had wanted the opposite: a succession of wild, sexy, reckless boys to prove over and over again that there was no such thing as happy ever after. And now, after a marriage that proved the same thing in a more protracted and painful way, but that has left her relatively secure, at least financially, she is more than ready for the grown-up version.

Maybe Ed saw that in her, a certain kind of hunger, a certain kind of damage. It hasn't been easy since they met: not alone had he had to sift through the Fogarty family entrails to find her father's murderer, he felt implicated in the subsequent suicide of her sister, Margaret. She told him it wasn't his fault, that if anyone was to blame, it was Anne for not simply letting the whole thing rest. Would she have done it all again if she had known in advance what it would lead to? But if she hadn't done it, she wouldn't have met Ed Loy, wouldn't have this voice in her head, this excruciating pain in her heart, this sense in her fortieth year of having been brought back to full, vivid life in all its stupid, sweet, throat-aching intensity. Would she have traded her sister's life for that? The older she gets, the fewer questions she wants to ask. She is afraid of what the answers might be.

She is afraid for Ed, too, and not just that he will one day take a beating he could not come back from, although that is not a minor concern: the state of his poor head after his run-ins with Jack Cullen's gang was like something from a David Cronenberg movie, one of the early ones with rubbish special effects. But more generally, she worries about Ed's relationship with booze. Not that he drinks too much, although he certainly drinks a lot. Anne still makes this distinction, which would probably make her look like someone who drank way too much to those who don't think there's a distinction worthy of the name. Americans, in other words. Maybe she does drink a lot. She doesn't drink as much as she wants to, but that's only because she has to get two girls to school every morning and get herself to work, and that's difficult enough without a hangover.

But she likes drinking, and she likes drinkers, and she is uneasy that Ed has stopped drinking, as she sees it, because he is trying to accommodate himself to a version of her that she doesn't want to acknowledge: in brief, the suburban housewife, the little woman, ever vigilant for signs of excess testosterone and wayward behavior in her male. He isn't a drunk. His drinking hasn't shown in his face or in his physique, it doesn't make him aggressive or angry or sloppy, at least, not with her. On the contrary, it loosens his tongue, and lightens his mood, and makes him fun to be around. As far as she is concerned, it isn't a problem. Worse, there's a sense that, in not drinking, he is somehow craving her approval, even if he isn't conscious of it. She doesn't want Ed Loy to need her approval. By the time a relationship gets to that level of weakness and dependency, it's probably fucked anyway; certainly, the best of the fucking has gone out of it. She'd rather see him less often but more intensely than have him popping in during the week, determinedly sober and not quite himself. She wasn't going to lay down the law: if he thought his drinking had become a problem, that was up to him. But she was going to make it clear that it was far from being a problem for her. Not only did she not want to marry the man today, she didn't want to change his ways tomorrow.

She hopes she can avoid the subject altogether, though. And if half what she has heard about Ed and Jack Donovan is true, chances are Ed is in the jigs somewhere right now, or in an early house, or in some bleary-eyed state of never again, never again. She likes him like that. Maybe she'll meet him for lunch back at hers, if he has the time, make it clear to him that he doesn't have to fit into what he imagines is her timetable, or become the person he thinks she wants him to be, that that is exactly what she doesn't want. She sends him a text in the spirit of the one he had sent her last night. She can remind him in person that he promised to bring her onto Jack Donovan's *Nighttown* set, and meet whoever was working that day—as far as she can work out, every Irish actor she's ever heard of is in the movie, and while she isn't exactly a starstruck teen, it would beat the hell out of the school run, not to mention commiserating with Southside ladies over the seemingly terminal demise of Dublin, the former gold-rush town.

Geri Foster appears in her front window and looks out. Anne is officially late. She gathers her things together, gets out of the car and walks up the driveway. After all, who knows what the future will bring? Miracles might happen yet. It could only be a matter of time before someone plucked up the courage and decided to hell with the expense and the social disgrace, there was nothing for it but to do up the living room.

CHAPTER 4

Jack's car drops me off in Holles Street, where I have an apartment on the third floor of an eighteenth-century house across the road from the National Maternity Hospital. I consider going to bed, but the swim has invigorated me, and in any case, I'm not going to be shamed by Jack Donovan: if he can follow a night's drinking with a day's work, so can I. I collect the papers and some eggs from the newsagent on Grand Canal Street. As I open the door to my building, three highly excited young children run squealing up the steps of the NMH, followed by what looks like their (no less excited) grandmother, while a glassy-eyed man in his thirties unloads a baby seat from an SUV. I have whiled away hours at my window watching the repetitive, endlessly enthralling drama unfold, day after day: the mothers exhausted and overwhelmed, the fathers proud and scared, the grandparents swaggering or blasé, the siblings excited and jealous; and then the notable exceptions in each category: the unaffectionate, the indifferent, the resigned and the bored; meanwhile swarming across the stage like jesters and like fools, the smokers: the boyfriends and uncles and sisters, but also in their peach and fuchsia, in their leopard skin and polka dot, ladies and gentlemen, in all weathers, on the steps and on the street and in the wheelchair entrance, the smoking mothers, seeking precious refuge from their infants in the slow, fatal kiss of a cigarette.

After a bout of bronchitis, at the urging of a doctor who told me if I didn't, I was going to die, I stopped smoking, but every day, the changing faces of these ridiculous women make me crave anew the stupid release tobacco brings. Tommy says it's the puritan and the scold in me, that I just love to torture myself, but then Tommy also accuses me of being broody for paying the NMH any attention at all. I don't know how to answer that. Maybe I am broody. Is that a sin? It's evidently a hanging matter in Tommy's book. But then, it's easy for him to say: he has a daughter, Naomi, seventeen she must be now. He has no need to brood.

There's nothing like a swim to work up an appetite. In the kitchen, I fill the moka with water and espresso and screw it tight, and while it's on the heat, I break some eggs and scramble them in olive oil and mix some chives through and put them on a plate with a few slices of smoked salmon. It's an indulgent breakfast, but the way I work, I can't always depend on eating lunch. At least, that's what I tell myself.

The papers are full of *Nighttown*-related stories, as they have been since news that the film would shoot in Dublin was announced. In an economy not just reeling from the worldwide recession but sucker-punched to its knees by the Great Celtic Tiger Property Bubble, a hubris-to-nemesis saga that has yet to run its course (I bought this apartment eighteen months ago at pretty much the top of the market, so the only thing in doubt is not whether it's now worth less than I paid for it, but by how much), the decision to film here was greeted as a vote of confidence, an omen signaling even better things to come and, at some hysterical level it seemed, proof that if Hollywood still loved us, we, the Irish, were still intrinsically lovable, the infants of the Western world, always landing on our feet no matter what manner of scrape we find ourselves in. The *Irish Times* ran a piece on the business page about tax breaks for film investment, and how the regulations here were not now as competitive as they were in the UK, and that certainly the costs were far greater than they would have been in Eastern Europe. The article concluded that Jack and in particular his producer, Maurice Faye, deserved credit for insisting that the movie be shot here, and Maurice was quoted saying something suitably flag-waving in which the word *brand*—as in, the Jack Donovan Brand, the James Joyce Brand, the *Birth of a Nation* Brand and the Ireland Inc. Brand—featured heavily. Which is I guess how film producers speak these days.

Nighttown was manna for the tabloids, of course, since the action takes place almost entirely in 1920s Dublin brothels, and therefore features any number of actresses wearing vintage lingerie, and often not much of that. The film's publicity office had initially refused to issue any "official" stills, but there were so many leaked shots from the set, which in any case was effectively a terrace of eighteenth-century houses near Mountjoy Square and therefore, given the less than salubrious nature of the area, impossible to keep entirely secure, and so many fetching extras only too happy to pose for the press at the drop of a hat, that a deal was worked out: in return for a small number of sanctioned photographs of the leading players, the tabloids agreed to limit their attentions to strictly arranged press calls. Of course, this was inevitably a deal more honored in the breach than in the observance, and as a result, the papers thought all their Christmases had come at once. The shots in general were not difficult on the eye, but I examine them with particular attention this morning until I find what I'm looking for: in the corner of an ensemble shot in what presumably is some kind of waiting or anteroom, three women with long black hair and deep blue eyes sit together, limbs interwoven, a three-headed entity. I thought of what Conor Rowan, Jack's first AD, had said about the missing extra, Nora Mannion: that Jack had wanted to use her with two other women of similar coloring. I couldn't tell which was Nora, and the shot was blurry, but I was struck by how closely each of the three Graces, or Fates, or Furies, resembled Jack's PA and girlfriend, Madeline King.

The other aspect of the newspapers in which I take an interest is the coverage of drug dealer and organized criminal Podge Halligan's appeal against his sentence for manslaughter. I have known the Halligans all my life, back from the time when they were disorganized criminals, you might say.

Podge Halligan is the most unpredictable of the Halligan gang, volatile and violent and quite possibly insane. The last time I was in his company, he pounded my head to a bloody mess and tried to finish me off with a scythe. He raped Tommy Owens, then told him it was "because he liked him." His brothers, Leo and George, were almost certainly relieved when Podge pleaded guilty, at their insistence, to the manslaughter of a drug-addicted county councillor for whom he had cooked up a hot shot. Since then, George, who among the brothers bears the closest resemblance to a normal human being, or at least, can give the most skillful impersonation of one, has successfully laundered most of his criminal wealth through a handful of small businesses and thence into a succession of property ventures. He has also become a noted racehorse owner. But the deal George made with the devil seems to have come unstuck in the past year or so.

It's true that the Criminal Assets Bureau, which can seize property and cash as the proceeds of crime if it cannot be accounted for legitimately, has never landed a glove on him. And he never borrowed large sums from the banks to finance his deals: he never needed to, such was his income from drug dealing. He has never had a difficulty with cash flow. No, George's problem now is that his wealthy friends, from whom he received deposits for apartments and development land and so on, have lost vast sums of money in the crash, and are reluctant to proceed on deals for properties and sites whose values have plummeted since they were signed. And while in the past, the Halligans rarely needed to issue more than an irritated reminder to see the brisk payment of outstanding accounts, they're now faced with employing more vivid forms of debt collection, involving the use, or so I understand, of carpenter's tools and garden implements. This is not what George spent many years climbing the ladder of business respectability for, and at a stroke would disqualify him from rubbing shoulders with, if not quite the great and the good, certainly the rich and the powerful, in the owners and trainers' ring at race meetings up and down the country. But dinars are dinars, and if the rumors were true that George had even been obliged to carry out some of the persuasion himself, well, maybe recession tears the motley off all our backs and reveals the essential man within: in George's case, the fact that beneath the pinstripe suits and the contrast-collar shirts and the diamond-tip tie pins breathed a brutal, violent, ruthless thug was no great act of dramatic revelation, to me at least.

Leo Halligan had got out of jail a couple of years back with the intention, if not of actually killing me, certainly of making me wish I was dead, as a way of avenging the part I had played in putting his brother behind bars. He ended up helping me out on a couple of cases and forming an alliance with my friend Tommy Owens that I viewed with unease and concern. Not so much for Leo, who is wild and cunning and capable of looking after himself, but for Tommy, who is none of these things.

But the prospect of Podge Halligan getting out of jail raised the stakes considerably; he was too wily to issue direct threats, but there was no doubt in my mind that once he was out, it would only be a matter of time. And with George having redis-covered his inner thug, and Leo always apt to value blood loy-alty above any other consideration, I could not expect a friend of any kind at the Halligan court.

By the time I get out of the shower, there are four messages on my phone. One is an extremely promising text from Anne Fogarty; the other three are voice mails from Madeline King, asking me to contact her as soon as possible in ascending degrees of urgency. I call her before I am dressed, but once I am dry.

"Ed, fair play to you, I thought you'd crashed out after your night with Jack."

"I'm wide-awake. What's up?"

Madeline is attempting a bright Galway jauntiness that sounds forced.

"Remember Nora Mannion yesterday?"

"The extra that went missing? Sure. What, has she been found?"

"No. What do you mean, 'found'? Nothing like that."

"Nothing like what, Madeline? You left three messages in twenty minutes, that sounds like an emergency to me. What are we talking about?"

There's a pause, and then Madeline exhales audibly. It sounds like a lament.

"It's a total fucking shitstorm. Kate Coyle—another extra, she was part of the trio with Nora and Jenny Noble Conor Rowan mentioned last night, you know, the Fates or whatever—"

"There's a picture of them in this morning's *Star*."

"Yeah, well, Kate didn't show up this morning, and Nora hasn't come in either, and everyone's freaking out, Jack wanted to sack Geoff Keegan, the second AD, and two of the trainee ADs *have* been sacked, I think mostly because Maurice was afraid Jack was going to kill them if he didn't get them off the set, there's blood on the fucking walls here—"

"I'll be there in ten minutes."

"I know Jack would really appreciate it. And Maurice Faye asked if there was any way you could—"

"I'll be there, Madeline. You can set it out for me then."

I dress and drink another cup of coffee and think about not having a hangover and how much better that feels than how I'm feeling now. I'm wearing a black linen suit and a white cotton shirt with French cuffs which I fold back but leave without links although I carry a pair in my coat pocket and plain black oxfords from Church's. On mornings like this, when the panic in the streets meets an alcoholically manufactured panic surging through my bloodstream, my habit of dressing like an undertaker or an orchestral musician is a reassurance to me, a reliable constant in an inconstant world. I think for a moment about the denizens of the film business and their necessary flair for the dramatic, and how it has a tendency to continue out of range of the camera. I think about pretty, careless girls who simply get bored being extras (because a film set is one of the most boring places on earth, where, as somebody said, nothing happens at great and painstaking length) and decide not only that they've had enough, but that they don't want to be hassled anymore by the maniacs who've been herding them around for the past while, so they turn off their phones and take care not to let anyone know where they're going. In short, I do everything I can to avoid listening to that voice in my head, the one that, as soon as it heard mention of Kate Coyle's name, preceded by that of Nora Mannion's, began to repeat, with grace notes supplied by the crashing waves of the Pacific Ocean and the roar of the Coast Highway traffic, at intervals as regular and ominous as the tolling of a bell: *Those girls are gone.*

CHAPTER 5

The *Nighttown* set runs along a terrace of three four-story Georgian houses on Gardner Street above Sherrard Street, extending back through laneways and yard space as far as Dorset Lane. Madeline King is waiting for me on the street and greets me with a wave. She holds her head inclined away from me and won't meet my eyes. Having had notably pale, milky skin yesterday, her face is thick with shiny bronze makeup today. I'm not an expert, but she had struck me as more than a few cuts above the orange-faced type of girl. She leads me down a side lane to a yard that runs the length of the terrace, crammed with trucks and generators. An old-fashioned double-decker bus does service as the film's catering truck. A couple of security goons in black T-shirts and baseball caps and shades with two-way radios loom into my path, then stand aside as Madeline smooths the way. One of the goons looks familiar, but then, if you hang around Dublin long enough, pretty much everyone looks, maybe even is, familiar; that is its blessing, and its curse.

"Mossy's waiting for you upstairs," Madeline says, and steps aside to let me pass, again holding her face away. I touch her elbow as gently as I can. She starts violently and turns on me, then her hand flies up to cover her cheek.

"What happened to your face, Madeline?" I say.

It isn't the most gallant of lines, but it can't be helped: Madeline's left cheek is bruised and swollen in ways makeup can't conceal. Madeline makes her eyes do a smiling thing that looks very close to a crying thing, and shakes her head in a cartoon manner, as if I'd never begin to guess how stupid she can be.

"Stop, I know sure, Madeline as in Mad, headless-chicken hour this morning and there's me running around the set trying to keep track of it all and don't I turn smack bang into a light stand, *whap*. I've been seen by the nurse and I'm fine, but that's why I have the mad orange face."

She is evidently shaken and upset, and who wouldn't be: her injuries look painful, and any blemish to the face is upsetting, especially for a woman. I tell her I'm sorry, and she makes a joke about it being her luck finally to look like a lady who lunches just when all said ladies have ducked for cover, and I smile and squeeze her arm and climb aboard the bus and hope she is telling the truth.

Maurice Faye, Mossy to friend and foe alike, not that he has made a great number of the latter, greets me with a laugh and an embrace, as if needing to consult a private detective to sort out a crisis on a movie set is the most delightful thing that has happened to him in weeks. Mossy is wearing a tan waistcoat over a collarless white shirt; his dark, silver-flecked hair falls in ringlets about his sallow, drawn face; his eyes sparkle with energy and life. He wears a Celtic-style wedding ring; his wife of twenty years or more, whom I have never met but feel I knew since she is a feature of the newspaper society pages, is a ferociously groomed blonde of indeterminate middle age who runs four or five children, a couple of cancer charities and an equestrian school from their farmhouse near Moycullen in County Galway; Jack once asked me, with a skepticism I didn't quite follow, "Has anyone ever seen them together?"

"Good man Ed, like the style, looking sharp these days. Welcome aboard. You're either on the bus or you're off it, am I right?"

"That's one way to look at it, I guess."

"Oh now. Equivocation, and it not even lunchtime? We'll have to keep on our toes with the Loy, won't we Maddy? No change there, we know this fella of old so we do. Sit down now like a good man."

The rows of seats on the bus have been rearranged to face each other and tables have been bolted in between. A smell of fried food and pungent spices hangs in the air. I sit facing Maurice; Madeline King sits across the aisle.

Mossy looks at me, frowns, rolls his eyes as if at the ridiculousness of the situation and then laughs again.

"God, it's mad though. Just when you think nothing can go wrong, ha? And everyone's delighted with the dailies, Jack's on massive form, massive. And we've just wrapped Josh Tyler, who is going to be HUGE, Ed, by the time *Nighttown* comes out Josh Tyler is going to be the, the next, the new, put it this way, by the time it comes out, we wouldn't be able to afford him. And now this!"

"And now what, Mossy? Set it out for me, will you? Two special extras missing, is that it so far?"

"That's about the size of it. Nora Mannion took a wander yesterday afternoon. She wasn't in the last shot but she was still on call. It's, you remember the way Jack always has a trio of women somewhere in the film, the Three Degrees, I always call them. Anyway, I think this time out, Jack decided he wasn't going to have them, you know the way, worried he might be repeating himself. And then sure when the extras come in, there are three young ones who are ringers for each other. And to be honest with you, ringers for Madam King there as well, this did not go unnoticed, I can tell you."

"Fuck up, Mossy," Madeline says sharply, pure Galway; Maurice Faye yelps in delight and winks at me. If I had been unfamiliar with Maurice, I might have thought he wasn't taking the situation seriously; knowing him, I understand the reverse to be the case: the more skittish and borderline hysterical he appears, the graver he is underneath. That hail-fellow Mossy persona concealed a shrewd intelligence and a surprisingly complex love of cinema; I'd heard him say his two favorite directors of all time were Andrei Tarkovsky and Michelangelo Antonioni, which is not what movie producers who actually make any money in the film business tend to think, let alone admit.

"Sling us over the glossies there so Ed can see what we're dealing with," Maurice says.

Madeline passes a file of photographs across, and while I look at three standard ten-by-eight head shots of Nora Mannion, Kate Coyle and Jenny Noble, Maurice continues talking.

"Anyway, Jack sees the three and says he, this was meant to be, and from then on, he's going to feature them as special extras."

"What does that mean?" I say.

"It means they don't have any lines, but they're shot in significant ways, you get to know the faces. It means they're key to the visuals."

"And presumably they get paid more as a result?"

Madeline King makes a sound somewhere between a cough and a jeering laugh; Maurice Faye rolls his eyes again.

"They should, you're right, we'll probably do something for them in retrospect," Maurice says, and flinchs, Madeline taking no care to disguise her laugh this time.

"Jaysus, your one is spoiling for it today," he says, grinning.

"Did you hear, Ed, she's already had a row with a lighting stand. Which one of us is safe, I ask you?"

"Get on with it, Mossy," Madeline says.

"No respect, Ed. That's what I get for hiring neighbors. Ah sure, it's Ireland, how can you avoid it, aren't we all neighbors anyway?"

It's Madeline's turn now to roll her eyes at this particularly heavy-handed piece of paddy-whackery. The bus is hot, and the smell of stale food is making me queasy. I slide open the top of the window next to me and breathe in some fresh air, and reflect that at least Madeline was telling the truth about how her facial injuries had come about. For this relief, some thanks.

"What we didn't do, I mean, they were all young ones with barely tuppence worth of experience between them, amateur dramatics about the height of it, I said to Geoff Keegan, he's the second AD whose job it is to run the extras, I said, see how it goes, Jack didn't want them to begin with, maybe it won't work out, no sense upgrading them before we have to."

"What difference would it have made? I mean, to their going missing?"

"Well, in the first place, there's the extra money they would have made, and the extra status they'd've had, which might have meant they wouldn't've gone for a wander, if that's what they've done. And second, Geoff could have kept a closer eye on them himself, or reinforced with the trainee ADs that they needed close watching and hand-holding and all the rest."

I stare at the three girls' photographs—and girls is all they are, really. They are each posed in classic cheesy head-shot fashion, two with their chins perched on their folded hands, one with her head tipped to one side, as if she's about to expire from cuteness. That's Nora Mannion. It's almost impossible to tell what they're like from these photographs, whose purpose is to make their subjects look as adaptable and castable and, as a perhaps unintended consequence, as bland and unexceptional as possible.

"I got hold of Nora Mannion's sister, Rose, on the phone last night," Madeline says. "She hadn't heard from Nora, couldn't get her on the phone. This was after I went out to where she was staying, a shared house in Killester with three young actors, the casting agent Debbie Moyers fixed her up there. They hadn't seen her, said she was very quiet, not really a party girl, if she came to the pub with them she'd have the one drink and that'd be it. Early to bed, early to rise. Rose said the same, Nora wasn't into partying, she was quite serious about acting, hoping to get a place in the Gaiety School, wanted to get some experience and see what it was all like. She was absolutely thrilled to have gotten work in a Jack Donovan movie, Rose said she got all his films out on DVD and watched them twice or three times each."

"So this is not a girl who is just going to get bored and wander off, or say to hell with it and do a runner; this is a serious, ambitious girl who wants to impress."

"That's how it's looking," Maurice Faye says. "Even when we couldn't find her last night, I had high hopes, whatever, she'd hooked up with some young fella, first time in Dublin, quiet ones you have to watch, didn't want big sis or anyone else to know, she'd scuttle back onto set this morning and nobody would be any the wiser. Instead, not only has she gone, we can't find Kate Coyle either."

"Just, before we go any further, the third girl, Jenny Noble, where is she?"

"She's on the costume truck. Jess O'Leary, the supervisor, said she'd look after her," Maurice says. "We can get her anytime, if you want to talk to her."

"She's going to be safe there, is she?"

Maurice and Madeline exchange an amused look at this.

"If Jess O'Leary looks after you, you know you've been looked after," Maurice says.

"Mossy's a teeny bit scared of the costume ladies," Madeline says.

"With good reason. God, they'd eat you now, Ed, I'm not codding you."

"They would not, don't mind him, Jess is lovely sure," Madeline says.

"Ah no, yeah, she is, absolutely, no, yeah, they all are, what I mean is, coming through, don't get in their way, they know how to get the job done, mighty now. In fact, if Jess and the girls had been in charge of Nora and Kate, we'd have them yet."

"And how are you managing? How's Jack?"

"Ah, grand. Toys are all back in the pram. We rejigged the schedule so he can do interior scenes with two or three principals. And once the two or three principals concerned have got over the schedule rejig, we'll be laughing," Maurice says, for once without even the trace of a laugh himself.

"Mossy's been running around like the Good Humor man all morning, trying to keep everyone happy."

"It's a great life if you don't weaken, isn't that right, Ed?" Maurice says, and dredges up a desperate chuckle from the depths.

"Tell me about Kate Coyle," I say.

Maurice lifts his hands up and looks across to Madeline.

"I don't really . . . day to day, Madeline's been on set more than I have, with Jack and the actors."

Madeline looks uncertain for a moment, and then nods decisively, as if some internal jury has finally returned its verdict.

"It's not beyond the bounds . . . Kate Coyle is a wild little yoke, a real party girl. So it's not beyond the bounds of anyone's imagination that she might stroll in yet, still trashed from a wild night out. And little Nora tucked beneath her arm. So—"

"So it could all be much ado, Ed," Maurice says. "I mean, it's all about money, when it comes down to it, what we can reshoot and what we can't, and the sooner we know, the sooner we can decide what has to be done."

"How wild can this girl be? She looks as if butter wouldn't melt."

Madeline grins.

"Ah, she'd play on that. Kate, she's brilliant crack actually. Her brothers are both actors, a lot of theater, the Abbey, the Gate, big drinkers the pair of them. Family's well-off, South-side, Kate got expelled from one of those posh girls' schools, Loreto or Holy Child, for, I don't know what, sex and drugs and rock and roll. Her folks wanted her to go to college, but Kate's in too much of a hurry. Not that bothered what she's hurrying toward, she's done some modeling, a bit of DJing, I don't think she had much of a sense of the script or of Jack either, she just knew Josh Tyler was in the movie and that was, like, wicked, y'know, Cool for Kate, yeah? Totally Southside, she'd make you laugh, but not thick."

"And when was she last seen?"

"She was at the party last night. And then . . . people I spoke to said, she was there and then she was gone. Didn't make it home, I spoke to her mum this morning. Who was totally un-derwhelmed, I called at eight in the morning, she said, Is this not what God invented mobile phones for? I said I couldn't reach Kate on hers, and her mum checked her room and there was no sign, and she just said, if my daughter has not made it back to her bed, it won't be the first time, she's over eighteen and there's nothing more I can do, I'm sure she'll surface at some stage in the game, please give her her mother's love and tell her to look after herself. And then she hung up on me."

"We should probably hear from Jenny Noble at this stage, see if she knows anything."

"She says she doesn't," Madeline says. "I'll get her for you now."

While she is gone, I tell Maurice what I charge, and Maurice does a lot of Mossy-acting about everyone's fee being negotiable in these hard times, and I say that's as maybe but last time I checked, he was a movie producer and if he's doing that job and he doesn't have any money maybe he should think about getting into another line of work. Maurice hums and haws and won't let it go, and finally as Madeline comes up the stairs with Jenny Noble, I tell him if he doesn't want to pay me, he can go to the Guards; in fact, why didn't he go in the first place? From the sudden pallor that spreads across his sallow skin, I see there must be a good reason; I just don't know what it is yet.

What strikes me most about Jenny Noble is not how much more individual or idiosyncratic she seems in the flesh than in her head shot, or, like most young Irishwomen, what a bizarre combination of youth and pseudo-sophisticated middle age she possesses, it's how closely she resembles Madeline King, or at least, Madeline pre-bruising and orange makeup. Her hair is raven black, swept back from a high brow, her eyes intense blue pools, her skin milky white; her head belongs on the prow of a ship. I would have trouble telling my Graces from my Furies, but if it came to ensemble goddesses, I would cast Jenny as a Fate, no question. But I wonder if Jack had the Muses in mind when he cast three women who look so much like his current love.

Jenny Noble speaks with an educated Cork accent, and in a let's-face-it-girls manner that belies her years. Initially she appears skeptical that anything sinister has taken place.

"Kate Coyle was fit to fly so she was. I said, Kate girl, shooting a film's the same as shooting a person: they need to see the whites of your eyes. And at the rate you're lashing into those Breezers, your eyes won't have any whites at all, and certainly not at six in the morning. But Kate was high as a kite, plotting and scheming how to drag Josh Tyler to Club 92 and work her magic on him."

"Club 92. Is that out in Leopardstown, at the racecourse?" Maurice says.

"That's the one. For the Canterbury and Dubes crew. Kate's home from home, I don't think she's missed a night there since we started."

"And did you see her go, Jenny?"

"Nah. I left myself around ten, couldn't say if she was still there or not. I'm telling you though, that's probably where she ended up. And if she didn't make it home, well sure, she probably did all right for herself. Clock was ticking like, sure it was only a matter of time before it all caught up with her. I wouldn't be surprised if she's still asleep. Or doing the long walk of shame into work. Although fair play to Kate, shame is just something she doesn't do."

"And what about Nora? Was she at Josh's party?"

Jenny shakes her head.

"She wasn't. Now Nora is another matter. You know, I'd've said it would take something major for Nora to miss five minutes, she just ate it all up. She'd be on set watching when it wasn't her scene, where the camera was, what the actors were doing. And any spare time she had, she was down the Irish Film Institute or at the Lighthouse, watching all the new art-house movies. Nora Mannion was an intense young one, her and Kate were like chalk and cheese. It was no surprise she wasn't at the party, but I would be worried Nora hasn't shown at all today. Maybe she's been in an accident?"

"Rose Mannion rang around the hospitals first thing this morning," Madeline says. "Nothing doing. She's going to keep calling every couple of hours. As far as she's concerned, it's completely out of character for Nora, she's . . . she was quite upset, to be honest."

The sudden talk of accidents and hospitals and upset blood relations lends the incongruous gathering on the upper deck of the bus a sudden air of gravity; for a moment, no one wants to pursue that line, lest fate perhaps be tempted; when the silence is broken, it's the grave-faced Fate herself, Jenny Noble, who speaks.

"On one level, it maybe feels a bit hysterical, two twenty-year-old girls not even missing twelve hours and everyone's freaked out. And when I was first told, I suppose I thought, if it was any other job in the world, you'd just say, bloody young ones, they don't know they're born, and get someone to cover and wait for them to show. I thought, God, what a bunch of drama queens, the way everyone was acting out. But I don't know if I feel like that now."

Jenny Noble turns her vivid gaze on me. Maurice Faye and Madeline King are looking at me anyway. The ball is in my court. But I'm not there, haven't been there since Jenny had deliberated and, in her considered, serious, yes, *fateful* way, had come down on the side of loss. I am far away, in space and time. I am in Point Dume, in Malibu, on the beach, in the ocean, on the bluff.

CHAPTER 6

Three extras, women in their late teens or early twenties, had gone missing from the set of *Ocean Falls*, Jack Donovan's 1994 movie, and I was sitting in a beach bar off Pacific Coast Highway having a version of this conversation with a different Madeline and the same Maurice Faye. To my knowledge, those girls had never been found. They certainly were never found by me.

Sweat prickles on my scalp and beads on my brow. My tongue feels as if it has doubled in size and been pressed dry, like a sponge. Finally, I manage to get a few words out.

"I'd like to be able to say there's no need to worry, but I don't know if there is or not. People act out of character sooner or later: being who we're not helps to remind us who we are. So it may well be that Nora Mannion got fed up with being a good girl and an apt student, got so sick of herself she wondered what it was like to be someone else. And she may well have woken or be waking this morning with the knowledge of what that's like, for better or worse. Let's hope that's what happened. It seems highly likely something like that happened to Kate Coyle anyway. The second option is that Nora has been involved in some kind of accident, or fallen ill, in a manner so serious she's not able to call and let anyone know about it. And of course, that could go equally for Kate. The third option . . . the third option is that some person or people are in some way holding one or other or both girls, and are preventing them from leaving. They've been abducted, in other words."

"And murdered," nobody says, but it hangs in the air like an unheard melody, like the red flash you see when you shut your eyes.

"Jenny, I don't want you to panic, but if there is something like this happening, obviously you're in danger. So we need to make sure you're somewhere safe, somewhere no one can get to you. Where are you staying?"

"I'm subletting from a friend in Trinity, she's gone to the States on a J1 for the summer. It's a flat in Rathmines, one of the houses the Celtic Tiger didn't touch. Old place in about twenty-four bedsits, very shabby, crumbling, damp, you could force the locks with the back of a spoon."

"Okay, well, if the other girls don't show up soon, we're going to have to get you out of there for a start. In the meantime, because I need to talk to Maurice about a few things, Madeline, could you maybe see that Jenny goes back to the costume truck for the time being, and then I'll be down to figure out where we take it from there."

One of the downsides of the way my mind works when I'm on a case is that I assume since I can make the connections, everyone else can, particularly those who are as well placed as me. Those who were in Point Dume fifteen years ago. But when Madeline King got off the bus with Jenny Noble, Maurice Faye holds his hands up as if to concede defeat, and lets a large laugh crash and rattle off the metal fittings of the bus, and nods his head ruefully.

"Fair play Ed, a thousand a day, you win. Let's just get it sorted out, search parties, smoke signals, the whole bit. Thing is though, we need to keep it under wraps. That's why there can be no Garda presence, Jesus, we'd end up all over the fucking *Evening Herald.*"

I look at him in a quizzical way, sure he must be able to see the parallels between now and then; he interprets it as my attempting to drive an even harder bargain.

"Look, a grand a day, that's what you asked for, and your expenses, don't push it any further now. Fuck, the trouble we've had with insurance on this gig . . . it's getting worse every time."

"How's that? I thought you had Universal behind you, their indie strand, what's it called—"

"Focus; we do and they're brilliant. But it's just . . . especially after *The Last Anniversary,* they're watching very closely. They want Jack back in his box. And as we both know, when you insist on putting Jack in his box, you get nothing but trouble."

The Last Anniversary was Jack Donovan's most recent film, a determinedly obscure epic that centered around a doomed love affair repeating itself with variations across seven different historical periods, from the twelfth-century Crusades to the Vietnam War. Characters moved freely from one period to the next; historical anachronism abounded, and although the periods seemed to have been chosen for contemporary parallels that might be made to wars in Afghanistan and Iraq, nothing of this came across in the script, nor, Jack insisted, was it intended to. The first cut of the film ran four and a half hours; after much hand-to-hand combat with Universal, Jack finally consented to a version that ran three hours and ten minutes. It opened to universally dreadful reviews, and from a budget of eighty-five million dollars, grossed one and a half million the first weekend, eventually ending up at just above five. It was the kind of extravagant act of folly Hollywood hates to back and directors love to make when coming off a big hit.

In Jack's case, that was his 2002 version of Philip K. Dick's alternative-universe classic *The Man in the High Castle,* which grossed over four hundred million and let Jack believe he could do anything he wanted. Which was briefly true; what he didn't realize was that, when he failed to do what he wanted well enough, he would get sent to Hollywood Jail, free to associate with inmates like Michael Cimino, Elaine May, Martin Brest and Michael Lehmann, but unlikely ever to leave. What saved Jack Donovan from shooting episodes of TV shows as a director for hire the rest of his career was the fact that Universal had insisted on putting a producer in over Maurice Faye's head on *The Last Anniversary,* so when Jack came up with the script for *Nighttown,* the low budget combined with Maurice's relatively unblemished track record on the hits they had together meant that Jack Donovan got a second chance. Not that he saw it like that. "Every movie is your first chance," he told an interviewer from *Rolling Stone.* "And your last."

"And the press are watching everything we do like a hawk," Maurice says. "So we don't want the cops anywhere near the production. Unless Colin falls off the wagon when he's in town and gets into a few rows, they love all that Hollywood Wildman thing."

"That's why they loved Jack so much in the first place, isn't it? He was Dylan Thomas, Richard Harris and Errol Flynn wrapped up in one."

"And he was making them money, Ed. When you start to lose them money, different story. Fuck, I don't know how many anniversaries we'll have to live through before we've heard the last of *The Last Anniversary.* Did you see it yourself, Ed?"

"I'm afraid so."

Maurice yells with laughter.

"You're afraid! Jaysus. Imagine how we felt. I think it took Jack two years before he realized, or at least admitted, what a mess it actually was. Maybe he'll do a director's cut someday and

they'll rediscover it, in France or some-fucking-where. Anyway. Forward, not back, isn't that right? The future is the only thing we can change. And the Guards needn't know, right?"

I shrug.

"The Guards won't be in much of a rush anyway—the girls have been gone such a short time they hardly constitute a missing person case."

"All right. Do you think you can find them, Ed?"

"If they don't show up themselves . . . in other words, if we're at option three, and they've been abducted, then chances are they're dead already. In which case, it doesn't make any difference to you; your budget is shot to hell. The only other possibility in that scenario is if the kidnapper contacts us. But if he contacts us, it may well be that he wants to mess with us, and he's already begun to kill them."

Maurice's eyes open wide, and he looks at me with a mixture of alarm and derision.

' "He's already begun to kill them?' What the fuck are you talking about man, a serial killer? We're making a movie, we're not in one. Fuck's sake Ed, this is Dublin, not L.A.—"

"Not L.A. Not Malibu. Not Point Dume."

"Not Malibu. Not . . . fuck . . . those extras on *Ocean Falls* . . . how many were there?"

"Three. You remember?"

"I do now."

"Three girls of nineteen or twenty. They were surfers, or surfers' girlfriends. They weren't that crucial to the shoot, they were just in crowd scenes, beach parties, so on. It wasn't like they were one of Jack Donovan's trios, his Furies or his Fates. And in real life, they were runaways, or they had no family, no one seemed to care about them, or even notice that they'd gone. Except for Jack's girlfriend of the time, who was the extras' coordinator, I think she pressured you into hiring someone to look for them. And Jack thought of me."

"In that beach bar off PCH, that's when I first met you. What was that, ten—"

"Fifteen. Ninety-four. It was one of my first cases on my own, after I'd taken over the agency out there. And it was not an auspicious start. I trawled through biker bars down in Long Beach, porn sets in the Valley, those girls left trails all over. But no beginning and no ending. They just vanished into thin air. Vanished back into the thin air they'd come out of."

"We got the cops involved on that one though, didn't we?"

"We notified them. But you know, the state of California reports between thirty-five and forty *thousand* people missing every year. And there's a fair number of those who already went missing from somewhere else, who came to California in the first place in order to disappear. So with the best will in the world, the LAPD will prioritize cases according to who is doing the reporting. And that means a tearful mom shades it over a private investigator whose client is a movie producer and a bunch of missing runaways with no known next of kin. So yes, they have the case on file, and I assume, technically, it remains open. But I doubt if you could describe it as active."

Maurice stares at me blankly for a while. He looks as if somebody has removed his brain for servicing. When it has been replaced, and all synapses are firing again, he begins nodding and gesturing animatedly, as if he has been fast-forwarded to a later stage in the conversation and is now keen to pursue me on points I haven't yet made.

"So what are you saying, these two . . . cases, fuck, I don't want to acknowledge this *is* a case—"

"So what am I doing here?"

"These two cases are *linked?*"

"I don't know. I hope not. It's one possibility. The first thing that flashed into my mind when Madeline called me was that bar on PCH, the head shots of those sunburned blond California girls."

"But what I mean is, if they are linked, we're the link, aren't we? Me and Jack."

"That would be a way of looking at it, all right. Whoever was on that shoot and is also on this one. You, Jack, Mark Cassidy . . . anyone else?"

"Conor. Conor Rowan, he's been Jack's First AD all the way through."

"Is that it? You haven't kept anyone else from the beginning?"

"Just the old Gang of Four. Are you going to tell us we're suspects, Ed?"

Maurice fires off a salvo of Mossy-laughs. I let my expression go blank. When the laughter abates, Maurice's face ripples with sudden anger and he jabs a stubby finger in front of my face.

"Are you saying one of us would sabotage our own work? Because if those girls are gone, and the costs are such that we can't recast and reshoot, or CGI them in somehow, or find some other solution I can't think of at the moment, this will bring the film crashing down around us, you know what I mean? This will be a disaster. Do you think any of us would do that?"

"Take your finger out of my face or I'll break it off," I say quietly. Maurice Faye's eyes widens and his mouth gapes. He snatches his hand back into his chest like I had burned it.

"I don't know what someone who abducts and, presumably, murders three girls for no apparent reason would or wouldn't do, Maurice. I don't understand that kind of person. No one does. All I know is, you guys were there, and there were lost girls, and now you're here, and there are lost girls. Don't waste my time, or yours, getting angry because I spelled that out. Or because you did."

Maurice bows his head. I humiliated him, and he deserved it, but I need him on my side.

"As regards the bigger picture, you're the common link, but the nature of the abduction has changed. In Point Dume, the girls were, from the film production's point of view, replaceable; here, they're not, or at least, not without great inconvenience and expense. So as you say, it's unlikely that any of you would want to do that. Isn't it?"

Maurice taps his phone and stands up.

"I need to talk to Jack now about this movie we're here to make. Just find those girls, Ed. You'll get whatever help you need from me."

"Maurice," I say. "It might be better if you didn't lay this out for everyone as bluntly I've laid it out to you."

Maurice's lips vanish inside his mouth and his eyes narrow, his expression as close to hostile as I've ever seen it.

"What, I should neglect to mention to them that they may be suspects?"

"I don't necessarily consider them—or you—suspects. There are any number of celebrity stalkers and fanatics who like to follow the carnival around. One possibility is that someone who was in Malibu in '94 could be in Dublin now, could have been in the pub last night, could have Jack, or you, or the Gang of Four, in his sights. Finding out who that might be will be hard enough without all of you closing down on me because you think I'm on your case. And I still don't even know what we're dealing with here: kidnapping and abduction, or accident and coincidence. So I need a little time and a little flexibility to explore every angle, and I'm asking you to do your best to allow me that. All right?"

Maurice stares out the window at a bunch of actors taking a smoke break in the yard, the men in military uniforms, the women in silk and satin wrappers. Grips in shorts are unloading a fat-legged Victorian table from a van, and a ponytailed technician is sorting through stacks of cable in the sun. When he turns back to me, his face is grave, and the gaze with which he meets my eyes is steady.

"If we can't wrap this movie, we're finished, end of. Whatever you need, you'll get."

We shake hands, and I follow Maurice Faye down the stairs of the bus and out into the heat of the yard.

Maybe it had been a mistake. Scratch the maybe, it had obviously been a fucking mistake, he knew the score only too well, special extras? Girls that had already been shot on? What was he thinking? Well, he wasn't thinking, was he? Driving back to the location, he spotted her coming out of a pharmacy, it was the work of a minute to pull up alongside her. The set was just around the corner but he knew she'd jump at the chance of a lift, of a precious moment alone with him. Not because she was some little operator, absolutely not, but because she was in love with the idea of the cinema, with the magic and the mystery, with the art of it all. And maybe that was all that had been on his mind, to give her a lift around the corner to the set, to bask in a little youthful adulation, but once she was in the car, once he'd gotten a good long look at her, once he'd gotten the scent of her deep in his lungs, he heard himself saying something about there being just one more stop he had to make, he was improvising, playing it by ear, at the outset he had no intention, she wasn't the kind of girl he did this to, he just wanted, in the moment, to be with her. They talked . . . what had they talked about? Michael Powell? Nicholas Ray? He can't remember. For one so young, she knew a hell of a lot about classic cinema, particularly in an era when most kids her age thought movie history began with Star Wars, *or at best,* Taxi Driver, *and balked at the very notion of seeing a black-and-white picture of any kind. Which made what he had done even more inexplicable.*

She was not the kind of girl he did this to.

He wonders what her reaction would have been if he'd said that to her.

He had felt bad about it all, even while he was doing it. He feels bad now, trying to make a joke about it. It was like . . . it was as if he'd been trying to kick the booze, had succeeded, nothing for years, actual years, and then one afternoon, the middle of the afternoon for God's sake, he suddenly decided to drink a bottle of whiskey. No prelude, no provocation, no great temptation, no sense of desperate urges being long suppressed and then at last indulged.

Maybe she had reminded him of the second Point Dume girl. He had liked her as well; she had been intelligent, she liked to read—he remembered he had given her new editions of Gavin Lambert's L.A. novels, and he'd had to break into her apartment afterward to remove the dedication pages. Not that there was any crime in giving a book to someone who subsequently disappeared, not that they weren't linked anyway by dint of working on the same movie, but still: any extra reason to connect him with her would have been unwelcome and unnecessary. He'd taken the empty blue bottle of Prosecco he had given her as well. And perhaps she was the only one he'd had to kill because he realized he'd told her more than was wise. The only one who hadn't disgusted him. Until now.

Of course there were many differences also. It's true all three Point Dume girls were extras, but they were just part of the crowd. They weren't even the only female extras. Whereas this one was so focal. For God's sake, he was jeopardizing the entire production. He really wonders if he has lost his reason. He has Broken His Pattern. That's how the criminal profilers, the Quantico brigade, would put it, he supposes.

Bunch of hucksters and faith healers, God alone knows what pseudo-psychological toss they'd come up with about him, especially since as a child he had never started a fire or tortured an animal or wet the bed. He would have to be the exception that proved their rule. But it's true, he's operating without a map now. He hadn't wanted to fuck her, he hadn't grown to despise her, he hadn't even plied her with Prosecco—after he'd located the bottles in Mitchell's, there wasn't a branch in Kildare Street anymore, he'd had to go all the way out to Sandycove, practically to the Forty Foot to get them. But they sat in the house, ignored, while he strangled her to death on the front seat of his car.

The question is, why? And it appears there is no answer more compelling than: he had felt like it. But once he'd pointed the car up the drive, with her chattering on about In a Lonely Place *or* Peeping Tom *and not for second doubting his intentions which in any case were not fully formed until he had crunched through the gravel outside the empty house and come to a halt, and in the moment, suddenly, almost abstractedly, as if she were a radio station he was changing, he reached for her tiny neck, he could have held it in one hand she was so slight, like a slender young bird, and squeezed and snapped and watched the light in her eyes gutter and fade and waited and waited and . . . nothing. Try as he might to summon it up, he couldn't feel the transfer of her light, the light of her eyes. There had been no contact, no transmission, no communion. And therefore, no salve of grace. Not then, and not afterward, when he reran it for himself. All he felt, then and later, was bad, like . . . like he always imagined a person who had killed someone would feel, like he had never really felt before.*

He knows that's why he decided to do it again as soon as possible. Or rather, he had decided against ever doing it again, had firmly resolved with the help of whatever grace he could muster, and then he had been at the party, had had a few drinks, and there she was, all Abercrombie & Fitched and Ugg-booted and candy-pink lip-glossed, in all her Southside Queen Bee glory. He knew he'd have no difficulty despising her, and he knew she'd leap at the chance to do a bit of starfucking, particularly once she figured out that Josh Tyler was mysteriously unsusceptible to her charms, so when he told her he was sneaking out the door to go drink champagne at Club 92 and he had room on the broom for one more, she had her tongue down his throat before he could get the car out of the carpark. He told her he wanted to stop off for something he'd forgotten, and she nodded, all the while leaning and stroking and kissing him whenever they came to a halt, and he found to his surprise that he was actually quite amenable to her charms himself, so much so that when he pulled in the drive of the house and she took his hand and pushed it down the waistband of her pink Juicy Couture sweats, he had to gird himself to resist.

She came into the house with him, clawing him every which way, breath hot and hands sticky. He insisted on the lights being kept off, and he led her down to the kitchen at the back of the house, and sat her at the table in the dark, and he found his way to the American double-doored fridge, and just as he opened the door, she asked him what he had forgotten, and he said, your friend, and the fridge cast a light across the table and there, sitting opposite her was her missing coworker, sleeping, or not sleeping, no, not sleeping, dead, in fact, and there, standing opposite the cold body was the living girl, shaking, screaming, tears and snot erupting from her face like boiling-over milk. He hit her on the back of the head with the Prosecco bottle because she was sturdy enough, a hockey player he guessed, and he didn't want to struggle with her while he strangled her.

He didn't feel quite so bad in that moment. He was drunk, to begin with, and so he had found it funny, not ha ha, but deeply, sublimely, poignantly comic, that moment beforehand, the last moment of hope, when the live one leaned across and touched the dead one's hand as if to nudge her awake, and the weight of her head tipped her limp, lifeless body onto the table with a dull thud. He thought the memory of her friend standing and shaking and howling would linger fondly with him always.

In the morning, he feared that it would: he had not slept, and he felt nothing but dismay and revulsion at his grotesque behavior. He hadn't even witnessed the second girl's eyes as she died, had sacrificed the very reason he killed for a cheap pantomime of stage-managed vulgarity, had forfeited the very possibility of grace. Worse, with two out of three Fates gone, and the amount of footage that was potentially unusable putting *the future of the movie in real doubt, he was beginning to wonder whether he had fallen in love with his own destruction (he had made a vow to himself way back: if not quite never again, certainly never in Dublin).*

It appears that he can make all the resolutions he wants, but to no avail: when it comes to action, he will do whatever he doesn't want, whatever he wants very much. And a part of him knows that he wants very much to kill a third time, because . . . why? Because it would be the final act that would give a wholeness, an organic perfection, to everything he has ever done? Because he wants very much to bring it to a climax, third of three and the last of all, Three-in-One, One-in-Three, to honor the sacred mystery of the Trinity, the culmination of his life's work in one vessel of flesh and bone and blood? Yes, but most especially, because he needs the balm, the salve that sanctifying grace would bring him, and he knows of no other way to receive it than from the dying eyes of a lost girl.

THE FILM ENCYCLOPEDIA, 6TH EDITION

THE COMPLETE GUIDE
TO FILM AND THE FILM INDUSTRY

edited by Ephraim Katz, Ronald Dean Nolan

Donovan, Jack (John). Director, Screenwriter. Born on June 16, 1964, in Dublin, Ireland. *ed* Trinity College, Dublin (Music); Royal Irish Academy of Music. A trained singer, he sang several tenor roles in opera productions in Ireland and the UK. His debut film was a low-budget, high-energy rendering of Verdi's *La Traviata* called *Scarlet for You* (1990) set in contemporary Dublin, which won much critical acclaim and proved a surprise American success. (Donovan himself sang the role of Alfredo Germont in the film, but has not sung professionally since.) He won international accolades with his next film, *A Terrible Beauty* (1992), a visionary tale of political violence and taboo sexuality which won an Academy Award nomination for best original screenplay. His first full American picture, *Ocean Falls* (1994), a haunting romance among surfers and Hollywood hopefuls, loosely adapted from *The Slide Area* and *The Goodbye People* by Gavin

LAMBERT, was much admired, and Donovan won the Oscar for best adapted screenplay. Studio assignment *The Armageddon Factor* (1995), an espionage thriller adapted from a bestselling novel, featured A-list stars and was a massive commercial success. This enabled Donovan and his longtime producer, Maurice FAYE, to raise the budget for *The Dain Curse* (1997), a dreamlike, disturbing adaptation of the Dashiell HAMMETT novel that divided critics and performed indifferently at the box office, though netting Donovan another adapted screenplay nomination. *Twenty Grand* (1999) was a mystical road movie set in the Sierra mountain range, described by the director as an homage to Michelangelo ANTONIONI. It pleased neither critics nor audiences. Donovan spent three years directing opera in New York and Rome and working as a script doctor before a triumphant return in 2003 with *The Man in the High Castle*, a provocative adaptation of Philip K. DICK's alternative history novel. The film was an international success and was nominated for seven Oscars, winning four, including best picture and best adapted screenplay. He followed this with a big-budget historical extravaganza, *The Last Anniversary* (2005), which has been described as a disaster on the scale of *Cleopatra* and *Heaven's Gate*. Along with producer Maurice Faye, Donovan has worked with the cinematographer Mark CASSIDY on every film (with the exception of *The Armageddon Factor*). Frequently ranked among other independent directors who came to prominence in the nineties, including Quentin TARANTINO, Paul Thomas ANDERSON and David FINCHER. Donovan is divorced, and has homes in Dublin, Los Angeles, New York and Rome.

FILMS (as director-screenwriter): *Scarlet for You* (Ire.) 1990; *A Terrible Beauty* (Ire./U.S.) 1992; *Ocean Falls* (U.S.) 1994; *The Armageddon Factor* (U.S.) 1995; *The Dain Curse* (U.S.) 1997; *Twenty Grand* (U.S.) 1999; *The Man in the High Castle* (U.S.) 2002; *The Last Anniversary* (U.S.) 2005.

CHAPTER 7

Maurice told me I'd get what I needed, so I tell him I need five minutes with Mark Cassidy and Conor Rowan. While I wait, I reread the text Anne Fogarty had sent me earlier. It would have made a dead man blush, among other things. I don't know if I am blushing when I'm greeted by the unlikely sight of Mark Cassidy with his arms full of orchids, but whatever my face is doing he takes as a reaction, and nods in eye-rolling acknowledgment.

"What can I say, sometimes you've got to play the exception to prove your rule. And I'd be lying if I said I never bought my wife the odd flower. But don't spread it around. A girl can lose her reputation so quickly on a set like this."

Had I known Cassidy was married? Perhaps I had formed the notion that he was not the marrying kind. But then it had been so long since I'd seen the Gang of Four, there were no doubt many things I had to catch up on.

"Are the flowers for your wife?"

"They're not, they're for poor Madeline. I feel a little responsible since it was one of my lighting stands she ran into this morning. Even if it was her own fault. Do you know where she is? I can't get her on the phone."

"I'm looking for her myself."

"Well, in that case, you wouldn't mind dropping these with her, would you? I need to get back on set. I have a trainee camera person holding the fort, but it's only a matter of time before Jack goes through him for a shortcut."

"Will do. Did Maurice talk to you?"

"No."

"He was going to ask you to give me a couple of minutes of your time."

Mark Cassidy, with blond hair cut like a public schoolboy's, short at the back and sides and long in front, bows slightly, as if to say *at your service,* and inclines his long, hollow-cheeked face in my direction, and pushes his fringe out of his eyes; the expression he presents is characteristic of him, somehow managing to appear polite and insolent at the same time.

"The *Ocean Falls* shoot in Malibu. There were three female extras, surfer girls? They would have appeared in the beach party scenes. And they went missing?"

Cassidy wrinkles his brow slightly, as if what I'm saying seems vaguely familiar.

"Their names were Desiree LaRouche, Polly Styles and Janice Holloway," I say. (I have never forgotten their names.) "Do you remember them?"

Mark Cassidy considers the names for a while, then shakes his head.

"No, those names are not familiar. But I would rarely even know the extras' names. Why are you interested? Oh, because of Nora and, ah—"

"Nora and Kate, yes. Because it's happened before."

"Isn't it a bit early to assume Nora and Kate are missing?"

"It probably is. But it's already caused chaos for you, no doubt." Mark shrugs.

"Nothing I can't handle. There are always fires that need to be fought. You have to expect it. Maurice and Jack like to get excited and stamp their feet. They must feel it helps. I react the opposite way. Whatever it takes. But going back to *Ocean Falls* . . . you know, I was all business in those days. If it didn't happen in front of the camera, forget it. The only reason I remember you is because you were in *The Dain Curse*. People used to have affairs and all sorts, and I was totally oblivious. I see a lot more now, of course. But we're all older, so what goes on has got a lot less interesting. Not to mention visually appealing."

"So no footage of the girls ended up in the movie?"

"There were two beach parties with about a hundred extras. It's possible. But at best, they would have been faces in the crowd."

"You didn't notice anything odd about Nora or Kate, did you?"

"I noticed they looked a lot like Madeline. But you'd expect that, with Jack. All for love."

Mark's two-way radio goes off. I wonder briefly if it has been triggered by the abrasive cynicism of his tone. No love lost any longer between Mark and Jack.

"Got to get back," he says. "I'm sorry I can't be any more help. I hope you find the girls soon, Ed."

I take the flowers from him and tell him if anything else occurs to him, to give me a call. I stand in the yard for a while, trying not to feel stupid while people beam at me they way they always do at a man with a big bunch of flowers. I feel stupid.

Madeline King appears from the direction Mark Cassidy has just gone, Conor Rowan by her side. Before I get a chance to give the flowers to Madeline, Conor pushes in front, gruff, surly smile in place.

"Mossy said you were looking for me. I don't have much time, Ed. And I don't remember those girls in Malibu. I remember they went missing, but that's about it. It was America, it was L.A., I think I thought shit like that was supposed to happen, you know what I mean? And it didn't really affect the day-to-day of the shoot. Not like this pair today."

"Anyone they might have had a fling with, a relationship, a drink?"

"I wouldn't have noticed. We were all flat out. Jack maybe, but I never know what Jack gets up to. Learned early on not to notice."

"Anything you can tell me about Nora and Kate?"

Conor looks at me through boiling eyes.

"Yeah. The only excuse they could have, the only one I'd be willing to accept for them not showing up today, is if they're dead."

Madeline snorts with nervous laughter. Conor's two-way goes off, and he points to it and walks back toward the set. His exit line comes over his shoulder.

"And they still should call and let us know where their bodies are buried."

I don't know if I blushed at Anne's text, but Madeline certainly blushes at Conor's remarks, and blushes again when I thrust the flowers at her.

"Oh Ed, you shouldn't have," she says

"Compliments of Mark Cassidy," I say.

"You've got to be kidding me."

"I didn't think he was the type either."

"And it was my own fault."

"Yeah, he said that."

"Of course he fucking did, I can hear him, the cynical bollocks," Madeline says, laughing. "Still. Nice flowers though. More than some people'd buy you."

"How *is* Jack, is he all right?"

"Ah, he's Embattled Man today. The world is agin him. A lot of temple rubbing and brow clutching. And groaning. Not to mention shouting and roaring. I don't blame him, given all that's happened, but . . ."

"But staying out all night on the lash wouldn't help at the best of times?"

"Something like that. He's being a pain in the hole, but he'll be grand."

"Do you have some time? I need to talk to you, ask you a few questions."

"Get your detective thing on? Sure. What do you want to do about Jenny?"

"Is she still on the costume truck? Don't suppose we can just leave her there, can we?"

Madeline shakes her head.

"There's not enough room, the ladies are getting grumpy and it's very hot. Fur will fly. What do you reckon, is she really in danger?"

"I don't know. It's hard to feel it. In the sunlight, it seems ludicrous. But we have to act as if she is. Two girls are still missing."

Madeline's hand shoots up to her swollen face, and her eyes widen, and for a moment I flash back to a darkened house two blocks back from Venice Beach, and a woman, not much more than a girl really, making the same gesture, betraying the same fear in her eyes, with pretty much the same kind of bruising. Only her marks didn't come from a lamp stand, but from a human hand.

"I can't think of anywhere she would be safe," Madeline says. "There's no one I could trust to look after her, no one I'd burden with it. I mean, they could put themselves in danger, right? Who'd sign up for something like that?"

I ARRANGE TO meet Tommy Owens in a café in Parnell Square. As I leave the *Nighttown* set, one of the security goons I had thought looked familiar smiles at me. When I nod back, he lifts up his radio and points it at me as if it were a gun and makes a plosive sound with his lips the way small boys do when they're playing soldiers. I can't work out whether his intention is to threaten me or if he's a bit simple; I finally plump for the latter, and give him a smile. My mistake.

It takes Tommy half an hour to get to the café, and it looks like it's going to take as long as that again to get him to stop moaning about the hot weather, which does not suit us as a nation and we're only kidding ourselves to think otherwise, and the latest chapter and verse on the misdeeds of the nation's bankers (complete with names, numbers and severance packages), in which Tommy (despite having lost no savings or pensions that I knew of and sitting tight in the family home which as an only child he has inherited outright), has taken an extremely personal, highly outraged and incredibly tedious interest. Once I had persuaded Madeline King, who had come down to the café to inspect Tommy, to go back and liberate Jenny Noble from the costume truck, I give him fifteen hundred of the three thousand advance Jack Donovan gave me. Not that this shuts him up, or at least, not immediately: the notion that you could soften Tommy's cough with filthy lucre would be intolerable to his dignity. But it might at least begin to work its slow-release money spell and bewitch him into channeling some recondite aspects of his better nature.

I say persuade in relation to Madeline because she made it clear that Tommy did not look to her like a person into whose custody you would release a stray dog, let alone a vulnerable young girl. And it must be said, Tommy, whose image was idiosyncratic at the best of times, looks especially unusual today: with Doc Marten boots that reached midcalf, three-quarter-length black combat trousers, a black short-sleeved combat shirt and a black Kangol beret, he resembles an extra in a modern-dress production of *Macbeth,* an effect mitigated by his slouching gait, his wispy beard, his native genius for anarchy and derision and his seeming inability to stop talking. I had laid out the basics of the case to Tommy over the phone, but I can't help feeling there is still a certain lack of engagement on his part.

"Tommy," I say.

"Yes, Ed?"

"Shut the fuck up and listen to me."

"I'm listening. Not hearing anything worth listening to, but miracles can happen."

"It may be nothing. But this girl could be in danger. Do you understand? Grave danger. I know I can trust you to make sure she's safe. Don't I?"

Tommy's reaction is everything I hoped for. He looks at me like I have lost my mind.

"Less of the fucking melodrama man, is this movie malarkey going to your head? Of course she'll be safe, what do you think? And I'll keep me eyes open, look-out-at-night type of thing. Have we anyone in the frame?"

"Strictly speaking, Maurice Faye, Mark Cassidy, Conor Rowan. And Jack Donovan."

Tommy looks at me like I've lost my mind for real this time.

"Are you kidding me? Jack? Abducting young ones? Mossy? No way. Sure even if they were capable of it, they'd only be harming themselves, wouldn't they?"

"They're the only suspects I've got at this stage. But as you say, it seems highly unlikely. It may be someone connected to them. Someone who wants to implicate one of them, someone who bears a grudge or who wants revenge."

"Extreme way of going about it. And you've no candidates for that particular post as yet?"

I think about giving Tommy a rundown on Jack and the case of the anonymous letters, but I decide against it: partly because I want to talk to Madeline, who is the common element in both cases, but mostly because I'm not yet convinced the let-

ters amount to anything more than some kind of narcissistic
Jack Donovan psychodrama. I'm not convinced, in fact, that he
hasn't written them himself.

Any anxiety on Madeline's part about how Jenny Noble will
fare in Tommy's charge is instantly put to rest by the following
brief exchange:

JENNY: Mr. Owens! What a surprise. How are you? Naomi's
nearly done, isn't she, she texted me last week in the thick
of it.

Jenny kisses Tommy on both cheeks. Tommy's face reddens.

TOMMY: (*Accent a rung or two up the social scale*) Hello, Jenny,
very nice to see you. Naomi's getting on grand, or so she
says. She's just got geography to go, then school's out forever.

It turns out that Jenny went to school with Naomi, Tommy's
daughter, and although Naomi lives with her mother, she spends
plenty of time with her dad. The girls were friends: Jenny is a
year ahead, and Naomi has applied to do the same university
course Jenny is doing. In Dublin, it sometimes seems as if more
than one degree of separation is too much to hope for. In this
instance, it worked out for the best, as Madeline reflected afterward.

"Jenny was not at all happy when I told her what we had
planned. Having had time to think, she decided that she was
more than capable of looking after herself. And to be honest, I
was anxious that she would be in safe hands. I mean, he has a
pretty strange vibe going on, doesn't he, your friend?"

We are standing on the street in a stream of office workers
flocking to eat their lunch in the sun, sunshine in Dublin resem-
bling a visiting dignitary from an exotic land whose appearance
you could not count on being repeated any time soon. I draw
Madeline in toward the palings that run along the terrace.

"I'd trust Tommy Owens with my life," I said. "In fact, I have, many times, and had cause to be grateful. I would not be here without him. He may look, he may well *be,* a little . . . unconventional. But he's rock solid, and we're lucky to have him on our side. No harm will come to Jenny Noble while she's in his care."

I believe every word of this as I say it, as indeed I should: it's true. But it isn't the whole truth, and I don't tell Madeline about pulling Tommy to one side while Madeline was slipping Jenny some petty cash for expenses and exchanging mobile and e-mail details with her.

"How's business these days, Tommy?"

"Grand, Ed. Grand."

"Still keep in touch with Leo Halligan, do you?"

"We're not in each other's pockets. But yeah, I still see Leo from time to time."

"Does he come to the house?"

"Of course he doesn't come to the house. What, you think . . . I mean, Naomi stays for weekends, you think I'm going to let my daughter anywhere near one of the Halligans? What's the matter with you, Ed?"

"There's nothing the matter. I just need to be sure—"

"You just want your mind set at ease. You're very happy to make use of any connections I have when they're useful to you, whether it's Leo or any other number of dealers and blaggers and crims, so you can keep tabs on gangland without getting your hands dirty. And I cultivate any number of those fuckers, at this stage almost entirely for your benefit. But you don't acknowledge that. And you don't trust me to have the wit, the gumption, the common *sense* to keep that part of my life separate from my daughter and her friends?"

Tommy shakes his head in disgust, his dignity wounded. I take my lumps. Maybe I deserve them. On the other hand, I happen to know for a fact that Tommy had recently been involved with Leo Halligan in counterfeiting designer bags and in DVD piracy; the reason I know is because Garda Detective Inspector Dave Donnelly warned me that the Fraud Squad were closing in on Leo, and that Tommy should step lightly in the other direction as fast as possible. I duly passed this tip on, and I assume Tommy took the necessary precautions, but it's hard to detect any of this amid the current self-righteous grandstanding. Let it go. I nod as if I have overstepped the mark.

"Of course I trust you, Tommy. Thanks for doing this, all right?"

Of course, as Tommy knows I know he can be trusted about as far as he trusts himself, a gratifying look of confusion and distrust now flashes across his face. Having worked himself up to a shouting match, he's deflated when he doesn't get it. There was always the danger the Guards might catch up with Tommy, but I feel reasonably sure, now that he doesn't do drugs in the volume he used to, that he is keeping his less-than-salubrious pals well clear of the house. Not least because his ex-wife, Paula, would have him killed if she heard anything to the contrary. Or rather, knowing Paula, who once stabbed a boyfriend of hers who was putting the moves on Naomi in the hand with a screwdriver and then expressed regret that she had missed what she was actually aiming for, namely, his balls, she would do the job herself.

I want to talk to Madeline there and then, but Jack needs her back on set, so, after warning her not to tell anyone where Jenny Noble has gone—and by *anyone,* I emphasize Maurice Faye, Mark Cassidy, Conor Rowan and yes, Jack Donovan—I tell her I'll catch up with her later. On my way out to Ringsend to interview Marie Donovan, I call DI Dave Donnelly of the Serious Crime Review Team, the Garda cold-case squad, and tell him who I'm working for, taking care to emphasize the anonymous letters over the missing girls.

"Such glamour," Dave says. "I read an article in the *Herald* there about Mr. Jack Donovan, numbers of homes he has, he's like a perfume company so he is. New York, L.A., Rome, wherever. Does he not have his own private police force?"

"You're speaking to it. I worked for him before sure, back in L.A."

"Well excuse me. Not sure you should be talking to a lowly inspector today, Ed, I think an assistant commissioner might be more appropriate to your status."

"Fuck off."

"That's what I just said. Anyway, if you didn't just call to boast, what was your point? Would you like me, as a public servant who has taken a hit on his salary because of the public service pension levy, to assist you on your high society case over there free gratis and for nothing?"

"Not only that, I'd like you to be a little less chippy and resentful while you're at it, thanks. There's no room anymore for the politics of envy, as you know, Dave. We should just sit back and wait for the bankers and developers who got us into this mess to get us out of it, as of course they will, in due course, once they've figured out a way to screw us all over again."

"What do you want, Ed?"

"I want you to check four names to see if they've criminal records. Maurice Faye, Mark Cassidy, Conor Rowan."

"And the fourth?"

"The fourth is Jack Donovan."

"Well now. Scandal in high places. Digging the dirt. It's a grubby way to make a living, don't you think?"

"You're breaking up, Dave."

"Come here, isn't your man in that film?"

Dave pronounces it "fil-um." There are only two people "your man" could be. In honor of Jack Donovan's first Irish movie in twenty years, pretty much every Irish screen actor of note had signed up to do something in *Nighttown*. As a result, taxi drivers and barmen and DJs had been referring to Colin and Brendan and Cillian and Gabriel and Liam and Colm as if they grew up around the corner from them. But if Dave is interested in an Irish actor, it's on his wife's behalf, and there are two at the top of that particular chart.

"Colin Farrell and Gabriel Byrne are both in the film, Dave."

"If I got their autographs for Carmel, that would give my domestic numbers a bump."

"Signed photographs?"

"Even better. Have you met them, Ed?"

"Are you kidding me? I'm just the help, Dave, strictly below stairs. But I know people who can get their feet under the big table. Anything for Carmel."

Dave clears his throat loudly, by way of alerting me to what's coming next.

"Ed, you know our friend Podge will be out this afternoon."

"No doubt?"

"It's a formality. They reduced the sentence sure. After a plea for lenience by McLiam's widow, can you believe it? She thinks Podge has found God."

"She's a very devout woman."

"She's a fucking fruitcake. But an influential fruitcake. They've been doing well to keep him in until today, trying to find anything to throw at him."

"That's what I was hoping for, Dave. Some charge like 'Being Podge Halligan.'"

"You'll have us living in a police state yet, Ed."

CHAPTER 8

There's a certain kind of Irishwoman who you feel is biding her time, waiting for the chance to land at her default physical type, which is that of The Nun. Maybe that won't be true in the future, now that nuns are less involved in education, are dying out, in truth, but among women of my generation, it's not uncommon. Marie Donovan looks like one of those women. She wears jeans and a blue polo shirt and purple Birkenstock shoes; her undyed, unstyled dark hair is short and graying around the edges; her elfin face bears no trace of makeup whatever, not even no-makeup makeup; her pale blue eyes are framed by oval steel-rimmed glasses. If I hadn't been told she had had an abortion, I might have discounted the likelihood of her ever putting herself in the way of one. She is slim and pale, physically easy but edgy in manner, quick to smile and to talk.

She lets me into her small house on Cambridge Avenue, a

quiet cul-de-sac tucked in between Ringsend Park and the R131 off Pigeon House Road, set across from the tip of the North Quay East. Marie Donovan's kitchen has pale boards and cane furniture and a wooden Spanish Mission crucifix of a kind I had seen in Santa Barbara and bookcases of plays and drama criticism and psychology and political theory and Indian and Latin American and African fiction and feminist theology.

She closes her laptop and smiles broadly at me for perhaps the third time, as if someone has said something hilarious.

"Is there something funny?" I say.

She shakes her head.

"No, it's just . . . a private detective . . . well yes, I suppose it is funny. Don't you think? And there you are, in your suit. You practically have a hat."

I smile, or grimace, irritably, unwilling to justify myself or my job or my dress sense, and thank her for the tea, which it quickly becomes clear I am not going to be able to drink because all Marie Donovan has in the fridge to accompany it is soya milk, and soya milk makes Irish Breakfast tea taste, to use the precise chemical term, like shit. She smiles at my dislike of soya milk also, a knowing, wise, somewhat smug smile, or so it seems to me; I appear to be building up quite a dislike of Marie Donovan and we have barely met; before I can get a question out, she irritates me further by taking control of the conversation.

"So my brother has hired you. How is he?"

I shrug.

"Under pressure, I guess you'd say. Budgets, actors, this and that. It's not a business I really understand."

"Oh come on, it's not exactly rocket science."

"You work in the same field."

"I work on a TV soap. But essentially it's the same. And I can assure you, film and TV people exaggerate every aspect of the business so everyone thinks it's impossibly complicated and mysterious. Which of course, it isn't. But you know Jack of old, you said. From school?"

"No, we met in L.A."

"Professionally?"

"Well, I do play a small role in *The Dain Curse*."

"*The Dain Curse*? Christ, what a mess. Hammett is such a misogynistic, patriarchal writer anyway, and the entire PI genre is basically preposterous boys'-own-wish-fulfillment fantasy, you couldn't possibly take it seriously, certainly not in this day and age. So there wasn't just an opportunity, there was an *obligation* to revisit, to revise, to look anew at tired old genre conventions. But what does Jack do? He makes it even more sexist and romantic than ever. Lovely girls getting rescued by strong silent men, glamorous women with runaway sexual appetites, wholesale violence, an ever-mounting body count. It's dinosaur time. Don't you think?"

I'm the one with the smile now, a patient one. It starts to hurt my face, and it doesn't seem to be having any positive effect anyway, so I let it fade to a blank stare.

"You disagree?" Marie Donovan says.

"I like those tired old genre conventions."

"Really? The misogyny, the patriarchy?"

"I like the glamorous women with runaway sexual appetites."

Marie Donovan wrinkles her nose and frowns, a frown that looks intended to be noticed and acted upon. She shakes her head briskly then, as if it's better that nothing more be said.

"You must think me very disloyal to my brother. But he's made so many movies, I can't be expected to like them all."

"Did you like any of them?"

Marie Donovan's eyes flash with what looks to me like anger, and I brace myself for what I suspect might be an onslaught. Instead, she bursts out laughing.

"I did. I do, actually. I just . . . it was stupid of me to go off on *The Dain Curse* like that, but it does get on my nerves, what he did with it. I think Jack's an amazing talent. I mean, doesn't matter what I think, he's Jack Donovan, Hollywood director, for God's sake. I'm the script editor on a soap, what would I know?"

"You know what you like."

"If only that were true."

Marie Donovan's voice falters on the word *true,* and she looks away, as if she has been caught in a truth she didn't expect and doesn't welcome but can't deny. The silence isn't comfortable, but it belongs to her, and I let her have it. She is an angry person, and like most angry people, she employs, consciously or unconsciously, probably the latter, a variety of alternating behavior patterns to help her retain her dignity. When she speaks again, she drops the strident and the confrontational for something more low-key and big sisterly.

"So look, Ed Loy, I doubt very much if we'd see eye to eye on many things, so let's not try. You're here on my brother's behalf. What kind of trouble is he in that he needs a private detective?"

"You don't appear surprised."

"I'm guessing you worked for him in L.A. I'm familiar with much of the trouble my brother got himself into in the years before that. Maybe we could have done with a private detective then; it would have saved me a lot of grief."

"What do you mean?"

"I mean, Jack has had people picking up after him for years. First me, now you. No doubt there were others. What is it this time?"

On my way from the *Nighttown* set to Ringsend, I stopped at a stationer's and made photocopies of the anonymous letters Jack claimed he had been sent. I show his sister the first three. She reads them silently, and then looks up at me.

"What are these?"

"Jack said someone sent them to him in the past few weeks, since he's been back in Dublin."

"And he thinks it's me?"

"He wonders if it might be. He didn't seem very sure."

Marie Donovan's face lights up with a smile of genuine amusement. She reads the letters aloud then, her voice injecting them with melodrama, as if they are the most ridiculous things she has ever come across. As a result, that's exactly how they sound.

" *'All praise to God the Father, all praise to God the Son, and God the Holy Spirit, eternal Three-in-One.'* That's a hymn, do you know it? It goes on, 'till all the ransomed number fall down before the throne, and honour, power and glory ascribe to God alone.' 'For All Your Saints in Glory,' I think it's called. *'Flanked by thieves, Jesus remained Lord. But all three died the same death.'* The power of three, do you see? And then: *'Once, twice, three times a dead man. He will know neither the day nor the hour.'* Is that supposed to be a death threat? It might be a bit scarier if it didn't echo a Lionel Richie song."

"The Commodores, I think."

"Same difference. What? Am I to take this seriously? Are you fucking kidding me? How drunk was my brother? What crazy lady has her hooks in him this time? Who advised him he needed a private detective, his *astrologer*? This is a joke, right?"

"He appears to be taking them seriously."

"No he doesn't. Do you know why? Because he's not an eleven-year-old schoolgirl or an old lady who lives alone with her fat dog. Come on. What does he want?"

With some people, you could spend hours going around the houses so they might say something unguarded. I reckon Marie Donovan is one of the other kind of people, the kind who match truth with truth. Besides, I can't think of anything else to say: she's right, on the basis of those three letters alone, the whole thing is ludicrous.

"He wants . . . this is basically what I used to do for Jack in L.A. I was starting out as a PI, and I didn't get to choose my cases. Not a lot has changed there, but . . . anyway, Jack would break up with some woman, without telling the woman. And it fell to me to say good-bye on his behalf."

"Nice work if you can get it."

"I know. And you're his sister, not his girlfriend. And . . . well, he told me some of the reasons you might have sent him these letters—"

"Really. Tell me them. Tell me the reasons."

"He said you had become something of a religious fanatic. Or that you were involved with people who were pretty far out there in that department."

"That might account for the content. For the sake of argument. But why would I want to send them at all? Did he give you any clue as to that?"

"He seems to think you've always resented him. That he has had the kind of career you wish you had, not literally, but in terms of scale, of success. That you feel somehow that he has stolen your luck."

"And in order to settle this karmic debt, all I'm prepared to do is send him a few not-very-sinister letters? That's it?"

"I think Jack feels there are certain not exactly veiled threats contained within the letters."

Marie Donovan sits bolt upright now, pale eyes glittering behind her spectacles, her voice taut and sharp as a whip. I can see why Jack didn't want to say any of this to her in person. What I have yet to determine is why he wanted any of it to be said at all.

"Is there more?"

I nod and produce a copy of the fourth letter, with its bloodred daubs of fetus and crucifix, and push it across the table. She looks at it quickly and then averts her eyes, almost flinching, and then turns back and focuses on it at greater length.

"And why did Jack think I might have sent him this?" she says, in a very careful, deliberate voice that makes me want to run straight out the door and give Jack Donovan his money back and wash my hands of him and all belonging to him. I don't answer her. I don't need to. She sits for a while, staring at the photocopy, nodding and shaking her head and pursing her lips and suppressing half smiles that aren't really smiles at all. Occasionally she summons herself, as if about to speak, then subsides and resumes her brooding, her bitter meditation. I don't know how long we spend in silence. For me, it telescopes back through many such silences, where I sit across a table from a woman to whom I have just confessed, knowingly or otherwise, something unforgivable, and I wait to be told just how I am not to be forgiven. And although it is Jack Donovan's transgression, not mine, it doesn't make me feel any less culpable.

Marie Donovan stands up and goes to the fridge and finds a half-full bottle of Pinot Grigio with a vacuum stopper in the neck and two glasses and sits back down and pours a glass of wine and I put my hand over the second glass to indicate that I won't have any. She drinks a little of hers, a sip, and rubs the edge of the paper with the fetus and the upside-down crucifix beneath her fingertip, making an insidious scraping sound.

"Did Jack ever tell you about our parents?" she says.

"Only that they died in a car crash when you were quite young. Fourteen?"

"Jack was thirteen, I was sixteen. Yes. Coming back from the opera in town. *La Traviata*. Which didn't inhibit Jack in any way when he came to shoot a film based on that particular opera; he just ignored the connection completely."

"Didn't he dedicate it to them?" I say.

"Very good of him," Marie says, and drinks more than a sip of her wine. "I found *La Traviata*, all of Verdi in fact, pretty much impossible to listen to ever since. The fact that his parents had died on the way home from a performance of a Verdi opera seemed of no consequence to Jack. But that's not relevant, of course, the pros and cons of Jack's glittering career, not relevant in the slightest. What is relevant is that that's when it all began. You know we lived on in the house together, Jack and I?"

"Just the two of you?"

"Just the two of us. I was sixteen, nearly seventeen, in fact, going on seventeen. I . . . and Jack was training, singing, his voice matured so early, and Mum and Dad had been so passionate about his blessed opera singing, and so that was, that became my, almost my obsession, in spite of the fact that every note he sang, or played, not alone of Verdi but opera in general, Puccini, Donizetti, whoever, all it did was preserve the grief, the loss of our parents. In my mind. Maybe it was some kind of . . . I was going to say, tribute in his. But I don't think that's true. Not in a bad way, just . . . the level of self-absorption involved, being so closed off to what anyone else might think or feel, Jack always had that to an extent that was enviable, almost frightening. His voice. That's what they say about a writer, you know, a really great writer, they talk about his voice, how it's utterly his own. I don't know how you get that, but Jack always had it. Even when the movies don't work, you always know they're his. How did he get that?"

She shakes her head. I have trouble telling if she despises or reveres him, hates him or loves him. It looks like she has the same trouble herself. She finishes her wine and pours herself a second glass and pushes the bottle in my direction in case I change my mind. I have changed my mind about her at least once, and I'm not done yet.

"So I . . . stood guard for Jack, I suppose you'd say. I made sure he was protected, so that all he had to concentrate on was his . . . was his art. Mum and Dad had left some money but not enough. So I sold the house, in 1986, well before the property boom, which wasn't very smart, but fuck it, Jack needed money for lessons. And I didn't go to college, I got a job straight from school, in the bank, to pay rent on a flat and keep us eating."

She looks at me then and sees my obvious surprise.

"Let me guess, Jack told you he'd bought me this house for me, but he didn't tell you why it was kind of right that he did?"

I nod, unable to speak.

"That's the other thing about the . . . *artist* . . . he does it all himself. It's all down to him. He kind of has to see it that way. I understand. Wishing you were one gives you great insight into what the real thing is like. I don't mean it in any humble or modest way, but I just don't hold myself in high enough regard. Maybe that's it. Or maybe it's that I don't have any talent."

Marie laughs loudly, surprising herself, and blinks, and pushes her wineglass from her.

"Stupid. Drinking at lunchtime. On an empty stomach. Would you like something to eat? Or are you afraid of what might be in my fridge?"

"I'm all right, thanks. I can come back, if you'd like. Or not."

"Oh Jesus, what makes you think I'd want you to come back?" Marie Donovan says with such frank disdain that I start to laugh myself, and after attempting a few slurred apologies, so does she, laughs until she has tears in her eyes. I wait until she recovers herself, wait until she's ready to say what she is burning to say. I don't much want to hear it, am dreading what I might hear, but that's what you have to put up with when you ask questions for a living. Marie reaches for her glass again. Maybe she has forgotten how fast the wine has gone to her head. Or maybe, with what she wants to say, she remembers all too well.

"Have you ever noticed, in all of Jack's films, no matter what the source, whether original or adapted, there's always a brother and sister, a brother-and-sister thing going on? Have you ever noticed that?"

I say that I have.

"Yes. Because then there was the time Jack decided he was not going to be an opera singer after all, opera was over, it was history, he wanted to be a film director. This, after my having not gone to university, and his having very much gone there, as well as expensive classes with Ronnie Dunne at the Royal Irish Academy, after we sold the house for half a crown and I . . . I got a place in RADA, you know, actor training, I . . . and turned it

down, and by the time I had the energy, the focus, the concentration to try again, it was too late. Not in age, in . . . what you
need, Ed. In heart, in spirit, in guts. Was that Jack's fault? No.
I probably didn't have what it takes. If I had, I wouldn't have
given it up for my little brother. But I did give something, a lot,
up. I made . . . what used we say in the Olden Days? Sacrifices.
And sometimes, that selfish big shite behaves like any trouble in
his life is my fault, like all I'm there for is to take the blame.

"So. That thing. The brother-and-sister thing. In the movies
of Jack Donovan. Have you noticed it, Ed?"

I say again that I have.

"It's quite strong, isn't it? I mean, a strong relationship between a brother and sister. Quite strong. And quite . . . pointed,
for it to be in every film."

Marie Donovan looks at me now. She removed her glasses
when she was wiping away her tears, and hasn't put them back
on. Her eyes seem filmy and out of focus, and one has a squint
of some kind, so that while she looks at me, she seems to be
looking elsewhere also, to the door, to the window, for help,
perhaps, or reinforcements. I wish they would come, too. I wish
they would come soon.

Marie holds up the page with the red-daubed fetus and
upside-down crucifix and points at it.

"Did Jack . . . I assume Jack told you why this might have
some kind of significance for me?"

My job is to elicit as much information as I possibly can from
whoever I'm talking to and then to get out fast so I can figure
out what to do with that information. I can only assume that
some inner determination to delay hearing what Marie Donovan wants to tell me accounts for my reply.

"I guess the crucifix has something to do with Catholicism—"

"That's very shrewd, Ed. Crucifix, Catholicism, well done.
And what does that make the fetus, Baby Jesus?"

"I don't know. Jack did say you had got involved with some extreme Catholic group, the SSPX?"

"The Society of Pius the Tenth? Where did he get that idea? They *are* extreme, they're a bunch of fanatics. Why would Jack think I'd get involved with people who want to take the church back to the Pre–Vatican Two years?"

"He said something about Latin masses—"

"In the Procathedral. Every Sunday, there's a sung Latin mass. But in every other respect it's perfectly ordinary. I like the music. It's a boys' choir. I like the Latin, too."

"And another group called Communion and Liberation—"

Marie nods wearily.

"Yes. Yes, they're . . . I don't think there's anything extreme about them. The last time I met Jack, I probably talked about them a lot. They're good people, they're not like Opus Dei or anything, they're not only interested in rich people. But eventually . . ."

Marie makes a gesture in the air with her hand to indicate futility and pointlessness, then brings her two hands alongside each other to help her make a point.

"The problem with a lot of Irishwomen my age is, you know, that Chesterton quote, having given up on Catholicism—for obvious fucking reasons, all of which I share—it's not that they believe in nothing, they believe in everything. So you know, a little Buddhism, a little Tao, a little Reiki, a little crystal healing, a little earth-goddess worship, a little Wicca . . ."

Marie Donovan's expression broadens into a grin as the list gets longer; now she picks up her glass of wine and giggles.

"A little white wine, a little scented candle, a little Enya . . . it's such bullshit, such a retreat into fantasy. I mean, men have their own fantasy world: it's called sport. With a revolving pantheon of deities, more gods than Olympus. Whereas for women, it's the exotic, it's the glamour . . . you know, massage is spiritual, perfumes are spiritual . . . *fashion* is spiritual . . . it's so narcissistic, it's pathetic, it's like a grown-up version of princesses and dressing up dollies. And not even that grown-up. And I . . . well, I believe in God, you know? The one I always did believe in, the one who is Jesus and the Holy Ghost and so on. Three in one, like whoever wrote your anonymous letters there. Not me, in case you're interested. And I'd like to worship God in many of the ways I used to, you know, like the mass, which is the perfect ritual if you do it right. I just don't believe God's that bothered about all the things He was supposedly so uptight about, especially in this country. Like sex, mainly. Christ, the only people who are as obsessed with sex as the Irish Catholic Church are the people who do it for a living: whores, and porn stars, who are whores on camera. And at least whores know how overrated it all is.

"And I thought I could just take what I wanted from the Church and leave the rest, do it à la carte, but it's difficult, not just because of the never-ending flow of revelations about sexual abuse among priests and religious, but because I'm a woman in the twenty-first century. And the Catholic Church's take on women . . . well, it's still struggling to get out of the nineteenth. And not struggling terribly hard. And I'm struggling back. Is that a crime? Does that make me the kind of sad old church mouse who'd send her brother anonymous letters?"

I shake my head.

"Has it occurred to you that he wrote them himself? Because he has a guilty conscience, my brother. Not that he displays it, but he's not an idiot, and he's not a moral idiot. He knows the truth. He knows what I did for him. And he knows what we did together. And I think he wants to confess. It's like with his movies, have you noticed, he'll almost always follow a success with a disaster, like he doesn't believe he deserves it, like he's compelled to drag himself down. Who else are you going to see? It can't be just me. I bet that little wife he had for half an hour is on the list. He treated her appallingly, too."

I have to stop myself reaching for the wine bottle. What Marie was saying has the ring of truth: you get close to Jack, and then too close, and then he would let you see something you didn't want to see and couldn't forget. Maybe that's what he wanted, to push anyone who cared about him away, to fall and keep falling, over and over, until the only one left at the scene of the accident was Jack.

I was ready to hear the worst. I pick up the page with the blood daubs on it and point at the picture of the fetus.

"Jack told me you were pregnant. He said the father wasn't on the scene, that you wanted the child, that he encouraged you to have an abortion, or at least that that was how you interpreted it. And so you did. Is there anything you want to say?"

Marie Donovan looks at me with no expression on her face.

"The father had a choice. He chose not to be on the scene. That had a bearing on everything else that happened."

"Who was the father?"

"Jack knows who the father was. I think you need to go back and ask him. I've told you all I want to tell you. He can help you with the rest. If he wants to."

I look at Marie Donovan for as long as I can, willing her simultaneously to tell me and to keep her counsel. She holds my gaze as steadily as her squinting eye will let her. She doesn't move as I get up from the table. I let myself out, and walk past my car and cross the main road and stand on the dock, watching an improbably large red ship sail out into the bay and wishing everything I have in my head could be stowed aboard that ship and cast adrift on the open seas.

CHAPTER 9

Los Angeles, 1998

Ed Loy hadn't been in the Sidewalk Café on Venice Beach for years. Well, that wasn't strictly true: he would occasionally find himself in the bar late at night, when the mist was in and the moon was down and holiday makers had been warned that the beach was liable to be used as the after-hours stage for the ongoing feud between the Latino Venice 13 and Culver City gangs and the African American Shoreline Crips, and LAPD surveillance choppers would keep a steady overhead presence just in case they forgot. In complete contrast to the tourist-trap boardwalk tables in full sight of the beach, the bar was a seedy dive joint frequented by bikers and dealers and lowlifes and drunks and the kind of women who found company like that congenial, and sometimes that was the kind of company Ed Loy sought out at the end of the day, not so much to take the edge off as to relocate it somewhere more exciting.

But sitting outside eating eggs Benedict and drinking coffee and juice as the sightseers mingled with the Rollerbladers and the skateboarders and the dog walkers, he realized the last time he had done this was in 1994, on the Tuesday morning the news of Nicole Brown-Simpson and Ronald Goldman's murder in Brentwood appeared in the *L.A. Times.* Loy remembered sitting in pretty much the same spot, facing the Santa Monica Pier, eating pretty much the same breakfast, poring over the details of the crime: the history of domestic violence, the bloodstained glove, the flight to Chicago—well, it wouldn't take the greatest detective on the force to nail that down tight, Loy remembered thinking as he turned the page and read the account of a man's body being found in a house on Westminster Avenue in Venice, and it occurred to him that that was where his boss and mentor CJ Ramsey lived, a split second before the dead man was named in the second paragraph as Charles J. Ramsey. He leaped to his feet and wiped egg yolk and Benedict sauce from his mouth and threw some bills on the table and ran up Horizon and across Abbot Kinney and Electric to Westminster and Sixth, all the time thinking, why had no one called him, why had no one let him know?

There were scraps of yellow police tape on the steel door frame of the modernist concrete bunker CJ had called home, and Ed Loy stood on the street staring at them, realizing the crime scene had been preserved and released and he had missed it all, missed it because, in those days before mobile phones, he had taken a date to a new movie, *Speed,* and then to dinner, and one thing had led to another and he had been at her place ever since, two nights without checking his calls or watching the news. He stood and caught his breath as the door opened and a woman in a black sheath dress with blond hair tied back beneath a black lace mantilla stood in the porch and waited for him.

As he sat here now, Loy remembered that moment so well, the look Barbara Ramsey gave him, grief-stricken but indomitable, wounded but forgiving, waiting for Loy to comfort and take care of her, and assuming he would, of course, assuming, at some level that could not be displayed, even between them, not yet, but that she took for granted, that he would take CJ's place, not just at the agency, but in this house, by her side, in her bed. And didn't she have every right to expect that? Hadn't he been in her bed, and she in his, every chance they got those past six months? Wasn't Barbara in love with him? So in love she had killed her husband so they could be together. When had he begun to suspect her? Was it after he'd gone in to be interviewed by the Santa Monica Police Department? Once he'd gotten hold of his girlfriend, a dental hygienist in Ocean Park, and she'd provided the cops with an alibi that convinced them he was, if not exactly in the clear, at least not involved in the physical act of murder, and once he'd made no bones about the affair, the cops made it very clear that they didn't just suspect, they wouldn't be looking for anyone else in connection with the murder. Oh, they had asked questions about recent cases the agency had worked, divorce, mostly, and Loy had suggested various candidates who had felt so aggrieved to have been caught cheating on their partners they might have been moved to violence, but he wasn't sure he believed in the likelihood of any of them having murdered CJ himself, and he suspected his lack of conviction communicated itself to the cops.

He knew they felt he was guilty, too, if only of standing to profit by CJ's death—the business, the widow—and he began to feel guilty there in that hot, stuffy room in police headquarters on Olympic Boulevard, guilty that he didn't and hadn't given a damn about Barbara, her hopes and dreams, about anything much beyond the momentary thrill, amounting to obsession, of what she brought to the bedroom. If she had killed CJ for him, then the cops were right: even if he didn't plan to profit from it, he bore his share of the guilt. When had he begun to suspect her? When she opened the door to the house on Westminster. In that instant.

It took him six months. Six months of looking like he'd been in league with her, six months of cocktails at Shutters and dining at Chinois on Main and taking every crack and threat the SMPD could throw at him, six months of seeing the agency almost go under because every regular claims adjuster and divorce attorney of CJ's had heard the rumors and refused to pass work his way. He found it hard suppressing his own grief, because for Ed Loy, whose father had been lost to him long before he disappeared for real, Charles J. Ramsey had been like an elder brother, in truth like a father to him. And of course, his guilt over the affair would have made it difficult for him to grieve in the first place, but this masquerade he had embarked on made it grotesque; he had found so many friends through Charlie, and to be blanked and shunned by each of them, often several in the course of one evening, was very upsetting.

The worst was one night in Mother MacGillacuddy's, the Irish bar he had worked behind for ten years. He had come there in the hope he could let his guard down and find a little slice of home. Admittedly he had been a bit drunk, but Mother M's was the kind of place where it wasn't important if you could hold your drink, so long as you could hold your glass. And they wouldn't serve him. Serve him, they wouldn't even look at him. Finally, because he had begun to shout, the manager, Brian O'Rourke, whose brother Kevin Ed had been at school with, clasped a firm hand on his forearm and swept him through a crowded bar—crowded with faces every one of which he had known for years—and out into the lane around the side.

"You should be ashamed of yourself, Ed," Brian said. "And because you're not, because you've lost even that, we have to be ashamed on your behalf. Go home."

We have to be ashamed on your behalf. With that broad York Road accent, as if he was speaking on behalf of the people of Dublin. It still made him plunge his head into his hands when he thought of it. Was that the worst? He would have had to compile a list of low points and compare and contrast, and in the intervening years, he somehow hadn't amassed the wherewithal of spirit and guts to do that.

Six months it took. And he hadn't elicited a single fact, a single hint as to how it had been done in all of that time. A burglary gone wrong was what it looked like: two cameras and twelve hundred dollars in cash and some jewelry stolen, Charlie wakes and interrupts the intruders, signs of a scuffle, Charlie gets shot four times, 9mm Parabellum cartridges, classic gang rounds. The alarm had not been set, but there had been a spate of alarms going off at all hours in that neighborhood, and local residents had been increasingly barring their windows and doors and hoping for the best, so that was not in itself suspicious. A window had been forced. Barbara had been at the Mark Taper Forum at a celebration party for Tony Kushner, who had won an expected second Tony Award in New York that day for his play *Perestroika,* the second part of *Angels in America.* Charlie had taken two Zimovane, had been asleep half an hour or so, and had a blood alcohol content of 0.23 percent, where 0.4 percent is generally a lethal intake. He had a firearm by his bed, but the combination of alcohol and sedatives had hindered his ability to reach it in time.

All of this was plausible: Charlie was an alcoholic who had trouble sleeping. There was no other physical evidence. The SMPD figured the reason he didn't go for his weapon was that he didn't think he'd need to defend himself against his wife, and wanted to bring a case against Barbara, but no one at the district attorney's office thought there was a hope in hell: as far as they were concerned, it just another gangland break-in; if Charlie had scarfed a third Zimovane or had another shot of Scotch, he'd've slept through it all. Token raids were made on Crip homes and hangouts; none of the stolen goods were recovered.

And then, through no great ability or endeavor on his part, through nothing but dumb luck, Loy caught a break. He had tracked down a girl from Ann Arbor called Karen Short, who had run away from her suffocating family, her controlling mother and passive father and perfect straight-A sister, had run away and wanted to run right back, now she had become Alicia Streams and her life had turned into a round of increasingly badly paid, increasingly extreme porn clips—there was a hierarchy even in the San Fernando Valley, and entry level mattered just as much as it did in the legitimate film industry whose infernal shadow it was, and if you started your career with group anal sex, there was only one direction you were headed.

The charmer who had introduced her to this world of glamour and distinction called his production company Ramrod, and it was Loy's good fortune that the 18 USC 2257 Records Keeping Compliance Statement that every porn producer is obliged to make, certifying that his performers are eighteen or over, was faulty in respect of Alicia Streams, aka Karen Short, who had traded favors with her elder sister's straight-A boyfriend in return for an extremely convincing forged ID, and was in fact seventeen years and eight months when she made, Loy didn't want to remind himself what it had been called, her debut, but it filmed her at seventeen doing things that could see Mr. Ramrod, who called himself D-Rod for reasons Loy didn't want to think about, locked away for a very long time indeed.

And D-Rod said, can we trade?

And Loy said, what have you got? (Because frankly, Karen Short had been seventeen rising, and she looked about twenty-five, and she wasn't on anything stronger than speed and coke and a few ludes, which in the Valley amounted pretty much to sobriety, so it wasn't as if D-Rod had done anything but make a genuine mistake. Apart from being a scum-sucking sleazebucket, of course, but that was all legal and aboveboard in the great state of California, hence the official system of compliance.)

And D-Rod said, I can give you that lady.

That lady being Barbara Ramsey.

In the time between first and second visits to the house in Glendale that was D-Rod's residence, D-Rod had done his homework on Ed Loy and made a startling discovery: that assorted business associates of D-Rod's had been on and off friends of CJ Ramsey's widow Barbara for many years, those years including the married years up until she met Ed Loy, on account of Mrs. Ramsey taking a special interest in the particular physical attributes of certain kinds of performers, if Ed knew what he meant. Ed said he did know what he meant, and D-Rod said no offense, and Ed said no offense given, and D-Rod said well, good for you, man, which wasn't quite what Ed had meant but never mind. In any case, one of the associates Mrs. Ramsey had been involved with about a year back, name of Richard "The Hose" Hill, had contracted the virus but was continuing to perform, with condoms generally but not always, and how Mrs. Ramsay found out was, she wanted to chug his load but he wouldn't let her and when she wouldn't take no for an answer the Hose had to come clean, so to speak, and alert her to his HIV status.

And within a few weeks, Mrs. Ramsey saw her opportunity. She told the Hose, who had a gangbanging thing going on both sides of the camera and was said to have Shoreline Crip connections, that she needed a piece. Otherwise she would tell what she knew and his life in porn would be over and he could be looking at jail time on account of some of the actresses he worked with getting sick. Piece needed to be an identifiable gang weapon that five-oh would connect straight off to local bangers, but would never find, because he would collect it from her after use. Some hassle would come down on the Crips, but strictly low level.

So the Hose got her a TEC–9 semiautomatic.

And Mrs. Ramsey blows her husband away and the Hose is waiting in a car parked at the Music Center that houses the Mark Taper Forum, and she parks back there and returns the freshly fired pistol to him. The pistol is clean of prints.

He had something on her but she had something on him. Crisscross, like in that movie. Only what she got on him is more powerful than what he got on her. It's only his word against hers, and what is he, some low-rent porndog with AIDS? She was so confident, rather than toss the weapon and risk being spotted by some passerby, she insisted the Hose take it back.

The Hose has still got it. Don't mean a thing without some way of connecting it to the lady.

No CCTV at the Music Center that night. That's how Mrs. Ramsey thought of the venue, she'd been there a couple weeks before, got into a conversation with the attendant in the booth on Grand Avenue, he said for safety's sake he'd recommend valet parking at the Hope Street entrance on account of how the closed-circuit system they had installed had all sorts of problems that would take months to resolve. The cameras were up, but they weren't shooting.

What the Hose did was, he got a cameraman buddy to park across the way and use a handheld camera to shoot the lady crossing to the Hose's car and sitting into the backseat. He couldn't pick up Mrs. Ramsey dumping the TEC–9, but he got her leaving, and then the Hose getting out of his car. The tape made the connection between them.

The Hose was ready to come clean about his status anyway: he had found God, and his pastor had advised him that it was not enough just to repent, he needed to make amends to everyone he had harmed, like you do in the twelve steps. And the Hose wondered whether it was right to tell what Mrs. Ramsey had done, because he wasn't supposed to make amends if they brought harm to anyone. But he reckoned the one who had harm done to him was Mr. Ramsey, on account of him ending up dead, so the Hose was ready to talk.

Was that enough?

Not quite.

Loy had spent a lot of time already trying to break Barbara's alibi for that night. Many of the guests at the Taper Forum's

Kushner party were too important or busy to consider talking to him; some of those who would meet him either didn't know Barbara Ramsey or didn't remember her that night; those who did remembered her being there but not when she left; three said she was definitely there at the end, and the coat check girl specifically remembered her, because there was some confusion over which coat was hers, and Barbara had gotten angry, before realizing she had forgotten herself which coat she had worn; she apologized and gave the girl a big tip. Loy realized now that this must have been a charade staged to nail her alibi tight. There would be no record of her leaving the car park or returning. Loy doubted very much that the amateur film shot by the Hose's buddy would be admissible in court, even if, as D-Rod claimed, the cameraman was one of the best in the business and well used to shooting scenes in car parks. The SMPD confirmed this to Loy when he went to them with everything D-Rod had told them. They also said since Richard Hill had gangland connections, it was more logical to assume that if he was in possession of the murder weapon, he had committed the murder himself.

In the end, Loy had worn a wire, and played the part of a jealous lover, and, sticking roughly to the truth, but avoiding any reference to Charlie's murder, charged Barbara with infidelity and Barbara, who was desperately in love with Ed Loy now and had jettisoned all her playmates and wanted to be true, finally, tearfully, confessed to a relationship with Richard Hill.

Was that enough? The cops had the murder weapon, they had the confession of a connection to the man who held the weapon, which automatically gave the Hose's testimony a credibility it would otherwise have lacked. They had no physical evidence, but they felt that yes, they had enough to make a case now, and the DA agreed.

The defense and the prosecution initially agreed on one thing: Barbara Ramsey's passion for Ed Loy lay at the center of everything that happened. The prosecution case was that Barbara

Ramsey's midlife passion for a younger man overwhelmed her judgment and caused her to plan and execute a ruthless murder. Initially, the defense sought to deny that Barbara had anything to do with the murder, and in cross-examination did as much as it could to implicate Richard Hill in the crime. Loy found himself cast by the defense as a feckless, callous figure toying cruelly with the affections of a vulnerable older woman who had been grievously neglected by her alcoholic husband. This was a pitch to the women on the jury, and it seemed to have some effect; Loy himself in cross-examination presented a shifty, shamefaced figure who denied any role in murder but was apparently content to be portrayed as a complete and utter shit.

But the prosecution had not rested, and with the help of D-Rod, uncovered at least three other porn performers with criminal sheets willing to testify to intimate relationships with Barbara Ramsey, and at least one who claimed the subject of firearms had been raised. It became clear that Barbara had been a regular in singles bars in North Hollywood and around the southern end of the Valley. And while none of this made her a murderer, it certainly complicated and qualified her image as a woman swept off her feet by sudden passion, and lent D-Rod's testimony enhanced credibility.

As the trial progressed, Loy found himself soul-sick with the reek of it all, with the thoughtless way he had behaved, with the memory of other women he had treated in this fashion, used just as functionally as Barbara used her playmates in the Valley. But Loy had dressed it up, had let Barbara believe he cared, had maybe even kidded himself on that he cared, too. He knew Barbara wasn't the victim here, that she hadn't been driven to the brink of madness by love for him, but she had committed murder, and that was a kind of madness he hadn't thought her capable of. And while she deserved to be punished, and he had worked hard to bring her to justice, he couldn't join the chorus against her.

He didn't need to. For all that the prosecution case was weak, and notwithstanding the defense's skill at casting Barbara Ramsey as a classic lost woman of a certain age, disappointed in love and in life, the fact remained that they had built a strategy around pleading not guilty to murder, and where a voluntary manslaughter plea would probably have succeeded, resulting in a much shorter sentence and eligibility for parole, the jury eventually found Barbara Ramsey guilty of murder, and she got life.

That was quite a wave of memory to break over a man's head and his breakfast not eaten. His eggs had gone cold, the fat had congealed on his ham and his coffee tasted bitter. The sun would burn the mist away eventually, but it was taking its time; there was a salt chill in the air, and the tourists on Ocean Front Walk looked like mutinous overgrown children in their shorts and their colored tops, promised a slice of Californian sunshine and bounty that was unaccountably being withheld from them; Ed Loy smiled at their confusion and disappointment and put his jacket back on. He pushed his breakfast away and lit a cigarette and thought about what had happened after the trial: how, once the guilty verdict was in, all the men who had shunned him welcomed him back with open arms, but how so many women had difficulty meeting his eye; how the agency soared on the back of its sudden notoriety, but attracted the wrong kind of clients, amoral sleazebags with too much money who assumed Ed Loy was just like them, and would be on their side if the price was right; how he went to work every day with rage in his head and shame in his heart. Most of all, he thought of the look Barbara Ramsey had given him across the courtroom when the jury foreman read out the guilty verdict. He knew what she had done, she seemed to say, but did he know what he had done? Did he know how he was going to live with it?

That was when Loy began to understand why Charlie had drunk so much, when he had begun to drink so much himself, not party drinking, not social drinking, steady, daily, whiskey-in-morning-coffee-and-take-it-from-there-drinking, drink-until-you-pass-out-and-get-up-when-you-come-to drinking. Jack Donovan, whom he met for the first time back then, had gotten involved in shooting some live Frank Sinatra shows in Vegas with a view to a concert movie that never happened, and told him the story of how Frank had one day encountered a music producer he deemed to have betrayed him in a hotel lobby. The producer approached, expansive, bygones all bygones; Frank blanked him, barking "Fuck you, keep walking" as he clipped past. That's what Jack told Ed he was doing, fuck-you-keep-walking drinking: don't look left, or right, or back; keep angry, keep drinking, keep walking. Denial, rage, booze: that was a surefire way to walk off a ledge, Jack said. And for all Jack Donovan's reputation as the wild Irish artist with a glass in his hand, he did a good job of talking Ed Loy back from that ledge in those times.

Ed later discovered that anecdote was pretty well known, and reckoned Jack had probably read it in the same book he had. But still, Jack had met, had talked, had worked, had got drunk with Frank Sinatra, that was for real. They'd even, Jack told him, after the show, having flown back to his place in Palm Springs, and sat up late the way Frank liked to do, they'd even sung together. Ed wasn't sure, but if there was anything cooler than that, he hadn't heard about it.

Somehow, the association—the "It's Frank's World, We Just Live in it" aspect—seemed to make what he was doing today feel a little less seedy, or at least, Ed kidded himself that it did. He had already called at the woman's apartment, a first floor on Horizon, just around the corner. He had a bag in his car with stuff she had left over at Jack's: clothing, shoes, books. He knew Jack had added a few pieces of jewelry, which was either generous or the worst kind of sorry present. Ed tried not to think about it. This would be the fifth of Jack's girlfriends he had seen off. Three had cried on his shoulder; one had bitten his ear.

From what he remembered of Amanda, he expected her to do neither. She was the kind of woman who didn't do scenes. Ed had assumed she would leave Jack: Amanda was way too cool and high maintenance and evolved for him. When he went round to collect her stuff, Jack seemed subdued, crestfallen, shamefaced even. Ed asked him how it had gone, and Jack said he didn't want to talk about it. That was when Ed got the first inkling that this might be even more difficult than usual. There had never been a single thing in all the time he'd known him that Jack Donovan didn't want to talk about.

He'd walk around there in a moment. First, he'd smoke another cigarette, drink another cup of coffee. There was time. He'd kept the day clear. There was plenty of time.

CHAPTER 10

It was difficult to make up rules about a situation she had con-
trived, and she knew well that if anyone was going to be un-
expectedly late on account of his job, it would be Ed Loy, and
it had obviously been a mistake to open the champagne as if he
was going to arrive right on time, because then she simply had
to have a glass, and then after twenty minutes she knew if she
didn't have a second she was going to have a headache, but since
she hadn't eaten in case her stomach started growling when they
started to get into it, she is now pissed, at lunchtime, wearing
expensive lingerie the only point of putting on was to have
someone else take off, and it's beginning to look very much like
the only man she is interested in letting do that is not going to
show, and the scented candles (Lime, Basil and Mandarin from
Jo Malone, a gift from Ed) are making her feel a bit queasy. The
point, though, is not to sulk, or blame someone else (him) or

get all pissy about it, although it did take a certain amount of chutzpah to get dressed up like a (she liked to think upscale) whore, and if there wasn't a fairly brisk and emphatic physical acknowledgment and reciprocation from an actual live human being, it's only natural that a girl might get a little demoralized. And it isn't fair to say he could have rung, or texted, because she knows he doesn't do the kind of job where he can just whip out his phone, God knows what kind of situation he might find himself in, and she did kind of spring it on him, but Jesus Christ, she does feel like a bit of a fucking eejit.

Lying here now, wondering if she should get dressed, or un-dressed and redressed, knowing she'd regret it if he arrived just as she had done so, and then getting mad at herself for obsessing about Him so much, like a character from a Doris Day movie or a Bacharach and David song. The danger now is he won't show and she falls asleep and is awoken by Bernie from the after-school dropping the girls off and she forgets how she is dressed when she totters downstairs to answer the door and that will give the other mums something to talk about For The Rest Of Their Lives.

The prospect of playing the lead in a lurid outtake from a Joan Crawford biopic panics Anne into sitting bolt upright and set-ting the alarm for an hour hence, just in case she does nod off. And she swears she can hear a noise in the attic. Nothing, just a creaking board.

Lord God Almighty, that was the scariest day of her life. It was the morning after they had moved in, and Kevin had to go to Riga (the Irish Pub franchise they ran together back then, she designing the interiors, he taking care of business), and there she was in the new house, packing crates and boxes everywhere, and the two girls. Five and three, they were, and high on the adventure of it all, racing from one room to another, finding old wardrobes and fireplaces and whatnot. It was a Georgian house, and rooms had been split and reunited over the years, so there were all sorts of nooks and crannies and strange doors and stud walls that would need to be sorted out eventually, but they had decided the thing to do was to move in and live in the space for a year or two and get the feel of what they wanted, otherwise they might rush into a conversion they'd repent at leisure. Happy days, back when her marriage was sound (although in retrospect, Kevin probably had a girlfriend in Riga, since as it turned out, he seemed to have one everywhere else—but she had believed her marriage to be sound, and she was happy).

She was downstairs, she remembered, trying to put some manners on the kitchen and hoping the plumber would come soon to get the washing machine and the dishwasher sorted, when Aoife trotted in and announced that she couldn't find Ciara. Anne said she was sure to be somewhere and why didn't Aoife just look harder, and Aoife said she had looked, and Anne followed Aoife back upstairs and together they looked for Ciara. For ten minutes. Twenty minutes. Half an hour. She wasn't in a wardrobe, or under a bed, or in or behind a box or a crate. The windows were all shut and Aoife said they hadn't opened any and Anne asked if she was sure, possibly in a shouty voice, and Aoife said tearfully that they had tried but they *couldn't* open them, they were too heavy. On the second floor there was a dumbwaiter Anne had not known about, and she began to shake at the prospect Ciara might have fallen into it, but getting the panel open proved so tricky that there was no way Ciara could have done it.

Having drawn a blank, Anne ran downstairs and checked front and back doors, but the back was locked and the latch on the front was too high for three-year-old hands to reach, and too stiff to manipulate if somehow they had. Breathing deeply, and insisting to herself that however old the house was, there were no such things as ghosts (and even if there were, all they could do was scare you, not make you vanish into thin air), she went through every inch of the house again, progressing up the stairs until she got to the room she was in now. And Aoife, who kept by her side and kept her from freaking out entirely, said:

"Listen Mum, that's Ciara."

And there indeed, drifting on the air, was the sound of three-year-old Ciara singing, to made-up words but the correct tune, "Edelweiss" from *The Sound of Music,* a favorite of hers. The singing seemed to be coming from above. Anne looked up and saw a square panel on the ceiling. Access to the attic, but the panel was attached by four rivets, and was in any case twelve feet from the floor. Ciara appeared to be in the attic, but how had she got there? Outside on the landing, there were two doors to the left, one leading to the adjacent bedroom and one which had opened onto a partition corridor but which was now locked to form part of the bedroom wall. On the wall which divided the second bedroom from the first, there was another door which connected the two rooms; Anne had noticed it from the other side when they had been listening to Ciara singing.

As Aoife approached this door, Anne began to tell her there was no point, that it just led back into the room they had come from, and anyway, it was locked. But it didn't, and it wasn't. It opened onto a narrow wooden stairway coated with dust and swarming with wood lice, and Anne threw herself up the stairs as if the woodlice-dust combination was very catnip to her, and at the top of the stairs was an attic space barely six feet in height at its tallest and there, sitting beneath the eaves on an upturned orange crate with an old cup-and-ball in one hand and a dusty yo-yo in the other, her smiling face smudged with dust, was Ciara, aged three, still singing, every morning we greet you indeed.

"Mummy, why are you crying?"

The ghost room, they call it now. A ghost door to a ghost room. The three of them hid on Ed Loy there once, freaked him out comprehensively.

Enough of that. Enough of the little darlings. Subsiding onto the pillow again, a little woozily, Anne tries to immerse herself once more within the not unpleasant erotic reverie she has been clinging to. But once you lose a mood, it's hard to recapture, especially since a) the underwire on the bra she's wearing (Elle Macpherson, half price in the never-ending sale the recession has spawned) is digging into her ribs, and b) the damp spot in the corner of the ceiling is spreading and getting darker. Oh Jesus, not the roof, she couldn't face the idea that she might have to get the tiles up again, and all that mess, but she can't see what else might be the trouble: there are no plumbing pipes there, and it's four feet from the window frame and eight from the blessed attic panel. Maybe the guttering?

She tugs on her bra as she tries to remember where she's left the number of the roof guy, then closes her eyes tight, furious at herself for dwindling from seductress to hausfrau. *Don't break the spell, don't break the spell,* she intones, but all that lodges in her head is a sour joke about the ceiling not being the right location for the kind of damp patch she'd had in mind, which is pretty labored anyway, since what she'd had in mind was not the damp patch itself, but oh for God's sake shut up Anne.

Her phone pings its text-message alert. The secret of good comedy. That will be Ed, canceling. She doesn't need to look at it. Of course she does, because it could be the after-school saying Ciara has a nosebleed or Aoife has fallen off a wall. Three ways she loses.

I'm really sorry, work got in the way. Later? Ed x

Well, she feels a total fucking eejit now. What the hell possessed her? She doesn't drink at lunchtime for a start, not when the kids are around, not even at weekends, it makes the rest of the day unbearable. Maybe it was because things had slowed down a bit since the first few months they'd met, when they couldn't get enough of each other, in cars, on floors, in a department-store changing room. Those weekends away where they'd barely leave the room. She knew that couldn't last, even if you did have the time to do nothing but fuck, it would slow down after a while anyway, and with kids involved, life was infinitely more complicated. But Ed had not exactly complained about that, not at all, actually, Kevin took the girls most weekends and a lot of the time there was just the two of them. No, she remembers what it is: she does not want him to turn into Suburban Man for her, partly because that's neither who he is nor who she wants him to be, but mainly because what would that make her? A fussy Suburban Mummy who can't lie in bed for half an hour without devising another round of home improvements. Maybe she had gotten carried away, rush of blood to the head and elsewhere, forced it big-time. She knows he can't just drop everything. But *he* had texted *her,* last night, he had got her all hot and bothered. He started it. God, listen to her, he *started* it, from self-loathing to shifting the blame, what is she like? That's the drink talking and no mistake. She certainly should have kept the cork in the bottle until he got here.

Other than that . . . fuck it, no more negative thoughts. She looks fantastic, she knows that. She isn't going to submit herself to full mirror scrutiny to check this point, or wonder why this bloody bra is digging into her when it had fit perfectly well three months ago, she is just going to take it for granted. Insist upon it, actually. And she isn't getting up to find the roofer's number or plan the summer holidays or do something in the garden or confirm her appointments for tomorrow. She is going to blow out the candle and lie here and not sulk and not be peevish and count her blessings. It's ten to two and the girls aren't due back until six and she has the whole afternoon, how often could she say that?

She could do as she pleased. Whatever that might be.

Maybe she could just focus on what she would have been doing if Ed had showed, what he would be doing to her, and then . . .

No no no, that isn't going to work. She doesn't have the patience. Or the interest. Or whatever. And she isn't going to beat herself up about it either, she just doesn't want to, that *would* only make things worse. Next.

She wonders if it was the *Nighttown* thing that has ramped things up a level. She isn't one of those mad women who thinks she is in competition with movie actresses and resents the idea that their men might find them more attractive than her, either on the screen or in real life, but when she found out Ed knew Jack Donovan, that they had been close friends before they fell out, over what, he wouldn't tell her, extracting that bare information alone had been like trying to get blood out of a stone, well, it was fair to say she had gotten overexcited one night on a little too much white wine (she shouldn't blame the drink but she had put away at least a bottle) and given a note-perfect impersonation of a mad neurotic bitch, replete with "dark insinuations" about how she was sure he'd find more congenial company among the lovely ladies of *Nighttown*. Of course, this had been provoked by her goading Ed into telling her everything about Jack Donovan, so once she had established that in the mid-nineties, Ed had not only met but hung out with Drew Barrymore and Patricia Arquette, among others (there hadn't been any others, and she could tell Ed didn't really know these women very well and had no especial interest in a woman simply because she was an actress, but the bottle of white wine—the *second* bottle of white wine—couldn't be bothered with such finely tuned distinctions), she had sort of gone off on one. Jealous rage (retrospective), and then tears, and then, because he had had the temerity to try and comfort her, or "patronize her," as she had styled it, more rage ("it's about trust, actually," she had heard herself saying) until the poor fellow had no option but to leave.

He had been lovely the next day, bringing flowers and fixing Bloody Marys and refusing to acknowledge that any harm had been done, and had never referred to it again and brushed off her apologies as if she was speaking in a foreign language. All he had said, looking her in the eye—he had told her once that he liked the fact she could look him in the eye, and she thought it was the most romantic thing she had ever heard, and the thing was, when *he* looked *her* in the eye, she filled up so that she thought sometimes she was going to burst, her heart began to race and a kind of prickly heat seemed to explode all over her body until she was sure she must look all blotchy but it had happened when they were at the bar in the Stag's Head one night and she caught a glimpse of herself in the mirrors and there was no sign of a blotch, which was a blessing and no mistake—all he had said was—

"Are you all right?"

And he had pitched it just right, a mixture of cheerfulness and solicitude, so beautifully tender, remembering all the things she had been through, her sister, and her father, bearing everything in mind and casting nothing up to her, giving her as many excuses and outs as she needed, that the least she could do was be honest, and say—

"I'm fine, I was just being a silly bitch. I know even if I gave you permission, you wouldn't slap me, so next time, I'll slap myself."

That had made him laugh. But she brooded about it afterward, not while he was there, bad enough he had to suffer through it once without his having to put up with her agonies of remorse and shame, that was like making him pay twice for her sins. She wondered what it said about her insecurity. Was she afraid she was the suburban mouse, and that at some level, Ed was out of her league? Maybe she felt a bit threatened after too much white wine, but deep down, she didn't think so. She felt—yes, this was more like it, she felt there was another woman she had to become. She didn't want to be Ed Loy's harbor, his place of refuge, the ready-made family he called sanctuary. She didn't want to do what he did, but a life of safety, with all decisions made and all doors closed against the storm, was not what she was looking for either. She knew he loved her, and she wasn't afraid of losing him. She just needed to keep raising the stakes. Today was an example of that. There'd be others. It wasn't a strategy, it wasn't manipulative, it was a way of making what they had live.

Christ, she sounded like a self-help book. You go, girl.

Well, no one else is listening. It's her afternoon.

And it came after quite a morning.

God, that was a coincidence. Or rather, that was Dublin for you. Her client, Geri Foster, turning out to be Jack Donovan's ex-wife. Wait until Ed hears that. On the plus side, she actually got a job out of it. The house is a thirties bungalow that had been designed in what most people would call an Art Deco style, but is strictly speaking Moderne or Streamline Moderne: all white, curved corners, occasional porthole windows, glass bricks, steam-liner railings and so on. Inside it had been decorated in standard minimalist fashion: bare floorboards, white walls, rooms that look like trendy art galleries or cool studio apartments. Anne had crossed her fingers and held her breath and prepared a series of sketches that embraced the Art Deco style full on: furniture, wallpaper, rugs, fabrics, lacquer, mirrors, the lot. And Geri Foster had squealed and clapped her hands and written a deposit check on the spot. Hadn't she heard about the global recession? Anne reckoned being Jack Donovan's ex-wife must have its compensations.

How she found out was, Geri had the papers on the kitchen table when Anne arrived, and a couple of the tabloids were open to *Nighttown* stories, and when Anne was talking Geri through the Art Deco references, she pointed to some textured wallpaper that you could see quite clearly in one of the newspaper photos.

And Geri Foster said:

"Oh yeah. Jack Donovan. We used to be married, you know."

And Anne said Oh My God and No and Serious?

And Geri Foster said:

"Here's the thing. If you're an actress, do anything you want with a director—anything he wants—except marry him. Unless you don't give a damn about your career. Which, sadly, I do. Or at least, I used to."

Anne quite liked that, because it sounded like something Eve Arden or Barbara Stanwyck might have said, in a hat, with a cigarette. In fact, there had been something old-school and good-old-girlish about Geri this morning, in contrast to the Southside spoiled brat she had appeared the first time they met. Anne couldn't figure her out at all. She fished for a little more Jack Donovan gossip, but Geri wasn't giving anything away. She ended up liking her a lot more than she thought she had, and way more than she needed to. What was it Tracy Lord said? "The time to make your mind up about people is never"? Anne remembers Ed quoting that to settle some question the girls had asked him, his face still bruised and swollen from Jack Cullen's thugs. That was when she realized that any man who did the job he did and who could then turn around and quote Katharine Hepburn in *The Philadelphia Story* was a man worth hanging on to.

Maybe she'll see him later.

She knows she'll see him soon.

She hopes, wherever he is, that he's safe.

It's not as if you made the rule to start with. Not even God had done that. You see what happens, how people behave, how you behave, and then you try to extrapolate some wisdom, some logic, some order, out of that human mess. In this case, he has acted on impulse, fine, not once, but twice, and feels a desperate urge to make it three, to bring all his work to a glorious crescendo, to achieve a, yes, an apotheosis. But now he has been to some extent thwarted, now the dread hand of the quotidian has intruded, he is obliged to step back and evaluate. You get caught up in the moment, in the frenzy and delirium of the day, in the heat and dust of the forest, and then you climb to a place of tranquillity, to contemplate, to weigh and measure and then to set down some kind of guide for the future. First physics: motion and velocity, the kinetic; then ethics: silence and certainty, the still point of the turning world.

That's why he is here now, taking some time from the melee, at the top of the house, in the attic room they've left untouched. From the tiny barred windows he can see right across Dublin to the mountains. He grips the bars and tears spring into his eyes. He promised himself, he prayed not to have to endure this kind of homecoming. Not in Dublin, not on this film. He knew it was more than could be borne, that—physics again—the system would overload. But it appears his will is not strong enough. Or is it his spirit that is lacking? Spirit, flesh, will. He doesn't know, he is not a . . . what? Theologian? Metaphysician? He does not know what he is not.

What he does know is that Ed Loy is on the case, and is looking at it as a case. And that he has arranged for Jenny Noble to be taken somewhere. There isn't much that happens on a film set that does not distill itself into gossip and bubble up and filter down until sooner or later everyone hears about it. A film company at work is as hierarchical and complementary and self-mythologizing as a medieval village. He just needs to be patient, and he will find out where they brought her. He cannot ask Loy—he knows he is a suspect, just as the others are—but he is sure Madeline knows, and it should not prove too difficult to extract the truth from her in due course.

But patience is not a euphemism for calm. Loy has already made the connection with Malibu, with Point Dume, with the three surfer girls there. If Loy is thinking on that scale . . . tears spring involuntarily into his eyes again. For God's sake, what is the matter with him, he is such a disgusting crybaby! The thing to do . . . because Loy is not going to be fobbed off, or diverted, or in any way deflected from getting to the truth . . . or is he? It's important not to mythologize people, to build them up into superhuman icons, he knows that only too well. After all, Loy had been on the case in Point Dume, and those girls had never been found, had they? Loy is formidable, but he is human. He came from out of the mire, just like the rest of us, and to the mire he can quickly return. So the thing to do, the thing to do is: not rush to judgment on the thing to do.

He remembers the Point Dume girls clearly. They were so utterly trusting, so easy, happy to go along with anything he suggested, however different each had been from the others. The first one—Desiree—she was so skinny, with boy hips and no breasts. She came from somewhere

in the south—that was the thing about them, they all came from somewhere else, but they all looked like California girls, all blond hair and
blue eyes and tanned skin—and when he offered her a glass of Prosecco,
she looked at it in wonder, as if the bubbles popping were fireworks, and
gulped it down before it could be taken away from her. Desiree was the
most direct of the three, not so much reluctant to talk as confused that he
seemed to want to, impatient when he wouldn't make a move and brisk
about initiating things herself. He became irritated by her because she
was stupid, and because her teeth were too sharp, and because the fug
of her patchouli oil wasn't enough to mask the strong smell of her feet.
She laughed at him, and he hit her, quite hard, he was pretty sure he
broke her nose, the bone had twisted to one side and the blood had come
gushing, and instead of getting angry—because the other two girls were
nice but pretty tough, it would never have occurred to him to hit either
of them—she just burst into tears, wailing like a little girl, and all sorts
of thoughts ran through his head in the seconds it took to get his hands
around her neck, thoughts and visions of her as a little girl, with her family, with her little-girl hopes and dreams, before she had run away, before
she knew what her life would be like, and how it was to end.

Unbearable thoughts, they made him so sad back then, he remembers
weeping, actually weeping as he strangled her, the hot blood from her nose
spraying onto his hands, hot salt tears in his eyes. He weeps again now
at the memory. It was the sudden howl of pain, and the wounded look
in her eyes, the eyes of a child, and even if he did receive their light, their
grace, it was not an unalloyed benison. The eyes of a child! It wasn't fair,
that he should have such a vision in his head. It really wasn't fair. He felt
shaky and remorseful for days afterward, even though nobody seemed to
notice she was missing. That was in part because he was smarter about
everything back then, both more cautious but also a little more deliberate,
and he had made sure she wasn't called for another week or so when he
made his move. But it was also that she simply was one of those girls nobody seemed to notice, one of those people whose feet don't make a deep
impression on the earth or kick up much in the way of its dust.

He wonders sometimes if he overcompensated with the second, Janice, *because of his unease over Desiree. But he is pretty sure that was not true. He knows he didn't waste too much time on the third because he was too upset after he . . . after Janice . . . passed. He was so sure Janice would understand what he was doing. But how could she have understood, when he barely had the tools to analyze it himself? It was rage, he sees that now, rage that Janice hadn't understood him, and that he had had to kill her, even though he didn't want to, more than mere rage, grief, yes, that's it, grief expressed as rage, that kicked over onto the third Point Dume girl, Polly, he barely had her through the door before his hands were around her throat, he remembers her necklace broke and the beads went flying everywhere, the sound so clear, a crash or a crack and then a brisk swishing as they sprayed across the wooden floor, like a blind flying up, it took him weeks to find them all, he'd stand on one late at night in his bare feet and convulse, so excruciating, the pain from such a tiny glass bead. He couldn't wait to kill her. No Prosecco for Polly.*

But with Janice . . . they liked each other. That was the extraordinary thing. Janice was, and he'd noticed this about so many Americans, hadn't progressed past high school level, he knew she hadn't even graduated, certainly had never been to university, but she was widely and well read, better read and more articulate than most of the supposedly educated people he knew. She had read not just the Gavin Lambert novels that Ocean Falls was based around, but his books on Cukor and crime fiction, his biographies of Norma Shearer and Natalie Wood. "It's the cheapest form of entertainment," she said. "Check out the used bookstore when you get to a new town. That's the place that will stop you getting bored." And her apartment was littered with bookmarks from One World on Venice Beach and Larry Edmunds on Hollywood Boulevard and from all the little stores on Main Street and Third Street Promenade in Santa Monica.

And they could just talk. She seemed to know everything about old Hollywood, not just the actors and directors but the designers, the technicians, the producers, too, how the whole studio system had worked at its height. They talked for hours. She was . . . she was very smart. No, that didn't do her justice, she was more than smart . . . she was perceptive, and sensitive, she had taste and judgment, she could marshal an argument, she . . . and of course, he made the mistake, because they had become so close, had shared many bottles of the blue Prosecco with no consequence more grievous than a sore head, and there never seemed a hint that she was keen to take things in a way he didn't want to go, never a hint she was impatient with him, sexually, it was . . . if he had kept his mouth shut, it could have been perfect. No. Not just if he had kept his mouth shut, if he had been someone else. Because how, if they were to be truly close, could he have kept a secret from her?

So—out of love—he tried to explain. The conquering army analogy. The Jews are in the attic and I am finishing my dinner, free. How it had to be done the first time, out of self-interest, because the girl had gone crazy, was a danger to him, self-preservation had kicked in. And then, after that, well, it was harder to excuse, but it had become a facility. Something he could do. And then perhaps a habit. Something he did. And he had begun to explain about the light in their eyes, the salve of grace, the eternal Three-in-One. But he faltered, partly because that was more difficult to explain—it was more an instinctual thing, a matter of conviction, of faith—and partly because of the expression on her face. She was smiling eagerly at first, even giggling, because she evidently thought it was some kind of joke, some outrageous satire, and then the laughter stopped, and the smile faded, and she looked . . . before she began to look angry, and scared, yes, this was the worst of it, he could still see the expression on her face, mingling pity and disgust. She looked disgusted at him. And the pity . . . he didn't know which was worse.

A line had been crossed.

Pity and disgust.

You can't base a relationship on that combination, can you?

She had caught him on the ear with the base of a lamp, and her nails scrabbled at his eyes, but it was always astonishing, it was, yes, truly pitiful, once his hands closed around their necks, how quickly the strength left them.

The tears come again now, just as they did that day. How he cried, wept as never before or since, howling over Janice's dead body. But then, the funny, the piquant, the human *thing.*

Then he stopped crying. He looked at himself in the glass, contem-

plated the light, extinguished in Janice's eyes, now blazing in his own.

Gift of vision. Salve of grace. He thrived by this sweet blessing.

Then he got to work: the disposal of the body (nobody has ever found a single body), the return to her apartment to remove the dedication pages of the books he had given, the preparation of a face to face the world, now that he had known true grief, now that he had been truly tested, weathered, had undergone trial by fire. He had known sacrifice and survived it.

That was the day that changed him.

That was the day that made him.

That was the day he had learned to harden his heart, just as Himmler had admonished the SS. Not that he has any sympathies in that direction, he is as appalled by the Holocaust as anyone. Useful and necessary advice, though, could come from any quarter.

Here come the tears again.

But that's all right. Tears are an essential part of any birth. And the more difficult the birth, the more urgent the tears.

That was what he must contemplate now. Were his impulsive killings of Nora and Kate abortive spasms, the death throes of a dying breed, or are they the first live births to herald a new dispensation? Would killing Jenny Noble round off his life's work, or be the harbinger of the next, irrevocable phase?

The next phase.

The new dispensation.

It's fair to say, he has harbored thoughts like this before.

Monumentalism, you might call it. When your work accumulates, until it becomes a body of work, an oeuvre.

Until your faith attains the breadth and gravity of a religion.

He shakes, almost giggles with the adrenaline, now he dares to think it through.

And of course, it is instantly clear that he has already embarked on the next phase. Where the timid spirit and the cautious mind had balked, blood and bone and sinew had acted. It is clear that the level of danger and self-destruction he invoked in killing Nora and Kate was an act of unconscious supplication: Let us move from private prayer to public wor-

ship. Let this work no longer be a private passion: let it be shared by an audience, a congregation. He had begun the process without consultation, all those years ago, when he killed the first girl; now he has raised the stakes. And the question he is asking of himself is:

Do you have what it takes to honor your own abilities? Do you have the courage to trust your best instincts? Do you understand that, though the inevitable end is your own demise, you can follow no other course of action?

His phone and two-way radio were flashing. He is always necessary to others. He is always wanted. Always in demand.

Let them wait a moment longer, until he resolves this in his head, until he attains . . . what is the expression?

A moment of clarity.

To embrace the truth, the deep and lasting truth of paradox.

That a man must lose his soul to save it.

That to act counterintuitively is to act with the keenest intuition.

That character is tyranny, that tyranny must be overthrown, that to act out of character is a consolidation of character.

That he has been toiling in silence and in secrecy for fifteen years now, in darkness, and the time has come to let in the light.

Better, the time is ripe to bring his light to the world.

He lifts his head to the barred window and looks across the city of Dublin to the mountains. His thoughts turn to the man who was killed on a mountain flanked by two thieves, the man in whom he still believes, always will, despite his own unworthiness, even if he thinks of Jesus more as a rival than an idol.

Someone not so much to emulate, as to outflank.

(He sometimes wishes he believed in demons, for then he could invoke the name of Lucifer, the light bringer, the fallen archangel. But try as he might, his faith is not inexhaustible. He believes in God. Demons are the stuff of fairy tales.)

Jesus said, Follow me.

He worked in silence and secrecy for thirty years, and then emerged from darkness into the light, knowing it would inevitably lead to His death.

And that is what he would do.

He would step into the light. More. He would meet it with his own.

He will call Detective Donald Coover. Coover had been at Point Dume. He had followed Coover's career. Coover knew Ed Loy.

And then the entire world would bear witness.

And there is still Jenny Noble to come.

And who knows what, to follow?

CHAPTER 11

On the drive from Ringsend to Foxrock, I send Anne Fogarty a text saying I'm sorry I can't make it for "lunch." I'm not sure if it's possible to convey total sincerity through the medium of SMS, but I know if I ring and hear the breathy husk of her voice, I'll be unable to resist, and I can't drop the case now, not for a minute, certainly not for an afternoon in bed with a beautiful woman. Why hadn't she got this idea last week, when all I was doing was working insurance fraud cases and would have had no trouble taking an entire day off? I stop off at a florist's in Donnybrook and arrange to have some flowers sent around to her house.

For now, I need to pursue this thing. Momentum is always an issue, and if I wondered whether the anonymous letter and drawings were a wild-goose chase before, I certainly don't after hearing what Marie Donovan had implied about her relation-

ship with her brother, and about the parentage of her child.
Everything is connected. If Jack set these letters up himself, or
has—as I certainly suspect—greater knowledge of them than he
chose to share with me, then I need to see all three women he
suggested knew something about them as soon as possible.

I park outside Geri Foster's white Art Deco house on a leafy
avenue in Foxrock. I still drive the racing-green 1965 Volvo 122S
my father, a motor mechanic, had unknowingly bequeathed to
me. It's a big old beast of a car, the Amazon; Tommy Owens,
who is a mechanic by trade, and had once worked for my father,
keeps it on the road for me; I often look out into the yard at the
rear of my apartment and see Tommy burrowing beneath the
hood. He doesn't feel it necessary to warn me when he's coming, or to let me know he's been there; at some essential level, I
think he feels the car belongs to him, and I'm just the nominal
owner; I probably feel the same way. I didn't get along very well
with my father, but the fact that the car was something he loved
and that I drive it around the city he lived in means something
to me, although it would probably take a Jack Donovan to tell
you quite what that something is.

Geri Foster wears flat round-toed shoes with ankle straps and
white pleated trousers and a silk top in a green that matches the
Volvo; her short, reddish-brown hair is cut in a loose marcel
wave; she seems to have been styled to go with the house. I sit
on a chair to one side of the hearth in her open-plan living room
and thank her for the cup of very good coffee she brought me
and wonder why, since I was pretty sure I had noticed Chanel
No. 5 when she greeted me at the door, I can smell Jo Malone
Lime, Basil and Mandarin, Anne Fogarty's scent.

Geri Foster sits on the sofa across from the fireplace and looks
at me expectantly. I had spoken to her on the phone, and when I
mentioned that I wanted to talk to her about Jack Donovan, she
had told me that in that case, I must come over, in such a careless
manner that I was taken aback; that same cheerful carelessness

is the overwhelming impression I get now. After all I have been told, I find it a little unsettling. On a set of shelves by my side there's a framed photo of two small girls riding a toy car along a funfair track. They look like miniature grown-ups in the car, their faces set in solemn concentration, as if they were two old ladies driving to church together. I pick up the photo and smile, and turn the smile around to Geri Foster, and her face lights up.

"Alice and Daisy," she says. "They're five. Started school last September, God, the time goes so fast. The crèche picks them up in the afternoons."

"Alice and Daisy?" I say.

"That's right. What did Jack tell you, Jackie and Joanie? Set me up as a total bunny boiler, did he?"

Still reeling from the level of misinformation my old friend has armed me with, I can do little more than shake my head.

"Maybe you could tell me . . . your side of the story," I say.

"Maybe you could tell me why," Geri Foster returned. "I mean, you're working for Jack, fine. I said I'd see you. Notice I don't have a solicitor here, which I probably should have. That's not the way I work. But why are you here? Is Jack trying to reduce his maintenance payments? Do you intend to poke around, see if there's any sign of a man in the picture? I mean, that's how people like you make their money, isn't it?"

I'm not sure how comfortable I am being lectured about how I made my money by a woman who continues to make all hers from a man she was married to for a few months, but then again, I can't necessarily be sure that anything Jack has told me is true.

"It's not how I make my money."

"Oh no? Dublin's a small town, Mr. Loy. I happen to *know*, was at *school* with someone whose husband divorced her because you provided him with evidence of her infidelity. And there was a prenup, and she landed hard on her ass with fuck all. So don't paint yourself as some kind of service to widows and orphans, some knight in shining armor."

I don't think I blush, but I can feel the heat on my brow. In recent months, I have felt the city shrinking. Part of my excitement at Jack Donovan's return is that he is a link with outside, with L.A., with the wider world. I try to do as little divorce work as possible, for the same reasons I try to avoid organized criminals if I can: because the people are depressing, and what they do makes you sad, and if you catch them out, they invariably want revenge. Not that the kind of people who hire private detectives for divorce work are as dangerous as organized criminals. (Although once the wife of a Dublin gangster tried to hire me to catch her husband with a woman she suspected was his younger girlfriend. I said I was too busy, whereas in fact I was too scared. I don't know if she hired a different kind of operative or took the job on herself, but three months later her husband and a twenty-three-year-old woman were shot dead in bed at the woman's apartment, thus vindicating her judgment, and mine.) But they are often influential in legal and security circles that it's not in my interest to alienate. Equally, they talk to the press and the press run stories, mostly speculative, on what I do. Dublin is a small place for a private detective to be a public figure, and I'm already too well known for my own good. The city is shrinking, and I wonder, not for the first time, whether I'm running out of road.

"All right. I'm not here at Jack's behest to snoop around and catch you out. I can assure you of that. I'm here because . . . because Jack has received a series of anonymous letters, and he's worried you might have sent them."

I pass the letters and the drawing to Geri Foster and finish my coffee while she examines them. Unlike Marie Donovan, Geri doesn't show the slightest glimmer of amusement; when she reaches the daubs of the fetus and the inverted cross, she emits an involuntary squeal and thrusts the bundle of paper back to me as if it was red hot.

"Oh my God, how *creepy*!" she says, in fluent Foxrock. "Some kind of Bible basher. Jack thought they were from me? Why would he think that? My *God*, that fetus and the crucifix, it's like *The Omen* or something."

I'm not sure what age Geri Foster is, somewhere in her mid-thirties at a guess, but she seems to have regressed from South-side sophisticate to agitated teen. She dips her head and tugs at strands of her hair, teasing them in the direction of her mouth. When she looks up at me, her face is flushed.

"What's the matter with him, Mr. Loy?"

What's the matter with you? is what I feel like asking.

"It's hard to say. I think he's feeling anxious about . . . about things in his life. A sense of unease. Maybe a, you know, a midlife sense. And the letters, while not specific, seem to suggest guilt and maybe retribution, in very general terms. And since there is a drawing of a fetus, he seemed to think that maybe . . . because you and Jack were at odds over the, uh, the girls there, the birth of the girls, I think he was interested in what you might have to say."

Part of my own stumbling unease is genuine, but the bulk of it is a kind of performance intended to relax Geri, and to an extent it seems to work; by the time I've finished speaking, she has regained composure and allows the trace of a smile to play around her lips.

"So what are you saying, you're, like, a go-between?" she says, her voice gently mocking.

"I guess that's what I'm like. To be perfectly honest, Geri, and I don't know how much you know of this, but I fell out with Jack myself, I haven't seen or spoken to him in ten years, and when he approached me with these letters, I didn't know what to think. I still don't. But I can tell you he's upset and anxious, and I said I'd try and help him. That's as much as I can tell you."

Geri Foster considers this, getting off the sofa and walking to the front window and looking out through the narrow wooden blinds.

"Cool car. Jack used to talk about that car."

"No he didn't. I didn't have that car in L.A."

"Well, he used to talk about some cool old car you had."

"A '63 Cadillac Eldorado. Same color."

"He used to talk about that. He used to talk about you. A lot."

"We were friends."

"You hurt him very badly. He said you would have nothing to do with him."

Back at her apartment on Horizon Avenue, the sun had burned the clouds, scorched the mist away. My hair was matted by the time she opened the door and I saw . . .

"That's about right. Did he tell you why?"

"He said you'd fallen out over a woman."

"I suppose we did."

"But it's all right now?"

"I don't know. Maybe enough time has passed."

"But the reason you fell out, the details . . . they don't seem important anymore?"

. . . and I saw Amanda's face . . .

"No, they do, I just . . . I guess I was glad to see him."

"He never told me what had happened. But he said it was all his fault. A couple of times . . . a couple of times, he broke down and cried about it. Said it was no use, he could never, should never be forgiven for what he had done. I couldn't believe it. Jack Donovan, such a tough guy, such a bear of a man, crying in my arms."

"Was that on *Twenty Grand*?"

"In the Sierras, yeah. God, I was such a fucking . . . I bet he told you I was a silly little bitch, working with this famous director, this amazing costume designer, and I hadn't the wit to realize opportunities like this did not fall out of the sky."

"Something like that."

"Well, he's absolutely right. I was an unspeakable little fool. And the only thing I can say in my defense is, I wanted to be an actress. And you know what you should never do if you want to be an actress? Work in production, or administration, or design, or in a technical department. Better off being a waitress. Because it's like being the bridesmaid and wishing you were the bride, the actual bride, marrying that actual guy. I had done some work here, fifteen years ago, theater stuff, I was okay. I was good, actually."

She pauses, as if to let how good she had been settle in the room. She is still at the window, her hair catching the light that filters through the half-shut blinds. About five eight, with a slender boy's hips and chest and a dancer's steady, supple posture, she is certainly good at finding a place to stand that makes her look elegant and graceful.

"But I was doing costume as well, in the theater, and then I was doing some styling for people I knew, to make some money, and that led to an ad, and then I worked in costume on a couple of small Irish movies and one went to L.A. and I just went on a holiday while the guys were out there and they met Jack and everyone and I got, I think it was through Maurice Faye, I got the chance to do it. And because it had happened so haphazardly, without my, you know, waiting in my room, oh my God I really hope I can do this, because it was so not my dream, I just took it for granted. I was like, if I hang out with the actors, I'll somehow get acting work. But of course, I totally pissed them all off as well, because it's on location in the Sierras, and everyone needs to do their job, and what did I think? They're going to write a part for me? So I was sacked."

"But at that stage, you had gotten together with Jack."

"That's right. Not Conor Rowan or Mark Cassidy, Jack Donovan, the director himself. Case closed."

"I don't know what the case is yet. You tell me."

Geri turns from the window and closes the blinds and walks back and sits where she had been sitting in one fluent movement that looks like it had been rehearsed. Her manner is not theatrical but somehow her overall *affect* is. I can't take my eyes off her.

"Of course, it might spoil a perfect little showbiz fable about a gold-digging actress who gets her director in her sights and then nabs him to point out that Jack made all the running. All the moves came from his side. I wasn't . . . to tell the truth, I don't think I really fancied him to begin with."

"He did say something along those lines."

"Along what lines?"

"That you didn't seem to like him very much, and especially, you didn't seem to like having sex with him."

Geri Foster cups her hands and thrusts her face into them as a high-pitched shriek issues from somewhere deep inside. When she reemerges, she looks chastened, as if the truth is hard to admit but you can't avoid it.

"Well, basically, that was true. I didn't fancy him at all, I . . . not then . . . but he was so keen, you know, and he was funny, and charismatic, and . . ."

"He was Jack Donovan."

"Ye-ah. In spades. Private-jet-at-the-weekends-to-go-to-Palm-Springs Jack Donovan. And I was just-been-fired Geri Foster. So it was all a bit . . . imbalanced? I mean, I *liked* him, but . . . and the other thing was, he was out of his face pretty much all the time. Self-medicating. I mean, there was booze and coke and Valium, up down up down all day and all night. I didn't really think that much of it then, I guess I felt, since he was the only famous director I'd ever met, and he'd won Oscars—Oscars, for fuck's sake—I just felt this was the way you did it. You were an artist, on drugs, what was the problem? And I really don't want to sound like I had an eye out for the main chance. It was just very hard to refuse him. And I had nothing, you know? And I reckoned, well, I'll get to fancy him. It's not like I actively dislike it, it's just the . . . the spark? The smell? Whatever it is you need. Which is weird in the light of what happened later. But I just want to say, in the weeks leading up to, and at the moment of, the wedding, I was not thinking, I'm going to take this guy for what I can get."

Geri looks around the room ruefully, as if the evidence tends very much the other way.

"So what happened?"

"What happened was, virtually the day after we got married, which was the day after the shoot, Jack started pushing me away, literally, as in, go back to Ireland, go back and find a house, our Irish house. And he'd come over when there was a break in postproduction. And I thought that was really nice, and I went back, and I found this place, quite near where my mother lived, I picked it because it had an L.A. kind of feel to it, and he said he loved it, and bought it within six weeks, and he never came back, he said he was under too much pressure and what was the problem and all the documents were made out in my name. And I was kind of so giddy with the excitement and the stress of it, that I didn't notice how weird it was. To buy a house without even looking at it. But at the time, I was like, hey, these movie directors, they're wild and crazy, they're so different from us. I thought, if this is going to work, it's going to work in a way I've never encountered before. The only thing was, he wasn't there, and pretty soon I was having trouble even getting him on the phone because he was so busy. And you know, shooting a movie he'd had time to start an affair with me, but editing the thing he's suddenly under pressure? I don't think so. And I started to feel a bit foolish, you know? All my friends were, what's the deal? Where's your husband? I mean, you get married, it's a public thing, right? So I flew out to L.A., unannounced . . . you're nodding your head, what, did he tell you?"

"He told me, yeah."

"He did? What did he tell you?"

"He told me that you walked in on him . . . with somebody else."

"Is that what he said? Well, I guess that would make it more understandable. No, I walked into the house on Amalfi Drive and he was sitting in a chair, looking out the window, down across the hills to Pacific Palisades, that view I'd been looking forward to, that I'd heard all about. And he turned to me—he didn't even get up—and he said, 'Hi.' Not 'Hi, Geri,' not 'Why didn't you tell me you were coming,' not 'I can't believe you're here!' Hi. Like I'm . . . I'll tell you exactly what it was like, like I'm someone he met on holiday and told, if you're ever in L.A., be sure and drop in, knowing there's no way the person would. Well, the person did. And he completely ignored me. Wouldn't even talk to me for the first evening, he showed me to a bedroom and vanished. I was just wondering, is he depressed? What's the matter with him?

"The next day, I get up, he's outside by the pool, I go out, and he's ready to talk. But all he has to say is, he gets really low after a shoot, it's a big comedown, it's better if he's left alone to regroup. And I ask him if he wants me to go back to Dublin, and he says he thinks that would be best. And I ask him—this is such a surreal situation, I swear to God, I've just gotten up, I'm by this pool, you can see down the hills to the Pacific Ocean, and I'm talking to this man who I thought I wasn't so keen on, and it's obvious he doesn't want me anywhere near him, I mean, how did this happen to my life?—I ask him if he wants a divorce. And he says yes, he thinks that would be best. And I say, what about the house? And he says, it's in your name, it's paid for, keep it. And he named a sum he wanted to offer in maintenance. And I said, no way, I don't need maintenance, I won't accept any, it's bad enough I get the house.

"Well, that was even more surreal, three hours, he becomes animated, it's like he grew back into himself, the old Jack, energy and wit and verve, calling his lawyer to draw up papers, all in the service of making me take some alimony. I say I don't want a penny. He eventually convinces me to accept by claiming I'll save him money, because any divorce attorney worth his salt would screw him for five times what he's offering, so I say yes and ask for a taxi to LAX. And the divorce is handled like the house purchase was, documents couriered back and forth. He drove me to the airport, and he cried when he said goodbye. And then we didn't have any contact in five years. And every month, the maintenance payments. Do you understand Jack Donovan? Because I sure as hell don't."

I shake my head, and trust that my face is a reliable guide to my feelings, which are genuinely and decidedly that I don't either. Geri shoots a smile in my direction that is just a little too bright, and that flashes off abruptly like she has turned a switch, and suddenly all that's left in her eyes is wounded pride, and confusion, and loss. Well-heeled loss, for sure, the kind of loss that people who in the last year had lost things like their pension, their job or their home would gladly plump for. But loss is loss wherever you sit, and it doesn't much care how worthy you are of universal sympathy. I nod at Geri, encouraging her to pick up her strange Hollywood tale.

"It was just bizarre, afterward. I think a lot of people, a lot of my so-called friends, thought I was fantasizing about the whole thing. But the divorce went on the record, you can't do it in secret. So they thought I'd snared the ultimate catch, especially for an actress, and royally blown it. Around then, it occurred to me that to suit my new life, I needed a new set of friends. Or at least, I needed to cut the old ones loose. And I tried to get back to normal, or to what had passed for normal. It was tricky though. The kind of theater companies that used to give me acting work thought I was some kind of rich bitch now and wouldn't give me the steam. And I was invited onto the boards of all these charities, you know, the ones for AIDS and MS that all the businessmen's wives organize, so they must have thought the same. So it was tricky. I know, I didn't exactly have it tough. But it was . . . here's the thing, having been unsure about Jack,

I'd found, during the time away from him, that I had completely fallen for him. So that trip to L.A. . . . the way he kept me at a distance, the way he humiliated me . . . it shook me. I . . . I didn't see anyone, I didn't see another man for years, I didn't have a relationship. I . . . I went from being a silly little girl to, to someone who thought her life was over.

"And of course, I was self-indulgent, I could afford to be, I didn't have to pull myself together and put on a face for the world, I could let the whole thing drift. Drift, that's the word. And then . . . and then I regrouped, to an extent, I got a couple of jobs, I got a small part in *Fair City,* and it was coming up to Christmas, and I went out to a club.

"And there was Jack."

"And everyone was whispering, you know, the people I was with, the cast were whispering, because it was still like some urban myth, like, remember people used to say Stan Laurel was Clint Eastwood's father. Type of thing, that was what me and Jack were, a fucking urban myth. And the town had to be Dublin.

"And we were all in a booth, and he was at the bar, giving it Life and Soul Jack, you know, Brendan Behan Jack, this was after *Man in the High Castle* and Jack Was Back, and all I could think was, is there a window I could crawl out, maybe I could hide in the ladies' until he leaves, why hasn't he gone in behind the velvet rope with Bono and the Corrs, and everyone with me is ever so subtly ignoring him by staring at him nonstop with blank expressions on their faces like they don't know who he is, and finally, inevitably, Jack spots me, and his face, well, he looks pleased, and there's a lull in the music, I find out afterward because he asks the DJ to stop playing, and he heads for me, and as he's walking he starts singing, that thing Pavarotti used to sing at the World Cup in Italy—"

"*Nessun dorma.*"

"That's the one, he's singing that, and everyone's looking,

at him, and all the celebs are piling out to see what's happening, and people are clearing a path as he goes, and he's heading straight to our booth, and everyone's looking at him, and then everyone's looking at me. And he hits the top, the high C, is it, and everyone is clapping, and he goes down on his knees in front of me and says, mouths, really, in a whisper: *'Forgive me. Forgive me. Forgive me.'"*

Geri Foster pauses, full, high at the memory, visibly moved.

"A Hollywood moment," I say.

"A moment of pure bullshit," she says with considerable passion, but her face is glowing and her eyes shine. "Why do we fall for his bullshit, Ed?"

I smile, and shake my head, and she answers her own question.

"Because reality isn't enough for us. Or too much for us. And Jack is so good at making it seem as if we can break its bonds. There was everyone clapping and cheering. It was very hard to resist. Too hard for me."

"You got back together."

"And I got pregnant."

"Jack thinks you were pregnant to begin with."

"Jack . . . Jack has five-year-old twin girls he hasn't seen. He says they're not his. Isn't that what he told you? Jackie and Joanie. You know what that was, that was the week we spent here. He said if I had a baby boy, I was to call him Jack. And I said, what if I had twins? And he said, well then, Jack and John. And I said, what if they were girls? And he didn't say anything, so I said, Jackie and Joanie. But God Almighty, do you think I called them that, after what he put me through? He kept referring to them by those names, as if I was trying to, I don't know, trade off his name. He says they're not his. But every year, on their birthday, he transfers what anyone would call a substantial sum into my account. They could get through Harvard on what he's given them so far. But he's in Dublin for ten weeks and he won't see them. What do you think that says about Jack Donovan? I'll tell you what it says, that he's a fucking disgrace, that's what, a disgrace with a guilty conscience. Because if he genuinely thought those girls weren't his, why would he do that? But this way makes us all . . . degraded. I haven't touched a fucking penny of it. And you know, I tried to get out of the marriage without taking a penny, why would I turn into some fucking breadhead chippy now?"

"Why didn't you just have a paternity test?"

"Why the fuck should I? How dare he? He made the running! Each time he's approached me, and then he's run away. Why is that my fault? Why does he have the right to accuse me of being some gold-digging whore who'd . . . this, yes, can you believe this story, who'd get pregnant by another man, and then go to a nightclub to snare a man she doesn't even know is going to be there, who in any case hasn't spoken to her in five years, but who will inexplicably get the hots for her there and then and go home and spend a week in bed with her expressly so that she can claim he's the father of her child. Fuck off! I mean, I know the plots of Jack's movies aren't his forte, but that wouldn't even work for a porno. He's . . . and it's up to me to prove I'm not! How is it up to me? How dare he?"

Geri shakes with anger. I can't answer her, largely because I agree with her. The revelation that Jack is paying her extra money for the children makes me want to throw the money he paid me in his face and tell him to sort out his own problems with the aid of people who are actually qualified to deal with them. It strikes me all the more forcibly that he has manufactured the letters himself, that he is having some kind of elaborate nervous breakdown and that there is very little I can do for him, particularly since he is not going to be frank with me.

Geri has moved from rage to tears; it's as if someone has cut the strings holding her up; she crumples onto the couch, weeping. I don't think she wants to cry on my shoulder, but apart from that, it's the same old Jack Donovan scene. I want to leave, but I can't move. I feel responsible. And there is one more question I need to ask.

"I'm sorry," Geri says, breathing deeply. "I'm really sorry, I just . . . I was so stupid to, to hope . . . to hope that, because Jack was going to be shooting here, he might at least want to see the girls. So stupid. I even hoped, maybe, because he'd sent you around . . . it's the hope that . . . that's the worst thing, isn't it? Because there hasn't been anyone else, you know. People think I'm weird. 'You've got to get on with your life,' they say. But I've two girls to look after, and anyway . . . actually, never mind the girls, the girls have nothing to do with it, who decided the normal thing is, when one relationship doesn't work out, get another one that will? What does that say about the relationship . . . I hate that word . . . what does that say about love? About your heart? That it's like something you buy, and if it doesn't work out, or no longer suits, you can return it to the store and get a replacement? That it's inexhaustible? I think if your heart is inexhaustible, it means you haven't been using it right. That you've never really been in love. We used to read stories about women who died for love. About widows who would never look at another man. But now, women say, forget him, move on, he's not worth it. But love isn't about the other person being worth it. It's about what you give. You have no right to expect anything in return. I'm sorry. You want to say something. Here endeth the lesson."

"Geri, did Jack . . . was Jack ever violent to you?"

"No. No, never, never a hint of it. Why?"

"When he broke down crying, remember, and said there were some things he could never be forgiven for, what do you think that was about?"

"I don't know. But it never occurred to me that he would be violent. Why?"

"I just . . . needed to ask."

"No. And I've been with men . . . with one man, who was, so I have an antenna for it? I never got the slightest vibe that way from Jack. He's a mad wayward bastard and a cruel, coldhearted prick, but he wouldn't lift his hand to you, I'm sure of that."

. . . and Amanda's hand flashed to her cheek so that I wouldn't see the bruising on her face. . .

I stood up.

"I have to go. Thank you for talking to me. I'm sorry to have brought all this up. It's no consolation, I know, but for what it is worth, I think Jack has behaved very badly."

Geri Foster stands too, and wipes her face with her hands and looks at me with anxious, grateful eyes, and I see again how worn away her confidence has become, how underneath the careless facade she had presented when I arrived is a woman whose life has been flung every which way by Jack Donovan's genuine carelessness. The tang of Jo Malone perfume catches me again, and heightens the sense I have of outrage on a woman's behalf by making it personal. I think of Anne's girls asking me what life was like in the olden days. It seems to me that Geri Foster could tell them a thing or two about what love had been like then, the kind of love that puts its object before itself, that is selfless, that deals in sacrifice. They'd probably understand that as the kind of love a parent has for a child, but not that a woman could, or indeed, should, have for a man.

"Do you think Jack is mentally ill?" Geri says, and the degree of solicitude she exhibits for the man she has been railing against moments earlier is poignant.

"I wouldn't be qualified to make a judgment like that," I say. "But it seems to me that, as I said earlier, Jack is experiencing a certain amount of unease about key aspects of his life, you being probably the most significant. And while he doesn't seem to want to tell either of us directly what he thinks or what he wants to do, it appears he's maybe hoping we can figure it out and . . . I don't know, somehow solve it for him. I don't know."

I'm not used to confiding in the people I interview on behalf of a client, but then, I'm not used to trusting them more than I do the client. Geri Foster sees me to the door, and I thank her and wish her well.

"Tell Jack . . . despite what he might think . . . I know he's in love with his own guilt, with his own shame . . . tell him I'd like to see him. And tell him the names of his children, Alice and Daisy. Tell him their names, would you?"

I say that I will. And as I stand in the doorway with Geri Foster, I feel the hope that her love brings, and I join in it, in hoping that Jack will see her, and see his children, hope for that, at least. This June afternoon, as the sun spills through the front door of Geri Foster's darkened house, it doesn't feel like too much to ask.

CHAPTER 12

My phone had rung a couple of times while I was in Geri's house; I had set it to silent. There's a photo message that looks like spray-painted graffiti on a concrete wall, but I can't make out the details. The call I had missed has a 610 area code; the message I retrieve is from my ex-wife in L.A., saying she needs to speak to me, nothing bad, but the sooner the better. I hadn't heard from her in a while. There was a time that I couldn't speak to her at all, couldn't hear the sound of her voice without remembering the death of our daughter, and the way she had betrayed me. I resented the life she had made with another man, the man with whom, it turned out, she had always been in love. I resented the son they had had together, the happiness she had found. But I had gotten past my resentment before it destroyed me; I had wished her well and meant it, and we had stayed in touch. I've never been much of a letter writer, and that extends into my not being much for sending e-mail, but she knows this, and is happy to send me long missives and receive my perfunctory responses. Lately, for one reason or another, mainly the frequency with which she has begun to reminisce about our marriage, I have started to wonder whether her domestic life is as happy as it had been, and that is very much on my mind as I get the Amazon on the road and call her.

"Good morning."

"Ed. Thanks for calling back so soon."

"You're welcome. It's what time there? Eight? Early."

"Not when you've a four-year-old boy."

"Right."

"Hey, I was thinking about you a few days ago."

"I should hope you think of me every hour on the hour."

"That would be the four-year-old."

"What's so special about being four? I was four. Piece of cake. And it only lasts a year."

"I'll just go out and come in again, shall I? 'I was thinking about you a few days ago.'"

"'Really? How come?'"

"There's this new Sandra Bullock movie, where she has a nude scene."

"The things these women do for attention. Is she not afraid her mother might see that?"

"And I thought of *Speed,* remember? Seeing it on opening day down in Third Street Promenade? Can't remember was it the Laemmle or Mann's. That was her first big movie. And our first big date."

"I do remember. It lasted an entire weekend. The book says you're not supposed to do that on the first date, big or otherwise."

"I mustn't have finished that book. Or maybe some of the pages were stuck together in mine. An entire weekend, you say."

"That's the kind of girl you were. I wasn't complaining."

"And then we didn't see each other for five years."

"You were too impressed by me. You were scared I was out of your league. You were—"

"You were screwing the blonde who murdered your boss."

"Yes. Well. Nobody's perfect."

"Ed, I got a call this morning from Donald Coover. You remember him?"

"Don Coover. LAPD detective? Robbery homicide?"

"That's the guy. Says he's with the Cold Case Unit now."

"Still part of the same division. He call you?"

"He was looking for you. I think he thought you might still be in town."

"Did he say what it was about?"

"No. He said you'd know, it was something you'd remember. But you'd need to call him fast, as it was . . . I think he said this, it was going to break big."

"Wow. Okay. I'm out and about, could you text me his number?"

"I'll send you his desk and his cell. He's going to be out and about himself today. When he thought you were gonna be here, he was hoping you could come out with him, out to Point Dume."

We might have said some other stuff to each other, but I have no idea what, and any notion I might have held of gleaning something about the condition of her romantic life had gone out the window. All I can think is the following: that I first met Don Coover at the Detective Support Division in Parker Center, where he was toiling in the Missing Persons Unit, some sort of career bottleneck before he made the grade at Robbery Homicide. I reported the three extras who went missing from the *Ocean Falls* set at Point Dume State Beach. Coover took their details, and they went into the system, and that's where they had stayed. And now he wants to meet me at Point Dume.

I hold off until I get back to Holles Street; I don't want to be at the mercy of international cell phone reception. I get into my office and sit behind my desk and make the call.

"Coover."

"Detective, it's Ed Loy."

"Ed Loy. Long time. How's life treating you in the Emerald Isle? My wife and I have wanted to visit for years."

"My advice is, get here soon, before they close the place down."

"I heard that. I heard you folks had a hell of a party all right."

"Someone told us the bar was free. Now the bill is here. Where is that guy?"

"I hear you. I think we need to find that guy in California, too."

"I heard you were out in Malibu this morning, Don. What is that, a day on the beach? Are you out on your yacht? Maybe *you're* that guy."

"I wish. No, I'm out here on a bluff above Point Dume State Beach, Ed. I have a small unit digging the earth at a set of co-ordinates, one of the map references I was given. They are in the process of uncovering at least one, and more likely what I suspect are three sets of human remains."

"Three bodies?"

"Is my belief."

"You think it's the three girls?"

"That was quick. I think it could be. I don't have . . . I checked missing persons for Malibu going back twenty years, they're the only ones who connect as a trio."

"Desiree, Janice and Polly?"

"You remember the names."

"You always remember the ones that got away. Funny, Jack Donovan is in Dublin right now, shooting a movie. I'm working a case for him and Maurice Faye. Just the same as fifteen years ago."

"That's a coincidence all right."

A coincidence. I wonder if Don Coover believes in coincidence. I don't.

"So you said, a map reference you were given? How where you given it?"

"Anonymous tip-off to Parker Center. Requested me specifically. I'm assuming . . . hold up a second there, Ed."

I hear the low burr of the breeze off the ocean. It blows cold down the line, colder than it ever gets in Malibu.

"All right: we've got three heads."

"Jesus."

"They were buried in the earth together, no wrappers or tarps, so we're talking bones here. Need to wait on DNA for an ID, unless we can find something in there that will point the way."

"Anything else in the message?"

"Yeah, the . . . I don't know, too early to say if this is some sort of tag, you know, like the killer's signature, or is it literally three bodies in one grave, but there's the expression, 'Three-in-One, One-in-Three.' That's the Holy Trinity, three persons in one God, right? Ed? You still there?"

I'm still here. I'm simply struck dumb.

"Hold up, looks like we've got something else. Here, I'll keep you on the line. They're removing it now, looks like a . . . it's wrapped in plastic. It's . . . it's a crucifix. One of those, you know they sell them in all the antique stores up in Santa Barbara, it's Spanish Mission style, plain soft wood with a mild stain, unvarnished, rough-hewn, asymmetrical . . . oh boy. Oh boy."

I hear voices now, an urgent conference, sense excitement mounting.

"What? Don? What is it?"

"What it is, maybe we don't have to wait for DNA to have some idea of what we're talking about. We've got, on the reverse of the cross, someone has marked the head and the two arms with a knife, and then stained in ink, or used a pen to dig deep into the wood, either way, the marks are of three initial letters: D, J, and P."

D for Desiree LaRouche, J for Janice Holloway, P for Polly Styles. The names of the lost girls.

CHAPTER 13

I try to get Don Coover to talk to me some more, but he closes the call too quickly. I don't blame him; there would be a circus at Point Dume soon enough, with media helicopters roaring above the bluff; only a matter of time until I can watch it on TV. It was good of Coover to have included me at all; he didn't have to; it wasn't as if I had anything crucial to bring to the table that morning. I asked him why he had wanted me along for the dig, so to speak.

"You're the one who connected those girls, and you're the only one who gave a damn about them, Ed. Nobody else ever reported them missing. Nobody else noticed they were lost. Although no doubt once the TV gets going on the Three-in-One Killer, all manner of traumatized parents and siblings will emerge, weeping and wailing for the cameras like a bunch of bought-and-paid-for whores."

The Three-in-One Killer. That was the first time I'd heard

it, Coover the first person to have said it. Within twenty-four hours, it would feel like we'd never lived in a world without it. The thing I didn't get to say, the thing that was on the tip of my tongue to ask when Coover abruptly rang off amid the sound of approaching sirens, was about the map reference. He said he had a unit at Point Dume digging at a set of coordinates, and described them as "one of" the map references he was given. Initially I assumed this meant the same thing, that the map references were two or more coordinates. But it could mean that this is one of several locations where the killer had buried bodies. I call Coover back but his phone goes straight to message. I ask him my question, but I don't expect him to call me back. Either way, I know I will find out soon enough: this is not a story that's going to unfold in secret.

I look at the photo message on my phone again, but it's still unclear; I open my laptop and send it via Bluetooth so I can view it in enlarged form.

The image is of my mother and father's roughcast granite headstone in Shanganagh Cemetery. The headstone has been defaced with a spray-painted amendment:

ED LOY RIP JUNE 2009

I phone the Garda station in Shankill, the cemetery itself and the stoneworks nearby who had carved the headstone and report the act of desecration. I suggest to the Garda on duty in Shankill that this probably has something to do with the imminent release of Podge Halligan, and he says, "Podge who?," and I put the phone down. I call Tommy Owens and ask him if Jenny Noble is safe. Then I tell him what has happened, and ask him to talk to Leo Halligan. Then I go into the kitchen and pour myself a glass of Tanqueray over ice and splash some bitters and squeeze a wedge of lime. I look at the drink, and I think of the Three-in-One Killer, and of the lost girls in Point Dume, and of Nora Mannion and Kate Coyle, and of everything I have done so far and everything I need to do. Then I pour the gin down the sink. This does not make me feel any better.

By the time Leo Halligan calls, I am in the Volvo on the way to Quarry Fields, where the house I grew up in has just been burned to the ground.

"Ed."

"My mother's grave, Leo."

"I'm sorry, Ed. If he's changed at all, it's for the worse."

"My mother's *grave*? My *house*?"

"I'm sorry."

"What are you gonna do?"

"What can I do? I can't move against him, he's my brother."

"You and George bullied him into pleading guilty. Why doesn't he burn down your houses? Is he out yet?"

"I'm down here at the Four Courts waiting for the fucker."

"So all this is by remote control? Don't you think the least I deserved was a warning?"

"He's not doing any of this through me, Ed. He doesn't level with me or George, he has his own crew, always had. The dregs of the dregs, they make the common or garden scumbag look like Brad Pitt. You had your run-ins with them Ed, beyond in Redlands."

Redlands. George Halligan's house. Trapped in a garage with Podge's men. Dessie Delaney. Nose Ring, no longer with us. And Blue Cap, whose nose I broke. I had forgotten all about him. But the face takes shape in my mind—a face I have seen somewhere recently.

"Leo, George's security company, Immunicate, is that still to be had?"

"Still going strong. Or at least, its books are very healthy, if you know what I mean. But no, it does all right. I think it's doing the security up there on Dorset Street for your buddy's movie."

A face I saw today, when its owner grinned at me as he shot me with his two-way radio.

"Working a case, Ed, are you?" Leo says.

"I am, yeah, which is why I don't need this. Of course, that's not the only reason I don't need this."

"Dangerous case, yeah?"

"Always the potential for danger, Leo."

"You might be wise to carry a piece, Ed. For this completely separate case you're working."

"I might be . . . what?"

"Unmarked, semiautomatic, compact, lightweight. No way of tracing it."

"You're offering—"

"For self-defense. In this completely separate case. Because many of us believe self-defense, aggressive, first-strike self-defense, would make all our lives a lot easier. In general. And, if necessary, in particular."

I say nothing for a while. Leo is suggesting I take Podge out. That isn't something I can even consider doing. On the other hand, the only way Podge has of raising the stakes is to mount an attack on me, so a weapon would not go amiss.

"I could use that. Leo, is Tommy safe from Podge?"

"No one is safe from the cunt. Fuck, here he is now, I've got to go. How will I get that thing to you? It wouldn't be wise for us to meet up."

"You know where I live, Leo. Does Podge?"

"I don't know, Ed. I don't know."

I DON'T STAY long in Quarry Fields. I speak to the fire brigade and thank them for their service. I make sure that my tenants, Maria and Anita Kravchenko, are safe, and that they have somewhere else to stay. They can bunk in with friends in the short term, they tell me. I promise to help them find something more secure when I can. I see a couple of neighbors I remember from childhood, now very elderly, staring across the road at the smoke. They knew my parents, and would doubtless remember me if I approached them. I don't want to talk to them. I don't want to let the reality of what has happened infiltrate my consciousness. A Garda car from Dun Laoghaire arrives, and I chat briefly to the two uniforms. At least they know who Podge Halligan is, and are familiar with most of his crew; one, Sergeant Mary Fleming, worked with Dave Donnelly, and is familiar with the part I played in capturing Podge. I ask Fleming if she remembers an associate of Podge's who wore a blue baseball hat; she asks if he's the one whose nose I broke in Hennessy's pub, and I nod. Fleming tells me his name is Brian Joyce, and he has a record that started when he was twelve and kept on spinning: on top of the usual drug offenses, he has convictions for sexual assault and rape. I tell the Guards about the desecration of my parents' headstone, and they say they will alert all units to challenge any of Podge's gang on sight. I thank them for the support, although I know it doesn't amount to much in practical terms: if Podge wants to kill me, short of my going into hiding, he won't be short of opportunities.

The flames in the house have been extinguished, for the most part, although one occasionally sputters into life. When I find that my eyes are smarting and starting to stream, I tell myself that it's the smoke, get in my car and leave. On my way back into town I call Tommy Owens.

"Tommy, it's Ed. Listen, they've burned down Quarry Fields."

"They've what? The fucking *bastards*. I'll call Leo—"

"I've already spoken to him. There's a limit to what he can do. In the meantime, you're a target."

"No way."

"You're a way to get to me."

"If they burn this house down—"

"I'm not so worried about houses. Jenny Noble—"

"She's fine, Ed, Naomi's here with her. Oh no—"

"Is exactly my point. Is Paula around?"

"Yeah, she dropped Naomi over sure."

"Better drop them both back, Tommy, and fast. Would they know where Paula lives?"

"She just moved to Enniskerry, some haulage contractor. But they're after you, they're after me; Podge's crew aren't going to be chasing Naomi, or Jenny Noble."

"You're right. Take a taxi anyway."

"To Enniskerry?"

"I'll cover it. Have you got somewhere to go?"

"Sure I do, Ed. It's a place called watching your back."

"You don't need to—"

"You gave me a grand and a half, Ed. So far, I've sat around all afternoon while Jenny and Naomi watch *Bones* and *America's Next Top Model*. Even with my relaxed work ethic, that's called taking the piss. They'll be safe out with Paula, if your snatcher tries to come near he'll get more than he bargained for, rottweilers and electric fences they've got, I don't think your man is a hundred percent legit, to be honest with you. But I'll be on you, know what I mean man? Don't forget, I owe Podge myself, nothing'd give me greater satisfaction than to see him go down."

I DRIVE STRAIGHT to the *Nighttown* set. Maurice Faye has given me a pass so I can park in the yard. I drive through and find a spot and get out. I spot Brian Joyce almost immediately, and as soon as he sees me approaching him, smiling, making a gun of my hand and shooting at him, he begins to run. He can't run as fast as I can. I catch him before we hit the street and nudge him headlong into the wall and hold the back of his head and tap his face off the wall a few times, or maybe more than a few times; no one has ever established satisfactorily what the difference between *a few* and *too many* is, but I possibly extend the terms of the debate. In time, a couple of Joyce's security colleagues, who sound Russian, get hold of me and secure my arms and frog-march me into the back of an unmarked security truck where a large man with a shaved head sits at a bank of screens. He wears a black T-shirt with IMMUNICATE SECURITY printed on the left breast, like a designer logo; attached to the right breast he has a badge with *Head of Security—Barry Holmes* written on it.

"I seen everything. Call the Guards," Barry Holmes says.

"I don't think so," I say.

Instead of answering, he stands up and punches me hard in the stomach. I expect it, so I manage to hold on to some air, but it still hurts like hell. He shapes up to bring some blows into my head.

"Brian Joyce is a member of Podge Halligan's gang and a con-victed sex offender," I say.

Barry Holmes looks at me, then waves his Russian operatives out the door.

"All right lads, I have this one. Everyone as they were. See Brian's all right, ha?"

The Russians leave, and I turn to follow.

"Where the fuck d'you think you're going?" Holmes says, tugging at my arm. "I can't have you just throwing your weight around like that."

I don't turn around, though every sinew of me yearns to, yearns to turn and head-butt his fat face until his nose gives. But I think of the gin I poured down the sink, and I tell myself to play it smart for once, and I bite my lip and take a deep breath.

"I don't know what the lines between the Halligans and Im-municate are like these days. In other words, I don't know who told you to turn a blind eye to the hiring of a convicted sex of-fender and criminal gang member like Brian Joyce. So I'll give you the benefit of the doubt: that somebody told you to employ him, and to ignore the basic vetting procedures you'd normally use. Am I right? Because frankly, I'm happy to call the cops myself if it turns out you're one of Podge Halligan's men too, and more than happy to let Maurice Faye and every actress and female crew member know a rapist is loitering around the set looking up their skirts."

I turn now and look in Barry Holmes's eyes. They're ugly gray eyes, flecked with red. They look mean, and they look scared.

"All I know is the connection with George, George Halligan," he says. "He's not supposed to be involved but everyone knows he is, type of thing. And occasionally you find a place on a job for someone, you just don't do the paperwork for them. Joyce was one of those. I . . . I wasn't happy, I knew what he done, I asked about it, word came back, it's for Podge. And Podge is getting out, so everyone's on red alert."

The yelp of a siren sounds outside. I look quizzically at Holmes. He looks at the screens.

"Ambulance. He needs it."

"Could have walked him to the Mater from here. Not cut out for the job."

Holmes almost smiles at that one.

"Podge is out. Today. This afternoon," I say.

Barry Holmes's eyes widen.

"And you choose now to break his boy's face? What have you got, a death wish?"

"May be. I'm off the drink as well, so that's done nothing to help my mood. But he threatened me, and then my parents' grave was vandalized and their house was burned down, so I'm not at my most magnanimous. I'm asking you: Have you any connection to Podge?"

"No."

"Any other member of your crew?"

"No."

"Right so. You'll need to think of a cover story for this."

"Cover story for you?"

"Cover story for *you*, the man who hired a rapist. Because I don't mind telling Maurice Faye. And then you'll be out of a job."

I make to leave, then turn back.

"Just so everyone is clear: my name is Edward Loy. Very fussy about credits in the movie business."

CHAPTER 14

Maurice Faye is waiting for me when I get off the Immunicate truck, shaking his head and beaming. Down the lane, I see Brian Joyce being helped by his colleagues into an ambulance.

"Jesus Christ, Ed, you're an awful man," he says. "What happened?"

"Barry Holmes'll tell you."

And indeed, Barry Holmes is at my heel, and takes Maurice Faye aside and speaks quietly to him for a moment, until Maurice nods him away and laughs loudly and claps me on the shoulder and ushers me around the corner and down a set of steps and into the basement at the rear of one of the three houses. We're in a cold, damp room whose walls have been painted a deep, burgundy red; the ceiling is navy; the floorboards are white.

"Art students," Maurice says by way of explanation. "House was all in bedsits. State of the place. If they'd done these up ten years ago, would have made a mint. Too late now. Good for us though."

Through an open door, two girls are photocopying different colored pages of script and fastening them together in rainbow sequences. Maurice shuts the door and sits against the table in the corner of the room that houses his laptop and an unwieldy satchel spilling contracts and scripts. He picks up his phone and holds it out for my inspection.

"Good news, Ed. These came in about ten minutes ago."

Maurice shows me two text messages:

Copped off w/ two fine things all luvved up back tomor
sorry for hassul gurlz I b gurlz xox kc

Embracing inner slut thanx to kate c sorry if we messed
up hope not fired but heard about fun and wanted to
have some N x

As I read them, two text messages arrive on my phone: the same messages. I look quizzically at Maurice Faye.

"They sent them to Jenny, Jenny Noble. She's passing them on."

I ring Jenny's number as it appeared in the text.

"Jenny Noble?"

"Jenny, it's Ed Loy. We spoke this morning."

"Ah God, did you get the girls' texts? Major relief, yeah? The dirty yokes! I got your number from Mr. Owens, and I forwarded them to Maurice and Madeline as well. God, I hope they don't get fired, but they deserve a right rocket!"

"Did you call them?"

"I called them both, just to get the gossip. Their phones went straight to message."

"Did you text replies?"

"Of course."

"What did you say?"

"Eh. What, like in detail? We were getting a bit girls only, if you know what I mean."

"Never mind about that. Did you tell them where you were?"

"Did I tell them where we were? God, not sure if I know where we are. In a car somewhere. Enniskerry? On our way to Enniskerry, Naomi says, to her mum. Because Mr. Owens has to go and work for you."

"That's right. Did they ask where you were?"

"Hang on. I've got a couple more messages."

There's a brief pause and then Jenny Noble comes back on the line.

"Yeah, they've both just asked where I am—if I've been fired, or am I on the skite, too, am I at home or what."

"Okay. Jenny, listen to me. I hope those texts are from the girls. But there is a possibility that they're not, that whoever abducted the girls is using their phones to try and trap you. Could you please just not reply to any more of their messages? Jenny?"

"Oh My God. Okay. You're freaking me out there, Ed Loy."

"You're perfectly safe. And I hope they are, too. But just to make sure, all right?"

"All right. No more texts?"

"No more texts. And I'll let you know if anything comes up."

I close the call. Maurice Faye is shaking his head, but this time he's not beaming.

"Ah Jaysus, Ed, you're some fussy fucker, is nothing good enough for you? Text messages from the girls?"

"But they're not available to talk. Did you hear what I said to Jenny? Do I have to repeat it?"

I don't take much care with the tone of this response, and a glitter appears in Maurice's eyes.

"Ed, go easy man. First, you're busting heads, now you're going off at me—"

"I'm going off at you? You employ a rapist as a security man.

You show me text messages from the girls and you think everything is fine. Are you fucking stupid? Do you think I am? Where *are* the girls? You're so fucking relieved, how much have they cost you today, Maurice? Thousands? Tens of thousands? Why aren't you screaming at them to get in here?"

"The schedule's already been altered, we don't need them today."

"That's convenient. How do I know you didn't send those texts?"

"How do you know I didn't kidnap the girls, is that what you're asking?"

"Yes, it is."

"Because I'm telling you I didn't. Is that good enough?"

"I suppose it'll have to be. For now."

Maurice is very still. He looks at me as if I am volatile material, which in some way I seem to be. Maybe I should have taken it out on Barry Holmes.

"I've sent Nora and Kate a message, telling them to report to the set immediately," Maurice says.

"Good. Any sign of Nora's sister?"

"I wasn't keeping tabs on that . . . Madeline would know."

"All right. And I'll need to check out Club 92, I think that was Kate's regular haunt, see if anyone can remember spotting the girls there."

I look at Maurice and raise my eyebrows and make a face, as if to say, *I know it's not you.* I don't know this at all.

"How has your day been?" I say.

Maurice gives me a hard stare, but can't sustain it; he subsides into a what-can-you-do grin and rolls his eyes.

"Wouldn't you know who've chosen today to pop in on a flying visit, private fucking jet, two associate producers . . . you know how many associate producers there are on this movie? Well, neither do I. As many as . . . since none of them are worth a tuppenny fuck . . . someone's girlfriend, someone's stepson, someone's personal, yes, this is good, someone at Universal married his personal trainer, divorced her, and now she gets to be an associate producer . . . do they give these credits out as alimony? And then occasionally there's a couple of guys who have some knowledge of the business, and even of this particular film. Which is the case with these boys, but I don't want to talk to them about the schedule changes, or what they're going to cost, not yet, not in person. Will you come with us? I have to bring them out to dinner, Jack and a few of the actors. They'll like you, you'll be a change, someone who does a real job. You can distract them. Tell them some war stories. Anything but what happened today. Come out, Ed, bring your lady. Tell her Gabriel and Colin will be there."

"Will they be there?"

"If I can persuade them to go. They're very good about things like that, but you can't blame them if they'd rather go home."

"Are Conor Rowan and Mark Cassidy going to be there? I want to talk to them again about Point Dume."

"There you go again. Mark is coming. I don't know about Conor. But part of the point of this dinner is to keep the studio thinking everything in the garden is rosy, so if you're going to go on about Point fucking Dume all night . . ."

"Have you seen the news, Maurice? Turn on your laptop there, put Sky or the BBC or something up."

Maurice flips open his gray steel laptop.

"Takes a while for the old Wi-Fi to kick in, I think it's the damp in the walls myself. There we are. All right, Sky News . . . Bankers . . . Iran . . . Obama . . . Malibu Mass Grave, oh good Jesus . . ."

I walk around and took a look. There are photographs of the dig on the bluff above Point Dume Beach, with LAPD and media helicopters circling. There are photographs of body bags being wheeled across the grass on gurneys. There are photographs of two of the three girls, Desiree LaRouche and Polly Styles. There's a shot of Don Coover, who had been lean and blond fifteen years ago, and is now lean and gray. THREE-IN-ONE KILLER HAUNTS MALIBU ran the headline. The story doesn't tell me anything I don't know already—LAPD were led to the burial site by an anonymous tip-off. There is no mention of any other sites. Coover had not let it be known that the girls were extras on *Ocean Falls;* the bare LAPD release simply states that the girls had been reported missing in 1994. The Sky News report describes them as surfers. It's always difficult to know in these cases what has been leaked and what the press has gleaned from "sources," including old boyfriends and distant relations who want to get in on the act, the people Coover described as "bought-and-paid-for whores."

Maurice looks up at me, his eyes blurry with shock.

"That's as much as I know, Maurice. I spoke to Coover this morning. As far as I'm aware, he's not looking at the *Ocean Falls* company, at least not at this stage," I say. "Tell me, has anyone talked about Point Dume?"

"Not to me. Jack is all in the present tense, you know, I need it now, all he's been doing is getting it done. And Conor is reinforcing that all the time. So not a lot of room there for reminiscing."

"How about Mark Cassidy? I did mention it to both him and Conor."

Maurice yells a Mossy-laugh and claps his hands.

"Good question. And when you get the answer, send it to me on a postcard."

"Meaning what?"

"Meaning twenty years, I don't really know the same Mark. You probably know him as well as I do. Never stops working, no conversation except movies, doesn't seem interested in anything else. No kids, no family—"

"He told me this morning he was married."

"God, that's right. Is she Brazilian? South American somehow. Anyway, typical you'd forget, you'd rarely see her."

"I had always vaguely assumed he was gay."

"Same as myself. If he was anything. We used to make up stories for Mark, that he had a secret wife stowed somewhere, or that he was in the CIA and had to keep things undercover. International man of mystery. Lovely fella, mind."

And a welcome alternative to Jack as a candidate for the Three-in-One Killer. If I need to look for candidates. Although not the only one.

"How about Conor?"

"Conor does his job, and when he's not doing it, he goes home. Has a house up around Churchtown there, bigger version of what he grew up in not far from where he grew up in it. Sees mates he's had since school, goes to see Leinster, the Irish rugby team. There's the occasional lady, then there isn't. Not exactly the life and soul. Enjoys the few pints. Might be a bit of a drink issue there, just the face of him, taking its toll. But you'd never know from his work. Keeps . . . Jaysus, sounded like I was digging a grave for him there, 'keeps himself to himself' is what I was going to say. But he does."

Maurice looks at me, his expression poised somewhere between amused and aggressive.

"Well, Ed—that's Mark and Conor. And you know Jack. Do you want the full lowdown on me?"

"Maurice, I'm going to level with you. If it is the Three-in-One Killer in action here, I doubt that you're the guy."

"You doubt I'm the guy. But you're not sure?"

"I'll be sure when I get him. Or when Nora and Kate show up, and we can rest easy that he's not on the loose in Dublin. That's what you're paying me for, remember?"

"I remember."

"All right. I'll need to talk to the others again, watch their reactions. So what I want you to do, organize it tonight, wherever we're going . . . where are we going?"

"Eden, there in Temple Bar."

"All right. Can you contrive it that I'm sitting near Conor and Mark? And I want to talk to Jack beforehand—"

"Drinks in the Clarence at seven thirty. Don't mention the *Irish Times*."

"Why? What's in the *Irish Times*?"

"There's a column there today, your man who knows everything about everything, Derek Doyle, he's having a pop at Jack. After the *Late Late*. Fair enough, not Jack's finest hour, but still, this is mad stuff. Says Jack would be the most annoying Irishman alive today if it wasn't for Bono."

"That's very modest of Derek. Does he not think he has a claim on the title himself?"

Maurice nods, too morose for any Mossy-action now.

"He used to drink in the Norseman, you know, with all the Film Base crowd, Jack and the lads. He wanted to make movies too, made a couple of shorts. He was a friend of Jack's. I always thought he was a sneery piece of work, looking down his nose, but you know what Jack is like with people, as if life is an election campaign and he's conducting a never-ending canvass. But he didn't make it fast enough, Derek Doyle. He gave up and became a journalist.

"And now he turns around and he has a go at everyone who has succeeded from that time, filmmakers and writers and musicians and actors, no one's quite good enough for Derek, Derek's standards are too high altogether, you have to be from New York, or Finland, or Brazil to impress Derek. And it's all from this perspective, he's on the side of the little people, the man in the street. All these artists with their subsidies and their tax exemptions, let them pay their taxes in these hard times. And him forgetting he's sitting on a hundred grand a year from the paper and a pension and all this stuff we never had. And it's not even for me, or Jack, he can't really hurt us, it's people starting out, people in the early stages, he's on them like a ton of bricks, willing them to fail, like the worst kind of begrudger. You know, just once, I'd like to see someone nail the cunt, tell him the reason he's like this has nothing to do with, what, critical judgment or artistic standards, no, it's because deep down he knows he's a failure, you know, a fucking failure, he tried to be something, and he failed, and rather than accept it, and own it, he just lashes out at anyone who stayed in the game."

Maurice's face is red and his slender shoulders are shaking; I have never seen him like this. It's as if the pressures of the day have all been combined and laid at the door of the unfortunate Derek Doyle.

"I mean, we're shooting here, in Dublin, we're probably los-ing money as a result, the studio definitely is, but we made that decision, and fair play, the *Irish Times* has praised us and the film people there have always supported us, but this fucker treats us as if . . ."

Maurice's hands are raised into fists; I had never noticed be-fore, but compared to his slight build, they are unusually large. Noticing me staring at them, he seems to come to, and gives a snort of Mossy-laughter.

"Ah. Fuck him. Long day. And miles to go before we sleep. Just don't mention it to Jack, is all I'm saying."

"I'm sure some other kind soul has broken the good news to him by now."

CHAPTER 15

I try calling Madeline King, but her phone isn't picking up. On my way out, I pass a dark-headed woman who looks familiar.

"Nora? Nora Mannion?" But as soon as I say it, I realize my mistake.

"I'm Rose, her sister," the woman says, her voice low and uneasy.

"I'm Ed Loy. I've been hired to find her. Jenny Noble says she got text messages from Nora and Kate today."

"I heard nothing from Nora. What did they say?"

"That they'd gone out to a club, picked up two guys, had a big night."

Rose nods, trying to smile but not quite making it.

"Well, it's not like Nora, but there's a first time for everything. I just don't understand why she hasn't been in touch, I left three, four messages. So did Madeline sure. Have you seen Madeline? I was supposed to meet her an hour ago."

"I've just been trying to call her myself."

"I just . . . I don't know what to do. I've been out to Nora's house, there's no sign."

"All right. Come with me and we'll check on Madeline at least."

I walk Rose Mannion through the yard and down the steps and catch Maurice Faye holding two telephone conversations at the same time. He sends one of the office girls onto the set; she comes back minutes later to report that Madeline hasn't been seen since lunchtime.

Rose Mannion looks so dismayed by this news that I suggest she accompany me out to Leopardstown Racecourse where Club 92 is located. The beginning of rush hour, it isn't the greatest time to be immersing ourselves in traffic. Rose's face is drawn, and she is not keen to talk; I put on the radio to dispel at least some of the unease. Amid the grim welter of property debts and bank bailouts and imminent cuts in public spending and increases in tax, amid the hand-wringing reproaches and the somber predictions that things would have to get worse with no guarantee they would get better, amid the rotting carcass of the Celtic Tiger and the newfound humility at large in the little country that thought it could, but as it turned out, can't, the producers of RTE's *Drivetime* program probably thought an item on the discovery of bodies in a mass grave in Los Angeles would come as a welcome and exotic, if macabre, distraction. The LAPD statement now includes one new piece of information, which so distracts me that I run a red light. I realize Rose Mannion has not been paying any attention to the radio because she only flutters briefly into animated life when a barrage of horns are directed our way. She slumps back into her seat, and soon we are in Leopardstown, and I turn off the radio and park the car and sit for a moment and wonder, when the LAPD press office said that there were "at least five" other sites they were investigating, just where exactly those sites might be, and if the Three-in-One Killer was consistent, does that bring the body count to eighteen in total.

Club 92 doesn't open until eleven; however, behind the bar at Fillies, I find Aimee, an amiably mindless gum-chewing girl with streaky blond hair in an up-do, who I am told was working in the club the previous night. It doesn't take long. I show Aimee the photographs of the girls, and she identifies Kate Coyle immediately.

"That's Kate Coyle, Lady Kate. KC and the Sunshine Smile. She wasn't here last night, no way."

"How can you be sure?" I say. "I imagine it gets pretty crowded."

"Because KC is my best girl, yeah? Ray of Sunshine. Simply No Way she's gonna show and not let me know. Never seen the other girl. Nice eyes."

"You sure? Take a closer look," Rose says.

"I may be thick, but I'm not blind," Aimee says breezily. "If she'd been in with Lady Kate, I'd've noticed. Something to drink?"

I shake my head.

"Then sorrreee . . . can't help ya . . . see you again, yeah . . ." she says, sounding as if she thinks it unlikely, and moves back along the bar to people who aren't as anxious or as old.

Rose Mannion is staying with a friend in Leeson Street; I drop her on my way back to Holles Street; we exchange numbers and I tell her I'll let her know if anything came up. If anything, Rose is somewhat cheered by her encounter with Aimee: as she sees it, if the girls didn't go to the club, maybe what happened was that they both completely disrupted their routines. In that context, their continued absence is consistent with some kind of girls-go-wild type adventure. It's a theory, but I can't summon up a great deal of faith in it.

When I back-heel my apartment door behind me, I call Jenny Noble, who sounds irritated that I'm interrupting her viewing of a *Gilmore Girls* rerun. She asks distractedly if I've heard anything from the girls, but I can tell she has stopped worrying about them. I call Madeline King again, and again her phone just tells me to try again later. I text Anne Fogarty and tell her to get a babysitter, that she's going out to dine with movie stars.

I take a hot shower and then a cold one and shave and dress in the black linen suit and the white double-ply cotton shirt with the French cuffs and the silver death's-head links and the plain black oxfords from Church's. I apply some Hermès Eau d'Orange Verte, the cologne I wear in summer, and I floss and brush my teeth.

Then, none of that having made me feel in any way calmer, I call Madeline King's number for one last time. I get Jack Donovan on the phone, and, having established that he doesn't know where Madeline is either, I arrange to meet him half an hour early, down the road from the Clarence. When I reach for the Tanqueray to make the drink I'd wanted and poured away earlier, I see that Leo has been in my apartment and has left me a gift: a Glock 26 subcompact about the size of my hand, with ten rounds of 9mm ammunition in the magazine. If I need it.

I pour the Tanqueray over ice and splash the bitters and squeeze the lime and stand at the window where the mothers of newborns come and go and smoke and I think about what I'd thought today when I'd seen Jenny Noble, and compared her to the missing Kate Coyle and Nora Mannion: how like Madeline King they looked. And I think about what I'd been told today by Jack's sister and by his ex-wife, and I remember what I saw he had done in L.A., and I wonder if my friend is capable of murder, and not just a crime of passion, not just a rush of blood to the head: murder on a grand scale. It takes me another drink to realize I'm not going to feel any better until I know the truth, and a third to tamp down the vision of my parents' desecrated grave, and the embers of Quarry Fields, and the specter of Podge Halligan on my trail. I shut the door behind me and walk down into the street.

Nice Voice, Shame About the View

It is a truth universally acknowledged that the standard of guests on the *Late Late Show* has deteriorated in recent years. We all remember the glory days when a David Niven, a Jimmy Stewart, or a Peter Ustinov could hold the floor for an hour or more with a mixture of wit, charm and downright storytelling fairy dust. In fairness, their likes are rarely to be found anywhere nowadays, and the chortling self-congratulation and studied inarticulacy of the modern celebrity is a pale imitation. And while it is also true that, in days gone by, we Irish were not above parading ourselves as horrid cute *idiots savants,* tottering beneath the joint burdens of infinite charm and vast melancholy, shouldering with a smile and a song (diddley eye), a solemn recitation and a brave sigh, the unfeasible weight of Being Irish, nothing, not Bono claiming joint credit with David Trimble and John Hume for the Peace Process, not Charles J. Haughey asserting his birthright to all of Ireland's four provinces simultaneously, nothing comes close to the riot of national humiliation and Celtic burlesque that was Jack Donovan's appearance on the *Late Late* last Friday.

I sometimes wonder if Jack Donovan is actually a paid minion of the aforementioned Mr. Vox: when the lead singer of U2 is having an especially difficult time due to, oh I don't know, everyone occasionally catching up with the fact that he is a pompous, self-regarding, vain, bombastic, tax-dodging, patronizing, caterwauling, do-as-I-say-while-I-buy-a-yacht chancer (take your pick, but you don't have to—he doesn't), the preposterous spectacle that is Jack Donovan emerges from whatever primordial bog or Celtic mist he usually inhabits, talking about "our innate spirituality as a nation" and our "instinctual love of great poetry" and littering his speech with constructions such as "man alive" and "with the help of God" and "it's a long road that has no turn in it."

Jack Donovan was born in 1965 and grew up in Sandycove, a middle-class suburb of South County Dublin. He is not a native speaker of the Irish language who was lured from the Blasket Islands to the mainland by a raw hunk of meat. Even if he were, he would have learned how to speak Hiberno-English correctly, not in the affected manner he currently favors.

The only conclusion one can draw is that this must go over big in America, and that Mr. Donovan has neither the ability nor the wish to modulate his Darby O'Gill tendencies for the more tender native sensibilities. We had fondly thought that Irish America had grown more discerning in its ability to sort the Celtic corn from the Irish gold, but then we remember the title of Donovan's first film to receive American financing: *A Terrible Beauty.* God help us all. A Yeats quotation so hackneyed from overuse it had lost its meaning almost entirely fifty years ago, but Donovan shamelessly appropriates it and gets an Oscar nomination for his pains.

And the perpetuation of these risible clichés continues throughout the films—in *The Dain Curse,* adapted from the novel by the great detective story writer Dashiell Hammett, the hard-boiled Continental Op *quotes Yeats*—but then, in Donovan land, everyone is always quoting Yeats, or Joyce, or Synge, everyone is a poetry-talking misty-eyed romantic with a violent streak and a desperate weakness for the gargle.

He is an altogether ridiculous figure, Edna O'Brien with a beer belly, and the fact that—and I cannot deny it, he has the figures on his side, even the absurd *Last Anniversary* was a box-office smash in Ireland—he is second only to the equally pre-posterous Bono in our national affections means we evidently love to be lied to, and to lie to ourselves, about the nature of our great little country. (The ways in which Bono and Donovan resemble one another are so numerous as to border on the supernatural; one that is worth noting, to qualify the justified praise the *look* of Donovan's films receive, is that, just as Bono would be nothing without the Edge's melodic and technical genius, so Donovan's films owe what power and beauty they possess to the uncanny vision of his cinematographer, Mark Cassidy, their success to the dynamism of his producer, Maurice Faye, and, if we are to believe what highly placed sources tell us, their fluency to his undersung First Assistant Director, Conor Rowan.)

In Jack Donovan's Ireland, no one is living in poverty as a result of the abuse of power by politicians or businessmen, or a victim of sexual abuse because of the disgraceful behavior of the priests and religious of the institutional Catholic Church. No gunman is a violent savage, no priest a cold-eyed pedophile. In Donovan's Ireland, everyone is too febrile, too impassioned, everyone is on the brink of some melodramatic revelation—we nearly had sex, but you're my brother!—everyone is carrying eight hundred years of poetry and history and nonspecific wistfulness around, urgent but passive, like lovely, friendly, stupid dogs.

At the end of the show, our host, for whom I'd never thought I'd feel sympathy but who deserved the nation's last Friday, our beleaguered host, visibly wilting under the epic tide of bullshit, encouraged Donovan to sing. And in singing "Danny Boy," magnificently, to these nonaficionado ears, at least we had the consolation of discovering something positive about Jack Donovan: that his career as a film director has been a terrible loss to the world of music. If only we could say the same of Bono.

Every plan has its limits, and there is a point when you have to give fate, or chance, or luck its due and say, and pray: let the will of God guide me, for I have done what I can. The only person he knew that he could ask about Jenny Noble was Madeline, and Madeline was . . . not evasive, that wouldn't be fair, just irritatingly vague. Someone Ed Loy knows, she can't remember his name, his daughter's a friend of hers, a house on the Southside . . . what use was any of that? Even if he had the information, he couldn't simply take the afternoon off, and since there were at least two girls, not to mention this friend of Loy's, the whole thing sounded far too complicated, and potentially dangerous, and in any case, the furthest he felt he could go with Ed was to ask in general about Jenny's safety and welfare; any direct inquiry regarding her location could only bring suspicion on his own head.

The clock is ticking though. It's strange: the decision to contact Detective Coover had occurred to him on the spur of the moment, but in one sense, it had been planted fifteen years before. He remembers when Coover came to the Ocean Falls set (even if he hadn't been interviewed by him directly, how could he have forgotten it!). Coover had been impressive, he remembers thinking: a worthy nemesis. And when Coover left, he handed out his card. He had kept that card, and over the years, he had called from public phones, ostensibly to report imaginary crimes, but in fact to keep tabs on Detective Donald Coover, and track his career from Missing Persons to Robbery Homicide, and now from Robbery Homicide to Cold Case Unit. Nice to have a face he knew, a connection, so to speak, almost a friend at court—so that when the time came—and now the time has come—the information would go to someone he had met. He didn't know why that had been important to him—hadn't known until today that it was important—but obviously, the fact that he had sustained the "relationship" over all these years spoke for itself. The truth of ourselves, the deepest truth, is not always, is rarely known to us. That is the mystery, and the power, of art, of course: How does one element, of story, or of visual material, that seems insignificant or random, in time assume crucial significance, become in fact the hook upon which the entire film's meaning hangs?

Yes, the clock is ticking now. After the Point Dume information, he waited to see what would unfold, and when he was satisfied that Coover was not going to file it with the astrologers and the cranks (he had kept faith in Coover, of course, but you never know), he had entrusted the other locations to him. Such a precious, such a volatile cargo! It was a gift that he had bestowed, and Coover would perhaps never know what he had done to have earned such grace. Of course, he had barely done a thing, just been in the right place at the right time. But that's the point of grace, surely: we put ourselves in the way of it, but there is little we can do to earn it—God does not judge us in such a primitive way, and His grace is not susceptible to any moral or logical pattern.

Indeed, never was the proof of that more keenly felt than now, and by him. He had made a generous compromise—after all, the three girls, the Fates, had all been cast because of their resemblance to Madeline King— there had never been any attempt to hide that—so why did he not simply *jettison the Jenny Noble option and plump directly for Madeline? Well, there had been considerations . . . but he told himself once more: harden your heart.*

He set Madeline a task—no, that was to give himself airs, he had asked a favor of her—to meet someone at the airport. The two associate producers were coming anyway, so it had been easy to add a third, claim he was arriving separately, give her a flight number and impress on her the need for the personal touch. Of course, she would wait and wait and eventually despair of him arriving, and she would phone him and he would tell her there'd been the most dreadful mix-up but that the producer was here now, at his home, he felt it was his fault, he wanted to make it up to her, everyone else was gathering here for drinks before dinner. He wouldn't take no for an answer. Madeline would come, he knew that. He doesn't know her well—could you ever know any of them "well"?— but he knows her well enough. Madeline would come, and that would be the end of it, or at least, the end of that particular chapter.

But she didn't come. She hadn't even phoned. Well, she texted him, once, to say she was in the airport. Nothing since. He had called her three times—he didn't want to call any more often, didn't want to leave too vivid a trace—but all he received was a message from her service provider telling him to try again later. He can't understand it. At the very least, Madeline is reliable. Has she been in an accident? Has she gone on the tear? He almost laughs when he realizes he is asking the questions every-one else has been asking about the missing girls. He almost laughs.

But it isn't funny. There is a time for humor, and this isn't it.

This is . . . this is simply . . . a problem with the ending.

That's better.

Never look at a situation from one angle only.

Never have just one ending for a story.

If Madeline is not to be the third . . .

Then maybe it is time to consider other, untried options . . .

To break the rule of three . . .

To raise the stakes.

To make the last a glorious, a sacred, an unprecedented Three-in-One.

CHAPTER 16

Los Angeles, 1998

Loy didn't know the bags Jack put his soon-to-be ex-girl-friends' stuff in were called Birkins, were manufactured by Hermès, and were dreamed of and lusted after by a certain kind of woman in the same way a certain kind of guy lusts after a Ferrari. But after he'd done it once, shamefaced on Jack's behalf, he realized there was something special about them. Mossy Faye said Jack wouldn't even give the poor girls the kiss-off himself, and Ed liked the expression "the kiss-off" because it made him feel like a fully fledged L.A. PI and not some shabby creep doing another shabby creep's dirty work for him, but he had felt the shame receding that first time when, midway through his prepared speech about how Jack felt it would be better for both of them and the problem was all on Jack's side, he noticed the girl had fallen into some kind of trance over the bag, and he'd had to ask her if she was listening to him.

"Yeah. Sure I was. Better for both of us," she said loudly, as if reassuring him that she hadn't fallen asleep. Within seconds, however, she had dropped eye contact again and was caressing the leather of the bag and seeing if her clutch purse would fit in the inside pocket. When he made to leave, she barely registered his going. Come to think about it, even the fourth girl, the one who had bitten Loy's ear, succumbed quickly to the bag's charms, even quicker than the others. In fact, maybe there was nothing to think about there at all, except to be very careful indeed with the kind of girl who might bite your ear.

Amanda Cole looked at the Hermès Birkin as if it was something an African despot might fill with diamonds and baby-seal furs and give to his mistress, and tossed it across her apartment without looking at it and said something in which the words *all his whores* were discernible and sat on a sofa in the corner of the darkened room. But then, Loy knew Amanda was not like the other girls. The "Cole" had been Koller, and she had changed it when she moved here in the eighties. Surprised, he said he didn't think people changed their names anymore; characteristically, she said she didn't care what "people" did. Her slender grace and dark blond coloring and intense blue eyes were very much what Loy thought of as German qualities; her accent was almost entirely American, but sometimes her phrasing hinted at her origins. The way Loy remembered it, he had noticed her face in the doorway, but that wasn't true; nor was his memory of her hand flashing up to conceal the bruising. Amanda Cole didn't do unconscious movements; she was the most highly controlled woman he had ever met. And initially, Loy had been so taken aback, almost to the point of outrage, at the cavalier disregard Amanda had shown for Jack's titanic largesse that he hadn't noticed anything else awry.

And then Amanda looked at him with such a penetrating gaze that he had to turn away. She had the gift of seeing a man as he was at his worst, he had known that, and reflecting that worst right back at him so he could share the view, and in that moment, in her eyes, he saw how deeply he had internalized his role as the hired help, how pathetic he had grown, how, if he didn't even appreciate his now degraded station, he was in danger of losing, yes, it seemed to him at that moment in the darkened room on Horizon Avenue as he deludedly attempted to tidy up somebody else's life, in danger of losing his soul.

"You don't have to do this," was all Amanda said.

"It appears that I do," Loy said, and willed himself to meet her gaze again. "I'm sorry," he said, and that was when he saw the bruising on her face, around her left cheekbone. He made an involuntary sound, maybe a gasp, and Amanda smiled in derision, a woman laughing at a child, although she was younger than him. Maybe her laughter, her contempt for him, contributed to his anger, but he didn't think so. He remembered seeing marks like that once on his mother's face, remembered his father's drunken anguish, remembered the stillness of the house for months afterward. He was prepared to change his mind about many things, but there was only one way you could think about men who hit women.

"Did Jack do that?" he said.

Amanda Cole made a willowy gesture with her hand, as if by doing so, she could dispense with reality, or so it seemed to Loy.

"It doesn't matter. It was my fault."

"How could that be? Did you hold a gun on him? A knife?"

"You don't understand."

"What is there to understand?"

He went closer to her, and saw that her arm was bruised also, yellowing bruises where a hand had gripped and shaken. His fist went into his mouth to stop himself from crying out. Something of his reaction communicated itself to Amanda; her stillness was a little shaken, her face a little flushed; she set her lips and broke Loy's gaze now.

"Don't . . . he's not a brute, he didn't . . . we got into something, something heavy. I just . . . I don't think I'm the right person for Jack. And I guess he agrees. So . . . so thank you, Ed, and thank him, and just go."

"I can't just go. Because . . . because if I do, it's to go around to Jack's and give him what he gave you."

"No!" Amanda's low voice suddenly came so shrill Loy got a fright. She was on her feet, her hands shaking as she approached, desperate for him to understand.

"How well do you know your friend?"

"Not very well, I suppose. We . . . I know he used to be a singer . . . he used to be an opera singer . . . he has a sister."

"He has a sister, yes. You know nothing about him, do you? Not really."

"I like him very much."

"You 'like' him very much. You . . . men! You can't even say 'love' in case people will laugh at you, or think you're gay. You love him. And he loves you. Two lost boys who never had a brother, found one in each other. I think it's very fine. But you don't see . . ."

"Don't see what? Maybe we don't confess our deepest fears to each other. Way I always understood it, that's what a guy gets a girlfriend for."

"You're very good, Ed. You have an answer for everything. And for those things you have no answer for, you have your fists. 'Oh, he beat up a woman. Now I beat him up. I am man, hear me roar.' And where will that get you?"

"It's not supposed to get me anywhere. It's supposed to . . . point out to him the error of his ways."

"And who made you the judge? You're the detective, not the judge. When the detective starts to think he is the judge, nothing but trouble. Believe me."

Loy was struck by this, and by the ghost of the accent in which it was said, and fell silent.

"Listen to me, Ed. There is something in his past, deep in his past, something wrong. Do you understand? I know you don't, but from the way I'm saying it to you, please believe me, it's immense. It . . . and I think he needs to see someone, psychologist, psychoanalyst, psychiatrist . . . but he won't. He says it's where everything comes from . . . his 'art.' I said you can't justify a sickness in the name of art."

"What did he say to that?"

"He just laughed, and said, that's what all the others did."

"All the other . . . artists?"

"That's his trip. He suffers so we don't have to."

The irony of this fell heavy in the room. Loy turned to Amanda Cole and held a hand up to her bruised face.

"I'm sorry. I don't think I have what it takes to make Jack feel better about himself."

"It's more than that."

"Maybe. But I can't find anything that would be an excuse."

"An explanation."

"An explanation is not an excuse."

Amanda Cole smiled, not unkindly.

"Then don't make things any worse, Ed Loy. I will keep the peace offerings. Even the horrid bag. And know your friend will miss you, but that you will miss him, too. No matter what he did. He is not a bad man."

Loy remembered feeling as he walked away from Amanda's apartment that he had left something behind. He couldn't quite put a finger on what it was, or maybe he refused to let himself. He didn't call Jack Donovan again, and wouldn't return any of his calls. When Jack called at his house, Loy wouldn't answer the door. Eventually, the calls stopped. Not long afterward, Loy took up seriously with the woman he had gone to see *Speed* with back in '94, and they married. The next time Loy saw Jack Donovan was in Dublin, in a nightclub, during the shooting of *Nighttown*. And that night, Loy remembered Amanda Cole telling him he would miss Jack. She was right. He had.

CHAPTER 17

Anne knows it's a spur-of-the-moment thing, and Ed has only been asked himself, but honest to God, an hour. An hour to get the girls fed and used to the idea of her going out, to find a babysitter (Kevin was in Krakow, the recession having failed to quell the Irish Pub epidemic thus far), and most important, To Find Something To Wear. She's too old now to underdress and get away with it like she could in her twenties and thirties: nine nights out of ten, if she just throws on a pair of jeans and a wrap top, she'll look like she's popping up to Spar for a carton of milk, but go too far in the other direction and she'll morph into a total desperate housewife. And, inevitably, tonight is the night Aoife chooses to reveal that she and her best friend since Junior Infants are not friends anymore, and Ciara, not to be outdone, says that she doesn't know what it is, *she* just "feels a little sad" and the only cure, apparently, for this sadness, is fastening her little arms around Mummy's neck and clinging on like a marmoset, if marmosets are the things that cling, Anne can't remember, koalas, perhaps, except not nearly as cute as koalas, certainly as the clinging continues.

Finally, mercifully, Molly, her fantastically cool and self-assured babysitter who is sixteen and looks twenty-four, arrives and whirls the girls off into a world of Mary-Kate and Ashley and *Hannah Montana* and *Zoey 101,* and after that, Anne might as well be in another country for all the attention her daughters pay her. She doesn't know whether there'll be any actresses there tonight—come to think of it, she isn't entirely sure which actresses are in the movie. She has the notion Mischa Barton is, but that might just be because she had that thing with Josh Tyler, who definitely is, and she's pretty sure Kirsten Dunst is in it, and that English one, not Kate Winslet, the other one, Emma Thompson. No, Emily Watson. Or was it Emily Blunt? Oh God, she's hopeless, she sounds like . . . and as Anne considers her makeup in the bathroom mirror, and considers equally the prosecution evidence it's intended to counter, and wonders grimly, how long, O Lord, how long, it comes to her exactly what she sounds like: somebody's mother.

At which uplifting intelligence, she decides that, having successfully slept and steamed and flash-facialed the two glasses of champagne she'd had at lunchtime away, if she has to play the part of some suburban matron among a crowd of glamorous young things, the least she is entitled to be is a bit pissed. So she nips downstairs before she puts her heels on and rescues the Veuve from the fridge and finds a glass and sits in the window of her bedroom and drinks champagne until the taxi arrives, all the while trying to retrieve and reorder the space in her mind that she used to use for talking to other adults.

CHAPTER 18

The city feels close tonight, with barely a breath off the river; the glare of the exhausted sun dazzles my eyes as I turn onto the quays. I'm carrying the Glock in case I run into anything Podge-related; as if in sympathy, Tommy Owens calls.

"The girls are good with Paula, yeah?"

"Yeah. How are you?"

"I think I'll watch outside your gaff, Ed. Don't know if Podge has a crosshairs on it, but it shouldn't be too difficult to find out, even for a thick fuck like him."

"Tommy—"

"Leo says he's got you Glocked up, are you carrying? Ed?"

"Yes. Tommy—"

"Good. Because we do not need any misplaced fucking Council of Civil Liberties bollocksology here Ed, do you understand me? You get the chance, you plug the fat fuck in the head, empty the magazine to make sure. You know who's going to care? Nobody. Leo is praying for you to do it. George sees Podge as a walking bad debt. And what do you do with bad debts? You write them off. Tell you what, why don't we do a drive around, the cunt is up in Redlands, we get him out front on some fucking pretext—"

"Tommy, I'm wondering is it wise for you to get involved with this one. I mean—"

"I know what you mean. And that's not going to impair my judgment, any more than what he done today is going to cloud yours. Are you up to it?"

"Am I up to what? I'm up to defending myself, that's why I called Leo. Am I up to taking him out first strike? Of course I'm not. And we're not going to drive around looking to hit someone like a pair of coked-up skangers, get sense. Don't ask me about it again. It's nothing to do with civil liberties or bleeding hearts or anything else, it's just not what I do. If that's what Leo wants, let Leo do the work. And for God's sake don't get tempted into doing it yourself. Tommy? Because just as Podge's gang of maggots are happy to spray-paint a headstone or burn down a house, they'll be just as delighted to take revenge on you, either in person or through the people close to you. Through Naomi. It's not what you do either. It's what makes the difference between us and them—"

"Yeah, yeah, Ed, there endeth the lesson, there's a lot of parishes down the country looking for priests, you won't ever be short of work if you're losing the bottle for this job. Or maybe you'd be happier buying organic vegetables at the farmers' market with your ladyfriend. Get yourself a Barbour jacket and a pair of fucking Birkenstocks. Meanwhile, I'll be watching out for you. Down on the street. Don't forget, I've killed for you before. I didn't much like it. But it would be a pleasure this time."

Tommy closes the call, the bitter last word successfully his. I've been waiting for a crack about Anne. I wonder if he's right, although my wondering runs counterclockwise to Tommy's: Does my reluctance to contemplate full-scale gang war led by myself and Tommy reflect . . . well, obviously, in the first place, what it reflects is my sanity. Tommy's blood is up, and he wants nothing more than to feel he's doing something, even if it means driving around like fools with a death wish. But also, he's been hanging with Leo. The lines are blurring. At this point, Tommy sees us as a gang too, just one with right on our side. I can't look at things like that.

And if I have a shot at happiness, or some kind of life, or more, with a woman who isn't crazy or dangerous or both, that doesn't sound the clanging cell doors of bourgeois complacency or suburban smugness, whatever Tommy, the eternal scourge of the middle class, might say. It's barely an argument worth considering, but I'm finding it difficult to wrestle it to the ground. That's probably because of my counterclockwise perspective: in the past, the only person who could be endangered by my job was me. If I take on other people, how can I ensure their safety from the kind of people I might encounter? How could I ever protect Anne Fogarty and her daughters from the likes of Podge Halligan? And if I can't, am I faced with a stark choice? Can I have my job or a life, but not both?

I stop by Butt Bridge and look down at the Liffey as it flows out to sea, and the commuter trains roll and creak overhead. I think of the night of my mother's funeral, my first time back in Dublin in over twenty years. I stood and looked out to sea, and watched a train flash past, hurtling into the night, and wished that I was on it, going somewhere, anywhere. I don't feel like that now. This is my city, my home, for good or ill. But nothing stays still. I want to find happiness, love even. But that doesn't come for free. I don't know yet if I'm willing to pay the cost.

JACK DONOVAN IS waiting for me in the dark wooden bar in Mulligan's of Poolbeg Street. I say waiting for me, but that is not in fact how it appears. He's installed at the counter, holding the rapt attention of two barmen who look indecently excited in his presence, particularly when the default mode among the bar staff generally oscillates between morose and taciturn, Mulligan's being the kind of Dublin pub where it is understood that at some level you are being served drink only on sufferance, and that your demeanor will be closely monitored for expressions of excessive optimism or geniality. I love the air of dreamy melancholy here, and feel that King-of-the-Hill, Top-of-the-Heap, Freeman-of-the-City Jack is somehow the wrong scale for the place, as if his motorcade is stalled outside and everyone is waiting for him to shake hands and leave so that mournful tranquillity may once more descend. But nobody appears to share my unease: the other customers are variously stealing glances and unabashedly staring at Jack. Joining him at the bar, my disquiet intensifies: Jack is showing the barmen how to fix Red Hues.

"For fuck's sake Jack, Mulligan's is a pub, not a fucking cocktail bar," I mutter, giving a note-perfect impersonation of a furious old man whose sanctuary has been violated by the filthy modern tide of drinks best left to women. Jack smiles silently and indicates the barmen, who present the drinks. They are smiling also. I look around. Everyone is smiling. It's like something from an Irish tourism ad, or a Hitchcock film.

"Take them down there, Jack, and we'll bring the pints through when they're ready," one of the smiling barmen says. Jack picks up the drinks and a newspaper he has been reading and walks along the bar and into the large wood-paneled snug at the back, and we sit around the table in silence and Jack's smile fades as he sips his drink, then flares up again when the other smiling barmen brings us our pints, then vanishes altogether when the door shuts behind him.

The paper is the *Irish Times,* and it is open to Derek Doyle's column.

"Ed," Jack says. "I want to ask you a question, and I want a completely honest answer."

"No you don't," I say.

"I do. Why would you say that?"

"Because nobody wants complete honesty. Complete honesty is what you feel slither across your soul at four in the morning. That's too much for anyone to carry around all day."

"I don't want it about everything, just one particular . . . aspect of my life."

" 'Aspect of your life.' "

"Fuck off. Now. Did I, or did I not, make a cunt of myself on *The Late Late Show*?" Jack said, and he tapped the *Irish Times*.

"Ah Jack, you don't want to mind Derek Doyle—"

"I don't mind Derek Doyle. Derek Doyle . . . do you know something about little Derek? He sends me scripts. He has been giving out about me for ten years now, but after each . . . episode, I think we might call it, he writes me a letter of apology, as if, I don't know, Mr. Hyde got out of the pit again and wrote that week's column for him. And then a couple of months later, he sends me a script! A screenplay. And I read it, I read them all, six, seven over the years, and I say positive things, and I get them to people who I think might like them, and some of them do, although none of them like them enough to get the fucking things made. And no doubt the fact that my things get made and his don't is an ongoing outrage in his mind. And do you know the worst thing about his scripts?"

"They're dreadful."

Jack shakes his huge head, his eyes begin to glitter and a grin creases across his face.

"*They're not bad*. That's the worst thing. That's what will kill the poor fucker in the end: they're actually not bad."

Jack laughs, hard, until tears of malice course down his face.

"Ah Jaysus. Poor Derek. May the Lord have mercy on him. And on us all. Now. Ed. Do you agree with Derek?"

"I think Bono is a national treasure who improves with age. The last album was the best yet."

"I agree with you."

"And I think your films are great. Even over the last ten years. Even when they don't entirely work."

Jack is taken aback by this confession, but I feel, in the light of what I want to say to him, that I owe him that, at least. Besides, it's true.

"What can I say? Thank you."

"And yes, I'm afraid you made an epic, Queen Maeve–size, Paddy Irishman cunt of yourself."

Jack begins to shake with laughter again.

"Oh Danny boy . . ." he began.

"Yeah, you should have started with that."

"And left right after. That's the future, Ed: forget talking, let the actors do that. I'll just rock up and sing. That can be, that *is* my USP."

We fall silent for a while, and I move in my seat and feel the Glock in my pocket and my sanctuary door blows open with a crash.

"Any word from Madeline?" I say.

"I was going to ask you the same thing."

Maurice hasn't told Jack about the discovery of the bodies at Point Dume, so I take him through it myself, tell him how Jenny Noble had received texts that were ostensibly from the missing girls, that they hadn't gone to Kate's usual club but that still left the possibility that they'd been somewhere else, but that neither had actually spoken to anyone, not Jenny or, more to the point, to Nora's sister, Rose. As I speak, I watch for any sign I can interpret, a flicker on Jack's part that might give me some clue to his possible knowledge of, or participation in, any of these events. I suggest that the reason Nora, Kate and Jenny had been cast was because of their similarity in coloring and look to Madeline, and speculate as to whether their abductor, if there was one, frustrated by his inability to locate Jenny Noble, has plumped for Madeline King to round out his "three-in-one." I alert him to the fact that he, Maurice, Mark Cassidy and Conor Rowan are the only people around now who had been at Point Dume. I tell him that the killer's signature, at least in the Point Dume case—because the LAPD had announced they were investigating at least five other cases—is a crucifix with the girls' initials carved on it, hence the "Three-in-One Killer" tag, and I note how this chimes with the frequent use of this motif in the anonymous letters.

And I wait for his reply.

And Jack, whose expression has not altered at all during the time I was talking, says: "Even if we got the money to recast the three girls, and reshoot all the scenes they were in, which is doubtful, Josh Tyler's starting a picture for Wes Anderson next week, and he's not going to be out of that for months, so I'd have to recast him completely, which is out of the question, as he is going to be a major star and this film will rise with him, or find some way of using a body double and then reinserting his performance with CGI, which will almost certainly send the budget into the outer reaches of feasibility. However it falls, Ed, I think it's safe to say, *Nighttown* is fucked."

I stare at him in silence for a moment, but he appears not to notice there is anything amiss. I mistakenly think he has not understood me.

"Jack? Did you hear anything I said?"

He looks at me closely, his face a mask of amused curiosity.

"Of course I did. But I wanted to be clear that you knew what you were asking. Which was, Jack, are you the Three-in-One Killer? Have you abducted Nora, Kate and Madeline? Did you kill the girls in Point Dume and bury their bodies? And if I've got that right, and please set me straight if I don't, maybe it's a two-guys-walk-into-a-bar-one-walks-out-a-serial-killer joke and I've misplaced my sense of humor, let me roll that ball right back to you, Ed. Do you think I'm the guy?"

"I think you haven't been honest with me. I think you're not in a very good place in your head. I think there are things to do with your sister and your ex-wife that you need to get clear, and you need to get them clear with me, because you invited me in. I think you wrote those letters and daubed that drawing yourself so that I could do some of your emotional dirty work for you, just the way I used to. And the last time I did such a thing, I found a woman who had been beaten up. And I should have had the guts to confront you on it, to let you give me the explanation, if not the excuse. But I was too young, and too angry, too consumed by my own certainty over right and wrong. Well, ten years has put paid to that certainty. I'm sorry it took so long. You were my friend, and I owed you more. But you owe me more than this fucking disrespectful bullshit, sending me out with a pack of lies to talk to an ex-wife who is raising your children, obviously your children, who grew to love you and is wasting her life away for the lack of you, and to see a sister who gave up her life for you, and who more or less told me . . . you know, for a long time, I couldn't remember anything about the day with Amanda Cole except the bruises on her face, it was like my eyes were dazzled by the glare and I was blind to everything else she said. She loved you too. And she told me I knew nothing about you. Well, this is the time, Jack. Tell me what I need to hear. Tell me about yourself."

CHAPTER 19

After a reviving glass of champagne, Anne's spirits rise to the point where she decides that whatever she might sound like tonight, she is not going to look like anyone's mother. She wears her navy Bolongaro Trevor leather jacket over her white Vivienne Westwood shirt and skinny black Zara jeans and the All Saints boots with the double straps, reckoning, after more than one mutton check, that she is still the right side of forty, just about, to get away with rock chick and not look completely deluded.

In the Octagon Bar at the Clarence Hotel, or strictly speaking in a private room off the lobby, she is glad she hasn't gone the skirt-and-heels route, partly because she would have felt too self-conscious, particularly because the Famous Irish Actor she was hoping would be here *is* here, although apparently just for a drink, he can't come to dinner, and when he says a drink he means water because he doesn't drink anything stronger now, and he shakes her hand and smiles at her, and she burbles something about the American TV show he does that probably makes her sound half-witted but he is so sweet, and talks to her quite openly, standing with his head to one side, quite grand, really, like an old style actor, a Barrymore, perhaps, beautifully dressed himself, and then those boy producers from L.A. try to fold him into some private conversation, excluding her, and he won't let them, he insists she be part of things, and there follows a long, rather stilted exchange about how Ireland has changed and yet stayed the same that none of them could in truth think very interesting, until Anne concedes that since the prospect of her and the Famous Irish Actor taking off into the sunset or even getting a room are slim, she should probably get a few more names on her dance card and leave him to the boy producers, who are wearing suits but look like they should be in short pants, and the Famous Irish Actor looks genuinely alarmed as she moves off, but that's probably only because he doesn't want to be left alone with the boy producers, although, Anne thinks optimistically, you never know.

She spends a while with Maurice Faye, who is very Galway and lovely and says Ed is the coolest man in Ireland and would, Anne suspects, say mass if he was let, and even if he wasn't, and Maurice introduces her to Conor Rowan, Jack's First AD, and she asks Conor Rowan what a First AD does and Conor Rowan, who has a red face and a blunt, direct manner and a smile that doesn't reach his boiling eyes, says the First AD directs the movie and gets none of the credit and Anne laughs, thinking it a joke, but Conor, who it now seems to her is not so much blunt and direct as angry and rude, does not laugh, and his smile looks like an affliction, and he does not reply in anything more than grunts to any of her sallies about Jack's earlier films (she has done her homework) or his opera career (Anne once saw him in a Dublin Grand Opera Society *Tosca*) or the current economic crisis, and Anne looks longingly across the room toward where the Famous Irish Actor had been but was no longer, and she wonders whether Colin or, indeed, Cillian would appear, and when their glasses are refilled she decides to try once more with Conor Rowan and if he can't find the manners to reply she will turn on her heel and ignore him, it's like first term at university, and all she says is if there is such a thing as bad champagne she has certainly never drunk any of it. Well, Conor Rowan suddenly embarks on a monologue about the snobbery over champagne, which of course is a region not a drink, and is vastly overrated and ridiculously overpriced, perfect of course for the kind of yahoos and yobs who have made money in Ireland in the last fifteen years and have no idea what they like on account of their having no taste, so the only way they can mark what they think of as their success is by spending more money than they could afford on things they think they're supposed to like. What Conor recommends is an Italian semisparkling Prosecco, at eleven euros fifty a bottle, he has been drinking it for fifteen years now, Mitchell's in Sandycove stocks it, she'd like it, he says smarmily, it comes in a very pretty blue bottle.

Then he asks her if she has any children, and when Anne says yes, she has two daughters, Conor's smile intensifies and he says, "Three girls together." A creepy smile, Anne thinks. A creep, anyway, definitely, and she is relieved to be rescued by a slender fair-haired man in a pale linen suit who says he is Mark Cassidy and asks her if Ed is coming and she says he asked her to come so she assumes so but you can never tell with Ed and Mark laughs like she has said something funny and Anne laughs, too, just in case she has, and her glass needs refilling again and Conor Rowan fades away and Mark starts talking about Nicholas Ray and what a strange career he had and Anne fears she is going to be a long way out of her depth, and too pissed to start bailing, and then she remembers a Nicholas Ray movie because Kevin had been a mad Humphrey Bogart fan and she says something low-key about *In a Lonely Place* and Mark gets very excited and they talk for a while about how dark and unsettling that story is, a doomed love affair, with Bogart playing a screenwriter prone to bouts of uncontrollable violence which, Mr. Hyde–like, he is unable to recall. Mark starts to talk excitedly about a screenplay *he* has written around the same themes, or maybe Anne misunderstands him, she isn't really listening now because Ed has appeared with Jack Donovan.

It's strange, shocking, what she feels in that moment, what she *sees*—both men so different, physically, Ed tall and slender and ramrod straight, Jack broad and bull-like, with the huge head, the mane of hair, but around the eyes, the identical glow, beneath the brightness and the swagger, and they have *swaggered* in, the pair of them, no show without a pair of Punches, but it's there around the eyes, a dark, haunted look, as if the worst is inevitable, and you can prepare all you like, no matter, it will end in tears. She has noticed traces of it in Ed before, a sense that he has lost something he can maybe never get back. She loves that chink in his armor, that glimmer of vulnerability. She wants to work on the maybe. But tonight, with Jack Donovan, he looks as if there is nothing left to heal, nothing to look toward, nothing except darkness. It makes her fearful for him, and for herself, and for her girls. It is as if someone has walked across her grave.

CHAPTER 20

I don't know what I was expecting. I never do, in those moments when I am driven to confront a suspect or a less-than-cooperative client, or in Jack's case, both. Did I think he would delve deep into the past and present me with The Answer, like an analysand in a movie? Unlikely, given the subject in question: Jack Donovan's movies are delirious with the *lack* of answers, with the notion that asking the question is in itself the answer. Did I hope he was so soul-sick he would want desperately to confess? And if so, to what? Did I fear he would rear up against me and fight, or flee? All of the above, or none. I needed anything I could get, even while I knew that none of it would make easy listening.

Across the room, I see Anne Fogarty's bright head, her crooked, sexy smile, her flashing eyes. I want to go straight to her, to share in her laughter, to join with her against the world, citizens of the independent republic of lovers. But I am carrying what Jack has told me, carrying Jack Donovan, what he has done and what he, or another, might yet do. I see in Anne's eyes the wit that understands this, and the care that worries on my behalf, and I smile in a way that convinces neither of us, that is probably not even intended to.

"Did you see the children?" is the first thing Jack Donovan says in the back room in Mulligan's. He has called for more drinks, so I can't be sure if the tears in his eyes are distilled from pure emotion or alcohol, but they take me aback. "Joanie and Jackie," he says, and the uncharacteristically hollow tone betrays him. Jack can make any falsehood sound plausible, convince himself of the truth of any lie—if he wants to. He has the singer's gift of conviction, of feeling the feeling, never mind the truth.

"Alice and Daisy," I say. "Geri told me to tell you their names. She also said that she knows you're in love with your own guilt and shame. But she'd like to see you, in spite of that."

"She said that?"

"She did. And she said, despite your refusal to acknowledge them as your daughters, you send so much extra money on their birthday, way more than any kind of maintenance settlement would demand, that it's clear you know you're their father."

Jack's eyes fill up, and his great frame begins to shake with emotion, and he rests his brow in his hands. There is something so grand about this gesture that, whether heartfelt or not, it appears bogus, and I am moved to anger.

"What the fuck is the matter with you? Your children, your fucking *children* . . . and that woman . . . you don't know the first thing about her. Maybe she was a spoiled little brat back then, when you met first . . . but you had that week together . . . you chose her . . . and you know something? She loves you. She only hates you as much as love entitles her to hate someone who's behaved the way you have. Any man . . . after five years, and then another five, and she still . . . any man would be, luck isn't the half of it, unworthy of such a . . . and you know, she's not a saint, she's bitchy and vain, with good reason . . . she's an amazing woman, any man would . . . what the fuck is the matter with you?"

Jack looks up at me through blood-flecked eyes. His face looks like a clown's, stripped of makeup.

"I ran away," he says. "I ran away twice. I was . . . frightened. Because I thought I had made a mistake, the first time. And then . . . the second time, because I knew the divorce had been the mistake, and I couldn't turn myself around to admit that. And frightened both times, all the time, of what I might do . . ."

"What you did to Amanda Cole?"

Jack nods, his eyes on his drink.

"Because I didn't understand it then, and I don't understand it now. And as a result, it could happen again at any time."

"What about willpower, Jack, what about making sure it doesn't by an act of will?"

"Will? Do you believe in will? I don't. I believe in fate, Ed. I believe in the things we do, and the people we are as a result, being beyond our control. And you can look at me like Derek Doyle, with mockery in your eyes, you can say I'm a buffoon and a clown and so on, but my voice . . . where does that come from? The stories, the characters, the films . . . you can say they're crap, or not you, Derek and all the Dereks, all the sneering, eye-rolling, give-me-a-break merchants who live in The Real World and are enraged at everyone who won't buckle down and join them there, they can say the movies are nostalgic and clichéd and not 'relevant' but they can't say where they come from and neither can I. It's like . . . it's like it's all already been written, and I'm just chasing after it, trying to get it out."

"That's art, Jack, that's not life."

"It's all the same to me. So I don't feel 'in control.' And I find . . . I found it very hard to take the risk. That I would beat the, the mother of my children."

"It's not good enough. In fact, it's ridiculous, and so are you."

Jack subsides into silence again, whether conceding the point or not it's impossible to tell. I write Geri Foster's name and address, along with the names of her daughters, on an index card and push it across the table at him.

"Did you like the house? I chose it, she sent me three possibilities and I picked that one, you know why? Because it's like the white house in Sandycove, by the Joyce Tower there. I used to dream of that house when I was a kid, swimming in the Forty Foot. And I liked the Art Deco shape of Geri's house, the house I bought for her, the way it looks like a house in California. I thought that would be good, you know, a way of linking the two places, Dublin and L.A."

"And then you broke the link."

Jack stares at the index card.

"Did you write the letters yourself, Jack? As a way of getting me involved with this?"

"No."

"Because if you did—"

"I didn't. I . . . what did my sister say?"

"She laughed at the idea that you were taking the letters seriously, and then she suggested that you had probably written them yourself."

"Do you think she wrote them?"

"No, I think you wrote them. The three-in-one stuff connects with the way you shoot the girl trios in every movie, the Fates or the Furies."

"And now it connects with the killer in Point Dume Beach, and possibly beyond."

"That's right. And the crucifix they found in the grave. And the fetus."

"The fetus. Yes. What does that mean?"

"I asked your sister about it."

"Did you? You're not shy about what you ask, are you?"

"And she said if I wanted to know who the father of her aborted child was, I should ask you."

"And are you asking me?"

"I was circling around it. I was interested in how close the two of you were. The way she described it, sounds like she played quite a maternal role. She gave up opportunities of her own . . . in order that your career would flourish. And she stuck with you when you changed courses, when you gave up singing. She passed up the chance to go to university, to drama school, she supported you by getting a job, she paid for your education. That's a lot of devotion, sacrifice, you might say. I suppose I'm confused, the way you sought to portray her when you hired me as this embittered, spurned figure constantly leaching off you while making it clear how hard done by she feels."

"And how does it seem to you, in fact? Like she's the one more sinned against?"

"I think that's how she sees it. And that these letters are very much your bid to confess the truth about what she did for you. Make no mistake, she admires, reveres you, as a creator, as an artist, a lot of the times she was talking she sounded like a muse, more an ex . . ."

Jack sits and looked at me as I lapse into silence, and an unpleasant smile twines around his lips.

"More an ex what? Less of a sister and more an ex-wife? Is that what you wanted to say? Feel free, Ed. I invited you in, after all. Just as I did back in L.A., back with Amanda Cole. Of course, you didn't follow that through. You ran away, and stayed away for ten years. You didn't have what it takes. But you're ready now, are you? You gonna ask me? Because I can tell you, whatever way I stretched the facts about Marie, emotionally, I was down with it. Emotionally, I owe her nothing, she owes me. And if all she has to ponder is a bit of career disappointment, then hey, I think she's the winner. Because she was, she'll always be, my big sister, four-year gap, she led the way. I was thirteen when Mam and Dad died, thirteen, and Marie . . . she was so glamorous, such a beauty. And it was such a shock, and she . . . she stood guard."

"That's exactly the expression she used."

Jack nods.

"And let nothing intrude. My world was music, and her. I didn't look outside, I didn't have 'groups of friends' . . . I didn't have *friends*. I had my sister. And . . . have you ever wondered about the women? I mean, when you were cleaning up after me, did you ever wonder, what the fuck is this guy's problem? Set aside that I could hire you to do my dirty work, the indulgence, the decadence of that, did you wonder, you know, Oscar Wilde, to lose one girlfriend is carelessness, to lose four or five in one year is taking the piss. Did you ever ask yourself, Hollywood director, girls form a queue, can he not just fuck them and forget them? Why does he have to try and fall in love with them?"

Jack stops here, genuinely interested in what I think.

"Sure. And there were several who I think would have preferred it that way, too, a quick fuck and a designer bag and good-bye."

"Of course they would. But I couldn't do that. I couldn't do without the song and dance. I wanted something more, something different, something . . . eventually, that I couldn't have. Something forbidden. When it was offered to me, I found I had no palate, no appetite. My taste had been . . . corrupted."

Jack looks directly at me now, almost smiling, almost triumphant, daring me to ask the question I do not want, do not need to ask. Part of it looks like taunting on his part, but pleading surely plays its part. It's a crucial moment, and it turns out that I am not ready to meet it, or at least, that when faced with the rival claims of friendship and professional duty, duty wins.

"I've run well past the limits of my abilities as a detective there, Jack. If you want to talk any more about this, I think you need to talk to a different kind of investigator."

There is a moment when betrayal flickers in Jack's eyes, a moment when we both hear the crowing of the cock. Jack shakes his head to dispel it, and pantomimed disappointment spreads across his face instead.

"I don't know. I paid you to find who sent these letters, and you don't appear to have done that, Ed. How do you think that reflects on your professional ability?"

"Poorly. The third person I needed to talk to is Madeline King. Is there anything you'd like to tell me about her?"

"That she is at this stage as disappointed as every other woman I've ever known. That she is a nosy cow who will not leave well enough alone. And that if you'd been around and willing, I'd have armed you with a bagful of treats and asked you to kiss her good-bye for me."

"What do you mean, leave well enough alone?"

"Poking her nose where it doesn't belong. I mean, at least I asked you to do it. I deserve what I get. I never asked her to try and . . . fathom me. Figure me out. 'I can't figure you out, Jack.' 'That's not the job description, babe.'"

"And now she's disappeared—"

"Maybe she's taken the initiative. She's a bright girl. Penny finally drops. She shouldn't have to put up with me. Maybe she's worked it out for herself."

There's nothing more to be said, or at least, nothing either of us wants to say. We walk down the Quays in silence. When we reach the Clarence, it's time to go straight on to the restaurant. I join Anne as she steps out onto Essex Street, and she pushes her fingers through my hair, and we hold each other as if it's months and not days we've been apart, and slip into a doorway and inhale each other's scent, and we kiss, at first the way we both want to, and then I kiss her in a way that tells her there will be less than either of us wants until I come through all this, and she holds me to let me know that it's fine, though not so fine that she isn't disappointed.

CHAPTER 21

Eden had been Anne Fogarty's favorite restaurant, had been "her" restaurant, hers and Kevin's, but infidelity violates more than just intimate memories of your lover; it tarnishes the places where you thought your happiness unfolded, the pubs and clubs and restaurants where you gazed in each other's eyes, where the staff got to know you, where you acted out the necessary public rituals of your marriage: all ruined, like the wedding photographs she scrawled obscenities in black highlighter pen across, drunk, the night she found out. For a while, the very city that served as the backdrop to your love becomes an unfriendly and unwelcoming zone, a doom-laden landscape of omens and portents. Anne hasn't been back to the Morrison, or Odessa, and she's not convinced she could ever cross the door of Thomas Read's, where they had met.

But here she is in Eden, and maybe this is the way to go, location by location, breaking the claims the past makes on her. She has especially missed Eden because it is such a beautiful room, with its great glass wall looking out onto Meeting House Square, its open kitchen the length of the ground floor, its swimming-pool tiling and the way the mezzanine level is perfectly integrated into the open-plan whole and yet secluded enough for privacy. When it opened, back in 1997, she remembers the astonishment that such a place could exist in Dublin: it felt like a restaurant in San Francisco or L.A. There was much about the Celtic Tiger that had been overpriced and overrated, but Eden got it exactly right: it had style and confidence; it said, we're stepping up here. We're ready. Because Anne and Kevin had been in business together, they had taken it as an inspiration.

They sit upstairs. There are two twentysomething actresses, one American, one Irish, both very pretty, neither of whom Anne recognizes. Maurice has seated them with the visiting boy producers in an obvious manner Anne would have called gauche, but presumably when Maurice does it it's cheeky, or Galway, or some such; the Americans don't seem unduly worried, at any rate, about anything other than what kind of sparkling water is available. Anne has worked hard at avoiding Conor Rowan, whom it appears Ed wants to sit next to anyway, and she ends up between Mark Cassidy and Maurice Faye. She would have been opposite Jack Donovan, only Jack Donovan, who stumbled on the cobblestones coming up the lane, has vanished. Anne wouldn't be surprised if that was it for the night, as he looked completely drunk to her, but he returns beaming, and kisses her hand and looks at her in some strange and knowing way that makes her feel like she is not just the only person in the room but the entire purpose of the evening, and that big bull's head of his suddenly seems positively dashing, and then she notices Ed grinning at her and realizes this is it: this is the legendary Jack Donovan charm. It's quite something.

When the wine list goes around, she can hear Conor Rowan

still talking about the Prosecco from the blue bottle, to Ed this time, and begins to wonder if he has some kind of high-functioning Asperger's, but then Maurice and Mark and even Jack take up the refrain. It turns out they had all come across it in L.A. on their first American movie together, and it seems to have acquired a kind of sentimental, even a totemic, significance for them all: bottles have to be on hand for the wrap of every film the Gang of Four work on together, Prosecco dei Colli Trevigiani, someone says it was called. Eden don't stock it, so they take the Prosecco they can get, which is priced at forty euros; Mark Cassidy recognizes it and tells Anne it's to be had for nine-fifty in Oddbins in Blackrock, a three hundred percent markup, and, charming (and handsome) as Mark is, Anne can't resist a shudder: for some reason, a woman pointing this out would not have been remarkable, but the whiff of meanness off a man always gives her the creeps.

But Mark is sweet, really, and asks about the girls, and Sandymount, which he knows, and where exactly on Strand Road Anne lives, because he has friends who used to live there, near the Martello Tower, and the Irish actress is down the other end of the table spinning the Americans some line about the Irish and the Catholic Church and sexual repression, which, given she is spilling out of a flimsy silk dress that is barely there in the first place, seems to Anne to have had little impact on the actress personally, but the Americans are lapping it all up, the history and the view, sure isn't that what they come here for, and Maurice is taking it all in and nodding and laughing along and saying very little. Anne wishes she could have some time with Ed, who is on Mark's other side, but she has never seen him so grave, even if he tries to nod and smile in her direction every now and then, although the way he looks at Mark Cassidy occasionally she wonders whether he is jealous: the very idea.

For a while, Anne sits saying nothing, just listening as the conversation swirls around her. Ed is talking to Conor and Mark

about three bodies that have been found in a mass grave in
Malibu, and how they may have been extras on a film Jack had
made there fifteen years ago called *Ocean Falls,* which Anne
watched last week on DVD and loved. Conor seems briefly interested but disengaged, as you do when you hear about terrible
things that have happened to people you vaguely know but have
trouble remembering; Anne smiles when Conor says that when
he wasn't working sixteen-hour days, he drank so much tequila
and smoked so much dope that summer he can barely remember
making the film, and has no recollection whatever of the girls:
he says it in such a gruff, dismissive way, it seems to sum up perfectly his apparent disregard for what anyone thinks of him. Ed
sounds as if he doesn't quite believe Conor, and Conor sounds as
if he doesn't much care.

Mark Cassidy seems more affected by the news, and says that
now, on reflection, he does remember one of the girls, Janice
Holloway. Ed looks at him like he can see beneath his skin, and
they have the following exchange:

ED: I thought you didn't remember extras.

MARK: I don't, as a general rule. But . . . I've been turning it
over in my mind since this morning. And I could be wrong
about which girl it was, of course, but I think it was Janice
who approached me and asked if I had seen *Big Wednesday,*
and I said of course, and she asked what I thought of Bruce
Surtees's camera work. It was unusual, or I thought it was,
for an extra to even know a DP's name.

ED: So what, did you guys hang out?

MARK: No. We had a brief chat. To be honest, I think she was
trying to curry favor, because she didn't really have much to
say. I mean, she knew the name, but not a great deal more.

ED: And you didn't take the relationship any further?

MARK: (*Laughing*) No. The extent of the "relationship" was a five-minute conversation at the end of the day's shoot.

Ed nods, staring hard at Mark, like he knows there must be more but he can't get it out of him. If he looked at Anne like that, she'd tell him anything he wanted to know and maybe a lot he didn't, but Mark just laughs and makes the Monty Python joke about not having expected the Spanish Inquisition. All the while Jack is staring and saying nothing, which strikes Anne as strange, since he directed the film the girls had been in, but then Anne supposes he has worked with so many extras over the years, it must be difficult to remember them all.

At the other end of the table, Anne thinks she hears a remark about extras going missing from the film set in Dublin, and the Californian boy producers seem startled until Maurice assures them there's no problem at all, and Jack leans across and says people are confusing the Malibu extras with the Irish ones, and Maurice seems a little cross with the Irish actress, as if she has spoken out of turn, but Anne can't be sure, and in any case it's quickly forgotten because of what happens next.

Ed has been in close colloquy with Conor, and just as the starters arrive, Conor pushes his chair back and stands up and nearly knocks two plates out of the waitress's hands. Conor is even redder of face than usual.

"I don't have to take this, and I'm not taking it. I live my life and it's none of your fucking business. So . . ."

Conor shakes a fist in Ed Loy's face, and drains his glass and stomps off. There's a shocked silence, and the Americans' eyes are out on stalks, and Maurice claps his hands and lets fly a bout of nervous laughter, and just as the boy producers look like they have questions to ask, Jack says:

"Conor is mellowing in his old age. Time was, he'd've turned the table over. Remember the Mexican place in Silverlake?"

And Maurice and Jack are off, telling tale after tale of Conor's alcohol-fueled rampages. Soon the Americans relax. But the atmosphere is tense. Cabin fever, Anne supposes. She checks in with Ed, who makes himself smile at her. He is miles away—in Malibu, perhaps.

Anne has the haddock smokies and the monkfish; the actresses both have chicken; the men without exception have fillet steak. Jack asks her about the girls now, and seems fascinated by the fact that she has two, and she feels somehow she's been maneuvered into being exactly what she didn't want to be, somebody's mother. But fuck it, she is getting tired, and she doesn't know what else to talk to them about, and she *is* somebody's mother. She remarks on the coincidence that she has been at Geri Foster's house today, and that she has been hired to redesign the interior. Jack seems utterly taken aback by this information, and she wonders if he is the father of Geri's two girls, and worries that she has spoken out of turn, then feels relieved when Jack orders champagne (not Prosecco) before the dessert is served, and says he has an announcement to make. He seems very emotional, not to mention pretty drunk, and Anne can feel waves of tension emanating from Ed. There's a turbulent, chaotic feeling at the table, as if the evening could easily spiral out of control. Anne stares at her place setting and plays her napkin through her fingers. Jack tugs on an index card which, as far as Anne can see, contains names and an address written in Ed Loy's hand.

"Esteemed colleagues, dear friends, distinguished visitors, Ed Loy . . . who is all of these things and more, who remains, as Duke Ellington said of Ella Fitzgerald, beyond category . . . many of you know I was once, briefly, married. So briefly, it seemed like a dream. Its brevity was no fault of the lady concerned. As many of you know well, the general principle holds good: when something goes wrong, Jack's to blame. And so I was, very much. And I walked away . . . and I got lost . . ."

There is a long pause, during which Jack seems overcome with emotion. Anne twists her napkin into a tight rope. The sound of other diners seems to get louder and louder, like the menacing roars of an approaching mob.

"And then . . . and then . . . our paths crossed again. And . . . as most of you do not know . . . I became . . . I am . . . the father of daughters. Twin girls . . . who I have not . . . but whom I'm going to . . . whom it is my task to . . . my duty . . . to be their father."

Jack looks around, beaming. He looks a little foolish. Everyone smiles desperately, and a crackle of applause sparks but doesn't catch. Anne is mortified for him, and hopes he will just sit down.

"I rang her," he said to Ed. "I rang her just there. She spoke to me. I'm going to see her. To see them all. I, who was an outcast, have escaped, alone, to tell you . . . I want to tell you all . . ."

The clapping starts up again, and stops just as abruptly, but Jack still stands there, beaming, nodding his head, looking like a man in the midst of some great crisis, or a man who has come out without his wallet and has forgotten where he lives.

And then he begins to sing.

At first, Anne thinks it will be the single most embarrassing moment of her entire life. Jack is swaying, and he starts in the wrong key and has to correct himself and start again, and Mark groans and sighs and mutters. But the voice, my God, the voice, he's barely two lines in and the room is completely hushed. It's *Tosca, Recondita armonia*, her father used to love it. Anne tries to control herself, but there is really no possibility of that; the raw shock of such unearthly beauty pushes tears into her eyes in a molten rush. Jack doesn't quite make the last high C. He leaves his mouth open in silence, and points into it with a finger, a cartoon O of outrage, as if the note has been stolen, but Anne swears she can hear it anyway.

And then the entire restaurant erupts, and it is as if the night has been elevated, and then, this being Dublin, Anne hears someone shout, "Pity he didn't sing that on *The Late Late Show*," which brings the house down, and Jack raises his hand and nods, ruefully conceding the point. The boy producers look entirely stunned, and Anne wonders if they think this kind of thing happens in Dublin all the time, and reckons they probably do, and realizes that this is what people love about Jack Donovan, that even though the movies are shot through with sentimentality and corn, he can make you believe in something bigger, bigger than just The Way Things Are. Jack Donovan can make you believe in love everlasting, and life after death, in fate, and in grace, and in miracles. Jack Donovan can make you believe in a Dublin where men announce out of nowhere that they are reconciling with their long-estranged wives and children, then sing Puccini arias and bring packed restaurants to an unearthly hush. Jack Donovan can make you believe, and, Anne thinks, as she walks arm in arm with Ed on their way to the pub for the after-dinner drink without which no trip to an Irish restaurant is complete, everyone wants to believe. Everyone.

CHAPTER 22

In the pub, things start to catch up with me. I feel exhausted, having had no sleep last night, and emotionally exhausted in any case from the rigors of the day. I know momentum is the big thing, sometimes the only thing, on a case, but I'm not sure I can function usefully through a second sleepless night. All I want to do is go home and go to sleep and start afresh in the morning. But that's not going to happen.

The TV in the pub is not tuned to the sports channel like it usually is, it's on Sky News, and Sky News is focused exclusively on the Three-in-One Killer case, and a map of the greater L.A. area flashes up on the screen with a graphic of a crucifix marking six separate locations where bodies had been discovered, making eighteen in total. Mark Cassidy says, under his breath but loud enough for me to hear, "Weird one, we shot a movie pretty close to most of those locations," and Maurice Faye over-

hears, and realizes it to be true. As it happens, the boy producers, whose names are Ben Epstein and Todd Carter, are about
to fly out on the studio's private jet. Maurice looks at me, and I
nod my weary assent, and Maurice lays out crisply the possible
implications of what Mark has said to Ben and Todd, and suggests that a man on the ground who knows the case and knows
Don Coover would be in the studio's interest. And the upshot
is, instead of going home and going to sleep, I am going to fly
to L.A. tonight.

Ben and Todd's car is waiting, so I kiss Anne good-bye, and
tell her to take care of herself. Because of what I knew of the
killer's MO, I discount the possibility that she might be in any
danger: if he is operating in Dublin, he is looking for a dark-
haired young woman to complete his trio. Nonetheless, when
Mark Cassidy offers to see her home, I say that won't be necessary, and insist she ride along with us until we hit the taxi rank
on Stephen's Green. It isn't just Mark: I wouldn't have let Maurice or Jack or Conor see her home either. I know she is vaguely
irritated that I am being so protective, but I don't care: I have
slipped firmly into Do The First Thing You Think Of. I can
make it up to her later. I hope.

We have to swing by my apartment to get my passport. I tell
Ben and Todd I'll follow them to the airport, and give them my
details so they can alert the Department of Homeland Security.
I pack a light bag with a change of clothes and my laptop computer. I duck out back and stow the Glock in the glove com-
partment of my car. Tommy Owens appears out of the shadows
and I bring him up-to-date. With typical directness, he asks me
what the point of going to L.A. is.

"What are you going to find? I mean, the cops'll be all over
the burial sites, there'll be media everywhere, rubberneckers
and ghouls and probably hawkers selling Three-in-One Killer
fucking baseball hats, and you don't know, is your man going to
have time to deal with you? Detective Coover, did you say? Not

if he's just caught himself a case the size of that, Jaysus, they'll be writing true crime books about this cunt from now until doomsday, he's not going to have time for some PI from fucking Dublin, are you joking me? Take a number, get in line, we'll see you sometime next September."

"I know. You're probably right. But . . . I have to do something, Tommy, what's the alternative? I've talked to the four lads, I've more or less accused Jack . . . if one of them is responsible for, looks like eighteen murders, if there's three in each grave, and if this is happening in Dublin, well, this guy is not just going to burst out crying because I confront him. I have to make a case. And if they don't know what's been happening here—there's no telling whether they've made a connection to the film company, to Jack. If I can make that connection, Coover will have to see me."

"Do you think it's Jack, Ed?"

"Honestly? I don't think so. But he's in a weird place right now. There's so much I don't know about the guy, nothing would surprise me."

"On the other hand . . . Naomi said Jenny's been getting texts from the missing girls. What happens if they show up tomorrow morning?"

I look at Tommy.

"I don't think that's going to happen," I say. By the look on Tommy's face, neither does he.

I'VE FLOWN ON a Gulfstream before, back in the days when I was Jack Donovan's carousing buddy, and there's no doubt that walking straight onto the plane and it taking off within fifteen minutes is preferable to the tedious alternatives. But I'm not really in the mood to appreciate the luxury; all I want to do is, in the first instance, turn over the case as it stands, and once I've taken that as far as I can, I hope very much that I can get some sleep. Ben and Todd have other ideas, however; I don't know what exactly Maurice Faye has told them (he enlisted Jack's help also), but evidently my polling numbers are soaring with Hollywood boy producers that night. We face each other on cream leather chairs. It's like sitting in the bar of an old-fashioned, expensive hotel.

They kick off with some corporate boilerplate about not bringing the studio into disrepute, and alerting the press office if any connection between the Donovan movies and the killings were to be made, and I assure them that I will do everything I can to be discreet, and that the number of camp followers and trade suppliers—from groupies and fan boys to craft services, security, transportation, etc.—that Jack's movies have attracted over the years means it would be impossible to narrow it down simply to the creative personnel on the movies. And since I don't mention, and since Maurice Faye has succeeded in keeping from them, the major reason I suspect exactly the people who would bring unholy scandal crashing down on the studio's heads, the disappearance of Nora Mannion and Kate Coyle, they are operating at a lower level of panic than I am.

"The thing about you is, you don't look sleazy," Todd, who is blond and oversize and freckled and goofy-looking, says.

"Tact, Todd, nice," Ben, who is very dark and slight of build and short, maybe five four, says. "What Todd means is—"

"I thought we had a guillotine on the expression 'What Todd Means,' like I'm some moron in need of an interpreter—"

"We had a *moratorium* on that expression. But that was in Ireland. And we're no longer in Ireland."

"We're in Irish airspace."

"Whatever. What Todd Means is, Hollywood PIs tend toward the slick and the sleazy—"

"I wasn't a Hollywood PI. I just did some work for Jack."

"Back in the day," Todd says excitedly. "My dad—"

"We were trying to keep that expression to a minimum also,"

Ben says drily. "'My dad.' On account of its somewhat less than cool flavor. My dad is picking us up from swimming. My dad owns a beach house. "

Todd shrugs.

"So I'm not cool. So I got this job because of my dad. You did, too."

"Did not."

"Forgive me, your mom."

"Boys," I say.

"Back in the day, my dad told some great stories about Jack and his crew," Todd says. "The Irish guys, the famous Gang of Four. So many stories. So it was just unbelievable to meet them all tonight."

"Hard to get to know Mark and Conor," Ben says.

"Mark's all right. You can talk to Mark. Impossible to get to know Conor," Todd says.

"I never managed it."

"It's weird, though," Ben said. "I mean, a good first—and Conor is, right, he works with other people, too, he's in demand—at some stage, they tend to move up, they want to direct. And from what we've been told, he never has."

"Maybe he's afraid his natural charm will get in his way," Todd says, and laughs at his own joke.

"Maybe it's just a lack of ambition," Ben says. "And all that boozing can't exactly help."

"I think there's also the Jack factor," I say. "I mean, he is unusually charismatic, he's a phenomenon, a force of nature. It must be hard to feel you can measure up to that. And maybe there's a magnetism about it, that you would never want to pass up a chance to be in his presence. Maybe Conor is happy to be where he is. It doesn't have to be a lack of ambition. It's just, he has his place on the team and he's content. And he is, I find him a surly cuss and no mistake, but if Jack says jump, Conor is still, how high?"

"Of course, Mark is a totally other kettle of fish," Todd says. "My dad—forgive me, O Gods of Cool—my dad was at the studio for *A Terrible Beauty* and *Ocean Falls,* and he said Mark was really champing at the bit, trying to set up shots and even talk to actors. And I mean, some DPs do set up the shot. But Jack just wouldn't have it."

"There was also a thing where Mark was writing his own scripts, and suggesting to Maurice that the next project they do should be one of his."

"Like a drummer joke: hey guys, why don't we do one of my songs?"

"It's the Jack Donovan show, dummy."

"All that."

"I never knew that," I say.

"Oh yeah," Todd says. "Because then Mark went off in a huff around the time of *Armageddon Factor.* And Jack shot that with someone else."

"Jack shot it with two people, he got these Brits in, and they have a different system, where the DP is like a lighting director, and then the camera operator handles the framing. And each was competing with the other, and Jack had real trouble getting his way," Ben says.

"*The Armageddon Factor* is not A Jack Donovan picture, it's a . . . hate to say this, but it's a studio picture, it's product. Efficient product—"

"Very profitable product—"

"No denying. But it's not a hundred percent Jack proof, even if he gets his little incest thing and his older-younger woman thing in, but they're like, so oblique, like, did that just happen?"

"So Jack was more than happy for Mark to come back on *Dain Curse.* And they've worked together ever since."

"No one knows what Mark did during the time; for a while he seemed to just slip off the radar. There were rumors he did some porno in the valley. And of course, the fact that *Armageddon* was so different, that opened a whole kettle of worms."

"Fish."

"Excuse me?"

"Kettle of fish. Barrel of worms."

"Keeper of the clichés. Whatever. To the effect that because Mark worked on all the *true* Jack Donovan pictures, he's like the power behind the throne."

"That used to be just industry gossip, but like every other piece of insider knowledge, it's now the talk of the backblogs."

"It's funny," I say. "I was around during that whole time. I was *in The Dain Curse.*"

"We know!" Todd and Ben carol in unison. "Irish Man in Bar."

"But I never picked up on any of that. I guess it's not surprising, though. I mean, Jack just . . . has no time for any point of view other than his own—"

"You say it as if it's a bad thing!" Ben says.

"So he either wouldn't have noticed or wouldn't have cared. Being Jack Donovan is a thousand-yard stare of a job, and it doesn't require a great deal of peripheral vision. And I wasn't really interested in anyone else but Jack at that stage."

"Well, the story is, Mark's done what he had to do for Jack, but the resentment hasn't diminished. And he's tried to get scripts going himself, but nothing's ever happened," Todd says.

"It's weird," Ben says. "It's like, he's not content to be a DP anymore. Never works with anyone else now. But he can't take the step up as a director. He's in this . . . career limbo."

"The Curse of Jack Donovan!" Todd says.

"Can he afford not to work?" I ask.

"The Gang of Four were all on gross points from early on," Ben says. "I mean, Jack and Maurice got more, but Conor and Mark made a truckload of bread for themselves. So unless they developed big gambling or coke habits, they can afford to do as they please."

"It's just unusual for a DP not to work," Todd says. "Those guys are so driven, they're obsessed with what they do. Mark could work year-round. That he chooses not to . . . is strange."

We talk a little longer, but start to double back on what we've already said, and I can tell they're working up to asking me about the case, and I don't want to talk about that yet. I plead tiredness; each of them as if by reflex produces a satchel of bound scripts and begins to work their way through them, and I sit back and think about what they'd just said, and about what had happened in the restaurant that night, and what it all might mean.

It isn't difficult to follow Todd and Ben's car, and to insinuate himself into Loy's backyard. It's one of the things he knows about: light, and the absence of light. You could say he's dedicated his life to it. He watches Loy talk to Tommy, Tommy Owens. He feels sure Tommy is the key to finding Jenny Noble. And in the absence of Madeline, he insists on making Jenny his last, his best of three. He realizes, too, he can't lie to himself, he can't break a pattern in the middle, he simply cannot be inconsistent in that way. It would undermine everything he has ever tried to do, set it at naught.

Loy leaves, and Tommy returns to his place in the shadows. Tommy will be armed, but there is no need for confrontation: shadows will see to that. And only the minimum violence required. That, he believes increasingly, in terms of moral force, stands to him—that he has never succumbed to brutality or sadism, never felt the slightest desire to see blood, or inflict excessive suffering—which is as much to say, he isn't some kind of freak or psycho, he has relatively normal wiring, there is no sense in congratulating himself for simply being the way he is.

Mind you, he does have his eccentricities.

Mustn't laugh.

Time to make a move.

He lobs the small weight through the window of the car nearest Tommy Owens and then feints to the blind side by the Nissan truck, and as the alarm squeals and Owens runs in the direction from which the weight came, he crosses the patch of yard illuminated by the building's stairwell light, where it's not too difficult to catch him firmly on the back of the head with a Maglite. He hopes he has got the force of the blow right; he has no wish to kill. Apart from anything else, he would be at a loss to know how to balance a dead man in his forties; who else would he have to murder to round that out? He goes through his pockets and takes his phone. The blow and the fall have knocked a handgun onto the ground. He doesn't like guns, and has no idea what type this is, but in light of the new phase he is about to enter, with the need to control and discipline three in one at the same time (even if two out of three are children), he feels it might be prudent to take it with him. He is in the car before the residents of the apartment block are out of their beds.

He checks his phone.

He sent a text immediately before he stepped into the yard, informing Jenny that Jack has rescheduled for an emergency night shoot, that Nora and Kate are on their way, that a car had been sent but she was not at her address, signing the text Geoff Keegan. He also sent backup texts from Nora and Kate's phones.

He knew Jenny would check her moves with Tommy Owens first.

On Tommy's phone, there is one missed call from Jenny, and a voice message.

Hi, Mr. Owens, I'm just checking, they've rescheduled on the move for a night shoot, and they want to send a car to pick me up, so I just really, is it cool to tell them where I am, let me know soon, thanks. This is Jenny, Naomi's friend, by the way.

He texts her back on Owens's phone:

Can't talk am at work that's fine if film crew are in touch
go for it Tommy

Jenny Noble texts him immediately with an address in Enniskerry. He can't use a Nighttown *car, for obvious reasons, so he arranges for a cab to pick Jenny up and bring her to his house, using Geoff Keegan's name. Jenny Noble evidently has the jitters, however; minutes later, she calls him.*

"Hi, Geoff? This is Jenny Noble?"

He is no mimic, but he has a similar vocal timbre and accent to Geoff Keegan.

"Hi, Jenny. Glad we found you. I've just arranged a car."

"That's great. Only I was kind of wondering, isn't it all a bit last minute?"

"Well, it's all pretty spur-of-the-moment, hands-on stuff tonight, we're working with an absolute skeleton crew, no assistants or ADs, just HODs all mucking in, doing each other's jobs. It's like the old days, just the Gang of Four and a camera or two in the great outdoors. Guerrilla style!"

"Oh, right. Sounds exciting! Just, also, I tried to get in touch with Madeline King, too, but she's not answering her phone."

"Sure Madeline barely has time to turn around. You have to hand it to Jack—when he gets an idea, he really runs with it. Wrote a new sequence set in a garden at night. Madeline's had her hands full copying it and marking it out for the various departments. She'll be there, you'll see her soon enough."

"And Nora and Kate—"

"And Nora and Kate. It'll be one big reunion. So anyway, thing is, when you get here, the cab won't be taking you to the set, it'll drop you at a house in Milltown, old house with a long driveway, we're using it as a location. A bit spooky, but don't be frightened—there's nothing scary about the person who lives there."

"Why, who lives there?"

"I do."

CHAPTER 23

My plan is to settle back and review the case, but since I don't have enough in the way of concrete new evidence, or even substantial conjecture, to add, sleep overtakes me. I awake to find the plane on the ground, and mistakenly think we've arrived, but we've only stopped in Teterboro, New Jersey, to refuel. Ben and Todd find this hilarious, and kick into a movie trailer routine:

"After *The Exorcist* came *The Omen*. After *The Omen* came . . . *New Jersey!*"

"He thought there could be worse fates than waking up in Jersey . . . He was *wrong.*"

I fall asleep again, waking slowly as we make our descent into Burbank. Gathering my thoughts, I find an extra item of information in the shape of a phone message I didn't pick up in Dublin. Inspector Dave Donnelly of the Serious Crime Review Team ran the Gang of Four through Garda criminal record files, and, apart from two not very surprising drunk-and-disorderlys and a dangerous driving-while-under-the-influence on Jack's part, the only other item of note is that Conor Rowan has twice had charges of violent behavior and assault laid against him by two separate females, one of whom subsequently sought and received a barring order forbidding Rowan to come within two hundred meters of her home. So Conor Rowan has been violent toward women; he has a famously bad temper, and overreacted to my questioning him tonight: he could be a killer. Although, would the killer be so uncool and draw so much attention to himself simply because he was asked a second time if he remembered anything about the Point Dume girls?

Jack has been violent toward women as well, or at least, a woman, and he has a complicated relationship with them at the best of times, which may have its roots in an abusive relationship with his sister. And he has a temper, and he's volatile and unpredictable.

Mark Cassidy said he didn't remember the girls, but then changed his story to say he does remember one of them, Janice Holloway. Would the killer have corrected himself? Why would he draw attention to a minor conversation like that, unless it was simply the truth? The fact that Mark has apparently become disenchanted with his career is interesting, as is the contradiction between his alleged resentment of Jack and his refusal to work with anyone else.

Maurice Faye is a hail-fellow-well-met family guy, hard to rouse to anger. On the other hand, he got very worked up over Derek Doyle's column in the *Irish Times*, and he has unusually large hands for a man of his slight build—the kind of hands that could fit easily around a woman's neck.

It all adds up to nothing. Not even a hunch. I guess if I had to plump for one likely killer above the other three, based on what I know of their backgrounds, I'd choose Jack. But I can't believe Jack did it either. From what I know now, he did not go easy on himself after he was violent toward Amanda Cole—indeed, he claims the fear he might strike a woman again has kept him from his children and their mother. The idea that he might kidnap and murder young women is grotesque.

Perhaps it is so for them all. You can't extrapolate from someone's childhood and background that he would step over the edge and act in this particular way. That's what I find so problematic about criminal profiling: it's magical thinking, when you boil it down, a kind of elaborate system of guesswork and hunch-playing. Nothing wrong with that, I operate pretty much the same way. Every detective does. Reading the runes and going with your gut are part of the job, along with gathering evidence. We just don't dress it up the way the criminal profile boys do, calling it behavioral science and making claims for its near infallibility. If an abusive father or a sadistic mother or an inappropriately young exposure to pornography contribute to the formation of a serial killer, how come so many kids survive these experiences and live harmless, peaceful adult lives?

Reading the runes and going with your gut and gathering evidence, and the greatest of these is evidence. Evidence is what I just don't have. Evidence is what I need.

It's been a while since I was in Burbank Airport—Bob Hope Airport, to give it its other name—the last time was with Jack Donovan—but its thirties country-club dimensions feel as instantly familiar as the stands of palm and yucca spread about like Californian landing beacons, part of a Los Angeles that dug deep into my bones and has never left me. Even at dawn, the heat of the Valley is intense; I feel a Santa Ana wind on my brow and on the back of my neck, serving notice that the normal rules have ceased to apply.

Ben and Todd grab copies of the *Los Angeles Times,* where the case is the main story; they look at me expectantly and I reassure them that I'll holler well in advance if things are looking bad for any of their employees, past or present. There's a Town Car waiting to take them to their homes; they offer it to me for the rest of the day, courtesy of the studio. It's tempting, but I reckon, for however long I'm going to be back, I had better drive myself; in any case, I don't like the idea that my movements can be monitored. I thank them, and take their cards, and wish them well. Maurice Faye is paying for car hire, so I rent a black Chevy Camaro. Before I pick it up, I call Don Coover's cell and leave a message; then I buy an *L.A. Times* myself and get a cup of coffee and sit and read my way into the latest developments in the Three-in-One Killer case.

The headline reads:

MASS MURDER IN LOS ANGELES
THREE-IN-ONE TIMES SIX

Beneath that, there's a map with the six burial sites marked on it. As well as Point Dume in Malibu, the sites are in the Sierra Mountains on the Californian banks of Lake Tahoe; in the garden of a house in Venice by the canals; in the garden of a house on Mulholland Drive by Laurel Canyon; in waste ground by the Los Angeles River where Ventura Boulevard meets the Hollywood Freeway; and beneath the floor of a house near Coldwater Canyon. On the second page there's a montage of photographs of every secured location with LAPD technical and forensic teams examining the scenes, each with an accompanying photograph of Detective Donald Coover. It's starting to look like I might have a better chance of meeting Harrison Ford for a beer than getting an audience with Don Coover. I call again, and leave a message that I hope might be a little more persuasive. He calls me back within five minutes.

"What do you mean, you think he's in Dublin? Dublin, Ireland?"

"Yes, Dublin, Ireland."

"You're kidding me. You sure? You got a profile of the guy?"

"It's one of four people. I haven't narrowed it down yet. But I'm getting more and more sure all the time."

"What's the connection between Dublin and here? Jack Donovan?"

"What makes you say that?"

"Because yesterday when I spoke to you, you told me you were working for Jack Donovan."

"Well remembered. It's a bit more complicated than Jack Donovan. Look, meet me for breakfast and I'll tell you."

"Very funny. Breakfast in Dublin? I'm kind of busy here, in case you hadn't noticed—"

"I'm in Burbank Airport."

"You're in Burbank right now?"

"That's right. I flew out here to speak to you."

"Well, speak, Ed, I'm listening."

"I need a face-to-face."

"Ed, I've barely been to bed, do you have any idea how big this case is—"

"I haven't been to bed in two days. And I'm saying I can help you to crack it. And you can help me. Because you can't get your photo taken arresting the Three-in-One Killer in Dublin, Ireland. And the FBI must be on their way—Malibu? Tahoe? No way are the LAPD hanging on to this. Now, where do you want to meet? I can be in Parker Center in maybe an hour if I take the 101 before the traffic builds."

There's a silence. I can hear Coover's breath. I press my case.

"Come on, Don. You know none of this would have happened if I hadn't knocked on your door fifteen years ago, you said as much yourself. And now look at you. You the man. You got any leads?"

"No. No ID on any of the bodies but the Point Dume three and they're not confirmed. Yes, the FBI is coming in to steal my case, I mean, offer their assistance, I mean, steal my case. Strictly speaking, all I have today is a press conference in the afternoon.

More like another photo op. Not to mention sit and play brief the feds until we all go crazy. Meanwhile we wait for the phones to ring and sift through what people tell us until some of it, any of it, makes sense."

"So what do you say?"

"I say let's steer clear of police HQ for a start. Doesn't matter that we're not releasing any more information until the afternoon, and I doubt if we'll have anything to say then either, the press and the cameras are in 'rolling news' mode, they're just waiting for anyone they recognize so they can stick a mike in their face and fill some airspace. All right. I imagine you want to head over to Point Dume yourself, since that's where it started for you."

"That would be the plan."

Coover names a diner called Patrick's Roadhouse just above Pacific Coast Highway at San Vicente Boulevard. It's one of those places that's hard to forget: with an exterior painted garish bright green and covered with shamrocks, it looks like the owners have forgotten to take the St. Patrick's Day decorations down. I get on the road, and instantly regret not taking Ben and Todd up on their offer; there are things in your life that you push to the back of your mind and hope will never again intrude on your consciousness, and the infernal machine of torture by heat, light, sound and physical agitation that the L.A. freeway system constitutes is one of those things, even this early in the morning. I take the Hollywood Freeway by force of habit, but I'm in plenty of time; I'm not meeting Don Coover until nine.

I get off and onto Cahuenga, then hook northwest onto winding Mulholland Drive. I want to ride Mulholland for the great views it affords, of L.A. west to the ocean, and back across the San Fernando Valley to the San Gabriel Mountains, but also because two of the burial sites are in the vicinity. The first is at a Spanish Colonial mansion just after the turn down into Laurel Canyon. I can't see the site. I can only barely see the house.

But I know I'm approaching a mile before I hit it on account of the melee of photographers, press helicopters, cops and other interested parties. Many of the latter have assembled already with sandwiches and sodas, ready for a day of hanging out at the scene of a mass grave. I don't know what they think or hope might happen—a resurrection? Or simply the chance to appear on TV, flaunting their empathy with people they don't know? That's my first reaction, and I almost immediately regret it; on closer inspection, many people are holding up banners and placards with the names and photographs of people they once knew; each sign carries a date, and the word *missing*. Never lost, which has the ruthless air of finality about it; always missing, which leaves room for that great faithless friend, hope. I feel ashamed of myself for having been so quick to judge them, and pity for them, and as I ride on, the great expansive grid that is Los Angeles stretching out on either side, I feel desolation, in the bright morning light, that so many should have lost so much in this sunlit, dark city; in the Santa Ana heat, I feel the chill of fear.

The scene is not dissimilar when I cut down into Coldwater Canyon. The helicopters alert me to the location, and as I approach, I see the same placards, the same faces, the same desperate hope. Between thirty-five and forty thousand people in California go missing every year; here is a chance that their daughter's or sister's body is buried in one of these graves—and many hold signs with men's, with boy's, faces, for the sex of all the bodies found has still not been determined, or announced. Of course, not everyone is distinguished by the dignity of their grief; there's a fair sprinkling of T-shirt and trinket sellers, ice-cream vendors, and assorted cranks seeing an opportunity to push their arcane worldview or conspiracy theory of choice. And plenty of cops and private security to keep them all in line, especially in an expensive neighborhood like this.

I come out on Beverly Drive, hang a right onto Santa Monica, and ride straight down through Beverly Hills, Century City and Westwood, cutting onto San Vicente at Sawtelle and riding around and down, down to the blue of the ocean.

Patrick's Roadhouse looms above PCH like a chemical dream in an azure world. I can't face it yet, and feel badly in need of fresh air and exercise, so I park in the lot across the street and cross the highway and walk along the bike path and climb up onto a patch of scrub and find a spot to sit and stare out at the ocean, the ocean I haven't seen or smelled for five years. I stare out at Santa Monica Bay, where we scattered the ashes of my daughter, Lily, who would have been eight years old had she lived, the same age as Anne's younger daughter, Ciara. I stare and stare, and I think my thoughts and I say my prayers, and at nine o'clock I walk back across Pacific Coast Highway and into Patrick's Roadhouse to meet Detective Donald Coover of the Cold Case Unit of the LAPD.

Coover sits in a darkened corner of the roadhouse near the back exit. Not only can you not see the ocean from here, you can barely see the bar. There are pictures of famous actors who are allegedly regulars hung up all around, but this is no balm to Coover, the most famous man in L.A. as of this morning. He has a haunted look on his face, and from his furtive sidelong glances, I can tell he has already been recognized.

"In hiding?" I say. "This is your moment, Don. Step up."

"I reserve the right to eat breakfast first," Coover said. He is a tall, lean, sinewy man with a tanned face and lank, side-parted hair which was California blond when I saw him last.

"Ed Loy," he says, standing up and shaking my hand and making a big deal of scrutinizing me closely. "A gray hair?"

"A gray head wins," I say. "It suits you. Distinguished."

"Distinguished. That's liar for 'old.'"

"Well. We're all headed in the one direction."

A blond waitress comes and takes our order. She doesn't look Irish and she doesn't sound Irish, and right now that suits me fine. I order lox, eggs and onions, because that's what I like to have for breakfast, along with whole wheat toast, orange juice and coffee. Coover has granola, yogurt and decaf, which I guess is how he stays lean and sinewy.

Once we've ordered, he looks at me.

"Jack Donovan?"

I suppose I've been harboring some vague notion that I can keep secret the possibility that my friend might be involved in the case, might in fact be the Three-in-One Killer, until I have a clearer idea myself. The logical corollary to this, however, is that I might consider showing mercy, or seeking mitigation, for a man who has killed eighteen people and counting. Sitting across the table from Don Coover, I understand enough about who I am and who I am not to realize that just isn't going to happen.

"All right. First thing. I have . . . I think I have a link."

"For the murders? The burial sites?"

"Yeah."

"And the link is Jack Donovan?"

"Keep your voice down. There's always an actor or two hanging out in here, or at least there used to be."

"Nah. You can be sure, once they put the photos on the walls, the only people who come here anymore are the actors who wait tables for a living. And tourists, like you, of course," Coover says with a guarded smile.

"Just wait until you hear, then you can decide what kind of tourist I am. All right, on the *Ocean Falls* set at Point Dume, there were four people who have worked together now fifteen years, half a dozen movies: Jack Donovan; his producer, Maurice Faye; cinematographer Mark Cassidy; and first AD Conor Rowan."

"And what? Each of these locations . . . is a location? Was used as a movie set? For a Jack Donovan picture, that each of these four guys worked on?"

"Hey. You must be one of those shit-hot LAPD detectives we see on TV."

A black Moleskine notebook appears beneath Coover's slender hand and snaps open, a steel ballpoint poised above it.

"What have you got?"

"Okay, 1997: *The Dain Curse*. Ended in the San Gabriel Mountains, but started out in Venice, along the canals?"

"Okay. Were you in that movie?"

"I was."

"I thought so."

"But do you see me on the wall here? I think not. All right, next: *Twenty Grand*. 1999. Shot in the Sierras, near Lake Tahoe."

"You're shitting me."

"I shit thee not. Next, *The Man in the High Castle*. 2002."

Coover looks up from his notebook.

"Mulholland Drive? A Spanish Colonial castle, it was, I remember. Great movie. Fuck, this is amazing. You won't be wanting a credit here, Ed, will you?"

"Where do you think we are, L.A.? *The Last Anniversary*. 2005."

"I left halfway through. I'm guessing Coldwater Canyon."

"A lot of it was shot in the studio, which is down in the Valley, but there were two long sequences shot in period houses in the Canyon, where the eternal lovers were a silent-era Hollywood couple and then a pair of Joni Mitchell/David Crosby–type rock stars."

"And the fifth?"

"The fifth. Now, I don't know about the fifth. The only other movie Jack made here was *The Armageddon Factor*, but I'm pretty sure that was all shot on location up in San Francisco. 1995."

"Where Ventura meets the 101, by the Los Angeles River there, it's close to Studio City, too."

"Right. Because I know they did postproduction on *A Terrible Beauty* somewhere there, would have been '92. That was their first time in L.A."

"Did they all come over?"

"Good question. Obviously Jack would have, and I think he

used to have Mark Cassidy in the edit suite back then. And Maurice would have been there at least some of the time, taking care of business."

"No need for a First AD once you're finished the shoot, though."

"I wouldn't have thought so. But they were very much one for all, all for one at the time, so there's a fair chance Conor would have come as part of the gang. The Gang of Four, they called themselves."

"Okay. Who can we ask? Not any of them."

"Well. Three out of four, but which three? And that's the thing about *The Armageddon Factor,* Mark Cassidy did not work on that picture at all. So if the Ventura/Hollywood Freeway site is linked to *Armageddon,* that's Mark out."

The waitress brings our breakfast, and we eat for a while in ruminative silence. Coover makes a few notes.

"Okay, well, on *A Terrible Beauty,* we can check studio records, expense sheets for the production, if . . . Conor Rowan came, he'd've been on the clock. And then find out which movie used that Ventura 101 site."

"You sound excited."

"It's good, Ed, even if the fifth doesn't hang in there. By which I mean, the sixth, counting the Point Dume three."

"Is there a crucifix in every site?"

Coover nods, his mouth full of granola.

"Three bodies in each. That's eighteen. All female, we weren't certain, but they're pretty sure as of this morning, they worked through the night."

"That's the job for me. Jesus Christ, eighteen."

"Tell me about these guys. Some kind of profile of each? Biographies?"

My phone rings; it's a withheld number, but I answer anyway: Tommy.

"I have to take this," I say, walking out of Patrick's and climbing up onto the side of the highway.

"Tommy? Whose phone are you ringing from?"

"A throwaway. I was rightly done, Ed, someone cracked me on the back of the nut, just after you'd gone to the airport. Woke up in Vincent's with a nappy on my head, concussion, ten past three this afternoon. Fuck, they even had Paula in there, and Naomi. I'm lying back, feeling all out of whack, not so much what is wrong with this picture as what *is* this fucking picture, know I mean? And Paula, you can see, now I'm alive, she's getting her scowl on, ready to give out, and Naomi, all tearstained, and the first thing I say, Ed, the first thing out of my mouth, is: 'Where's Jenny Noble?'"

Tommy says something else, but I don't hear it; the sound of an LAPD helicopter overhead drowns out even the sound of the cars on the highway. It's headed north toward Malibu, where through the haze I can see another two or three choppers hovering like hungry insects, I guess marking the spot at Point Dume where the lost girls' bodies were discovered. I tune Tommy in again.

" . . . Naomi said Jenny texted her to say Nora and Kate were back, and that she was going to her flat. But there was no sign of her there, I checked myself out of Vincent's, got Jenny's address from your man Geoff Keegan—was looking for Madeline but I can't find her either. No sign of Jenny on the set. She's gone, Ed. All three of them are gone."

Those girls are gone.

"It's time to get the Guards involved."

"Maurice Faye has done that, Store Street Garda are on it. But what are they gonna do?"

I tell Tommy to take care of himself, that I'll get back to him soon, and end the call. When I get back into Patrick's, Don Coover is on a call himself.

"Yeah, 1992. No, that was when the movie was released, you want to go back to probably '91 for the production. Yes. Thank you. And then *The Armageddon Factor* . . . yes, that would probably be '94. Just, if there were any studio pickups, and, and where postproduction was done. Yes. Thank you. The first number is my cell, call me anytime, I mean anytime. I appreciate it."

Coover closes the call and meets my eye.

"You look all shook up."

"The other reason I made the connection: two girls had disappeared off the set of *Nighttown*, the movie Jack is shooting in Dublin. One on Wednesday afternoon, one Thursday morning. It's not enough time for anyone over the age of eighteen to be considered missing, but these girls were a trio in scenes that had already been shot, so for the movie, it was an emergency. I thought of Point Dume immediately. So I got an associate of mine to keep the third girl, Jenny Noble, in a safe house. Our guy put my associate in the hospital, tricked Jenny into thinking her friends were back and there was a night shoot, sent a car for her. Now she's gone."

"Three-in-one. Man. You think it's him?"

"On the negative side, why would one of those guys do that when it would mean jeopardizing his own movie? They may not have the budget to shoot those scenes again. It's against his interests. But maybe there's a reason for that. Maybe he just doesn't care anymore. All right, say I think it's him. What do we do? They've reported the girls missing. That's the scenario I came to you with, all those years ago. Just three missing girls. Nothing to see here."

Coover flinches, maybe bridles a little.

"There was no way I could have known—"

"I wasn't saying there was, Don. You did what you could. What do we do now?"

"I think you have enough legitimately to request a police investigation. House searches, questioning of suspects. Lay it out for them. If you have good Irish police connections. If you like, I'll do it, maybe take it up the food chain a bit. No offense."

I think about it, and then shake my head.

"If this is our guy, his work is done. Three-in-one, every

movie, the end. Maybe he's taking more risks than he used to, but I can't see how the Guards are going to catch him out. And if we alert him, we could lose him."

"There is that. All right then, profile. Give me a sense of these guys, who we're dealing with. Could I get some nondecaf, please?" (This last to the passing waitress.)

"In the olden days, we used to call it coffee."

"The olden days. Wasn't this a tar pit?"

"You have a few years on me. Okay, profile. Well, if you want a serial killer with built-in motivation flashing like a neon sign, Jack Donovan's your man."

The waitress refills both our cups, and I take Coover on a ride along the roller coaster that is Jack Donovan: the strong possibility that he had an incestuous relationship with his elder sister that resulted in the termination of a pregnancy, his disastrous relationship with women, culminating—for me—with his physical abuse of Amanda Cole, his bizarre marriage and refusal to acknowledge his own children, and the anonymous letters he allegedly received, apocalyptic in tone, that seem to refer to the three-in-one motif used by the killer. Coover looks at me in amazement.

"That is one awesome profile. Sounds almost like he's overqualified for the job. You sure about the incest?"

"Not certain, but . . . that's the way I'd go on it. Against all that, Jack Donovan's an artist, and a very complex, troubled guy, who's in a period of major transition at the moment. I've sat down with him, I've pushed him on all this."

"And what did you get?"

"What did I get? That's he's a damaged, messy, wayward, willful man who's alternately the most thrilling, enthralling companion you could imagine and an absolute nightmare to be around. Do I think, do I really think he could murder eighteen, twenty-one women and dump their bodies in mass graves? No, I don't. But this is where I think you can't simply translate personality traits or behavioral patterns into actions. Otherwise, why doesn't every abused child become a pedophile? It's bullshit."

"Well, up to a point. I mean, you've got an angry guy, he's a loner, he's got a history of violence against women, that's gonna move him up in line from Mr. Family Man two kids a dog and a cat."

"Well, that's Conor Rowan you've just outlined, Jack's First AD. Angry, probably alcoholic, lives alone, girlfriends who come and go, no family, goes drinking in his local bar with people he's known all his life."

"He could fit the bill."

"I can see how Conor Rowan might fit the bill as a guy who'd lose his temper, maybe drunk, and beat his girlfriend to death, who'd even, drinking all the time, plan to kill her. But that's run-of-the-mill, maybe we could all fit that bill. We've all imagined someone we don't like dying, how convenient it would be—it's a short trip through a glass darkly to acting on that thought. But this is a whole different bill: eighteen, maybe twenty-one bodies, twenty-one women, left in mass graves with crucifixes carved with their initials. I mean, you can even quote your whatever, your McDonald triad, ask if this guy wet the bed, tortured animals and set fires, but even if he did, how does it go from that to here, to three-in-one, to this spectacular carnival of murder?"

"So what are you looking for?"

"A fact. A detail. A mistake. Something that leads me to the guy, not the *type* of guy. There's a hundred and one Conor Rowans in every neighborhood, disappointed, angry, alcoholic middle-aged guys, pissed off about so much they've lost track themselves. Even in the unlikely event that they were all capable of murder, they'd never be capable of this. Then there's Mark Cassidy—supercilious, sneery, clever, aloof, smart-aleck, maybe thinks he's the real power behind the throne, the brains of the operation, feels aggrieved because he's underappreciated.

Resents being in the great man's shadow, but lacks the balls to strike out on his own. I bet there's a Conor Rowan and a Mark Cassidy in every workplace, bet you work alongside one or two yourself."

"Sure I do. Don't work alongside any Jack Donovans, though. What's the deal on the fourth guy, the producer, Maurice Faye?"

"In a way, Maurice is the most opaque to me. He's a kind of hail-fellow-well-met guy, all business, but everything's an adventure, everything's a joke, everything's hilarious, even the calamities . . . and then he'll get very angry about something trivial, some adverse criticism in a newspaper, say, and you see beneath all that joviality and backslapping and charm, he's kind of in a rage . . . now that I talk about him, he's actually a very characteristic Irish type."

Coover smiles.

"I was gonna say. You guys have a habit of making a hell of a lot of noise to cover up a broken heart."

"Maybe we do. Maybe we do. But none of that . . . I mean, Maurice could be the killer. Jack could be. The point is, any of those guys, it's going to be a shock. Anyone who doesn't live in a cave on a diet of maggots and blood, it's going to be a shock."

Coover can't stop smiling.

"I'm sorry, Ed, but that's a big case we got here. Looks to me like, from nowhere, we've got this down to four suspects. You should feel good."

"I'll feel good when we get it down to one. Have we got any, you have IDs, at least provisionally, for the Point Dume girls, have you got any relatives? Wasn't there a brother?"

"I made some calls yesterday. That was the thing, back in the day these girls were already runaways and you were the only one to report them. We found nobody for Desiree LaRouche or Polly Styles, but for Janice Holloway, yes, we had a brother, Keith, we got his address in her apartment in North Hollywood, kept his details on file. I called him yesterday and he's coming out this morning. He wanted to see where his sister had been buried, so I arranged to meet him along at Point Dume— thought you could see him there also. They've closed the beach. And then I'm gonna need you to come in, talk on the record to me, maybe to the feds, the Irish police, too, whatever way we're set up on this, get the whole thing moving forward."

Before they let us leave Patrick's, they take a photo of Coover by the bar holding the *L.A. Times* "Three-in-One Killer" cover. All the stars in heaven.

CHAPTER 24

I follow Coover north on Pacific Coast Highway for almost twenty miles. It's a drive I've always loved, this stretch of coastline bound for Malibu, with the hazy ocean glistening on one side and the jagged red rock of the Santa Monica Mountains on the other, the canyons drifting up through green hillsides and parks and then shimmering out of sight. But today the sun's glare seems too harsh, the roadside stops too garish, the trippers and bathers and skaters positively indecent witnesses to a funeral cortege headed for an unmarked graveside.

As we approach Point Dume, it's as if the sun slips behind a cloud: the placards and signs with names and pictures of old and young suddenly line the highway. Coover still hasn't released the names of the girls, and won't until he has confirmed their IDs. So the same principle applies as at the other burial sites: anyone missing in Malibu could be one of the bodies found. There's a limit to how many people can fit on the side of the road, and the highway patrol are pulling in on motorcycles and urging people to move on, whether for their safety or to prevent traffic delays. It looks like a cross between a mass protest and a pilgrimage, although the effect is maybe less overwhelming than those I saw on Mulholland and in Coldwater Canyon. But the iconography of loss and the dedicated communion with the missing is still deeply affecting.

At the approach to Point Dume State Beach, the cops have effectively mounted a roadblock. Don Coover leans out his window and shows his ID, and the cop on duty calls to his colleague, who knocks on the window of a beat-up old Toyota. A skinny man in his twenties with long dark hair in black jeans and T-shirt emerges from the tragic orange heap: Janice Holloway's brother, Keith, I presume. Keith nods to Coover and shakes his hand and sits into the passenger seat of his unmarked Ford Taurus. I follow them down Wildlife Road and we wend past the luxury houses through the evergreens and park down near the bluff on Cliffside Drive.

The pungent scent of pine and eucalyptus lingers with me like incense from a censer as we climb the bluff. We walk a quarter of a mile through pampas grass and scrub and gorse and down to a small depression shaded by greenery. An LAPD technical team in paper suits have taken down a forensic tent to reveal a mound of freshly dug sand and earth, and beside it, a grave about four feet in depth.

Keith Holloway looks at Coover, who inclines his head toward the grave and nods; Holloway stands by the grave and bows his head in a prayerful attitude. No matter that this is not a cemetery, that his sister's body has been removed and has not yet been identified, he is relying on the rituals of mourning to get him through. At times like these, ritual is sometimes all we have. I stand still in the salt breeze and look out to the ocean. It would make a beautiful last resting place. My thoughts turn to my parents' grave, with its view of the sea, and then to what has been done to it, and I, too, bow my head, but in rage. All the way to Malibu, and Podge Halligan has come with me. I turn away and leave Keith Holloway to his thoughts. Coover closes a call on his cell phone and beckons me up the bluff a pace.

"The FBI is requesting my presence. I want you to come in, get all your stuff on the record . . . how long are you here?"

"As long as it takes."

"That could be a while. I need to clear the ground with the feds first, bragging rights, jurisdiction, all that good stuff. But there was some stuff I was thinking on the way out. Some pro-filing stuff, if you'll indulge me."

"Anything that works is fine by me."

"Well, this is all just serial-killer 101, but it's worth consider-ing. Okay, on the one hand, as you say, he's hit his target, three girls gone, he's done: not quite forget about him, but the softly softly approach is sensible, try and snare him somehow now we've narrowed the field of suspects to four."

"Two days ago, we didn't know we had a field to narrow."

"And why do we know now? First, because you made the connection, Ed: you joined the dots between Point Dume, and Dublin, and Jack Donovan. But second, because the killer tipped us off. Tipped me off. Now, why would he do that if he's happy to just go to ground again?"

"So what, he's reached some kind of crisis point?"

"Well, it's like you said, if it's one of these four, why would he put his own film in danger? Why would he kill actresses who had already been filmed? Unless he's getting that way people get when . . . I don't know if it's that they want to be found out, or to close a particular chapter in their lives, or the only way they can really function is under the adrenaline gun, and each time they have to risk failure, to flirt with disaster. I've seen a lot of cops go to that place, usually with the help of booze and pills and powder. But it's the same idea, you blot out the lows, and become addicted to the highs, but each time the highs get harder to come by, so you end up always having to raise the stakes. And there's only so high you can raise them."

"Before what? Disaster? Self-destruction? Are you saying he wants to be caught?"

"No. Well, yes and no. At its simplest, maybe it's that, after fifteen or twenty years of secrecy, he wants us to know what he's doing. In the e-mail, which we're trying to trace—although it's been routed through a chain of remailers, so it's not gonna happen any time soon—he laid out each burial location, with a grid reference, and he rounded it out: Three-in-One, One-in-Three. So he was self-branding, bracing himself for the attention."

"The attention he would get when the movie connection with the Three-in-One Killer was made and the missing girls were attributed to him? That sounds like he was inviting disaster."

"Or the attention he would get when he said: that's what I've done so far, the Dublin girls are what I've just done, see what I do next. Which is also inviting disaster, but on a more spectacular scale. And to the question, why would he do that? Well, you answered it yourself this morning: Why would he kill all these people? We're not dealing with normal psychology here. As it stands, he could be ready to do just about anything."

COOVER LEAVES, AND I ponder the implications of what he has just said. Because the age of the Point Dume girls—late teens, early twenties—matches the ages of Nora, Kate and Jenny, I have pretty much taken for granted that as the killer's range. I have assumed he would act with a certain kind of logic, in other words; I have trusted to his profile. I had been anxious for Madeline King. It has never occurred to me that Anne could be in any kind of danger. But if he is ready to raise the stakes, then any female might be fair game. It's midday now: eight o'clock in the evening Irish time.

I call Anne, but her phone won't take a message, instead asking me to ring later. I don't have her landline number, the mark of a modern romance. I could call directory inquiries, but I know she never answers the landline anyway, and that after four rings it goes to a message minder that doesn't record any messages. "Anyone who knows me has my mobile," she says. I don't have Tommy's number either, as the killer took his phone and I haven't got the new one. I try Dave Donnelly, but his phone is ringing out, and there's no one answering at the Serious Crime Review Team number. I leave a brief message; Dave takes long weekends off during the summer and goes down to a caravan in Courtown with his family, but I leave a message at his home in any case.

The only other senior Garda connection I have is a superintendent in the National Bureau of Criminal Investigation called John O'Sullivan. I don't know him well, but I've been on his wrong side in the past, and have come through unscathed: he's smart and fair, and if he doesn't entirely trust me, I think there's a certain regard there. I call and identify myself, and once I establish that he's willing to listen, I give him the rundown. Like the rest of the world, he's been watching the case unfold on television, but didn't know there was an Irish angle.

"Strictly speaking, there's not a lot to go on there, Ed. I mean, it would be a case of having a chat, letting the four guys know we're watching them, as opposed to hauling them in."

"One of them has three bodies. Either he's buried them already, or he's working up to it. You might catch him in the act, or provoke him into doing something stupid."

"Right. And so what are you doing out there? Sure the LAPD are all over that," O'Sullivan said skeptically.

"Well, I've just had breakfast with Detective Donald Coover. He's the lead on the case so far, but the FBI are coming in, so I think they get to argue about who's in charge. I know Coover of old, and I've briefed him on the Irish situation, so if you'd like me to put you in touch . . ."

That has the desired effect. When Superintendent O'Sullivan speaks again, it's with a noticeably higher degree of interest and intensity, not to mention a tone verging precipitously on the respectful.

"Fair play, but you might have briefed us on the Irish connection a bit sooner, Ed."

"As you said, at one level, there's not a lot to go on. And anyway, it takes eleven hours to get here, and I've been kind of busy since I arrived."

I give O'Sullivan Coover's details, and phone numbers for the Gang of Four, and he says he'll arrange visits to each of them tonight, even if he has to carry them out himself. I thank him and finish the call.

The LAPD forensic team are waiting to fill in the grave. Keith Holloway says his final farewell to his sister's temporary resting place and we walk back to our cars together. The screeching and keening of seabirds cuts through the dull roar of the wind and the surf, a discordant Dies Irae for Desiree LaRouche, Polly Styles and Janice Holloway.

"I'd like to thank you," Keith says. "Detective Coover said you were the one who reported Janice missing. All those years ago."

"Well. I was only doing my job. You were pretty young back then."

"I was seventeen. But I was on my own. We kind of got scattered as a family. So I didn't even know Janice was missing until someone saw the police alert."

He has dark eyes and pale, unshaven skin and his long hair is thick and dark with a natural wave in it.

"I wonder, do you have anything of Janice's? Any possessions, keepsakes?"

"She didn't have a lot in the way of possessions. She lived in a rented apartment. There were some clothes, but I got rid of them. I figured, even if she showed up, she's a woman, she wouldn't want her old clothes."

"Did you think . . . did you hope she was alive?"

Holloway looks out to sea and considers this.

"You know, she was missing to me long before that. Maybe that's why yes, I always sort of thought she would come back. I was so used to her being away."

His voice is low and delicate, ethereal, if you were being grand, dreamy if you weren't. He strikes me as quite a dreamy person. Not a bad way to be, if you ask me.

"So there's nothing of hers left?"

"There's a box of books. Paperbacks, mostly. I kept them. Sometimes tempted to sell them, but they're not the kind of stuff my customers would go for."

"Do you have a store?"

"Comics. Keith's Komix. With, I regret to say, a *K* and an *X*."

"You didn't have a choice."

"I think there's a federal law."

"I thought part of that law said you had to have a goatee, and a beer gut, and a Slayer T-shirt, and a baseball cap on backward."

"Although I choose not to, I can put my hair in a ponytail. Otherwise, what can I say? I Am Not Like the Other Comic Book Guys."

"Do you think I could . . . would you mind letting me see Janice's books?"

"Not at all. The store's in Venice, on Market, between Riviera and Main. I live above it. You can follow me if you don't know the way."

"I know the way. I've been there before."

CHAPTER 25

There's a duty to be cheerful, she acknowledges that, and there are many blessings to be counted, but honest to God, there are some nights where she feels she has had enough by eight o'clock and needs to go to bed and sleep for a year and wake up, if she's lucky, in the middle of somebody else's life, and tonight is one of them. It has been a grim day, for a start, not helped by how she and Ed had parted the previous night. Christ, he could be so brusque sometimes, rude, in fact, and almost rough, the way he insisted, because suddenly *he* had been called away somewhere, he wouldn't say where, and she didn't ask, didn't pester him, but why *she* had to march out on the street and get a cab straightaway just because *he* was leaving she didn't understand, she had just started a conversation with one of the actresses, the American, who had been in *Gilmore Girls* and was *lovely*, and she had suddenly contracted a real thirst and could have put three or four more away, it wasn't as if she got out that often, and Maurice and Mark were in such good form and you never knew what Jack might suddenly do, God if he sang again she'd *die,* and all in all Anne was feeling the stardust of the evening on her cheeks and in her eyes and suddenly the lights go out. So . . . *paternalistic,* and no question in his mind but that she'd agree, and she had been so swept along by his forcefulness that she had consented, meekly (God, of all the words, *meek.* Blessed are the meek? Yeah, because they are fucked. And not in a good way) and he had kissed her on the cheek, a peck, as if he was her brother or something, and said he'd see her soon, and the cab was in Ringsend before her annoyance even attained coherent form and then she had almost ordered it back to Temple Bar.

She knows she likes that forcefulness sometimes, that decisive quality, but not when it was used so . . . brutally, that's what it was. God, she's raging yet. Although if she had just said no, he would of course have said okay. So rationally, it takes two. But Anne doesn't feel like being rational, and hadn't much felt like it last night when she got home and, instead of going to bed, asserted her independence and autonomy by sitting up at the kitchen table drinking white wine and listening to the new Bat for Lashes album and flicking through back issues of *World of Interiors* magazine, telling herself she was working, even though her eyes were beginning to swim halfway through the second (of five) glasses.

The Second of FIVE. On top of . . .

Not surprisingly, this morning was Hell. So this was the perfect morning for Aoife to decide she was old enough to have juice out of a glass, not a plastic beaker, then to prove she was not old enough not to break the glass on the kitchen tiles, the glass smashing into a thousand shards, only one of which Aoife needed to step on in order to cut her foot, and the *weeping,* and the *wailing,* and the *blood,* and the tissues and plasters and kisses, and by the time Anne successfully got the pair of them to school she felt the day surely couldn't get any worse.

Then Geri Foster calls and says she isn't sure she wants to proceed with the design commission, she really likes the ideas but she just needs time to think, and Anne, who is feeling rather Down On Men, wants to tell Geri she's only saying that because of Jack Donovan suddenly coming back to her and what business is it of his, sure he probably won't notice one way or the other but since she doesn't really know a) Geri Foster, or b) the half of it, she simply says fine and okay and tells Geri she should really let her know as soon as possible, otherwise Anne will run into scheduling difficulties. With all those other jobs she has lined up. How many? That's right, none.

And if that all seems grim enough, it's merely the overture for the grand opera that is the evening performance. First, the girls have been sent home from after-school with a note declaring that they have nits, possibly head lice, bizarrely a not uncommon occurrence in Irish schools high to low. This means the washing of the hair with the Lyclear and the leaving it in for ten minutes and the painful combing with the nit comb, with more cries and yells and tantrums and tears until the house feels like full moon in a women's penitentiary, and then Anne decides she had better give herself the treatment as the girls spend half their lives in and out of her bed and God knows how long they have had nits.

While she is doing this, in her own bathroom, Aoife, who likes very much to have a bath, and has felt obscurely cheated by the imposition, for medicinal reasons, of the shower, has taken it upon herself to run a bath for her and Ciara (the bath is the forum for all sort of story making and role playing, and, since it's one of the few places the girls can be guaranteed privacy, is also a great place for secrets). Under an entirely separate piece of legislation, since the battery in Aoife's phone has died, Anne has given permission for games to be played/amusing videos to be filmed etc. on her phone. The unauthorized conjunction of these two privileges results in an eerily quiet house as Anne emerges from her bedroom, freshly rinsed and, she trusts, deloused. Fearing the apocalyptic worst, she runs to the bathroom, to find two girls properly naked in the bath, Ciara at one end, wrapping the phone, which has Fallen In The Water, of course, in a facecloth, Aoife at the other end, crying softly and steadily.

Oh, the *shouting*. The red-faced, foot-stamping THIS IN-STANT shouting, and the furious toweling dry and the enraged blow-drying of hair and the door banging as Anne retreats to her room, delirious with exasperation and exhaustion, a headache flaring like magnesium fire behind her almost blinded-with-rage eyes. And then the wailing of the girls, and the unbearable guilt, and everyone into Anne's bed for making-up hugs, and everyone comfortable except Anne, and carrying the now rather heavy little brutes back to their beds.

Later, much later, Anne is awoken by a stone on her window and a voice calling her name, in singsong fashion, a not unmelodious voice. She gets out of bed and lifts the blind. It's Jack Donovan, swaying, drunk, insensate: he raises his arms up to her when he sees her face, his own beatific:

"Anne, Anne, Anne!" he sings, louder each time.

"Shusssh!" she says.

"I didn't want to wake the house by ringing the bell," Jack says.

"What do you want, Jack?"

"To talk to you, Anne. To ask your advice. About Geri. About . . . marriage. Women. You and Ed. A Good Thing. I have kept my own counsel long enough."

Jack delivers the last line as if he is in a Shakespeare play. Anne looks at the clock. It's half two in the morning.

"Jack, it's half two in the morning. Come back tomorrow."

"Anne, Anne, Anne!"

"Shusssh!"

"Anne, I need your advice."

"You need my advice?"

"Yes."

"All right. Here's my advice."

"Yes."

"It's half two in the morning."

"Yes."

"Fuck off, Jack."

He has forgotten about digging, how grueling it is, how hard he has to work. He has forgotten also: how chastening it is of the spirit, how mortifying of the soul, especially since it is toward that grim end, the burial of the dead. It always feels like this, and he always forgets, and then he always remembers. In this, as in so much, he is all too human. He remembers why he stopped killing: because the unspeakable physical facts of handling decomposing human flesh were almost too difficult to bear. But he can't remember why he started to kill again. Not at this stage, not with the pungent ammonia smell in his nose, the taste of rank humanity in his mouth. He smells it for days, weeks afterward. When they did Macbeth *at school, he remembers the teacher saying that Lady Macbeth trying and failing to wash her hands of blood was such a sublime metaphor for guilt and so on. But it isn't. It barely rises above the level of the documentary. He knows pathologists use nose plugs and surgical masks and so on. He doesn't want to do that. He feels that would be to pro-*

fessionalize his crimes. That way he would lose his bearings altogether. This is the right way, he knows: to atone through suffering, or at least, to suffer. Once he is done—and the pit is almost deep enough now— he will know, as he knows each time, the other condition of absolution: a firm purpose of amendment. But it's never been firm enough, has it? Like an alcoholic in the morning jigs, it's never again, never again, and then midafternoon turns into evening and that insatiable thirst arises, whispering: better to quench me than to suffer.

He knows that craving, too. He has never conducted any of the burials sober. For a start, there are two bodies already stowed somewhere, and since he rarely has access to refrigerated rooms or even ice, decomposition is always in progress, and handling the bodies is complicated and unpleasant.

And he always feels as if the third girl is one too many, but too late he always feels it: the craving is so intense—is it physical, or mental, or spiritual?—but in the act, in the moment, he always regrets it. Above all else, he does it to see the look in their eyes when they die. It gives him immense—not pleasure, but a sense of great, occult power. The last glimpse of life, of light, that she has is her own death, reflected in his eyes. It is the perfect danse macabre, the ultimate duet. It has a kind of perfection, a spiritual communion, that no work of art can match. But the third time is once too often, it sickens him, he sickens himself, his own greed. The glutton's need for satiety leads inevitably to self-disgust. He should remember this: that life is about longing, in the greater, but also in the lesser things. Rather wish for another drink than end up in the gutter as a result of it.

He wonders about the killing in threes, about the concept of the Three-in-One Killer. It is preposterous, on one level, like something from a comic book. And yet it springs from an authentic place within him. He remembers an interview with a colleague, who said you make your first film to see if you can make a film, and your second to check whether the first wasn't some kind of fluke. It's only on your third that you begin to feel, even though you probably only feel it unconsciously: Now I can take a risk or two. Now I am expressing myself fully. Now I can speak from my soul.

And there is the crucifix with the initials carved on it, standing at the graveside, waiting to go down. Because he does believe in God, in the Trinity, three persons in the one God. He just does. If that sacred mystery is at the very core of your psyche, then inevitably it shapes your philosophy. He doesn't know how to explain that in any greater depth, any more than he can explain what being Irish, or being an artist, means to him. It Just Is. That's why he included it in the anonymous letters. It's central.

That's deep enough. He goes to the shed and drags the bodies out, one by one, using a tarpaulin he has bought for the purpose. He disposes of that later, along with the girls' clothes. He insists they go into the pit naked. It isn't a sexual thing, not at this stage, far, far from it. It's just . . . like any part of a ritual, fulfilling it bestows a kind of calm. Perhaps that feeds into the Three-in-One business: compulsion, he must call it: that once there is a ritual to be observed, it's injurious to the soul not to observe it. To the letter.

Yes. That is as much consolation as he can take. No matter that the third girl felt excessive, no matter that the burial was arduous and nauseating, he could no more shirk his duty than a priest could refuse to say mass. He takes the crucifix from the ground where it lay and tosses it down, looking about him the while.

He is not overlooked here, and there is sufficient light from the conservatory. This is only the second time he has buried the bodies where he was staying. The first time was on The Last Anniversary, *the house on Coldwater Canyon. Each time he has rented anonymously, through an agency; in the Canyon, he had rented two: one to live in, and one to bury the girls. He doesn't need to do that here; his own house, where the Guards visited him last night, is a mile or so around the corner. He wonders if they visited the other three, expects they did. Loy is in L.A., but he hasn't found anything conclusive. He doubts if he will.*

But it is running down, there is no doubt about that. Flinging the first shovelful of earth down onto the twisted limbs, the matted hair, the unseeing eyes of the three lost girls, he feels such an intense burst of self-loathing, of self-disgust, of petrifying shame. He falls to his knees at the graveside, crying, a cawing, drizzening kind of cry. He has already vomited; now in his weakness he loses control of his bladder. He feels the hot piss seep down his crotch and along his thigh and nestle in his ankles where he crouches, hunkered down among the dead.

Now he has told them, they will find him, and put an end to it.

Is that what he wants?

It is, he knows at this moment, what he deserves.

But in the same moment, he thinks of the Garda Detective, O'Sullivan. Prying into his life. Asking if he can come in and look around. Of course, welcome, even without a warrant, what have the innocent to hide?

Who the fuck does he think he is?

Loy the same.

He would like them to suffer the way he has suffered.

He feels these both, within the same moment: shame, and rage.

Maybe they're the same craving, just as a drink quenches the craving for a drink at the same time as it creates the craving.

It is a paradox.

Three-in-One, One-in-Three.

It is his nature.

And maybe he is not going to get away with it much longer.

If they've narrowed it down to four.

If the LAPD and the FBI are involved, then just how badly could the Guards fuck it up?

And there is Ed Loy.

He could sit back and wait. That would take patience, and nerve, and courage.

He has those.

But does he want to?

How much longer can he endure this?

He has to consider his own welfare.

In another couple of years, another movie, the sap slowly rising, the old desires insisting on being assuaged, one girl good, two girls better, and then the squalor and degradation of the third, the inevitable letdown, the misery and self-laceration on some desolate hillside . . . it is a kind of hell.

Is he willing to continue, a condemned man?

He flings the last shovelful of earth on, pats the mound down, spreads the mulch from the adjacent compost heap in a haphazard manner, strews a few dead plants and a dried-out pine tree around and inspects the art-fully compiled garden mess.

Production design. Not his area, but anyone can lend a hand.

The first rays of dawn are starting to trickle through.

He needs a shower, and a drink, and his bed.

One thing has changed.

In the past, all the girls were lost girls, runaways, few had family con-nections. He always made sure of that. Although he notices with grim amusement how, in L.A., all sorts of human dreck has emerged from the mire with placards of their missing loved ones, as if he was to blame for them all. Where are they the rest of the year?

But he has not done that this time. These girls are not lost.

Could he stop?

He thinks of Macbeth again, a play he loves. He remembers his English teacher's horror at quite how much he loved it.

"But it's so dark, so nihilistic, so lacking in humanity, so devoid of the light. Even the children are murdered."

Yes, he nodded, it is so beautiful.

What is the quote?

I am in blood stepped in so far that should I wade no more,
Returning were as tedious as going o'er.

Something like that.
Yes, something like that.

CHAPTER 26

Keith's Komix shares dingy mini-mall space with a used-record store, a head shop dealing in all manner of joss sticks, herbal highs and hemp-related products and a Moroccan fast-food outlet. There's a pervasive aroma of patchouli, chamomile, falafel and that ripe late-teen and twentysomething pheromone, part sweat, part sebum, part why-don't-we-do-it-in-the-road. What there aren't in any great numbers are customers. Keith closed the shop to make the trip to Point Dume; he unlocks it now and leaves me waiting while he goes upstairs to collect Janice's stuff.

The store is not big, and it's shabby, if clean, but it has a wide range of stock, from Batman to the Hernandez Brothers, manga to Robert Crumb. I find a half-dozen old Teen Titans books which I know Aoife and Ciara don't have, and some Scooby-Doo comics for Geri Foster's girls.

When Keith Holloway comes down carrying a six-bottle

cardboard half crate with *Prosecco dei Colli Trevigiani—Bortolomiol* on the side, I get two shocks at once: one because of the wine, which Maurice, Jack, Mark and Conor had all extolled the other night in Eden as their trademark, their celebratory wine from way back; the other because Keith Holloway looks even paler and more drawn than he had out in Malibu.

"You okay, man?" I say.

He hands me the box.

"Kind of all catching up with me," he says. "Didn't really sleep last night. Shock, I suppose you'd call it."

"You want to get a bite to eat? On me."

"I need to open the shop. As you can see, business is not exactly booming. Can't afford to miss my customer of the day."

"I am that guy. Look," I said, and I show him my selections.

"You're a Teen Titans fan? I'd have put you down for Batman."

"They're for my . . ." I say, and falter at the cliché. Keith Holloway grins.

"Oh yeah? Your niece?"

"Forget it. Is this enough?"

"It's more than I did yesterday."

"Okay, then let's get out of here."

We find a dark old Italian place a block away, near the ocean. I have a pizza with anchovies, black olives, capers and green chilies and Keith has one with fresh basil and cherry tomatoes and mozzarella and we share a bottle of Chianti Classico and I have a Negroni up front and Keith has a Peroni. I did have some vague notion that I should stay off booze while I was in L.A., and driving, more to the point, but we have been at a mass grave, and there's a rule about having a drink even after you've been to an ordinary graveside, and I didn't make the rule, so don't blame me.

The box is half full of books. There are a few notebooks in there as well. I start to inspect them, but I want to ask Keith questions as well, so I ask him for a favor.

"Look. I think whoever killed your sister is in Dublin right now, and that's where I need to get to. There's a couple of flights leaving this evening—"

"I thought you told Coover you'd go downtown and make a statement," Keith says.

"Yes, well, it's always a good idea to tell cops what they want to hear. But the truth is, on this case, L.A. is the past. The present is happening—has just happened—in Dublin. I want to try and prevent there being a future."

"So what are you asking, you want to take these with you? They're all I have. I've been through them over and over, there's no reference to anyone, some even have the dedication pages ripped out—"

"I just . . . there might be something among them, however tiny, a detail, a glimmer, that I might spot . . . you'll get them back, I guarantee it, hey, I'm coming back anyway, I'll have to make that statement for Coover at some stage. Look, what I'll do is, we'll eat lunch, and then I'll sit here and work my way through the books, and whatever I haven't got through, I'll take with me. How does that sound? It's all in the service of getting this guy."

Keith agrees, and I make a call and get a seat on a British Airways flight out of LAX at 5:45 that will get me into Dublin, via London, by 2:30 on Saturday afternoon.

Over lunch, Keith tells me about his life: how his parents split up when they were kids and his dad got custody, how Janice had been six years older—they were half siblings, different moms, their dad was a deadbeat, frankly, not violent or unpleasant, just feckless and weak and generally useless at the basic stuff like keeping a roof over their heads and food on the table. Janice bailed when he was nine, and he didn't see her much after that. But up to that point, she looked after him, and loved him, like a mother, really. He didn't blame her for leaving, fifteen-year-old girls aren't supposed to be their half brother's moms, if it hadn't been for him she'd've been gone years before. It's why he'd always liked Jack Donovan's movies, they always have this murky fucked-up are-you-my-sister-or-my-mother vibe going on, not exploitative, more . . . you know, Adam and Eve, man, the original brother and sister, that's how we got going around here.

He did see her once more, when he was about twelve. She'd been in some movie, and she came around to give him some money, told him to hide it from his dad, who wouldn't even spend it on something you could measure and enjoy, she said, like booze, or women, wouldn't waste it with integrity, he'd probably just go and lose it, or buy more shitty furniture or another tragic car or the wrong kind of potato chips. She was funny, Janice. She was smart, too. She said she was hoping to make it in Hollywood, that she had dreams, not dreams like some silly little tramp that ends up selling her ass in the Valley, real dreams. She had read the history, researched the background. She said your dreams were like your conscience, they need to be informed in order to be valid. He's always remembered that.

He doesn't know whether she had it in her to be a star. He doubts it. She was twenty-four when she . . . when she disappeared, still working as an extra. That wasn't very promising, really, was it? He isn't going to make her out to be more than she was. And he's no one to talk, he doesn't know how long they have until they jack the rents on Market again and they'll all be out on their butts. But she was a good person. Not in any kind of moral sense, well, maybe that, too, he doesn't really know about that, although he thinks she probably was from what he has read in the notebooks. See, that's what Loy should start with, he can take the books to Ireland but the notebooks stay with him. What he means is, a good person, like the common good, you know, like a rounded person who gets the . . . gets the shape of things? The proportion. How they fit together, how everything is integrated? He isn't explaining it well. Wine at lunchtime, not a good idea. If Loy reads the diaries, he'll understand.

After Keith has gone back to the store, I order a large espresso and a bottle of San Pellegrino and I unload the Prosecco box and set three brown ring-bound notebooks aside and quickly inspect the books. They are all paperbacks, and all in one way or other have something to do with Hollywood. There are novels by Budd Schulberg and Nathanael West and Michael Tolkin and Bruce Wagner and Gavin Lambert. There are memoirs and biographies and histories of film noir and screwball comedy. There's *The Dress Doctor* by Edith Head, and a book of postcards of costumes by Adrian.

I set the books aside and start to work my way through the notebooks. They are handwritten, and filled with quotations Janice had selected, some from the books in the box and some from movies, along with recipes, beauty tips and motivational exhortations to herself. Some are typical of a girl her age, complete with exclamation marks: *Life is NOT a rehearsal!!!* Others feel like she'd come up with them herself: *Happiness is not the Destination, it's the Journey.* There are no smiley faces, or dog and cat stickers, or drawings of Pierrots or clowns. Every so often there is a list of infrequently used words—*attenuate, redact, compunction*—and their definitions alongside. I think the seriousness and earnest intent of these lists—*orotund, factitious, numinous*—moves me as much as anything else in the notebooks. I'd like to have met Janice Holloway. So would a lot of other people.

I can see nothing in the notebooks that makes any connection with a possible murderer: no names, no initials, no references to *Ocean Falls* or to any concrete aspect of Janice's life.

I pay the bill, leaving half the bottle of wine behind, and walk back to Keith's Komix. Keith is assembling a pile of reserved comics for a bearded guy in his sixties, evidently a regular, while several other customers—many, I am pleased to see, with shorts, or goatees, or reversed baseball caps, or metal T-shirts, some with all four—pore over the new arrivals. There are even a couple of girls. I like comics stores. I like the look of the comics, of course, the kinetic artwork and incendiary color schemes and the exaggerated sense of life they have, and I guess the fantasy aspect must appeal to my inner geek. I even like the smell of the paper and ink. Most of all, though, I like the way everyone seems so happy in a place that is not about being rich and famous, a place that doesn't care what you look like or how cool you are, a place that is devoted to something other than making money.

I give Keith Janice's diaries and shake my head at his raised-eyebrow inquiry into my progress thus far. I've asked him for a photograph, and he gives me a paper copy of a scan. I take his card and give him mine and tell him I'll be back.

It takes me longer than I expect to get to LAX, and though I had confirmed over the telephone that I could return a rental car at LAX that had originated in Burbank, this seems to come as radical and unwelcome news to the obdurate and very stupid guy at the rental desk; after many reluctant (on his part) discussions with his superiors, he is finally persuaded to do his job. I make it through security and get to the gate as the flight is boarding.

On the plane, I work my way steadily through Janice Holloway's books, page by page, line by line, looking for anything: a faded pencil mark, a significant underlining—she liked to underline passages or place exclamation points in the margins. There's a lot about the dark side of Hollywood, the difficulty of making friends and of finding and holding on to love, and of doing good work, but there's no clue to the man who murdered her. Two books—*The Day of the Locust* and *Inside Daisy Clover*— have pages inserted that look like they were pulled from her ring-bound notebooks, but each page just has a quote from the book copied out in Janice's handwriting. She did these on the fly, I guess, and with a certain amount of enthusiasm, as you can see the indentations from her ballpoint where she copied out the quote using the facing page as a base.

The other thing I do, while the plane is in darkness and the bulk of the passengers sleep, is power up my laptop and watch a DVD copy of *Ocean Falls* I got from Maurice Faye. I fast-forward through the bulk of the action, and concentrate on the beach parties. It's not long before I spot Janice Holloway, and though I think I see the backs of the other girls' heads, Janice is the only one who is focal. It's not as if she's given any close-ups, more that the footage is artfully constructed to make you feel Janice is the kind of standout "girl in the crowd" your eye is naturally drawn to. It seems to me that Mark and Jack should certainly have remembered this, and mentioned it to me. I think again of Mark correcting himself in the restaurant, saying he suddenly remembers Janice after all. Is that to cover himself in case I watch the movie? Or does this put Jack in the mix? He is the director, after all. I freeze-frame a shot of Janice dancing on the beach, her hair uplifted from her head, the glow of a bonfire behind her, her face abandoned to the ecstasy of the dance. It's very beautiful and immensely sad.

I sleep for a while before we touch down in Heathrow, and sleepwalk through immigration. TV screens are running non-stop on the Three-in-One Killer. I feel like I've flown around the world and back in thirty-six hours to learn no more than I could have had I sat at home and watched television. I think about powering up my dead phone at the charging pole, but our arrival from L.A. was late, and my flight to Dublin is already boarding, and in any case, I don't have any concrete information to communicate to anyone yet. I feel hot and shiverish simultaneously. To complete my sense of personal well-being, when I board the Aer Lingus flight to Dublin and sink into my window seat, hoping at least for an hour of sleep, a mother sits her excited five-year-old boy in the seat beside me. In fact, the boy turns out to be perfectly well behaved, and spends the entire flight coloring Spider-Man pictures in a book. And with his help, as we're beginning our descent into Dublin, I find out who the killer is.

In *On Cukor,* Gavin Lambert's book of interviews with the famous director, there's a passage during the discussion of the film *Gaslight* where Cukor talks about various cameramen he has worked with over the years. Janice had underlined their names, and placed asterisks in the margin. On the facing page, she had evidently written a note. The indentation this time is not quite so clear, but I could tell she had not copied out a quote, simply what looked like a list of the names of the cameramen. I ask my young co-traveler if I can borrow one of his coloring pencils, and he nods his smiling assent before his mother can have me seized for child endangerment. With a red pencil, I shade over the page, and the indentations reveal themselves in script:

William Daniels
Joseph Ruttenberg
Karl Freund
Robert Planck
Freddie Young
Oliver Marsh
Ask M.C. about their work!

A night's sleep, as it so often had, makes the decision for him.

He awoke thinking of the dinner in Eden, when the details of the next phase first began to fall into place. He had balked at the idea of harming children before, and doesn't condone it in general, but Jack's grotesque display of grandstanding sentimentality that night deserves some response. And when Loy's girlfriend revealed that she has two children as well, it seemed heaven-sent. Three-in-One, One-in-Three. He has no idea what age Jack's "wife" was now; he remembers her vaguely from the Sierras, when she seemed in her early twenties, the perfect age. Now she would be in her early thirties. That was old. While Anne Fogarty must be close to forty.

Old women. Jesus.

Still. The children would be the leaven in the dough.

"Sooner murder an infant in its cradle than nurse unacted desires."

Blake said that. One of Jack's favorite quotes.

That will come back to haunt him, won't it?

He isn't happy about it. Not deep down. He isn't looking forward to it. He doesn't want to see children die, who does? And old women, that would be as depressing. But where else can he go now? He knows it's all coming to an end. Entropy, is that the word? All energy dissipates. What he refuses to do is wind down. He has to go out with a bang, not a whimper.

Now he has a public in thrall, he can't just deliver the same old story. He has to keep moving forward, raising the stakes. Action and revelation, the future and the past. You can't give next year's audience last year's movie. He has learned that from Jack, at least. Now he is emerging into the light, he has to dazzle, to blind them with his own.

In fairness, he has learned a lot from Jack. In fairness. That is a piquant expression. For what has Jack learned from him?

Jack learned plenty, right from the first, right from insisting he always be in the edit suite, up until Ocean Falls, anyway. But Jack never wanted to pay tribute, to acknowledge his vital contribution.

Other people know what he has had to put up with. Even the other day, in the Irish Times, *Derek Doyle gave credit where it was due. It's not just that he is crucial to Jack's films—he's the reason they are the way they are.*

Look at Armageddon Factor—*it's obvious to everyone. Without him, it's Hollywood Hack time. Where was the Donovan poetry, the Donovan magic, the Donovan touch then?*

The irony of it: being the rightful owner of the Jack Donovan trademark and having the credit denied you.

Gall and heartburn, every day of your life.

It's all about Jack, when it comes down to it. And Loy, who is a kind of surrogate Jack, a shadow Jack, Jack's representative on earth. Loy had forced the pace. Without Loy none of this need have happened.

Maybe he hoped somehow the blame might fall on Jack's shoulders. Jack had behaved so abominably to women over the years, that's what made his guff about family and children in Eden so nauseating. Home is the wanderer, home from the sea, fatted calf served up without demur. Where is the natural justice in that? He has no right to happiness, less right than any man. The depraved way he treated his own sister!

But in fairness—perhaps he overuses that expression, but a man could have worse vices, could he not?—in fairness, he had not set out with the intention of framing Jack. And Loy only became involved after he had snatched Nora and Kate. He had followed his own lead, his own desire . . . yes, Blake again, he had never considered it before, but of course, Jack had used those quotes in black screen before A Terrible Beauty—*don't use Yeats, Jack said, the title will do that work, use one of the great influences on Yeats.*

"Those who restrain desire, do so because theirs is weak enough to be restrained."

Perhaps he had been an unconscious disciple, Jack's creature. Perhaps that was how it would be seen. Perhaps—no, without question—there would be a movie.

Never mind about that.

What he has found, in the void of sleep, is resolution.

He will not wait for the knock on the door.

It is too late for comfort, for safety.

He knows it is time to move beyond where he has been, beyond his own control, release himself from the tyranny of self.

It is time to place himself beyond time.

CHAPTER 27

Anne Fogarty thinks she is dreaming when the doorbell goes at eleven the next morning and there is Jack Donovan, large as life, with flowers and croissants and coffee and a boxed set of Wagner's complete *Ring* cycle, which Anne very much hopes he isn't going to ask her to listen to.

"I'm very very sorry," he says, dropping to his knees on the doormat.

"And so you should be," she says, laughing. Across the road, Sandymount Strand at low tide stretches out for what looks like miles. They need a dog, she thinks, not for the first time. Jack stands up, his expression an improbable, endearing mixture of sheepish and cheeky. He is a very bad boy.

"I simply had too much to drink," he says. "But if it is at all possible, I would like your advice. On a matter of the heart." With that, he places his hand on his heart, and thrusts his head back, and Anne suddenly feels like she has been propelled without warning, and still in her dressing gown, onto a very public stage, and rushes Jack into the house before he starts to sing.

The girls are in the living room playing on their Nintendos or watching TV or doing whatever they do: Saturday mornings at the Fogarty house are strictly free-range. The world looks two hundred percent better after twelve hours' sleep. All she has to do today is get a new mobile phone. And maybe see if anyone has called her on it. Her boyfriend, for choice.

Anne sits at the kitchen table with Jack and puts the croissants on plates and drinks some coffee and waits for him to begin.

"I suppose I'm really wondering what I should bring by way of gifts. I mean, it's a complicated situation, an incredibly complicated situation, and while we did speak on the phone, it would be easy . . . very easy to get things wrong."

"What were you thinking?"

"I was thinking . . . I was thinking, perhaps, of a new car."

Anne thinks he's joking, then sees he is serious, and bursts out laughing.

"No no no. God Almighty. That's ridiculous. She would feel . . . not that I have any experience of men trying to buy me cars, you understand, but I think, especially if it's a getting-to-know-you-again visit, she might feel a car would be just a little over-the-top."

Jack looks at her earnestly, but she doesn't feel he is getting it.

"Look. To put it mildly, you're going in there on the back foot. Ground to make up. So to a certain extent, all you want to be bringing with you are token gifts. Nice things, but nothing that says, See How Much I Love You, nothing that looks like it's trying to prove a point, nothing that makes her feel uncomfortable."

"So. Not a car."

"Not a car, not paintings, or jewelry, or bags, or designer gear or expensive gifts of any kind. God, I hope I'm not talking her out of booty here, but all that can wait."

"What will I bring, then?"

"Well. Something for the girls, of course. And after that, a version of what you brought me. Some nice flowers, something to eat, maybe something to drink, not champagne, looks a bit previous, on the other hand, who doesn't like champagne?"

"Champagne?" Jack says.

"Champagne. Not Wagner's *Ring* cycle."

Jack looks amused.

"I think Ed likes Wagner."

"Good for Ed. He can play it in his apartment. On his own. Anyway, you get the picture. The kinds of things you'd bring to someone's house if you didn't know them very well, but knew them well enough to like them a lot, and hoped they might grow to like you, but knew you were not going to endear yourself to them by grandstanding or showing off or being fabulous."

"I can see why Ed likes you so much."

"Did he say he liked me so much?"

"He wouldn't tell me. But I know he does."

"Get the girls—what are they, six?"

"Five."

"Get the girls fairy-princess dresses in Avoca."

"No question?"

"Hands down. And . . ."

"What?"

"Well, I don't know you well enough to be telling you things—"

"That's why I came here. People either know me too well or not well enough. No one will tell me anything. I'm too important to need to know how to behave, apparently."

"All right. When you get there, don't make big declarations, or look like you're going to make any. Don't prepare anything, it'll sound as if you're very pleased with yourself if you do. Pay a lot of attention to the girls. That shouldn't be hard. And then listen to what Geri says. She'll probably do a lot of talking. Don't pick up on points she's making, she isn't making them really."

"What do you mean?"

"I mean, there's no point trying to respond to what she's say-ing, she won't really be listening to herself."

"But I should?"

"Yes. I know, it doesn't make any sense. She'll just be talking to see how things go. Agree, but not in any major way, occa-sionally she'll tune into herself and think she's just prattling on, so you don't want her to think you're patronizing her by agree-ing vehemently with things she doesn't necessarily mean."

"But I kind of will be. Patronizing her, won't I? If I don't take what she says seriously."

"No, you'll just be . . . not taking control. There might come a point at which she'll want you to take a bit. But if you can get through the first half hour or so without giving the impression that you're doing her a favor, or that it's all very difficult for you, or that at any moment you might burst into song, I think you'll be doing well. And don't stay longer than an hour or so, unless things are going really well."

"What about the champagne?"

Anne shakes her head.

"She might offer it. Shake your head and ask for tea. Then the champagne won't look like a move. Even though you both know it is."

"I know some of this stuff."

"You probably know all of it. It's just so easy to forget. I'm an expert when it comes to other people's situations, of course, not my own."

"I'm sure you do all right," Jack says, and gets up from the table.

"And if you have an apology to make, make it when you're intending to leave, but not when you're on your feet. Again, that way, it's as if you're giving her the option of responding or letting you go, as opposed to giving yourself a big operatic exit line. Letting her know the apology is for her, not you."

As Jack walks down the hall, Aoife and Ciara pile out of the living room, still in their pajamas, their uncombed heads all tousled. When they see Jack, they fade back with a sigh.

"Uhhh," Ciara says. "We thought it was Ed."

"Rude," Aoife hisses at Ciara.

"This is Jack, a friend of Ed's," Anne says.

"Is he your secret lover?" Ciara says, barely able to control her giggles.

"Ciara," Aoife says, and puts her hands to her head in pantomimed outrage at her sister. "What are you *like*?" Then she bursts out laughing.

Anne, laughing herself, and maybe blushing, sees Jack to the door.

"Looks like fun," Jack says.

"It is. Sometimes."

The last thing she remembers saying to Jack Donovan that morning is "Good luck."

CHAPTER 28

I'm tempted to blurt something out to one of the Guards at Passport Control, but I hold off until I make it to the arrivals hall. Casting around for a public phone, I spot Tommy Owens waiting, his face drawn and pale, his tiny eyes glittering with anxiety and unease. He looks like I feel.

"Ed—"

"I need your phone. Now."

Tommy gives me his phone and I call Anne Fogarty—and get the runaround from her service provider yet again. What the hell is the matter with her cell? I get her home number from directory inquiries and call it. It rings four times before connecting to a voice mail service that informs me that this customer has no voice mail.

"We need to get to Anne's place. I think . . . I'm pretty sure . . . Mark Cassidy is the Three-in-One killer. Anne could be in danger. What are you doing, Tommy? We're in a fucking hurry here. Geri Foster, Geri Foster, I need to call her, too. Shit, all my fucking numbers are in my phone and the battery's dead. Tommy! Get out of the fucking way!"

Tommy tries to stop me getting out of the arrivals hall; now he's trying to prevent me from crossing the road to get into the car park.

"Ed, we're walking into an ambush. Listen to me man."

Tommy draws me to one side behind a line of passengers waiting to board a coach for one of the long-stay car parks.

"Podge Halligan knows you went to L.A. That prick who works for Immunicate, Brian Joyce, they got rid of him off the set, but Immunicate is riddled with Podge's men. There was all gossip going the rounds about the Three-in-One Killer because of the three girls going missing, and then it came out you had gone over."

"So they know—"

"And so they're waiting for you, your car—"

"What, they're going to shoot me in the airport car park? Have they not heard of CCTV footage? Do they all want to go to jail? How thick are these fuckers? I can't make allowances for fucking eejits. I have the Glock Leo gave me in the Volvo, and I want to get it."

"Which is what I'm saying man," says Tommy, slipping an identical Glock 26 into my hand. "Leo was very understanding, how I lost the other piece. These are from him." Tommy puts a hand in his jacket pocket to indicate he is carrying as well. "So we're ready, know what I mean?"

I know what he means, but I'm not really capable of focusing on it. Podge Halligan in Point Dume, Podge Halligan at the airport. Podge Halligan is not my concern. Podge Halligan is amateur hour compared to Mark Cassidy.

"I still want my car."

Tommy nods.

"If they come, we're going to have to get rid of them. We need to get to Sandymount, fast."

They don't jump us in the car park. I take the motorway and the Port Tunnel. Tommy tries Anne every five minutes, but there's no reply. What the fuck has happened to her phone?

"AH, THESE ARE fairly indestructible little guys," the young fella in the Vodafone shop tells Anne as he slips the sim card from her ruined phone and replaces it in the shiny new model. "Now, you'll need to give that a good twelve-hour charge, ideally, before you use it?"

"Has it any power as it is?" Anne says. "I'd kind of like to get my messages."

"A little trace energy from the battery. But it won't last. Plug it in when you get home, if you want to switch it on quickly and check, that's fine as long as you switch it off again."

"Okay," Anne says. "Let's go, girls."

Aoife, who has a phone, is drooling over a more expensive model; Ciara, who doesn't, is drooling over a phone.

"I didn't get mine until I was ten," Aoife says.

"Yeah, well, two girls in my class got them at eight. And all your friends got their phones when they were nine."

"That's true. Actually, Mum, maybe Ciara should get a phone."

"She will get a phone. When she's ten."

"Mum!"

"Home."

"Mum, with no phones until we're ten and no TVs in our bedrooms, we live like something from the olden days."

"I'm sorry."

"You don't mean that, do you, Mum?"

"No."

"Grrrrr."

Oh God, please God, help me, if you only get me out of this, I promise I'll never, never, never again. . .

> *All praise to God the Father,*
> *All praise to God the Son,*
> *And God the Holy Spirit,*
> *eternal Three-in-One. . .*

He has to hold on to logic.

That is all he has left.

He has acted impeccably for eighteen years: three-in-one, one-in-three.

And now, when he has the world's attention, he has sullied his record, and brought disgrace upon his name.

He will look like a rough beast, like a careless savage. What possessed him?

Overconfidence. Hubris. Delusions of grandeur.

What was Jack doing there?

He rang ahead, said he wanted to drop out some gifts for the girls, Jack had told him all about them, was that all right?

And Geri Foster said, sure. She sounded surprised, but . . .

But she didn't say Jack would be there.

The plan was, to get into the house, to disable the mother and weaken her, to shoot the girls quickly, in her sight, and then to strangle her.

One-in-Three, Three-in-One, raised to a kind of burnished perfection.

And then to shoot himself on the scene, with the last map reference in his hand.

That would have been immaculate.

That would have been immortality.

A valedictory death masque.

A Mark Cassidy Picture.

But when Geri Foster opened the door, the first thing he saw across the room was Jack Donovan, kneeling by the fireplace, holding shiny turquoise dresses out to the two little girls.

He wanted to run, but he knew that would have been shameful beyond bearing.

Jack had a strange expression on his face, as if he had figured it out, as if he knew. He left the dresses with the girls and started to walk slowly toward him, while Geri, looking toward Jack, began to retreat.

The idea that they had discussed him. It was unbearable, the humiliation.

He pulled the gun from his pocket but he couldn't shoot it, had no experience with guns, disliked them intensely, what made him think he could use one in such a high-pressure situation? The amateurishness of his own plan galled him. Jack was still coming, and Mark gripped the gun by the barrel and hit Jack hard on the right temple, once swaying, twice to his knees, a third time to the ground, writhing, gurgling. Geri froze, and he looked around at her, and at the children. Jack was still now, silent. He wondered briefly if he could continue, if he could steel himself to pull the trigger. Geri moved then to protect her children. He closed her down by the fireplace and tried again to use the gun but he couldn't, he hit her instead, clubbed her down with the gun butt until she, too, had stopped moving.

The children were crying.

He did not like that sound.

Macbeth had not killed Macduff's children, he had sent others.

At least allow himself that crumb of dignity.

He walks from the house, shutting the door on the weeping children.

He has blood on his shirt.

He doesn't know whose.

The light is dying . . .

What he needs to do . . .

What Jack has always done . . .

Is come back from the brink.

High Castle *was a triumph after* Twenty Grand.

Nighttown *would probably have been his masterpiece.*

(Has that ever entered his thinking? To deny Jack his greatest film? He will consider that later, be rigorous with his conscience. But that is for another time.)

If he is given the chance to speak, he will say, of this moment:

I asked myself a simple question: What would Jack Donovan do?

CHAPTER 29

Tommy thinks we're being followed, and then he thinks we aren't, and then he isn't sure. I just try to keep the car moving, and to spot motorcyclists on Tommy's blind side. If they're going to do it in traffic, it'll come from the pillion of a motorbike. All the while we call Anne Fogarty and call her and call her, and Vodafone won't accept our messages. At last I send a text, and that gets through. Maybe her phone works for texts but not for messages. I don't know. I don't understand mobile phones.

ANNE GETS HOME and plugs in her phone and dumps the papers on the table, and puts the coffee in the moka and puts it on the heat and warms some milk in a cup in the microwave and scans the front page of the *Irish Times,* the first mention Anne Fogarty has seen of the Three-in-One Killer, rumored to be in Ireland, apparently, and switches on her phone to see if she has any messages, and the doorbell rings.

She walks down the hall as her phone gets its signal, leaning into the living room on the way to check that the girls are okay. Aoife is playing the new Harry Potter DS game Anne was persuaded to buy because their trip back from the Vodafone shop passes Gamestop, and Ciara is looking out the living-room window.

"Hey, Mum, there's a man at the door with tomato ketchup on his shirt," Ciara says as the doorbell rings again, and Anne, not really listening, glances at her phone and sees a text from Ed. One text in two days? Cheeky sod. And as she clicks on the text, she opens the door.

And the text says:

Mark Cassidy is the Three-in-One Killer.

And Mark Cassidy is in the doorway with a smile on his face and a red stain on his shirt. And she sees him seeing that she knows, and a gun glows dull in his hand.

And Anne spins around so that her voice will carry and yells, "Aoife! Ciara! Ghost room! This instant!"

She feels the barrel of the gun against her spine. She thinks she might set it off by pushing against it. She is frightened, but not as frightened as she is that the girls might not pick up on her tone. That's why she says "this instant." It takes longer to say, but they know she really means it when she says that. And there they are at the bottom of the stairs. Their frightened faces.

"Go!" she screams.

She thinks at first that she's been shot, but all that has happened is, Mark Cassidy has smashed the butt of his gun against the back of her head. She stumbles forward and falls on the hall carpet. As she falls, she sees the girls rounding the first landing return. The white flash of Ciara's bare little legs.

And then Mark Cassidy is past her, thundering up the stairs himself, and Anne knows she needs to call the Guards but she can't let him go up there alone so she follows him up and hears him thundering in and out of the bedrooms on the first floor and it isn't as if she even thinks about it, she just continues up the stairs to the top of the house and past her bedroom and through the ghost door and locks it behind her, thanking God the girls know they are forbidden to lock it, and climbs slowly up the stairs and puts her finger to her lips so the girls won't cry out "Mummy!" when they see her and there they are, shaking with fear without really knowing why, and she can hear the footsteps and the slamming doors and the pounding up stairs beneath her as she huddles with her girls in the attic, as scared as she has ever been in her life, too scared to call the Guards in case she is overheard.

Instead, she texts Ed:

We're in the ghost room. Mark is in the house.

THEY'VE VANISHED.

Three-in-One, One-in-Three.

They've disappeared into thin air.

He has checked every room, every wardrobe, beneath every bed.

He has lost them.

Have they jumped?

It's like a dream. Is he losing his mind?

He looks out the front window of the top bedroom.

Loy and Tommy Owens are pulling up in an old green car.

He had thought that he could kill himself.

But that would have been the prize for glory.

There would be no dignity in this . . . humiliation.

He moves quickly downstairs, and out through the kitchen to the yard he has seen from the back bedrooms. There's a door out to a laneway that gives cars access to the rear of the houses in the terrace. He runs the bolt and steps out into the lane and doubles back around to the front of the house. He parked his car half a mile away, he was confused about which house was Anne's. He looks quickly into Loy's car, a heavy old Volvo. They were in such a hurry, they've left the keys in the ignition. This is perfect. He can drive to his house, collect his passport, pack a bag, get to the airport, and take the first available flight. Escape into the light . . .

ANNE HEARS DOORS opening and slamming and footsteps running, and dares to raise her head and look out through the Velux roof window she installed in the ghost room. She sees Ed's car out front, but she doesn't want to go down and open the door until the coast is clear. Then she sees Mark Cassidy appear at the front of the house and stand for a moment, as if trying to figure out what to do. He ducks his head in the window of Ed's car, then opens the door and gets in. Anne reaches for her phone to call Ed to tell him, but she ends up fumbling with the keys and pushing the camera slide back. As the engine of the Volvo starts up, she hears the roar of a motorcycle as it approaches and screeches to a halt alongside the car, and the pillion passenger, who has a full visor and a steroid-swollen upper torso, swings himself off the bike and stuffs what looks like his gloved fist through the driver's window and then Anne hears shots. The shooter gets back on the bike and the rider punches his fist in the air and the bike revs and revs and then speeds away up Strand Road toward the Merrion Gates.

CHAPTER 30

Jack regains consciousness within minutes of Mark Cassidy's fleeing the house. He has suffered memory loss, and is extremely confused to find himself in a house he doesn't recognize with two wailing five-year-old girls he's never seen before and a vaguely familiar-looking woman slumped on the floor with blood seeping from her head. He does what he would have done anyway, which is to call 999. By the time the ambulance arrives, he has recovered the missing minutes.

Geri comes to in the ambulance, and her injuries, while never life-threatening, take a longer time than Jack's to heal. The saving grace is that Geri has no memory whatever of Mark Cassidy's visit, or of the moments leading up to it, and so she gets to relive her reunion scene with Jack as if for the first time.

Anne Fogarty takes it upon herself to help Geri through her recovery. She tells me Geri and Jack are taking it slowly, but they're doing all right, which is about as much as can be said for me and Anne. Jack said to me: "The fact that she still loved me, that she never stopped. How can I ever live up to that?"

I guess he probably can't, but it looks as if he's going to try. I think Anne and I are going to try also, but it won't be any easier. I know that, while there was no way of legislating for someone like Mark Cassidy, the fact that Podge Halligan carried out the hit on her doorstep, thinking it was me in the Volvo, has made a deeper impression on her, and, indeed, on me. Anne inadvertently filmed the shooting with her phone, and while there was nothing incriminating in the footage, those of us who know Podge Halligan well are certain he was the shooter.

The following morning at dawn, the National Drugs Unit launch a raid on the hotel in south Wicklow where Podge Halligan has been staying since his release from jail. In a wardrobe in his room, they discover a package containing 8.5 kilos of cocaine. Podge, who is immediately rearrested, insists the drugs have been planted. I ask Tommy Owens, who vanishes immediately after the hit on Mark Cassidy, if he knows anything about the raid. Tommy says all he knows is that Leo Halligan wants his guns back, as I won't be needing them anymore.

The Guards find the location of the garden in Milltown where the remains of Nora Mannion, Kate Coyle and Jenny Noble are buried. The bodies are exhumed and returned to their families for burial. I go to all the funerals, as do most of the *Nighttown* cast and crew. Tommy helps steward his grieving daughter, Naomi, through Jenny Noble's funeral.

In the cellar of Mark Cassidy's house in Churchtown, the Guards find the corpse of a woman believed to have been his Brazilian wife; no passport or papers have been located, so as yet, no identification has been made. He left no documentation of any kind, no diaries, notebooks or computer records. We only have the notes he sent Jack Donovan.

Details of Mark Cassidy's life emerge. He was the only child of parents who died of cancer within a year of each other while Mark was at university. Former school friends and university colleagues line up to tell us nothing we didn't know before: Mark Cassidy was a charming, intelligent attractive man who was difficult to get to know outside of a social or professional context. He never alluded to any experience of abuse or displayed signs of mental derangement, never spoke disparagingly of women. A woman he dated briefly at university said that he was very gentle and didn't seem that interested in sex. None of it, and nothing else, explains why Mark Cassidy did what he did, or even what he thought he was doing. In many ways, how could it? Or to put it another way, what exactly could have? Family background, life experience, hard knocks and paths not taken: none of that is enough. At a certain stage, evil becomes a mystery, transcending all considerations of biography and motivation. Three-in-One, One-in-Three, it becomes a matter of faith.

That doesn't stop people trying; books and newspaper articles appear, some content to recount the mere facts of the case, others attempting to provide some insight into the psychology of the killer's mind. The result: we know almost all the facts; we remain terrifyingly low on insight.

The case slips out of my hands. I brief Kevin O'Sullivan and he deals with Coover and the LAPD and the FBI. They've only identified ten of the lost girls to date. On top of the three Irish victims, that leaves eight unidentified bodies.

No one has seen Madeline King since Thursday afternoon, when she left the *Nighttown* set. There is CCTV footage of her at the airport, and her car was found in the short stay car park. Her mobile phone details show three missed calls from Mark Cassidy that afternoon, and one further call which needs to be traced. There is no record of her taking a flight that day, or at least, not under her own name. I go to Galway, to her family home, I talk to her friends in Dublin, I track down ex-boyfriends: no one believes she would have simply chosen to disappear, and no one knows anything else that can help me find her. Jack Donovan tells me their relationship had run its course, and while Madeline would have wished otherwise, she was resigned to its demise: disappointed, but cheerful, and certainly not despairing or suicidal. Even though Mark Cassidy broke his killing pattern at the end, it doesn't make sense for him to have killed her. And *his* phone records show he was at his rented house in Milltown that afternoon, or on the *Nighttown* set, nowhere near the airport. It is as if she has vanished into thin air.

Like me, the Guards don't believe Madeline's disappearance has any direct connection to the Three-in-One Killer case, but I press John O'Sullivan of the NBCI to pursue the service provider of the number that made the last call to her phone just the same. In the meantime, I work through all the numbers I have called while working the case, and before the Guards get the details released, I find a match.

When I call to Marie Donovan's house, she sits me at the kitchen table where we sat before. She doesn't offer me tea this time; she simply takes a full bottle of Pinot Grigio from the fridge, fills a glass for herself and pushes a second glass in my direction, leaving the choice of whether to fill it or not up to me. The only other thing on the table between us is the Spanish Mission–style rough-hewn wooden cross I saw on a shelf here the last time I came. The kind of cross Mark Cassidy used as a tag, with the initials of his three victims marked on the reverse of the arms and head. Marie shows me that on the rear of this particular cross, there are three question marks, gouged deep in to the wood, stained red. Then she bursts into tears. By the look of her red eyes and puffy cheeks, Marie has been doing a lot of crying recently. I wait for her to stop, and to drink her wine, and to pour herself some more. Finally, she begins to speak.

"Mark Cassidy came here . . . a few weeks ago, when they were in preproduction on the film. He . . . we . . . we had a thing, years ago, not much of a . . . we would meet, for dinner, or drinks, and talk, about Jack, mostly. Bitch about Jack. I guess that's what our bond was. And . . . anyway, this time he came here, brought me this cross, as a gift. And he seemed really, he seemed very angry. How he was destined to live in Jack's shadow, how nothing he did received the proper credit, how he was a minor chapter in a book called Jack Donovan. And I . . . God forgive me . . . I rejoiced in his spite, I relished his bitterness, I encouraged him in his . . . hatred. I . . . I told him about the abortion . . . told him it was Jack's . . . "

"And so the letters . . . the drawing of the fetus . . . "

"He used what I told him."

"When I called here and showed you the letters, did you know they were from Mark?"

"I thought they probably were. I . . . but I didn't know . . . you didn't tell me the girls were missing. I didn't know . . . "

"Nora and Kate were already dead. But Jenny Noble was alive. And you could have spared Jack and Geri's injuries, never mind what their children went through. And Anne Fogarty and her girls. If you had just told me about Mark sending the letters."

Marie Donovan begins to cry again. It seems to me that her tears are for herself alone, but I might be mistaken. In any case, she's right: I hadn't told her enough. That doesn't absolve her though.

I have one more question.

"What did you say to Madeline King?"

"I told her that Jack and I . . . I told her that I had an abortion. That the child was Jack's. I told her she could not, should not love a man like that."

"And?"

"And she . . . I heard her breath . . . it seemed to rattle in her throat . . . and she closed the call."

"Why did you call her? Why did you tell her that?"

Marie Donovan looks me in the eye for the first time. It's as if telling the truth at last will come as a relief.

"I didn't want her to be happy with Jack. And I didn't want Jack to be happy. With anyone."

"Jack is going to be happy with Geri and his girls," I say. "And no one has heard from Madeline or seen her since."

Marie Donovan shakes her head, looks at me as if perhaps there is something I can say by way of solace or comfort. There isn't, and even if there were, I'm not sure I could rise to it. I know I'll feel sorry for her in time. That time is not now.

I rise to leave. As I reach the door, Marie Donovan stops me with her last revelation.

"I lied though."

"What?"

"I lied. To Madeline. I told her the baby was Jack's. But it wasn't."

"Whose was it?" I ask, not wanting to hear the answer.

"It was just one time. It was . . . a drunken mistake. He never knew what happened. And I never told Jack."

"Whose was it?" I ask again.

"Mark's. The baby I was carrying was Mark Cassidy's."

IN L.A., I made one stop between leaving Keith's Comix and arriving at LAX. My ex-wife was in the garden of her house on Westminster, not far from where CJ Ramsey used to live. She was sitting in the shade drinking a glass of cold mint tea. I had not seen her since the day we cast Lily's ashes onto the ocean at Santa Monica. There was a time I could not even speak to her on the phone, when her betrayal of me haunted my days and bled my nights white. Now I sat beside her, and while we talked, I noticed that my hands didn't shake, that my heart didn't race, that not once did I worry tears might spring into my eyes. Not even when she told me that her marriage, to the man who had been Lily's blood father, was over. Not even when she said she still loved me, and asked if I thought I could one day find my way back to loving her.

I didn't say that for many months, that had been my deepest wish. I didn't say that even though I had met someone else, I wanted to see her just in case I was still in love with her. I didn't say that now, I knew my future lay with Anne. I didn't say anything. I looked her in the eye, and I shook my head, and I took her in my arms, and we held each other, and let the sadness of our lives together drift away in the L.A. afternoon.

MINDFUL OF THE appalling crimes committed by its cinematographer, the studio decides to cancel the entire *Nighttown* project. However, it soon becomes clear that the Three-in-One Killer is the biggest media story of this or any other year, with many newspapers running a front-page story every single day. "The best publicity money doesn't need to buy," as Todd and Ben apparently tell Maurice Faye. Jack Donovan's entire oeuvre, or at least those parts of it shot by Mark Cassidy, attains a ghoulish allure. Demand for the films on DVD soars; in the press, there is condemnation of the societal decadence thought to underlie this demand, and celebration of the supposedly "transgressive" qualities the films are now considered to display. Jack leans heavily toward the first reaction and wants all the DVDs to be withdrawn from circulation. When the studio proposes a reshot version of *Nighttown* "to vindicate the artistry and dedication of the surviving members of the Gang of Four, and as a memorial to Nora, Kate and Jenny," Jack declares that it will happen over his dead body.

And then, about forty minutes of *Nighttown* footage, as shot by Mark Cassidy and featuring the three murdered girls, appears on the Internet. It is never clear who leaks it—Jack blames the studio; I have my doubts about Maurice Faye—but it quickly goes viral. Soon it's being mashed up with satanic heavy metal, horror movie soundtracks and extracts from Wagner's *Ring* cy-

cle. The girls' deaths dwindle into just another slice of Hollywood Gothic; Mark Cassidy's murderous insanity is transformed
into entertainment.

Jack is distraught. Finally, he makes a deal with the studio: if
they use their legal muscle to cleanse the Internet of any trace of
the *Nighttown* footage, he will reshoot the movie from scratch.

It takes a year.

The film opens at the Savoy in Dublin, with press and TV
cameras gathered from all over the world. It is a strange and
macabre night. The film, sombre and savage, makes uncomfortable viewing in itself; knowledge of the appalling circumstances
of its birth make it almost unbearable to watch. No one knows
quite how to respond until the very end.

Jack has crowded all the production credits into the opening
of the movie, to a particular purpose. The closing shot of *Nighttown* is a cityscape: Dublin, looking upriver from the bay, the
Four Courts a smoking ruin behind the Ha'penny Bridge, the
sun setting, the world on fire, the screen fading to black.

Then, over sepia-tinted footage of Nora Mannion, Kate Coyle
and Jenny Noble retrieved from the original shoot, and used
with the assent of their families, who are here tonight, as Jussi
Björling sings *Recondita armonia*, the names of the lost girls roll:

Rebecca Tull
Unknown
Unknown
Desiree LaRouche
Janice Holloway
Polly Styles
Kim Kovnick
Unknown
Madison Berkley
Unknown
Brianna Corbett

Unknown
Unknown
Alyssa Parsons
Lauren Bergeren
Unknown
Morgan Waxman
Unknown
Nora Mannion
Katherine Coyle
Jennifer Noble

THIS FILM IS DEDICATED TO THEIR MEMORY
AND TO OUR FRIEND
MADELINE KING
WHO IS LOST.

ACKNOWLEDGMENTS

Thanks first and foremost to Julian Plunkett Dillon; and then to David Highfill, Danielle Bartlett, Gabe Robinson and everyone at William Morrow; Roland Philipps, James Spackman, Anna Kenny Ginard and everyone at John Murray; Breda Purdue, Margaret Daly, Ruth Shern and everyone at Hachette Ireland; Alan Glynn; Sheila Crowley and George Lucas. Above and beyond to Kathy, Isobel and Heather.